Faking It

LOTTE DALEY

PENGUIN BOOKS

PENGUIN BOOKS

Published by the Penguin Group
Penguin Books Ltd, 80 Strand, London WC2R ORL, England
Penguin Group (USA) Inc., 375 Hudson Street, New York, New York 10014, USA
Penguin Group (Canada), 90 Eglinton Avenue East, Suite 700, Toronto, Ontario, Canada M4P 2Y3
(a division of Pearson Penguin Canada Inc.)
Penguin Ireland, 25 St Stephen's Green, Dublin 2, Ireland (a division of Penguin Books Ltd)
Penguin Group (Australia), 250 Camberwell Road, Camberwell, Victoria 3124, Australia
(a division of Pearson Australia Group Pty Ltd)
Penguin Books India Pvt Ltd, 11 Community Centre, Panchsheel Park, New Delhi – 110 017, India
Penguin Group (NZ), 67 Apollo Drive, Rosedale, Auckland 0632, New Zealand
(a division of Pearson New Zealand Ltd)
Penguin Books (South Africa) (Pty) Ltd, 24 Sturdee Avenue, Rosebank,
Johannesburg 2196, South Africa

Penguin Books Ltd, Registered Offices: 80 Strand, London WC2R ORL, England

www.penguin.com

First published 2011
1

Set in 12.5/14.75pt Garamond MT
Typeset by Jouve (UK), Milton Keynes
Printed in Great Britain by Clays Ltd, St Ives plc

A CIP catalogue record for this book is available from the British Library

ISBN: 978–0–141–04679–2

www.greenpenguin.co.uk

Penguin Books is committed to a sustainable future
for our business, our readers and our planet.
The book in your hands is made from paper
certified by the Forest Stewardship Council.

To Ger, for making my dreams come true,
and to Ellen and Freddie – I love you

Chapter 1

'He broke up with you in a text message?!' my best friend Danielle shrieks down the phone at me. London traffic whizzes past her in the background.

'Are you being serious with me here, like, swear on his life serious?' she says, her voice going an octave higher with each word spoken.

'I'm being deadly serious,' I sniff, unable to control my tears. 'Jack . . . broke up . . . with . . . me!' I cry.

'When?' she says.

'Early this morning,' I sob.

There's a stunned silence from Danielle's end of the phone, aside from the sound of her lighting up a cigarette. I light one up too. I hear her puff before she continues to talk. 'Oh my God, Katie, that is totally un-cool of him, I can't believe anyone would do such a thing, in a text!'

I grab a tissue and blow my nose into it. 'I know, he's just, so . . . so mean!'

'Spineless!' Danielle replies.

'Horrible, nasty, cowardly!' I cry.

'Have you, like, got a decent explanation out of him?' Danielle queries.

'No, no I haven't. I've been repeatedly calling him all morning. He won't pick up. All I got was this pathetic text,' I cough and clear my throat. 'It said, "It's not you, it's me, I'm sorry, Katie".'

'That's it?'

'That's it,' I sob, 'nothing else! Does he think that I don't know what those words really, actually mean?' I pause, letting the words between us sink in.

Danielle waits expectantly for further shoutage on my part.

'We ALL know what "It's not you, it's me" means!' I sob. 'It means it IS you!' I begin to cry some more. 'It's meeeee!' I wail, almost choking myself with snot and tears.

'Shit . . .' Danielle says slowly, before adding, 'after everything you've done for him as well . . .'

With no clue as to why Jack had dumped me, my hysterical mind had begun to conjure up favourable reasons of absence to explain why he had left. I tore round the bedroom opening now half-empty drawers of our things and slinging back coat hangers in the wardrobe, searching for his clothes, and groaned aloud with each empty space that met me as further proof he'd gone. To keep myself momentarily sane, I wistfully imagined things that didn't involve me at all, which for a brief moment made me feel better. At least with an external disaster, he wouldn't have had a choice in the matter of leaving me. Aside from being abducted by aliens, a sudden death was the optimistic reason for explaining his departure.

I paced up and down my living room going over and over the time we last spent together, searching for clues whilst furiously speed-dialling his number. He must have had at least fifty missed calls. By 9am, two hours after the text, I was frantic. My calling had so far remained fruitless, as I was going straight through to his voicemail. His answerphone led me to stupidly hope against all odds that this whole break-up text could actually be a hoax, and not him ignoring me, and that Jack could have been tumbled into the back of a van with a bin bag over his head on his way to work, bound and gagged, and his kidnapper was simply getting a sadistic kick out of hurting his poor girlfriend. I had visions of a man in a balaclava wielding a knife, ordering him to text me, to break my heart or have his bits chopped off and made into a soup. He'd be begging for mercy, 'Please no, don't do this to her, do anything you like to me, but not her . . .' whilst the kidnapping, murdering, female-hating man would bellow, 'Text or you die!' and then laugh in an evil way. Jack, of course, would have put up resistance to his heinous request and quite happily risked death by henchman. On second thoughts, he would never allow anything to go near his ridiculously good-looking face, or his £1,000 designer jacket. He'd willingly sacrifice me though, I thought, based upon this morning's efforts. I gave a heavy sigh and peeked out of the window. The street was filled with large vans and men wearing fashionable scarves and carrying cameras. Perhaps someone famous had moved into Lauriston Gardens? After all, the East End was always being touted as 'trendy' and 'up and coming' – which bits of it, I was still unclear, because to me personally, it made no sense. Last time I checked, I still had to dodge weird-looking men calling me 'darrrrling' with elongated Rs, asking for dates at the bus stop in broad daylight, when clearly, all they really wanted was a shag and to make a copy of my Visa. Not much different to Jack, then . . . sex and my Visa debit. I quickly drew the curtains to match my mood. In the reality of daylight, my whimsical fantasies of abduction and the like became painfully embarrassing, but with the curtains closed and the lights dimmed, I could keep up the pretence, at least, until anyone called round. Thank God I hadn't told anyone what was really in my head – they'd be slinging me into the loony bin within a blink of an eye. Jack's phone was now ringing out . . . a painful stab of rage grappled with my heart, as I knew that this meant his earlier phone issues were a mixture of cowardice and lack of signal. He had probably emerged from the Tube by now and was not dead after all. In reality, I would hazard a guess that he was probably sitting at work, a shot of espresso in his hand, phone on silent, reading *The Times* and scratching his balls, without a care in the world.

As for me – I was inconsolable and it wasn't even lunchtime.

'Fucking men,' Danielle continues, between puffs of smoke. I could hear her heels clip-clopping down the street. 'What a loser with a capital L! Listen, I'm on Brick Lane about to get a bagel. Want one?'

'I can't eat, I'm stricken,' I moan. 'But bring me a soft cheese one with pastrami, just in case . . .'

'OK, I'll grab the food and then I am so on my way over, I'll bring the choc– OH MY GOD!!' she screams down the line, nearly deafening me.

'What? What is it?' I squeal back at her. 'Are you being mugged? Are there celebrities in Starbucks again? Is it Jack? Can you see Jack?'

There's nothing but silence for a few moments before a sharp intake of breath. 'Give me that!' she hisses to someone. 'I'm serious, it's a matter of urgency!' she shouts. I hear her whip something from the unknown person. A few seconds pass before she says, 'I'm not being mugged, a credible celebrity hasn't been seen in Starbucks since forever and yes, Katie, my God, I've seen Jack all right!'

'Well, what's he doing?' I query. 'Who is he with, does he look OK, is he dead?'

'Oh my . . .' she says tepidly. I hear her rustling. 'Katie, he's not dead . . . what on earth . . . just please don't go anywhere until I get there, OK? Sorry, here's a tenner, keep the change. Just wait until I get there and I'll explain.' I hear her rushing out of the bagel shop and into the street.

'Why?' I question, losing my patience. 'It's like you totally know something I don't about Jack!' I had to know, I mean this was serious!

'TAXI!' she yells and I hear her getting into a cab. 'Can you take me to Lauriston Gardens please, number eight,' she says, 'and step on it!'

'Whoah, Danielle, I thought they only said that in films?' I attempt a laugh, but I'm still pretty freaked out by Danielle's emergency action.

'I'll be there as soon as I can, don't go anywhere!' she repeats breathlessly, and hangs up on me.

Puzzled, I stared at the phone for a few moments before laying it on the coffee table. Could Jack have left me for someone else? Is that what Danielle saw, him draped across the body of another woman on Brick Lane? I mean, he's hot for this little café down there that serves macrobiotic food and holds Bikram yoga classes on Wednesday evenings . . . but it was our haunt, he wouldn't dare take another girl to a place we go to together . . . no, that's just insane, especially as it's only been a couple of hours since we broke up.

If Jack was having an affair, I totally hadn't noticed. I sat on my sofa, in my house, which was now empty of any man-stuff and surveyed the room for clues. Everything Jack owned, which wasn't much aside from the designer clothes I bought him, appeared to be gone, and I wasn't even sure exactly when he'd moved out. As an up-and-coming actor, Jack Hunter was always on the go, schmoozing and booz-ing, living the dream, whilst I filed my life away in an office. I worked flat-out as an administrator in a PR com-pany to fund his lifestyle, which meant he could take acting jobs which were largely low paid or unpaid. Jack was a man of extreme leisure, he moved at a slow pace, every-thing was 'chilled, man', and would be done 'in a minute'. He was hardly ever seen without his trademark Wayfarer shades on and if he tried to lie to me, his ears, which stuck out slightly, went bright red. Now I come to think about it, bits of his stuff had been missing over the past fortnight, just the little things, like his electric mouth-moulding, gentle-vibrate toothbrush that I liked to use when he wasn't looking, his Liberty hand cream that made my hands feel super smooth and his Louis Vuitton vanity case that I hoped he'd tire of because, to the outside world, the dial was hovering on the wrong side of the sexuality gay-o-meter. Jack was effeminate. He even wore light make-up to casting calls. He began to take his new man-bag that he begged me to buy him, made of real distressed leather, to work with him. He took it with him most mornings, instead of leaving his essentials lying around my bathroom, much to my annoyance. His stuff was way better than mine.

I must admit, I had noticed Jack was a lot quieter than usual, but I simply put it down to stress, after all, it's tough trying to break into an industry that bases your entire worth on the symmetry of your face. I was, however, used to occasionally not being able to immediately get hold of him. His phone would sometimes be on silent or off altogether for castings and very important meetings with other semi-successful actors. It was rude, you see, to have it on, and apparently even ruder to take five measely minutes out to pacify your fretting girlfriend. As an actor, Jack was deep, he was brooding, and sometimes, if he didn't get a job he really wanted, he went into his metaphorical 'cave' (round to his mother's) and was impossible to talk to. Sometimes he'd stay there for days, with his phone off or on silent, and I would be left wondering if it was something I'd done wrong that prevented him from sending a simple 'hello, I'm fine!' text back to me.

After around six months of sitting on his backside in my house, learning how to throw his voice, he decided to make a bit of money for himself that didn't come from the Department of Work and Pensions. He took a part-time barista job in one of those organic patisseries in Primrose Hill. I told him to keep the small wage he took, otherwise he'd never begin to make a proper life for himself. He did this job for the flexibility it gave him to attend auditions for commercials and the fact that he didn't have to tire himself out working beyond sixteen hours, thus not affecting his benefits.

He had a part in the Hollywood bonkbuster *Cowgirls* with primadonna diva Jessica Hilson, star of numerous cheesy rom-coms, that was set for release this summer. It was, as far as I knew, a small part, but he hoped that this would be his big break. As a result of his experiences rubbing shoulders with minor celebs on set for the past three months, he had developed a very noticeable swagger. He yearned to get closer to the A-list actors, especially Jessica Hilson, whom he idolized. He had the entire collection of *My Fabulous Life*, a fly-on-the-wall show which followed Jessica and her mega rich, gorgeous Italian boyfriend Fabio Matravers around the world with zillions of cameras, as they swanned about sunbathing on yachts, or schmoozing with celebrities at Cannes. They often jetted off to Mimi Sparkles beach hut in Honolulu. Mimi Sparkles is the name of Jessica Hilson's pet tiger who lives in her own personal mini jungle garden, with monkey helpers to cater to her needs. I was forever reading about Jessica and Fabio in *Sizzle Stars*, and then, when I reached for my gossip magazine's television guide, it would be missing. A hunt would ensue and I would find it either wedged down between the wall and my bed (Jack's side) or next to the toilet. Heaven knows what he was doing with it. Jack was desperate to get close to Jessica or any other A-lister, but failed because they always had an entire security system circulating them at all times on set and, as such, it was impossible to catch a glimpse of a manicured fingernail, let alone get close enough to introduce himself. I didn't really blame him for obsessing over various blonde starlets because when I did complain about it, he very rightly pointed out that if there was a slight chance of my coming into contact with Gerard Butler or Hugh Jackman in the stationery cupboard at work, I would probably faint on the spot and/or attempt some manhandling of said celebrity hunks into the nearest hotel room. Perhaps . . . I could dream, right?

Jack's cute dimples, his cheeky grin and his to-die-for skin tone caught the eye of at least a dozen older actresses who were partial to his effervescent charms. These actresses worked on neighbouring sets as the mothers of lithe young beauties in teen soaps. Jack never stepped out with the younger actresses – if he did, he'd find himself missing certain bits of his anatomy, because even I had my limits. Despite his protestations that those skinny minnies could open doors for him, I had my suspicions that the only doors that opened would be the ones to their bedrooms. I mean, I'm all for career progression, as long as it's kept in public view and with clothes firmly on bodies. Jack sniffed around the Cougars, the older ones who actually, in all fairness, could help him. They hadn't always worked on Z-list soaps, some of them had trodden the boards of the West End, some of them had even been in *Dynasty* and knew Joan Collins and everything! For those women, he would happily forsake lazy weekend mornings in bed with me to eat crumpets with them on Primrose Hill. He would laugh at their jokes and make them fall in love with him; he would compliment them to death whilst they fawned and simpered over him, flicking their Barbara Cartland curls and always footing the bill.

He always went to these breakfasts without me. Most girls I knew wouldn't let their boyfriends have as much free rein as I allowed Jack. But there was a very good reason why I did. He told me that his ex-girlfriend, Megan Vodianova, a Russian-born, feline-looking girl, was a total diva who ruined their relationship with her possessive, bunny-boiling behaviour. There was no way I would lose Jack Hunter, love of my life, for anything or anyone. Megan was slender and beyond beautiful and worked as a fashion model. She had a small dog that she carried everywhere in her little handbag. She walked with a wiggle and had the most annoying laugh he said he'd ever heard. To me she sounded perfect, flawless, amazing. But he said she was an attention-seeking control freak who had to know where he was at all times or she would cry and scream in public and cut up his clothes. He couldn't even break wind without permission, and she always had to be on top. This led him into my arms . . . the girl who was happy to take a back seat, who would give him a knee-lift up on to his shiny pedestal and who would let him fart to his heart's content. I would hold his mirror up for him so he could check his hair wasn't out of place, I carried his vanity case for him on his weekend casting calls and I organized his life with practical precision. But most of all, after Jack had almost shed a tear recounting the trials and tribulations of his awful life with Megan one day, I had decided there and then that I would be the opposite of Megan Vodianova in every single way.

This wasn't hard, as Megan Vodianova flaunted a size eight perma-tanned body with two giant stuck-on boobs, and nails that looked like teeth veneers growing from her fingertips. Her hair was so white it was blinding to look at. I was more mouse-blonde, wore a 34B bra and went red in the sun before peeling. Bah, I was her opposite. In terms of what I could do for Jack that was different to Megan, I was the better option by far. For one thing, I would support him and never ever question his whereabouts. I would be an ultra-modern girlfriend, and that would make him love me more, right? After all, I wasn't clipping his wings to keep him with me. Since meeting in the staff canteen where I work two and a half years ago – he had taken a casual job washing pots – I, unlike Megan, had displayed wondrous perfect-girlfriend traits, such as the ability to be ultra understanding of his obsessions with female megastars such as Jessica Hilson, Sharon Stone, Madonna and the lesser known female cast of *Hollyoaks*. I was incredibly loyal, faithful, great in bed and paid for everything so he didn't have to do that grotty job after about a nanosecond of our second date. I was mesmerized by his energy, his big ideas and his dreams. I fell in love harder than I ever thought possible, and Jack swore he felt the same way too. Within a month, he had moved into my house in Bethnal Green and we'd bought our cat, Grum.

The only thing that bugged me about Jack was that he was a bit thick. I couldn't have a joke with him without explaining the punchline, in great detail. Also, as he spent the only free time I had to spend with him, without me, out gallivanting with other women on the weekends, and frequenting underground West End bars where he had no signal on his mobile to reply to my texts – where did that leave me? I sat happily at home revelling in my supporting role, comfortable and relaxed, eating biscuits and watching *EastEnders*. Now you could easily forgive a girl for getting fed up with never seeing her boyfriend, but when he reappeared in the early hours of the morning gently singing my favourite songs, 'our songs', I would melt and passionately snog him until his lips fell off. Then we'd have sex and it would be oh so worth it.

In general, I didn't mind paying for his nights out or for his new expensive boots with the slight heel to give him extra height, if it helped him secure his dream of becoming a household name. I had faith in him, and he promised to repay me when he hit the big time. Besides, he did other things for me which more than made up for my giant credit card bills. For example, it was thanks to him that I not only got to see Orlando Bloom in the flesh, but also got his autograph on a coffee cup. Orlando popped into Jack's work for a drink incognito, or so he thought. Jack immediately texted a picture of him sipping his drink in the corner with his cap pulled firmly down and I hopped on the Tube from work to catch him in action. The location of Jack's work in Primrose Hill meant that lots of cool celebrities chose his café to sip their coffees and read their books, which meant I'd seen plenty of famous folk I admired so much they'd made me giddy. So, Jack staying out late and acting erratic was not unusual for him. Anyway, he couldn't possibly be having an affair, we were still having sex. And he still laughed at my jokes, made me cups of tea and thoughtfully recorded Jeremy Kyle for me when I was at work. Any signs or distant behaviour I may have worried about were quickly wiped out by a longing glance over dinner or a cuddle before bed on the nights he wasn't out partying. Sometimes, I would joke that he was having it off with his agent, a shifty-looking cockney geezer named Joel Farthing, who, in my opinion, was a bad influence on Jack, leading him into Soho peep shows and the like. I hadn't seen his ears go red since I asked him if he liked my mother after their first meeting. He said he simply adored her, but his ears told a totally different story. He knows now that he can't lie to me and get away with it.

I was still racking my brain as to why he'd walked out on me, and also why Danielle shot out of the bagel shop, down the street and into the taxi faster than the day we went to see Michael Jackson live – God rest his soul – and had to race to the front to catch backstage passes. I decided to go and make a cup of tea, as that normally solved most things. En route to the kitchen I flicked the TV on and whistled the theme tune to the news as I opened a packet of biscuits.

The presenter's chirrupy voice was drowned out by the sing-song of my old-style, boil-on-the-hob kettle. I tapped my foot impatiently on the kitchen floor as I waited for Danielle to appear at the door with details of her mysterious sighting of the elusive Jack Hunter. I poured the milk into my mug and accidently dropped my spoon on the floor. I bent over to get it and as I resumed a standing position, I glanced over at the telly and received the biggest shock of my life . . .

Large as you like, there he was, his tousled dark hair falling slightly over one eye, winking at the camera. There was no mistaking the sight of Jack's face grinning back at me, in full Technicolor widescreen. He was plastered all over my 52-inch plasma man-telly that he begged me to buy, right alongside a picture of mega famous A-list actress Jessica Hilson! The two pictures next to one another looked like glamorous mugshots. A flashing caption read: LOVE SHOCKER! JESSICA HILSON CAUGHT CANOODLING WITH MYSTERY MAN!

'That's my mystery man!' I managed to squeak. According to last week's *Sizzle Stars*, Jessica was still with her billion-dollar boyfriend, Italian shipping heir Fabio Matravers! Swoon! He was the epitome of suave glamour. What was she thinking?

In slow motion, my mouth agape, I dropped the teacup in horror. Grum sprinted out of the way of the shards of china bouncing in all directions off the kitchen floor. The milk splashed all over the counter top, spilling down the sides like a milky waterfall coming to rest in a puddle by my feet. I stood absolutely gobsmacked with a teaspoon in my hand. I strained to hear what the presenter was saying.

A slinky yet serious-looking blonde sits next to a man with a beard in a bright suit jacket on a sofa with this morning's newspapers fanned out on the table in front of them. She stares vacantly ahead as she appears to process information being sent into her earpiece. Pictures of Jack's face, hand up at the camera, Jessica Hilson's head under his armpit in an attempt to duck for cover from baying paparazzi, were clearly visible on at least two front pages. So he finally got his chance, then, I screamed inwardly.

'We've just had news in right this second that Jessica Hilson's mystery guy is an actor.'

'Actor?' I squealed at the television. 'If you count one line in *Emmerdale* and multiple walk-on parts in crappy movies that went straight to DVD,' I fumed.

The presenter continued: 'His name is Jack Hunter . . . worked with her on *Cowgirls*, which is set to smash the box office in July.'

The words became blurred in my head as the two presenters effectively joked about the scandal that is my boyfriend leaving me for an impossibly thin blonde actress with supermodel looks who carries designer bags that are worth more than anything I have ever owned! It's the stuff of nightmares! I hear the words 'his girlfriend', 'wouldn't want to be in her shoes' and 'affair' before I almost lose the will to live. I could have died right there and then on my kitchen floor had I not needed to gather absolutely every single shred of information about this, this betrayal! As if I didn't have content for at least five nightmares already this week, this has to happen.

'OH MY GOD!' I screamed, as the next picture showed the familiar window box in front of my house! My house was on bloody national television. Christ, I was in my house, shit, could anyone see in? My heart racing, I quickly looked either side of me, and thanked God that my curtains were still drawn. This meant the whole of the UK thankfully couldn't see me, humiliated Katie Lewis who was heartbroken, bedraggled and with no make-up on to speak of, aside from faint mascara trails that lay upon my cheeks. I was now hideously aware of my unfashionable tartan pyjamas that my nan had bought me last Christmas. I quickly moved towards the kitchen window and pulled the blind down before running upstairs and doing the same in my bedroom and bathroom. Fuck, what on earth is going on? Why is he with Jessica Hilson? I raced downstairs and continued to gawp at the screen but the images of my house, his face and her highness had been replaced with the weather. I moved into the hallway and sat down with the cat in my arms and my back against the front door and tried to process what was going on. I could hear people talking outside on the pavement.

'Yes, dear, the lad lived in there with Katie, lovely girl . . . why do you ask?' I could clearly hear Mrs Bellamy from next door shimmy along on her electric wheelchair to whoever was asking her the questions, presumably a reporter. Now I understood why those vans were parked on my road, they were news teams reporting back to BBC-bloody-Breakfast about my stupid boyfriend and this ridiculous charade! It's one thing for your boyfriend to leave you, but another thing altogether if your neighbours are getting a first-hand, warts-and-all, blow-by-blow account of it. My street hadn't seen this much dramatic action since the Blitz. All of a sudden, there was a knock on the door and the sound of someone crouching down to my level on the other side.

'Katie Lewis?' a woman's voice said authoritatively through my letterbox. 'My name's Pippa Strong from *London Lowdown*. I'm looking for your comments regarding the relationship between Jack Hunter and Hollywood hot property, Jessica Hilson?' I shirked backwards and attempted to flatten myself against the wall so she couldn't see me. My heart was racing like the clappers. Relationship? So it's true, really, actually true? No, it simply can't be, the papers make stuff up all the time, especially the tabloids – secrets, lies and Paris Hilton sex tapes. No, this was just some hideous mistake. Not my Jack! The bed was barely cold, the sheets still had his stray pubes lying in them, and his organic water-activating, mineral-particles facecloth was still in my bathroom. He'd never up sticks without that.

'Shove it, bozo,' a familiar voice said, as the reporter with her big nose shoved firmly in my letterbox went flying.

'I'll have you for assault!' Pippa squealed. I opened the door gingerly to Danielle, wearing my giant comedy pink heart-shaped shades I'd found underneath the radiator whilst sitting on the floor. Jessica Hilson wasn't the only one who could do glamour! The glasses did a good job of almost obscuring most of my features. 'This is harassment and I'm a lawyer!' Danielle screamed, with such velocity that Pippa, who had now come forwards again to get a glimpse of me, jerked her head right back as though she was a tortoise retreating into her shell. She said nothing as Mrs Bellamy and other assorted neighbours of pension-drawing age and a couple of mumsy types who had no doubt spied their houses on TV gathered before my gate as though they were witnessing a macabre accident.

'Nothing to see here OK, so beat it!' Danielle continued to bark at them all, as I stood aside to let her in. Closing the door, double-locking it and sticking on the chain that I only use when I'm on my own overnight, I sank to the floor and cried big, fat, salty tears.

'Shh,' Danielle soothed. 'It's OK,' and she took me into her arms for a much-needed hug.

'I was hoping I would get here before that lot,' Danielle said sullenly, as she gestured towards the window.

My mouth was still hanging slightly open as I tried to process this morning's insanity. Last night, Jack was here, in my house, eating spaghetti bolognaise and watching *Antiques Roadshow* whilst I sat next to him on the sofa, polishing off a bottle of red. He left around 9pm to go and nurse his sick mother who had a cold that wouldn't budge. He was worried that she had pneumonia and therefore would need to take a rather large bag for an extended stay. *Did I mind?* he asked, chivalrously. *No, darling.* How could I refuse that beautiful face?

'I need a biscuit,' was all I could say, as I realized now exactly when Jack had left me. Coward that he is couldn't even tell me about Jessica Hilson, had to let the world tell me. On the inside, a zillion and one questions were pummelling my weary head from every direction.

'OK,' Danielle said to me, opening the chocolate digestives. She handed them to me, staring at my face, looking for clues as to how I felt.

'I have to know everything,' I said quietly.

Chapter 2

Handsome vest-wearing muscleman Jack Hunter has been seen emerging from The Dorchester by our eagle-eyed photographers several times over the past week. Wearing casual attire, Jack smouldered as he carried a distressed-leather man-bag whilst sporting designer stubble. Jessica Hilson, wearing a chic multicoloured Diane von Furstenberg dress and carrying this season's Balenciaga Giant City handbag in Maldives, was spotted leaving via the back entrance with her giant minders, before speeding off in a chauffeur-driven limo, which, on closer inspection, also contained Jack Hunter. Their elusive getaway was well and truly foiled. As *Sizzle Stars* went to press, no official announcement has been made regarding the status of their relationship and what this now means to their significant others, Fabio Matravers, 35, the well-respected businessman and shipping heir and the as yet unknown girlfriend of *Monsieur* Hunter.

'This just gets better and better,' I moaned to Danielle as we ate breakfast. Toast crumbs dropped down my front and all over the pages of the tabloid that I had pinched from Danielle, that she had pinched from some poor startled girl in the bagel shop yesterday morning.

'I know,' she mused, drinking her tea. 'The press are

still camped outside your door . . . I called work for you this morning. They understood you can't get out of your door, let alone into Leicester Square.'

'Who did you speak to?' I asked her gingerly, lighting up a cigarette.

'Richard Dewberry.'

'Richard will love this. I'm surprised he's not here now.'

As if on cue, the doorbell gave a loud shrill.

'Ignore it,' Danielle said, turning to an article about Tom Cruise. 'Did you know that Tom Cruise wears high heels?'

'Yeah, I bought the same ones for Jack. They're not like ladies' high heels, they have special inbuilt heels to assist a man in the height department,' I said. God, I knew so much about men's fashion now, I could run a specialist PR department.

'Darling!' The unmistakeable sound of Richard's estuary accent shouted through my letterbox. Then he turned to the gaggle of information-thirsty reporters.

'No, I am not going to give you any kind of quote on Katie, you horrible woman. Don't you think you lot have done enough to the poor girl?'

Pippa was still camped out on her knees outside my door, peering in my letterbox every so often and calling my name. I could hear her talking back at Richard, eager to misquote him.

'I'm just saying,' he continued, 'that Katie has had her heart broken on national television and that little turd Jack is off swanning around The Dorchester with Jessica silicone tits, living the life of Riley!'

I put my massive pink heart shades back on and tied my dressing gown tight around my middle. Flashing my grey underwear to the national press was not something I wanted to have happen today. I slowly unhooked the chain and opened the door, keeping as much of me as possible out of view. The flashbulbs went off as Richard made for the door. He turned round and stuck his middle finger up and told the press to 'Eff off'.

'Richard!' I squealed before pulling him in by the coat-tails. 'I don't want attention! At least, not until I have had some kind of extensive face-changing makeover!'

'Jesus, who died here?' he said, looking at me with his hand clasped to his face in mock horror.

'I'm supposed to look like shit,' I bit back. 'I've just been dumped and now everyone on my street knows that Jack's been having it off with Jessica bleedin' Hilson.'

'Um, the whole world knows, practically. I saw it on Sky news last night in The King's Head. I've been trying to call you ever since, Katie, why haven't you answered your phone?'

'It's on silent,' I lied. It's not on silent, it's on the loudest tone possible due to the fact I insanely thought that Jack hadn't meant to have this affair with Jessica Hilson. I thought that now that it's exposed, he would come running back to me with his tail between his legs and a plausible explanation, such as, he was using her to forward his own career, still loved me, never stopped in fact and could I just play along a little bit more because soon enough he's going to make it and we'll jet off to the USA, live in the Hollywood Hills, shop all day long and get fabulous-look-ing tans. I thought he would call me, make a midnight return, something more than the pathetic-looking text of yesterday morning. I ignored all calls on my mobile last night, which included a zillion from my mother Jo, my sister Janice and Richard. No doubt they'd all seen the unfortunate demise of Jack & Katie plastered all over the tabloids and, of course, the telly. I had briefly logged on to my Facebook last night to discover twelve emails in my inbox, multiple wall posts and one less friend on my list – Jack. Jack Hunter had not only erased the past few years of his life with me in favour of some American bimbo, he'd also severed virtual ties on Facebook, MySpace and Gmail chat, and he wasn't following my life on Twitter any more. Any shred of what we had, had been blown up in a puff of smoke and I, like our relationship, had been deleted.

'So, why are you really here, then?' I said sarcastically to Richard.

'To see you, darling, to check you are OK, I mean, the whole office is tremendously worried about you. Magenta sends her love too. She says to tell you to take some compassionate leave, we're all thinking of you. Even that snarled face Hanna Frost sent her condolences.'

'Condolences?' Danielle said, aghast. 'No one's died here, Richard.'

'Yet,' I said, as I shoved the grainy picture of Jack canoodling with Jessica in the back of a limo under Richard's nose.

'Youch,' he said, pulling a startled face.

'Magenta said I could have compassionate leave?' I asked.

'Yes, she said take as long as you want. She'll pay you too. To be honest, chick, she's probably over the moon at the ensuing publicity you're going to generate for Poets Field PR with this little media storm.'

'But it's hardly good publicity, Rich, is it? "Administrator at Poets Field PR gets dumped for super-rich plastic megastar" doesn't exactly have a good ring to it.'

'It all depends on how you conduct yourself from now on, darling. You could come out of this as the dignified, classy English Rose or the downtrodden, common Waynetta Slob.' He looked me up and down, taking in my pyjamas and tea-stained pink robe. 'Now, have you thought about getting some advice? I know a chap who could guide you through this whole to-do. You could make yourself a tidy sum out of it – pain equals pounds, darling!'

'Oh God . . .' Danielle groans from the living room.

'What?' Richard and I say in unison.

Danielle calls us in and Richard and I sit down together on my couch, transfixed by *This Morning*.

Holly Willoughby stands there looking boobtastic in a figure-hugging wrap dress whilst a giant picture of Jack and Jessica adorns half the screen.

'And now, let's meet Joel Farthing, a well-respected media agent, acting on behalf of Jack Hunter. Joel, how are you today?'

'Hi, Holly, thanks for inviting me on the show. Well, as you can imagine, things are indeed pretty hectic for Jack right now and, of course, for Jessica.'

'And where exactly are Jack and Jessica right now, the couple at the heart of the UK's most sensational story?'

'They're out of the country. They've gone on holiday because we knew there would be quite a furore over their clandestine encounters. Jessica Hilson is actually a very low-key star, preferring quiet nights in to glamorous nights out. Jessica prefers to shy away from the spotlight unless it's specifically to do with her artistic endeavours, such as *Cowgirls*, set for release very soon.' Joel taps his nose and nods to the camera. 'And of course,' he adds as an afterthought, 'they don't really want any more attention.'

'Hmmm, of course,' Holly nods vigorously and flashes a set of perfectly white teeth.

'Now,' she continues, 'what may seem like an obvious assumption, can you confirm for us, the question on the nation's lips – are Jack Hunter and Jessica Hilson an official item?'

'Well, I'd like to say watch this space, but they're definitely enjoying one another's company right now . . . you'll have to wait and see!'

And with that, Joel gives a smarmy wink to Holly and then to the camera. Holly's cheeks blush a furious red. She wrapped up the conversation by talking about another actor Joel represented who was staying in the Priory. The picture of the two hurtful figures in my life was replaced by a skinny-looking person with bad skin holding a guitar.

'What a rat,' Danielle said.

'Bastard!' I said.

'How on earth did he manage that?' Richard cooed.

We both turned to glare at him.

Richard got up and peeked out of the window.

'Richard!' I screamed. 'Shut those bloody curtains, I cannot have anyone seeing me in this state!' I instinctively reached for my shades and stuck them on my face, just in case.

'Whoa, sorry, I was just seeing if it was clear to get you out of here, that's all.'

'To where?'

'I don't know yet, but you can't stay here,' he said.

'Why not?' I asked.

'Because you have that big-nosed journalist living on your doorstep, about ten trucks with cameras perched on top trained on your front door and a bunch of old ladies on deckchairs, eating cheese and pickle sandwiches, handing round their flasks of tea to the thirsty press. They won't budge until you give them a story. Come off it, Katie, I'm a PR media account manager, I know how this shit works.'

'You work with lipstick brands and lingerie! It's totally not the same thing!'

'The methods of execution are the same,' he smiled sweetly.

'Well, what do you suggest I do, then? Creep out in disguise?'

'Well, yes,' he said. 'Either that or you get scurvy from lack of sunlight.'

'I guess I could go to my mother's . . . and then figure out what to do next,' I mused.

'Good idea. Now, for a distraction, do the press have any idea of what you look like?' he questioned.

'I don't know, perhaps, if someone has given them a picture of me . . . I never answered the door fully so they couldn't see my face yesterday or today, I wore these comedy shades,' I said, wafting said shades in the air.

'I doubt that the press are going to just go away, though, are they?' Danielle said. 'And they know I'm not Katie and clearly, as a bloke, you're not Katie either, so how do we get Katie out of the house without them noticing?'

'I don't know. Give me a minute to think.' Richard scratched his chin. 'I've got it! We get you out of the house with a pillowcase over your head with only eye-shaped holes cut out. My sports car is parked at the end of your road, we run out, past them, and jump into the car and I'll speed you anywhere you like. They won't catch us, they've got too many news vans and pensioners lining the street.'

'True,' I said. 'Plus, Mrs Bellamy and other nosey parkers have set their deckchairs in prime position in the middle of the road facing my house. They'll never move them out of the way, you know how slow old people can be at the best of times.'

'By the time they've turned their cars round and shuffled Mrs Bellamy out of the way, we'll be halfway across the city. Now, where shall we go?'

'My mother's house, in deepest, darkest Oxfordshire.'

'Right, well, get your things. Danielle, can you take Grum?'

'I'll just come round using the spare key and feed him, if it's all the same to you. I'm allergic to cats,' she said, sparking up another cigarette.

I ran around the house looking for a pillowcase I didn't mind cutting up, my make-up and sufficient clothing to last me for however long it took for this ordeal to die down.

I was lucky I had my friends around me, otherwise I could quite possibly have starved to death as I had run out of bread and milk that morning. I sighed heavily and rubbed my temples. Jack's departure had hit me harder than I had ever imagined. I loved him with all my heart, not despite his faults and mild annoyances, but *because* of them. I could smell him on my clothes and his aftershave lingered on my pillows, in my hair, in the living room. There were remnants of my boyfriend and our life together all around me and I could still feel him in the air. It was all

I could do to stop myself from crying long, drawn-out, incomprehensible sobs on to Danielle's shoulder as she stroked my hair and said the right things to make me feel a little bit better last night. It must have been a good four hours before I could stop sobbing yesterday. I managed ten long minutes of semi-dry cheeks at any given time last night, which was enough to light a cigarette and not extinguish it with tears. Danielle had no option other than to remain by my side, the Kleenex man-size tissues at the ready, mopping up my sodden face. When she left for those brief moments I would shamelessly wail in a totally over-the-top fashion, fuelled by my worst nightmare coming true and a vat of Blossom Hill. When we had sunk enough wine to inebriate an army, I climbed up on the kitchen stool and clumsily continued up on to the breakfast bar where I ran my hands around the rim of the shelving units. We then consumed all the emergency wine. Finally, in the early hours of the morning, exhausted from the day's events, we had collapsed in a drunken heap on my bed. I prayed with all my might that it – Jack leaving me for a Hollywood film star – had all been a bad dream.

But no, I woke up this morning to yet more intense scrutiny of my house, love life and stupid Jack Hunter. Just who did he think he was, ditching me like this? My heart-wrenching, guttural pain of last night was now somewhat absent with the presence of a banging headache, dry mouth, and intense fury for unwittingly being presented to the world as a 'scorned woman'. How dare he do this to me! I can feel the anger bubbling up inside of me, adrenaline surges through my veins. I angrily throw on my dressing gown and violently shove my feet into my slippers. Oh, it was all right for Jack Hunter, wasn't it! He was off sunning himself with my nemesis whilst leaving me here to deal with a bunch of hacks on my doorstep, plus I was totally going to be the subject of gossip at work. It was bad enough having Richard charge in and take control as though he was Max bloody Clifford, what with all his talk about getting my own PR adviser to guide me through this drama, but realizing Jack's dreams didn't include me was so much more terrible than I could ever comprehend.

Despite his flamboyance and scathing comments, Richard was one of my favourite colleagues at work. He loved fashion and designer labels even more than Jack. If people think Jack bats for the other side, it's fair to say that most people's first impressions of Richard are that he's an eccentric, image-obsessed gay. He doesn't correct their assumptions, because this is one of the tricks he uses to attract women. Richard often told me about the tricks that men use to attract women. He kept books and magazine articles dedicated to subliminal mind tricks with which to entice a woman into bed and he swore blind that they worked. He was like a romance version of Derren Brown. I was well inclined to believe him, based upon the fact he almost always had a stunning six-foot goddess draped all over him at any given time.

'Why,' I asked him one day, 'is it OK for a man to have it off with tons of women but it's not OK for a woman to have it off with loads of men?'

'Well,' he said, 'that's easy.'

'Explain,' I said.

'Well . . . for a man to have slept with many women he must be charming, sensual, attractive, funny and rich.'

'Well . . . that's not strictly true . . .' I grumble, thinking about my ex-boyfriends.

'For a woman to have slept with many men, she simply has to exist in the same oxygen space.' He smiles and winks.

I roll my eyes. He was forever expanding upon his laws of attraction theories, in the car on the way home, over coffee at work, during lunch, in emails, on the phone and in just about every other conceivable situation. He was obsessed with beautiful women.

'You chicks love gay men,' Richard announced one day, shortly after I made him watch *Will & Grace* round my house one night whilst I lay on my sofa dying of the flu. Jack had sensibly stayed away from me in case he caught it and potentially jeopardized his upcoming audition for the bartender in *Cowgirls*, the part that has now ruined my life. I should have sneezed all over him. From watching my girly box sets, Richard figured that women instantly put their trust in a gay man – all of us ladies want a Gay Best Friend as much as this season's Chanel lipstick. He also figures that lulling girls into a false sense of security by acting gay and discussing emotions, sharing and feelings talk, will result in a 10 out of 10 smash-up – his term for getting a woman into bed.

Richard talks about another man-technique that he uses to succeed with women, although he never stays with the women for any great length of time. A love 'em and leave 'em type, he breaks hearts and beds and narrowly escapes having bits of him broken by the scorned women. It's the Cat String Theory.

'It's like this,' he said, as he crunched on some of my

homemade tacos in front of the telly, 'you put some string in front of your cat and you dangle it.'

'Yeah . . .' I said, blowing my nose into a tissue, 'obviously, that's what cats like . . .'

'No, well, yes they do, and what happens when you pull the string away?'

'The cat goes nuts for the string. Oh, Rich, please tell me you're not comparing us girlies to balls of string!' I say, affronted.

'Kind of . . . What happens when the cat gets the string you've been teasing him with?' He gives a wry smile.

I sigh loudly and Rich squeals, 'He gets bored!' at me before slapping his thighs. 'AH HA!'

I grin back at him, shaking my head. I can't believe men operate on this level!

'Kitty gets bored and he loses interest within five minutes and searches for another toy to please him and I'm afraid, darling, that this is what men do to girls, all the time. Seriously, girls need to make themselves that little bit unavailable, that little bit mysterious. Us men, we're predators!'

Despite all of his arrogance, women flock to Richard, men flock to Richard, animals and children flock to Richard and all get a short shrift. He is charming and devilishly handsome with it, a wicked combination. He is a natural at Public Relations.

He's also bloody good at getting my backside out of the door and into his car at the end of the road. Without warning, he manhandled me up and over his shoulder, which was impressive considering how slight he is. He tumbled me down the street, one hand clinging on to his shoulder for dear life, the other holding on to the pillow-case which made me look as though I was about to either burgle someone or join the Ku Klux Klan. Reporters attempted to give chase but were prevented by the gaggle of fogies who had now all stood up to get a better view of my backside wobbling in the air. I gave a quick wave to Danielle, who stood on the doorstep giving little concerned hand gestures as though she was waving me off to sea. A tear escaped down my face, ruining the mascara I had freshly applied in case my pillowcase should blow away in the wind. I couldn't quite believe that Richard was giving me a fireman's lift away from a crowd that had gathered outside my house to get a glimpse of me. Was this what it was like being a celebrity? Would *Sizzle Stars* and *This Morning* now have images of the crack of my bottom and flowery giant Tesco pants? Which was inevitable, really, when someone hoists you up with no warning, you don't get the chance to pull up your jeans as high as they'll go to avoid what was probably happening now. I couldn't see a thing through my eye slits other than rows of terraced houses, cars and bemused-looking passers-by, wondering what on earth was going on.

Eventually Richard set me down, collapsed against the bonnet of his car, and clicked his key fob to open the doors. Sweat trickled down his face and he touched his chest with his free hand and sighed dramatically.

'Oh, come off it, Richard, I'm not that heavy!'

He raised an eyebrow at me and clutched his chest some more before taking out a hanky and wiping down his forehead.

'Get . . . in . . . the . . . car,' he said, breathlessly.

I clambered in, and sat back against the seat, chucking my rucksack of clothes and other bits and pieces into the back seat. Richard sat down next to me and put the radio on.

'Phew! Well, we did it. Keep that pillowcase on your head, we don't want anyone taking pictures of you with their long-lens cameras!' he said, as he revved up the engine and we sped off in the direction of my childhood home, the village of Little Glove, Oxfordshire.

'Thanks,' I said to Richard, as his face went back to a normal shade of peach and his breathing slowed.

'It's OK, chick, any time. Now, let's get you home.'

Chapter 3

The car rolled on to the gravel driveway of my family home two hours later and we came to a stop. I still had the pillowcase firmly on my head in case we were being tailed by any paparazzi. We'd twisted and turned through several routes with a number of suspicious-looking vehicles' bumpers halfway up our backsides. Richard had sped away and it looked like we had escaped them all.

As we parked up, I reached into the pocket of my rucksack for my cigarettes and lit one up. I didn't care that my mother, who was fastidiously against smoking, may quite possibly kill me for lighting up in the front garden.

All of a sudden, the all too familiar grainy picture of Jack with Jessica Hilson's head in his armpit, arms flailing at the camera, an eye throwing an accusatory glance backwards, was slammed up against the window of the car. My seventeen-year-old sister stood there with a copy of the offending tabloid.

'For goodness' sake, Janice, don't you think I've seen enough of that picture to last me a lifetime?' I scream at her. 'Besides that, you nearly frightened me to death!' I say, grabbing my chest for effect.

'What the fuck is going on?' she screams back at me. 'I've had to, like, field off zillions of phone calls all about you and Jack, plus my Facebook has been inundated with friend requests!'

She stands there, hand on hip as though my drama is her drama.

'There is no me and Jack!' I state defiantly, before thinking of suitable words to throw at her that best describe my feelings towards Jack, her and that huge chip on her shoulder. 'Not any more,' I add, with a lump in my throat.

'Bite your tongue,' Richard hisses in my ear. 'She's a kid, she lives and breathes celebrity gossip, you've probably just single-handedly elevated her in the popularity stakes in the sixth form for having a sister who inadvertently dated a movie star. She'll thank you for it when she goes into school tomorrow.'

'Well, this isn't about her, is it!' I spat.

And then it dawned on me . . . Facebook . . . zillions of new friends . . . could only be one thing!

'You didn't say yes to any of those friend requests, did you?' I asked, with a cold feeling in my blood. But I already knew. With a sinking heart, I realized that of course Janice had accepted every single friend request that came her way because having as many friends as possible, regardless of whether you knew any of them or not, was a badge of honour amongst her friends.

'Yeah . . . so?' she answered blithely.

'Well, didn't you think that some, if not all of them are from journalists digging for information on me?'

'No, I guess . . . I . . . I didn't think.'

'You never bloody think, Janice! Oh my God, those are probably the same journalists who have been camping outside my house for the past day and a half! The very same journalists who have hounded me out of my home and over Richard's shoulder disguised by a pillowcase over my head!' I was red in the face, close to tears and pointing at her furiously.

She took a few steps back, clutching the tabloid protectively to her chest.

'And another thing, how am I now supposed to get Jack away from her? How do you expect me to compete with a world-famous actress like Jessica Hilson with her dazzling white teeth and perfectly styled hair, when the whole world and their mother is now going to see your photo album of the two of us as bridesmaids, gap-toothed and podgy, at Aunty Fiona's wedding back in 1997!'

'Oh . . .' Janice says, looking at her feet. Richard flicks his fag out on to the driveway.

'What's so wrong with that, Katie?' Richard says. 'You can't have been all that old, the media aren't going to chastise a teenager for having dodgy style sense now are they?'

Janice rolls her eyes in Richard's direction. 'You so don't know anything, do you?' She sighs, as though he was the most ignorant human being to ever walk this earth. 'Don't you read the style section of *London Lowdown*?'

'Can't say I do . . .' he says, checking his reflection in the wing mirror.

'Well, trust me, bubble perms and puffball dresses, although fashion statements of their time, are not in vogue any more.'

'Were they ever?' I ask. 'But see, this is my point – I am going to be crucified in the press and it's all your bloody fault!' I spit at her.

Richard places his arm around my shoulders and squeezes me tight. I shrug him off.

'Listen, Janice,' Richard addresses my sister with the

same twinkly eyes he uses on women he fancies, 'why don't you go on inside and pop the kettle on for a cup of tea?'

'Milk one sugar, right?' she says bashfully, cheeks ablaze. I always knew she fancied him.

'Yes, darling,' he coos, knowing he's successfully wrapped her around his little finger, 'and how about you pour a little shot of vodka for your stressed-out big sister?'

'How about you just give me the bottle?' I mutter under my breath.

'No problem,' she says, as she flashes him a lip-glossed smile and wiggles her bottom towards the house.

'The girl's shameless,' I say, shaking my head.

'And cute,' Richard adds, as Janice throws a lust-filled look over her shoulder.

As Janice opens the door, my mother Jo waltzes out towards the car, swinging her brightly coloured pashmina over her shoulders, long necklaces with jangly bits clashing against one another, making tinkling sounds. I open the car door and stand up, ready for the full force of her maternal bosom; her long brown curls bounce against her shoulders as she thrusts herself upon me for a smothering hug.

'Darling!' she says, relaxing her embrace. She holds me by the elbows at arm's length, the way parents do when they haven't seen you in a while and want to measure how well you have fared without their home-cooked shepherd's pies.

'What on earth is going on?' she cries.

'Jack dumped me!' I throw my head back for effect and make loud gulping sounds as the comforting presence of my mother makes me cry big salty tears. Just seeing Mum again in this time of extreme crisis brought me back to 1988, aged four, with a skinned knee from playing leap-frog on the gravelled drive with Nicola Baxter from two doors down. Her mum owned a beauty salon in the village. Beauty being debatable, seeing as every time Mum goes for a makeover ahead of any family occasion, she always returns with so much rouge on her cheeks and cobalt-blue eye shadow you could easily mistake her for a transvestite. She cocks her head to one side, processing my tale of woe.

'He did it in a text message!' I blub. 'He left me for a Hollywood actress with supermodel looks!' I wail and launch myself back into her arms.

'Darling,' she sighs, 'I know it feels like he's left you for a supermodel, it always does, but I'm sure that's not the case.' She strokes my hair as I stand pitifully in the drive-way, wiping my nose on my jumper sleeve.

'I'm sure she has just as much cellulite as you do, per-haps even more!'

'Oh God!' I groan loudly as my knees buckle. Richard grabs hold of one arm and my mother takes the other.

'Let's get her inside,' he says wisely, 'we don't know who may be watching . . .'

'What do you mean by that, dear?'

'The paparazzi! They've been camped outside her house in Bethnal Green since yesterday trying to get her side of the story. Katie isn't being a drama queen, Mrs Lewis.'

'For once,' Janice sniggers, as she appears in the door-way, holding a shot of vodka. 'It's actually all true.'

The colour drains from my mother's face as she realizes the gravitas of my mini drama.

'Here, looks like you need it more,' Janice says, as she passes the little plastic shot glass towards Mum.

'I don't want that!' She pulls her 'insulted' face, as she snatches the shot and pours it on the flowerbed.

We go inside and position ourselves around the breakfast table and drink tea. I pour myself a triple vodka.

'Our Katie,' Janice announces in a stupid newsreader voice, 'has made a terrible mistake in her choice of man . . . chiselled muscleman Jack Hunter has only gone and upped sticks and left her for size zero Hollywood actress Jessica Hilson!'

'Wasn't she the lead in *Forever in my Pocket* with Will Ferrell?' Mum queries.

'The very one.'

'What's she doing with your Jack?'

'I wish I knew!' I say. 'He's not told me anything!'

'That's right . . .' Richard adds, 'although if we want to know the latest gossip on Jack Hunter, a quick Google search throws up some impressive results . . .'

'I know where he is based on which magazine has been stalking them with a long lens,' I reply.

'I never liked him anyway,' Mum furrows her brows. 'His eyes were too close together.'

'So, Mum,' Janice says gleefully, 'there's, like, a very good chance that the *Daily Mail* will be camped outside our front door in the flowerbeds trying to get shots of us all tomorrow morning! How exciting is that!'

'It's not exciting at all, Janice,' I hiss, as Mum looks ready to collapse with shock. The *Daily Mail* to Mum is what *Sizzle Stars* is to Janice and Prada is to Jack. Our neighbours in Oxfordshire were even worse for snooping than the ones in Lauriston Gardens. If I thought a couple of deckchairs and a cheese and pickle sandwich was a problem in London, I knew that the residents of Little Glove would be ten times worse. There would be the local press for one, then the regional and so on and so forth. But that wouldn't be the worst of it. Oh no! The gaggle of middle-aged busybodies who darned socks in their sleep and could recite passages of the Bible and then sugar lace them on to the tops of cakes were even worse than Mrs Bellamy and her cronies. We'd be confronted by a senior crowd fuelled by curiosity and organic jam tarts whenever we went anywhere in the village for the foreseeable future. We had lived in Little Glove for twenty-three years, but because my nan hadn't been born and raised there like every other member of the geriatric generation, we were still considered newcomers, and as every newcomer to a village knows, getting into the clique is no mean feat.

'Peter!' my mother says breathlessly, and as if by magic, my father appears by her side. He can't see a thing without his bifocal glasses, thick as milk-bottle bottoms, which means his other senses overcompensate, resulting in extra-sensory perceptive hearing. My dad communicates with a series of grunts and hand gestures that only my mother can understand.

'Paint the fence! Wash the windows! Mow the lawn!' she squeals, whilst fanning her face with the dish towel. 'We're going to be famous!'

Richard, Janice and I all throw looks of sheer horror at one another. My mother, however, has scuttled over to the phone and, diary in hand, is booking us all in for trims and blow-dries down at Betty's Salon, at their earliest convenience.

'Christ,' I say to Richard, 'fag time.'

We push our chairs out and retreat into the back garden. Swinging back and forth in the afternoon spring sunshine on the summer bench, I listen out for any suspicious rustling from the holly bushes. Nothing. Not a tweet.

'If Betty Baxter gives me a wonky fringe again I will positively kill her,' I laugh.

We spent the rest of the afternoon enjoying the sunshine and watching my father clamber up and down a ladder painting anything and everything so it looked shiny and new for when the media showed up. My mother, as mad as she was, was extremely house-proud and set about giving our house an industrial-strength super clean. I kept well out of the way. My head was already splitting from all the red wine Danielle and I put away the night before, and alongside the dramatic cupboard slamming, huffing, puffing and moaning about the state of our house (which was perfectly fine, trust me) it didn't help that I was constantly thinking about Jack.

This was a zillion times worse than when I broke up with Matthew Robinson, aged eighteen. Back then I had no clue what girl he might have been with when we broke up, or what he was doing. There was no Facebook and therefore no internet stalking could take place. There were no updates on the progress of his day on a newsfeed nor were there any tagged photographs detailing his nights out.

The Little Glove Community Centre on a Friday night gave me every opportunity to check up on him, with his gelled hair slicked back and his designer gear with the massive logos that shimmered in the darkness of the dance hall. He could have been shagging any one of the girls I regularly saw him with in the months after we broke up. One minute he was with Tracey, a girl who had mastered how to style her fringe into swirly little patterns that stuck without movement down the side of her face, and the next he was with Debbie from the year below, with her ginger hair and her platform shoes. Nicola Baxter, my childhood partner in crime, and I would stand in the corner eating strawberry laces and necking vodka from the quarter bottles we'd snuck in our knickers. When we'd got the Dutch courage, we'd strut over to where Matthew was standing with his equally moody and brooding friends, and dance like strippers in a vain attempt to get their attention. Sometimes they'd throw a grunt and a nod of approval in our direction and as soon as we got that, we told them to piss off, spun on our high heels and strutted off.

'Prick tease!' Matthew and his friends would shout in unison after us. We'd laugh until we cried and then share a packet of cigarettes behind the bowling club before spraying ourselves with Impulse and chewing two packets of Wrigley's to convince our parents that we'd remained on the Cola Pops all night. Those were the uncomplicated days of dating where the only sneaking about we did involved back doors, midnight returns and a bag stuffed full of make-up and flimsy outfits. I can't imagine Matthew Robinson off gallivanting with Hollywood starlets. The last I heard of him, he worked for British Gas and drove a Ford Fiesta. He's the kind of man who thinks he's grand for holidaying in a caravan.

Eventually, Richard and I had eaten enough Battenberg to satisfy a small coffee morning, and had exhausted ourselves on the whys and wherefores of Jack's behaviour. I stood next to his sports car as he sat in the driving seat, revving up the engine.

'See how this week pans out, darling, I'll be back for you in a couple of days,' he purred. He loved being the knight in shining armour, and right now, I totally needed someone to just charge in and take control of my life.

'I will report back on the haircut,' I said gravely. Richard winked at me, blew an air kiss and drove off down the driveway and into the sunset. I stood there looking after him, hugging myself for warmth.

'Brrrr,' I said to myself – there was a chill in the air. I heard the gravel crunch as my sister walked up to join me. She looked at me with her puppy-dog eyes before wrapping her arms around my shoulders and giving me a hug.

'You soppy thing,' I playfully pushed her. She smiled gently and we walked arm-in-arm into the house, which had been disinfected to within an inch of its life and now stank of lavender-scented candles. I grabbed a packet of paracetamol for my headache and steered myself away from the drinks cabinet to go up to my old bedroom.

'Night, Janice,' I said, as I walked up the stairs. She smiled at me before heading off in the direction of the television.

I loved the safety of my old bedroom, and as I creaked open the door and peeked round the corner, I was pleased to see it was exactly the same as when I'd left home nearly four years ago, and had remained so with each fleeting visit since. It was almost like a shrine in honour of me, the eldest child who had absconded to the big smoke of London. My mother never tired of telling anyone who'd listen that I was a successful, hard-nosed city type. She made me sound like Hanna Frost, which couldn't be further from the truth. I don't know why she makes such a fuss about the fact I only come home for family dos, because when I was living at home full time she never listened to a word I said anyway. She was forever muttering on about the state of the house, my dad's piles, her piles and playing dominoes with Betty Baxter, before coming home and recounting tales about how wonderfully Nicola Baxter was doing in her two-up two-down semi in Little Glove that she shared with her boyfriend. This, apparently, is what I should be aiming for, before I become too old to marry someone suitable and end up turning into a bitter and twisted, childless, cat person. Methinks she's been reading too much *Bridget Jones*. According to Mum, Janice was always out 'gallivanting' and my father barely lifted his head from the depths of his newspaper to communicate with her. He only put it down to fix something or other in the house at Mum's request. Never mind, I thought, as I wrapped myself in my dressing gown. Photos of Nicola Baxter and me mucking about on the last day of term were pinned up on my cork noticeboard and old toys Matthew Robinson had won for me at the local fair sat happily on my shelves. I gently thumb-stroked a picture of us in a photo booth, tongues out and silly grins on our faces.

Nostalgia took over as I pressed play on my ghetto blaster and listened to an old Take That album. As the sounds drifted up and around my bedroom, I flopped on to my single bed and snuggled under the duvet. Oh, to be a teenager again, where my biggest worry was the spot on the end of my nose and whether my right boob really was bigger than my left. I drifted off into a deep sleep, clutching my teddy bear, as Mark Owen, my favourite member of the group, warbled 'Babe'. I thought only of Jack, and imagined him sitting beneath my window sill, tears in his eyes, singing 'Babe' to me. I would launch myself from the window and into his arms, narrowly escaping death by trellis jarred in abdomen. A single tear trickled down my nose and landed on the pillow.

LOVE IN A TEACUP! screamed the *Sun* newspaper, in reference to Jack's bartender job in Primrose Hill. I rubbed my eyes and surveyed the headlines of this morning's tabloids as I stood half asleep at the breakfast table in front of a scene reminiscent of the very first moment I discovered Jack's affair. Just like they do on TV, Mum had fanned out the morning papers across the breakfast table. Janice leant over the *Mirror*, which screamed:

SEX BOMB JESSICA HILSON IN MARRIAGE SHOCKER!

'What!' I squeaked. 'He's MARRIED?'

'Calm down, dear, he's not married,' Mum said. 'It's the press sensationalizing the fact they were spotted dithering with intent outside Tiffany's,' she said, matter-of-fact. My heart leapt out of my mouth and into my cornflakes at the thought that my Jack could be on the point of making Jessica Hilson an honest woman! The pair of them intentionally scouting for engagement rings before skipping up the nearest church aisle was my ultimate Jack-themed nightmare.

'Do you think this means he's planning on popping the question?' Janice asked, wide-eyed.

The next headline from the *Star* screamed salubriously:

THREE-WAY LOVIN' FOR JESSICA AS SHE KEEPS MATRAVERS AND HUNTER DANGLING

'Seems as though Miss Hilson has yet to give Italian guy the heave-ho,' Janice said, as she spooned cereal into her gob. 'Give me Fabio Matravers over Jack Hunter any day!' she sang, as Mum busied herself with making cups of tea. Even Dad had succumbed to the soap opera unfolding within the family home and had lowered his newspaper to fully concentrate on our conversation.

I retreated into the back garden for a cigarette.

'It's not even eight o'clock,' Dad harrumphed, as he came and stood beside me with a cigar in his mouth, 'and they're screeching at the top of their lungs. Normally, I get at least an hour or so of quiet. Janice can usually barely string a sentence together at this time of the morning.' He sighed and lit up the cigar.

Dad only smoked cigars when something important happened, like a birth or his football team scoring a winning goal. Neither had happened since Janice was born, so this must be an occasion of sorts.

'What's with the cigar?' I queried, staring at him.

Ignoring my question, he said gravely, 'Sometimes in life we have to take these things on the chin. Hold your head up high, you're a Lewis, my girl!' He championed me with a shoulder squeeze as though I was about to step into the ring with Mike Tyson. I suppose I was in a way. Ready to fight for my dignity, which had been cruelly stolen the moment Richard flung me over his shoulder and I flashed my pants to the world. Dad sighed deeply.

And that was the end of the conversation. There seemed to be a 'moment' passing between us, and just as I was about to acknowledge that, my phone trilled loudly.

Richard flashed up on the screen.

'I have you a proposition of sorts,' he wittered down the phone.

'Hang on,' I said, as my dad turned and walked inside. I could have had a father/daughter communication break-through and Richard had gone and ruined it. It would take another cataclysmic family drama of epic proportions to evoke that level of emotion from my father again. I waggled a finger in my ear, and listened to what Richard had to say.

'Magenta has called you into an emergency summit at Poets Field asap, so I'm sending a car for you now,' he said, breathlessly.

'A car? What am I, the next Princess Di?' I joked.

'Of sorts,' he said.

'What do you mean?' I said, puzzled.

'Look, just get yourself looking more va-va-voom and less kaput and for heaven's sake, wax your tash. It was like looking at a spider's fandango on your top lip yesterday afternoon.'

I gave a startled cry. My top lip! 'I forgot!'

'Darling, you have a little over an hour to de-fuzz and sort your outfit . . . oh actually . . . hang on . . . are you serious? You are . . . OK . . . yes, yes, yes, will do. Katie?' Richard appeared to be taking orders from another source.

'Hmm?' I replied.

'Magenta says stay as awful looking as possible, and all will be revealed when you arrive!'

'What on earth are you talking about?'

'Just get your things together, you'll soon see!'

And with that he hung up on me.

Chapter 4

I stood by the living-room window, nervously tapping my foot against the skirting board, waiting for my driver. My driver! How posh am I? I pulled on one of Janice's old Primark jumper dresses with a dropped hemline and a pair of old woolly opaques that had seen better days from Mum's chest of drawers. As penance, I had to then spend a good ten minutes explaining to Mum that I had to look awful, and that my employers wouldn't think any less of her parenting skills for my turning up to the office in a snagged pair of tights. Janice had left for sixth form college right after breakfast, wearing the world's shortest skirt, complete with knee-high boots, her face covered in inch-thick slap and her hair styled to within an inch of its life. I swear she must have gone through at least two cans of Elnett. She looked as though she was going to a glamour shoot. Thankfully, Dad was in the garden picking up stray fag ends, which left only Mum to tut and sigh disapprovingly about what people would think of her for letting her younger daughter out of the house dressed like a hooker and how my sister would be one sorry girl when she caught a chill from the weather. Janice didn't care, though, as she was revelling in her newly found popularity at school, which had shot up thanks to Jack. Janice had been busy prancing about in her bedroom, posing for the camera, taking pictures of herself, pouting her lips and squeezing her boobs together suggestively. Her bra was clearly stuffed with socks. She'd even requested some highlights for her mousy brown hair ahead of the family visit to Betty Baxter's beauty salon this afternoon, which thankfully I will now not have to attend, courtesy of my summons back to the office.

With Mum still muttering in the background about misplaced values and how things used to be 'in my day', I stared at the stretch limo that was rolling on to our driveway.

'Jesus, Mary and Joseph!' Mum exclaimed, her hands clasped against her cheeks in surprise. 'The neighbours will think we've won the lottery!'

'Wow,' I said. This was something else! I was just the office girl at Poets Field PR, I wasn't anyone special or important, so why on earth had they sent a limo? And why did Richard tell me to dress down and make an extra effort to look shit when he was sending something as grand as this to ferry me back down the motorway?

'Why do you have to look like such a midden!' Mum tutted as she busied herself with smoothing down her wild curls and undoing her food-stained pinny.

My mobile chirruped with an unknown number. Could it be Jack? I immediately hoped, as my mind went into 'ex-boyfriend calling me from a withheld number' fantasies.

'Hi, Katie?' the unfamiliar male voice said.

'Yes?' I replied nervously, quickly realizing it wasn't Jack and must be my driver. 'Is this the posh car?'

'This is Bailey from Poets Field PR to pick you up for your scheduled meeting. If you'd like to come on outside . . .'

'Sure, sure.' Duh! How stupid of me, of course it wasn't ever going to be Jack. Still, my heart sank a little. OK, a lot.

I put on Dad's old skiing balaclava that Mum had him fetch from the loft last night. Covering my face to disguise my identity should any errant photographers be poised to take photos, which didn't seem to have happened so far, thank the Lord, I opened the door and stumbled down the driveway towards the car. In the bright morning sunshine, standing right there in front of me, I saw this Bailey boy, enormous brown eyes glinting in the sun, all six feet two of him.

'Whoah, call the police!' he joked, as he stood in a so tight it must be illegal white t-shirt, with his arm outstretched against the rim of the car door, laughing at my get-up. He gestured for me to climb in. I flashed him a smile that looked like a snarl through the black dense wool and quickly turned my head back towards the neighbouring houses. There was a ridiculous amount of curtain twitching going on.

As I settled in the back of the car with my seatbelt digging into the middle of my chest, I worked on trying to get my tits to look less like beach balls parted by the waves.

'I've not seen you around before,' he said, attempting small talk. I felt utterly ridiculous sitting in the back of a plush limo, with an Adonis driving me around like I was Lady Muck or something, looking like a thug with no fashion sense. This could quite possibly trump the pillowcase escapade.

'You can take that off now,' he said, gesturing to my headgear, his eyes meeting mine for a brief second in the rear-view mirror. I felt my heart unexpectedly skip a beat, as though he'd asked me to remove my underwear in order to ravish me. What was going on? It was far too early to be getting skippy beats and fancying gorgeous chauffeurs like this Bailey guy. He was a dish, though, with his rippling biceps commanding the steering wheel and his penetrating eye-lock that seemed to bore right into my soul. I was a little bit lost for words and I couldn't quite work out if it was down to being in the company of a man who looked like he could be modelling Calvin Klein pants, or the fact my life was turning increasingly into some kind of James Bond film, complete with ex-boyfriend espionage and covert meetings at work.

'Oh, sure, of course!' I said, bitterly regretting the absence of my make-up this morning. I sat in the back seat looking like death warmed up. I shouldn't care anyway, after all I love Jack, no one else compares. My hair had been subjected to some serious static underneath the woolly material and was now attaching itself to the inside roof. I looked like a scarecrow. I thought I'd better say something.

'I work as a PA for Magenta Rubenstein, and I also, you know, help out the other PR account managers, Richard Dewberry, Hanna Frost, Bowman . . .'

'I know Hanna well . . .' Bailey said with a wink and a smile. I wonder if that meant they were shagging each other? I thought Hanna Frost was a lesbian. She was known within the company and the canteen to have a feisty streak, a no-nonsense demanding approach and was well respected as a ball-breaking business woman – one of the best in her field, according to *London Lowdown*'s Office Awards on the South Bank in 2007.

'Hanna's nice, isn't she?' I probed further as we rolled over country lanes towards the city.

'At times,' he smiled sheepishly.

'Well, I don't really know her all that well . . .' I replied.

Annoyingly, Bailey didn't offer any more titbits of information about Hanna Frost. I started to wonder whether Hanna had anything to do with this important meeting of mine?

'Does Hanna have anything to do with this summons?' I blurted out, immediately regretting it, as Bailey shuffled his lovely cute bum in his seat.

'I know nothing . . .' he said, and I almost believed him, until he smiled at me and then looked away.

The rest of the trip passed quickly as we talked about music we liked (him, Kasabian and Jeff Buckley, me, Madonna and Britney Spears) and exchanged other exciting bits of information about one another. Interestingly enough, he didn't ask me one thing about Jack and Jessica, or this whole furore that seemed to be enveloping the country's media. For heaven's sake, we were at war, people were dying, we were in a recession, yet the only topic on *Loose Women* was much ado about my relationship.

Bailey never even touched upon the subject.

Refreshing, I thought, a man with sensitivity.

For approximately one hour and forty-five minutes or so until we hit London traffic and ground to a halt, I felt like Katie Lewis pre-Jackgate, the normal chatty Katie instead of the creeping about, badly dressed, crying woman *sans* make-up that I was beginning to resemble of late. I began to wonder if there was any point in wearing mascara when even the waterproof brands gave in to my turbo tears.

There was barely an hour that had gone by since this whole kerfuffle began that I hadn't had a mini breakdown. I smoked whenever I could feel one about to come on; my lungs must resemble a smoky blancmange. Luckily for me, most of my extreme crying was conducted in the dead of night under my duvet, or under my pillowcase/balaclava disguises.

'We're here!' Bailey announced as we pulled up into the staff car park. I must have dozed off for a minute or two, thankful that in Bailey's company I had enjoyed some slight respite from reality, and now I had a handprint mark on my cheek from where I had rested my head. Never mind, I thought, it was now time for the balaclava to make another sexy appearance.

Bailey had already released himself from the seatbelt and had shimmied round to my side of the door and opened it with a flourish.

'Why, thank you, kind sir,' I simpered, as I swung my rucksack over my shoulders and made for the back entrance. In keeping with the undercover nature of the meeting, Bailey led me to a set of secret stairs – stairs I'd not previously noticed, anyway – and into a sumptuous velvet-walled lift with lovely dim lights that made me look beautifully serene instead of like an exhibit in a crime lab. I was used to the strip lighting in the main lifts and ladies' loos, which made you feel positively suicidal, magnifying each and every micropore on the end of your nose, not to mention the bags under your eyes which glowed luminously no matter how many layers of Touche Éclat you put on.

'This lift is a dream,' I commented.

'It's used for the mega rich and important clients, so you ought to feel honoured,' Bailey said with a wink.

On the seventh floor, the doors parted to reveal a swanky loft-style apartment-cum-office. It was split on two levels with a clear glass mezzanine running along the perimeter. Directly ahead of us stood a gigantic table and sitting right at the head was my flamboyantly dressed boss, Magenta. Sitting on her left was Richard, and on her right, Hanna Frost.

'Darling!' Magenta cooed, as she stood up to greet me. Richard, Hanna and Magenta grinned megawatt smiles. They were all slick, polished and oozing glamour. On the other side of the room there were several odd-looking fashionistas, crowing at one another and pointing at a number of different whiteboards, each containing indecipherable patterns and bold lettering. This must be where they come up with their ideas, I thought, excitement bubbling up inside of me. Perhaps they have finally recognized my artistic talents and are now going to promote me away from my grotty desk and into this funky space of fabulousness!

'Now, Bailey, darling,' she addressed him, 'can we have a tray of skinny lacto-free organic Fair Trade mochas? And make it quick,' she said, snapping her fingers as she talked. I figured Bailey must be the office assistant for the bigwigs, to be bossed around like this.

Magenta came right up to me and embraced me like a long-lost friend.

'I am so sorry to hear about your loss,' she said, with an air of gloom. 'In time, you'll see it's for the best.' She hooked her arm through mine and positioned me at the far end of the table. I felt like a contestant in a game show, as all eyes descended upon me. I shuffled uncomfortably in my seat, aware that Janice's jumper had a bit of dried dribble on the lapel, from my accidental snooze in the back of the limo.

'Well, you did say come looking your worst!' I laughed nervously, referring to my unkempt appearance. Three pairs of eyes stared back at me, nonplussed.

'OK, I'm going to cut to the chase here, Katie,' Magenta said, with an air of authority about her. Friendly Magenta had been replaced with ball-busting Magenta.

'Richard, show her,' she wafted a perfectly manicured hand in his direction. Richard sheepishly pulled out a copy of what looked like *London Lowdown* and placed it face down in front of me.

'I think you should see this,' he said, gesturing for me to turn it over. 'But may I suggest you take a deep breath first . . .'

Cripes! I thought, what is it now? Jessica Hilson's Miracle Baby? Jack's sordid past being dragged up from when he was an eighteen-year-old adult film worker? He confessed one night after a game of spin the bottle and a succession of tequila slammers to having worked on three blue movies. Soft core, he said, meaning he groped some boobs and showed his dong but didn't go any further than that. Certainly no sex took place, so I doubt I'll be staring that in the face . . .

'OK,' I said. 'Deep breath, it can't be that bad . . . OH MY GOD NOOOOOOOOO!!!!!!' I wailed, as I looked at a giant, full-colour, double-page spread of my arse, complete with big flowery pants, my love handles spilling either side, legs akimbo, over the shoulder of Richard, who was visibly struggling to contain my weight. Various surprised and shocked faces held up camera phones in the background. Pippa bloody Strong, that big-nosed, frizzy-haired journalist, was to blame for humiliating me further than I ever imagined possible.

'What the fuck am I going to do NOW?' I screamed, forgetting boardroom etiquette, my cheeks burning as hot tears filled my eyes. *Please don't cry! Please don't cry!* I repeated like a mantra in my spinning head. Oh God, oh God, must keep control! I gripped the sides of my chair for support as I prayed to Almighty God that there was a secret trap door that I could command by the power of thought which would catapult me back into another dimension where none of this had ever even happened, or failing that, at least back to my own desk, within sprinting distance of the ladies' loos, so I could have this moment in private.

All three faces looked bemused at my diva-style melt-down, complete with high-pitched squealing and snot flying down my cheeks from my running nose. I gave up trying to contain the sobs and blubbered all over the magazine. Any shred of self-respect I may have had left was now lost, as I collapsed my head on to the table and tried to hide under my hands.

Five minutes later my sobs had subsided into little snif-fles and I was now able to hold a conversation. I looked around the room and realized that I was alone with Hanna and Richard. Magenta had wisely left the room – God only knows where she was now. Filing my P45 perhaps? After all, no one wants a liability at work, do they? Oh

Christ, I thought, I've gone and done it now, with my candid emotions. I give a massive sigh and a weak smile. My face is sure to be blotchy and reddened beyond redemption. If I had worn make-up today, it would have been a wasted effort.

'Darling,' Richard says gently, 'are you feeling a bit more in control now?'

'I'm sorry,' I say, blowing my nose on the tissue that Hanna has passed across to me. 'It's not so much the double-page spread of my backside, or even the pants . . . it's everything, I guess. I mean, it's every girl's worst nightmare to find out her boyfriend's left her, but to be left for someone who's practically Madonna is just too much to bear. Her backside is small and cute and would fit on a Twitter blog, whilst my backside takes up two A4 pages of this magazine.'

'Well, the photo was enlarged, Katie, so don't pay too much attention to bottom envy,' Richard says.

Hanna's face remains straight. She clearly has had so much Botox in her forehead she looks permanently startled. It had now been almost ten minutes since my public display of emotion – plenty of time to compose oneself and relax one's face back into a normal expression? No, Hanna has definitely had work done. 'As we were about to discuss before you, ahem, well, we have decided that you are in a wonderful position right now, Katie,' Hanna says, without a twitch.

'You have got to be joking, Hanna, how on earth can you possibly say that with a straight face?'

'Botox,' she says bluntly. 'Let's not waste time wondering whether I have or haven't. And see these lips?' she says, pointing to a full and wondrous pout. 'Filler.' She looks pleased with herself, before continuing, 'And yes, it is impossible to have breasts as curvaceously perky as mine with a 23-inch waist to boot – surgery.'

'Um,' I say, lost for words. Richard scratches the back of his neck and looks skywards.

'Katie, I noticed you staring at me, and I wanted to put you straight on a few things right away so that we have no issues in the future when working together,' she says, matter-of-fact. She got it wrong – I was staring at her when I came in to see how she reacted to the delicious Bailey.

'Working together? I don't understand?' My face contorts with confusion.

'This is what we propose to you,' she says, pushing a large A3 poster towards me. There is a picture of me, but it doesn't quite look like me. I am slimmer, shinier, I have straight teeth . . .

'I don't get it,' I muse. 'I mean, it's me, but it's not me.'

'Katie, you are going to get revenge on Jessica Hilson and Jack Hunter. No one likes a cheater, Katie, no one. Jessica Hilson may be popular right now, but you, my girl, have the potential to outstrip her at every single corner.'

'But how?' I cry. She's completely lost me now. 'How on earth can I get back at Jessica Hilson? Does it involve getting my beloved Jack back?'

'You'll get him back, in an instant,' Hanna says, as she clicks her fingers. 'You just have to listen very carefully to our proposal,' and with that, she sat back in her chair and pressed a button. 'Send them in now,' Hanna barked to the little gadget-type thing strapped to her wrist. Very futuristic, I thought.

Within a couple of seconds, three fashionistas trooped into the boardroom, carrying the boards I saw them working on earlier.

'Katie Lewis, you are a star!' the first guy says, clapping his hands together and doing a little skip.

'You are vibrant, you are amazing, you are incredible and you are going to take the media world by storm!' fashion guy number two says, somewhat less gay than the first.

'And this,' fashion guy number three says, 'is how we do it.'

Back to fashion guy number one. 'Since Monday morning when Katie Lewis found out love-of-her-life Jack Hunter, an up-and-coming actor who worked in Primrose Hill's Coco Caramels, was having intimate relations with Hollywood IT girl of the moment, talented actress Jessica Hilson, her private life and her knickers have been splashed across the media for all to see. Red tops to broadsheets have given column inches to the subject,' he pauses for effect before fashion guy number two picks up where he left off. 'And in less than a week, what are we on, day three now, websites have popped up all over the internet championing Katie Lewis. The elusive Katie Lewis, who shops in Tesco's and wears giant flowery pants. Katie Lewis had a bubble perm in the late nineties when she really ought to have known better . . .'

'Fuck!' I swore. Janice, bloody Janice, argh!

'Katie Lewis is a role model! She has conducted herself with a quiet dignity throughout this hurtful and very public relationship breakdown.'

I'm nodding in agreement here, I guess I have been a smart girl, I haven't screamed and hunted him down, I haven't gone to the papers, but then I have been doing my best to escape from this whole thing, I mean, who wants to be reminded about it? Not me, that's for sure.

'Katie, you have a following that's growing bigger by the hour, thanks to that picture of you going arse over tit on Richard's shoulder,' Hanna said, inspecting her long crimson nails.

'But how?' I query, still bemused.

'In times of recession, people are looking to each other for support, for reality. You aren't like those reality television ejectees, you actually are real, this is happening to a real woman, one of their own, and who wouldn't be able to relate to you, a girl after their own hearts?'

Fashion guy number three steps in. 'Normal women don't like skinny minnies either, darling,' he says.

Cheeky sod, I'm not that fat! God, do they think I'm fat?

'Katie,' he continues, 'you have a potential voice, you could make yourself a very wealthy woman, change the lives of others, change your own life, make a success, a difference, anything you want. I propose we fix you up and we do something so unique, so innovative, a PR exercise to end all PR exercises! We are going to make you a real reality celebrity!' He claps his hands together and all three of them make simpering noises and deliver high fives.

'In simple terms, please?' I turn to Richard and Hanna.

'We want to build the hype around you. We want to fix those teeth, get you hair extensions, a spray tan, a personal trainer, designer clothes, everything Jessica Hilson has, except you, my darling, will be the high-class version. We're going to put you with Danny Divine, Brit-flick actor of the moment. He's bisexual, loves boys, loves girls, but no one knows that yet, his commercial viability in the teen market would sink, so we are going to say that you are dating him. You're going to go to all the best parties, you're going to dazzle and you're going to shine, and all the while, you're going to give in-depth interviews on how you brought yourself back from the brink of a nervous breakdown – in short, we're going to style you into being the kind of girl anyone can be, with a bit of hard work and determination, and we're going to get you back with Jack.'

'But I won't be me, will I, and it won't be self-made, will it?'

'No, but we'll market you as if you are and it is,' Richard says, grinning. 'And the best bit is, we'll work in conjunction with products that you will lend your name to, you will wear what we tell you, shop where we tell you and you will say the carefully scripted words we will prepare for you.'

'And what do I get in return?' I say.

'How can you say that?' fashion guy two gasps, whilst fashion guy one elbows him in the ribs.

'You get £10K, a one-year contract with Poets Field PR, and the potential to make squillions. So, here's the contract, take it away and have a think and come back to us.'

'Or what?' I say dubiously.

'We'll let the media eat you for breakfast, lunch and dinner.'

'But I thought you said I was a media darling?'

'You have the potential, sure. The public like you, yeah, that's true . . . but the media? Fickle bunch . . . they will be digging up dirt from your ex-boyfriends, any school friends, ex-work colleagues, anyone and everyone you can think of, they will descend upon until they get a story. If they don't get a story, they'll make one up. You are far better off going with us and allowing us to market you, to guide you through, for however long this attention lasts, Katie.'

'So . . . whaddya think?' fashion guy one says. I look up from staring at my lap to see all three fashion guys with their heads cocked to the side in eager anticipation of my response, Richard with a massive grin on his face, Hanna with her smug frozen look and Magenta, who had reappeared with a fresh coat of lipstick on her plumped-up lips, smiling warmly. Bailey saunters over with a tray of coffees, putting one down before each person.

'Thanks,' Magenta coos, as Bailey almost curtseys in her presence.

'Well, it's a lot to think about,' I begin, 'and uh, I will need an hour or two and a stiff vodkatini before I make my decision,' I say, solidly, before adding quietly, 'if that's OK?'

'Sure is. Hey, guys,' Magenta says, turning her attention away from me and towards her team, 'let's reconvene at say . . . what time is it now?'

'It's just before midday,' Richard says.

'Midday, fabulous, OK, let's see, Katie . . . let's rendezvous back here at 5pm. That's plenty of time to go do what you have to do . . . Here,' she says, sliding some leatherbound A4-sized pads towards me. 'These are "look books", they detail all our ideas about your mega transformation, ranging from your hairstyle to your clothes. Everything you need to know, and then some more, you will find nestling in the pages of these beauty bibles.'

'Thanks,' I say, as I pull them towards me and stroke the soft leather with my fingers, 'they're beautiful.' I smile back at everyone. I suppose I ought to be getting used to feeling like a monkey in the zoo, what with all eyes being on me for the past few days. I would much prefer to be one of those beautifully elegant sculptures found in an art gallery, though. Perhaps this whole makeover idea is worth thinking about after all? Perhaps it could turn me into a masterpiece, instead of the bit of art a person really has to stare at to 'get'. I gingerly slide my chair back and, clutching the books, I make my way to the door.

'Wait a second . . .' Richard says loudly. 'Wait there, I just thought!'

'What?' I say, startled.

'You can't leave right now, not looking like that!'

'Oh, thanks a lot, Richard, but may I remind you, it was you lot, I mean, sorry, Magenta, it was everyone here who asked me to come dressed down and with no make-up on . . . which is why I look like this. God, we've been over this a zillion times so far!' I am losing my patience. I am tired, I feel like the most heinously ugly woman ever to grace their presence, and you know what? I feel like that most days working in a PR company which is filled with women with legs like whippets and wardrobes from *Vogue*. Maybe I could take on this ridiculous project, well, the project being me, and transform myself into a goddess who not only rivals Jessica Hilson, but trumps her. Good work that these crafty PR types have done on me, I already have their power buzzwords shrieking in my brain about being the best, the most fabulous, with the best shoes money can buy. I feel dizzy now – I must get some fresh air.

'Bailey,' Magenta commands and he appears. It strikes me how much their synergy reminds me of my mother barking at my father, who also appears from nowhere ready to take the next instruction whenever the mood takes her.

'Take Katie down to the guest room, make her comfortable, give her anything she wants.'

Bailey nods. 'Sure thing.'

'Anything I want?' I question.

'Anything you want,' she replies.

'As an afterthought, darling,' Richard says, dolefully, 'I meant don't go showing your face in public because the paparazzi will still be waiting to take pictures of you and we can't have that, darling, not if we're the ones who are going to make you a star.'

'Come on,' Bailey says, gently pulling my arm towards his body. His touch sends little shivers up my spine.

He hustles me out of the room and into the posh lift and as we descend, I give out a big sigh and fall back against the mirrored walls.

'Tough day?' Bailey says to me. His hands are awkwardly tucked in the belt of his jeans. I couldn't help but look down to where they were pointed, to his crotch area. And what a magnificent crotch he appeared to display.

'Uh huh,' I said, mumbling. I must focus . . . but how?

'Can I call anyone for you?' he said in concerned tones, as though he was addressing some kind of accident victim.

'Yes, yes, I need you to call Danielle Kingsley, she is my best friend, she knows what is going on here. She's a lawyer, you know.' I never tired of showing off my best friend's talents to the world.

Danielle was kind but firm. She was strong, but not in the ball-busting, shit-your-pants kind of way that Hanna Frost was. Hanna made you feel like you were the most inept human being known to the office with her passive-aggressive behaviour, she could command a room in an instant and woe betide you if you ballsed up at work. She had gone through at least a dozen assistants in the time I'd been at Poets Field PR. Girls would arrive all bright-eyed and bushy-tailed, eager to make their mark within the world of public relations, all were wannabe media princesses, most slept with Richard, and all of them were so worn down by the end of their first fortnight that they left, saying that PR was simply not for them. No one so far had managed to please her. Hanna was frightening. But today, I must admit, I'd seen a different side to her. She was more gentle, more personable . . . dare I say it . . . more human? Could this be because she was now, nearly, in a way, working for me? Perhaps she meant to keep me sweet . . .

Danielle, on the other hand, was different. She was firm, articulate and intelligent, just like Hanna, but she had that warmth about her that many scary women in power lack. I loved her for all that she was and all that she had achieved in her life. I had first met Danielle in a cute little book-shop in the East End of London that also served up hot drinks and blueberry muffins. It was the kind of place where you could lounge about on massive sofas or rest on beanbags looking indie-pretentious. It was tucked into a side street down Brick Lane and it was there I used to sit for hours on end on a Sunday, reading my books that I'd bought and admiring the clothes I had picked up from the quaint little vintage shops in the area. One Sunday morning, I sat down in my usual spot and saw Danielle. She was having a full-on meltdown on a giant floor cushion. She sat in a long flowing Pucci maxi-dress, her corkscrew curls bounced up and down on her head as though they were lovers romping in a barn, and her face contorted first with anger, then with pain. Heart-type pain, boyfriend-trouble pain, the very worst kind there is. People were looking, but this fiery little thing in six-inch wedges was still yapping ten to the dozen, pointing her arms and furrowing her brows until she reached a crescendo and with one violent shriek said: 'And you can go and fuck yourself, Stewart, because I sure as hell will never go near your horrible flaky-skinned, small-penis self ever again!' And with that, she ended the call with such ferocity she snapped her phone clean in half and her drink, which must have been cold by now, sprung up into the air drenching some poor sod next to her who was trying to read his paper.

'Oi!' the man said in alarm, clearly irritated.

'Fuck off!' she hissed.

And then she slumped back into her massive seat pillow and looked up to the ceiling, her fingers delicately placed beneath her eyelids to capture her tears. I just stared at her from the brow of my book, along with everyone else in the room, stunned at such a candid display of emotion in public. The girl had some balls. The waiter approached me with a drink. It was a hot chocolate with all the works, marshmallows and cream, everything yummy and calorific.

'For you?' he questioned, setting it down on my table.

'No, not for me,' I replied.

'It's for me,' the girl with the wild hair and beautifully wide-set eyes said, flatly, as she appeared at my table, hands outstretched to take it. Instinctively, I placed my hand on the mug – I decided quickly that I now wanted this hot chocolate, anything to do with chocolate provoked a reaction within me that was instinctive. Like a mother protecting her young.

'Well, I think it's mine really . . . after all, he did bring it to me,' I replied haughtily, before adding, 'he was probably scared witless after seeing you go nuts down the phone . . . but then, your guy must have done something pretty horrific to be told how small his penis was in public.'

We locked eyes for a moment, both unsure of how to take one another's humour. She threw me a smile and I smiled back at her, and we began to laugh, a proper belly-ache of a laugh, so I said, 'Hey, we'll just order another one, but I'm holding you fully responsible for breaking my diet.'

'I bet that's at least the fourth time this week, huh?' she said, as though she'd known me for years. 'You didn't exactly need a lot of persuading.'

'True,' I said, and invited her to sit down. Every Sunday for quite some time afterwards, Danielle and I would casually meet and have hot chocolates with the full works, and I would listen to her moan and whinge about slime-ball, small-penis Stewart, who was a big-shot media lawyer in the firm where she worked. Even though he was a cad, she loved him with such force that she was permanently skinny. Such was his power over her, she hardly ever ate due to the fact she was either in love with him or heartbroken. He was hot for her and then he was cold. He pushed her away and then he pulled her so close she feared she may burst with happiness. Stewart Smallthwait wined and dined and devoured her body like I devoured chocolate fudge cake.

When she joined the firm where she worked, she had no idea who he was, or how powerful his influence was upon her colleagues. I guess that was what drove him wild, her complete face blank when it came to how much power this guy in a grey marl suit had at his disposal. He was, of course, the firm's senior partner. But Stewart was the partner who worked from home or spent a lot of time abroad on business, so he was hardly ever in the office. He could have been the post boy for all she knew, and here he had found a woman who was his match. Almost . . .

'He's just bloody perfect!' Danielle simpered on one of our coffee dates. 'I think I'm in love with him . . .' she blushed furiously.

'Do you love his small penis too?' I giggled, as we talked at great length, well at least in Jack's case, about how much we loved the men in our lives.

Unfortunately for Danielle, Stewart Smallthwait turned out to be the world's greatest storyteller. He had told her solemnly he was separated from his wife and Danielle had seen no evidence to suggest otherwise. There were no cheerful photographs dotted about his office like her other married colleagues, never any reference to anyone else in his life aside from his dog Vince, a small black pug he had rescued from the arms of an oh-so-cruel owner. Until the day the pug came into the office, in the arms of one gregarious and very current wife. Lisa Smallthwait entered in a whirlwind of peachy-pink flowery clothing, wafting her expensive-smelling perfume all over the open-plan office and flashing her very-much-married-to-Stewart left hand, complete with enormous engagement ring and wedding band.

'The bastard is indeed married and, according to his

wife, very much in love,' she snarled one day, several months after continuous simpering about how perfect and manly Stewart was. He went from Stewart, the big strong hunk of power to weak with no balls and a small penis every other day.

'His wife Lisa crowed about him so much I nearly vomited right there on her moleskin shoes,' Danielle spat, whilst filing her nail down with a hint of violence. 'I swear she was one stop away from telling everyone which sexual positions they loved the most.'

'Arsehole,' I said, in between mouthfuls of blueberry muffin.

'I know, so I told him, that's it, ultimate betrayal, we're over, but he begged me, convinced me to stay with him . . .'

'You never forgave him!' I was shocked.

'He cried,' she said, 'and I just buckled.' She put her head in her hands. 'I stole another woman's husband,' she wailed. 'I'm going straight to hell when I am hit by the inevitable double-decker karma bus on my way to work.'

'So, what did you do?' I said, putting my arm around her.

'I am ashamed to say this but it's too late to leave him,' she said, looking up at me, tears glistening down her cheeks. 'I told him I loved him, he said it back . . . as far as I knew it was all mini-breaks and impending commitment.'

'I see,' I said, nodding with her.

'I've become one of those awful women who say that he's different to the rest,' she continued, 'but he is! I know him inside out.'

'Seriously, babe,' I said, remembering this is what all married men who are cheating on their wives and girlfriends do in *Coronation Street*, 'has he told you how he is in the process of gathering his thoughts before he leaves her?'

'Yes,' she sniffed, 'how do you know that?'

I gave a weak smile and continued, 'And that they never have sex although deep down, you're pretty sure that they do?'

She looked at me whilst it dawned on her that Stewart with the small penis made up for it with his big massive lies.

'Uh huh . . . he does . . . Oh God, you're right! He's totally playing me. How can I be so stupid?'

'It happens a lot, Danielle, you're not the first . . . I expect you won't be the last . . .'

'Heaven knows where he gets his energy from, Katie; did you know he is pushing late fifties?'

'No, no I didn't.'

'Ah, well he is . . . and another thing, if that's not bad enough, I don't know if I can forgive him for standing me up in the café that day I went bananas at him on the phone. You know, that was supposed to be the day he pulled up with his car jammed full of his man-things, ready to begin his new life, with me, and he failed.' Danielle stared wistfully out of the window.

'On the other hand,' she continued, 'I was a fool to believe it would only be a matter of time before he located his balls and did the right thing.'

'And then I guess once he stood you up, he promised it would be within weeks that you could start your super-duper new life together, yet those weeks turned into months and those months into years?' I queried.

'Got it in one,' she said.

70

'So,' I said, taking a sip of my drink, 'how many years has he been saying that now?'

'Three,' she said, sipping hers. 'Nearly four.'

'And he's still married?'

'As far as I know.'

'And the gifts?' I queried, knowing that there would be many, a girl who's addicted to her soaps knows these things, you see.

'Tiffany, Cartier, fresh flowers almost daily, love letters, poems . . . the man pursues me with the hunger of a vulture circulating a fresh meat carcass.' She looked forlornly at her near-empty coffee cup.

'Ah, but you're so much prettier than a rotting piece of flesh!' I said jovially, in an attempt to lift her bad mood.

Eventually, we swapped numbers and began to go places other than the café. We became firm friends and I have seen her through two boyfriends since Stewart, an event well remembered in any girl's emotional calendar. First, we had Joe, the Wanker Banker, who liked a finger up his bum and cocaine up his nose, and then there was Seth, at the other end of the wild spectrum. Seth was a librarian whose only dream in life was to abscond to Scotland with Danielle and live in a croft with a menagerie of animals. Both men had failed to ignite the same amount of passion as I saw flowing from her perfectly manicured square-tipped fingernails the day she broke up with Stewart-small-penis.

Unfortunately, Danielle still saw Stewart-small-penis in the biblical sense now and again, even when she went through man detox, which involved changing her mobile number, her MSN and her hair colour, in an attempt to reinvent herself and extradite him from her life. As a result of this, Danielle only ever had two contacts in her phone (myself and her mother), a succession of Hotmail accounts to check for wayward ex-boyfriends' emails and split ends from all the hair dye it took to go from blonde to flame-haired and back again. Yet she continued to see Stewart and then she would get sick of his indecisive no-balls behaviour, scream at him, they'd part and the whole shebang would begin all over again.

Meanwhile, back at the ranch, Bailey had led me to a darkened room and for the second time today sexual thoughts crept into my mind.

Must. Not. Think. Rude. Thoughts. I chastised myself. It was way too soon to be imagining another man naked next to me, let alone someone sent to take care of my needs.

'Whoooooo,' I squealed, as I accidently tripped over my own feet into the dimly lit basement room.

'Steady there, Katie,' Bailey said, reaching out a hand to catch me. 'Mind how you go, you'll have a crocked leg if you're not careful.'

'Oops,' I said, feeling my cheeks flush, 'silly me!'

'Right, OK, here is the bed area if you need a lie-down. I bet you must be so tired, what with all the excitement.'

'Excitement?' I said, wondering whether Bailey had read my thoughts.

'Yeah, you know, from Magenta, the fashion guys, crazy bunch they are . . .' He shrugged his shoulders.

'Yes, a bit excited, and tired, very. Now, where is the phone?' I said.

'Here,' he said, pointing towards the kitchen area, which was neon pink with white tiles, fifties themed, *très* cool.

'Thanks,' I said, as I dropped my rucksack on the floor and made my way into the kitchen.

'There's vodka to calm your nerves and nibbles to line your stomach in the fridge, and Sky telly over there on the wall. Go make yourself at home, I have to nip out and pick up some clothes from Harrods for Magenta, I'll be back by five,' he said, as he backed out towards the door, threw me a devastating smile and turned on his heels. As I flopped myself down on the sumptuous bed, I stared right up at the ceiling and counted the spotlights above. I wondered just how much of my life was going to fall under one very big spotlight . . .

Chapter 5

Jack took my hand in both of his and pulled his lips on to my fingers, kissing them gently one by one. I sighed dramatically. I had to pretend I was over him, even if I wasn't.

'I love you, Katie cakes,' he said, as he then blew gently into the palms of my hands. 'It's all over now,' he said, his scent overpowering me. It's Acqua di Parma . . . mmmm . . . 'It's all over now, baby,' he says, stroking my hair.

'Katie?'

'Hmm . . .'

'Katie? Are you there? Wake up, Katie? Katie!'

'What? What!' Oh fuck, I realized, I was dreaming, Jack isn't here and the screaming of my name wasn't coming from his lips but those of Danielle.

I sat up bolt upright and attempted to spit and smooth my crazy hairdo which hadn't seen a pair of GHDs for nigh on two days. My head was fuzzy from one or two, OK, six calm-me-down vodkatinis in the kitchen whilst watching a bit of Oprah. Between her and Dr Phil I had rested against the plush furnishings and fallen asleep.

'I'm coming, I'm coming,' I said, with what sounded like a mouth full of socks. I unlocked the latch and slowly opened the door to Danielle, looking frizz-free and fully made up.

'Hey, you,' she said gently, before pulling me in for a hug.

'I smell,' I said, 'plus I'm hairy. Please don't look at me unless you have to.'

'I brought you some brand-new, top of the range, very plush designer make-up,' she said with a wink, as we moved into the kitchenette. A half-empty quarter bottle of vodka and umpteen empty packets of honey-roasted peanuts lay strewn across the table.

'Stewart-small-penis?' I mumbled in reference to the personalized bag. I took the brand-new, baby-pink, Juicy Couture leather make-up pouch engraved with her name from her hands.

'Good afternoon?' she said, ignoring my Stewart quip and taking in my food carnage.

'Uh, I just had a dream about Jack,' I said, rubbing my temples.

'I'd say that was a nightmare,' she chuckled.

'Very funny. What time is it?'

'It's four o'clock.'

'Shit, I have to be upstairs in the big posh meeting room with Magenta and her assistants for, like, five, with a contract, ideally signed.'

'So, what's the deal, then, Katie?'

'The deal is this: some madcap idea that I, size fourteen Katie Lewis, could outstrip Jessica bright-eyed and bushy-tailed size zero Hilson, and thus win my Jack Hunter back and achieve world domination.'

Danielle's face said it all. It was an outrageous idea. Completely unbelievable and what a waste of time and energy on every single person's part.

'Amazing!' she said slowly, before breaking out into a sunny smile. 'Katie, this is just fabulous; you are so going to nail that bitch from here to kingdom come. And as for Jack? Well, yeah, toads like him will always come crawling back if they think they can get something out of it so you will not, I repeat NOT, go anyplace near him, you understand me?'

I nodded unconvincingly.

'I'm serious, Katie, he's bad for you, and he has as much sincerity as finger-bum Joe!'

'Not a lot, then,' I giggled.

'Bordering on being a soulless creature from the deep!' she grimaced.

'Seriously, you are well rid of him.'

'Then why does it hurt so much?' I whinnied.

'Because love sucks. Now, where can we smoke?'

I smiled. We moved on to the bed and flopped back against the giant pillows as I pulled a chrome ashtray from the bedside table.

'Loving the bed,' Danielle murmured, as she settled herself into the plush duvet cover.

'Yeah,' I agreed. 'You want to see this guy who's ferrying me around, Bailey his name is, God, he is beyond gorgeous, stunning in fact, could very well be a tight-pants model in his spare time.' I made a mental note to ask him about that.

'Good . . .' she said, 'takes away wasted thoughts about Jack.'

'Oh great, thanks, now I'm thinking of him.' I pulled a face and reached into my rucksack for the contract.

'Here,' I said, thrusting it into her lap. 'This is the contract. Basically, if I sign it, they'll make me gorgeous, and if I don't, I get eaten by the press.'

'You're already gorgeous, Katie, so I'm not sure what you mean by "making you" gorgeous.'

'They mean they'll fix up my face, my clothes, my hair and my teeth.'

76

'But there's nothing wrong with you! OK, you want to make the most of what you have, I get that, but don't go crazy, OK?'

'Sure,' I said, already planning my first boob job. I looked down at my pair of modest 34B boobs; I'd love a D cup! And a nose job. Ever since I got smacked in the face by a netball in PE when I was twelve, I had a small bump in the bridge of my nose. My teeth had seen better days too.

'OK,' Danielle said, as her reading glasses perched precariously on the top of her nose. She studied the contract intently. 'So, it seems that by signing this you're giving up all rights to go elsewhere with your story, including that of your makeover and your weight loss.'

'Weight loss? So they do think I'm fat!' I said, clasping my hands to my mouth.

'Ahem,' Danielle said, coughing.

Bailey stood in the doorway.

'Hey,' he said casually, the way cute guys do in the movies, all sexy and smouldering.

'Hey,' I replied, the way girls who fancied boys in the movies do, all ridiculously high-pitched and silly.

'I know I'm a bit early, it's just I got off the hook from Magenta. Seems I got it right first time with the clothing deal, so no sweat, huh?'

'No sweat,' I thought, apart from my armpits, I *so* needed a shower.

'Listen, Bailey, this is Danielle, my friend,' I said gesturing to her, as Danielle did what I imagine most girls did in the presence of Bailey – a coy smile, girlish giggle, with her fingers elongated into a cute little wave. Bailey, seemingly oblivious to this, continued to stare across at me intently. He must be able to see the massive spot on my chin. Self-consciously, I covered said spot with my hand.

'Danielle is a lawyer,' Bailey's eyebrows raised high in admiration, 'and she's looking over my contract right now so . . .'

'Could you maybe go do something else,' Danielle interjected, 'and come back here at five?' she said sweetly.

'Okey dokey!' he said, and saluted us farewell. 'Till five,' he said and backed out of the door, closing it gently. Danielle's face said it all.

'Sex,' she said, fanning her face with the contract, 'on legs.' And with that she threw the make-up bag she brought for me at my lap. 'Slap up, girly, he's gorgeous.'

'What are you talking about, you silly woman!' I cried. 'He's not that special,' I lied.

Danielle raised her eyebrows at me and I knew she could tell that I actually fancied Bailey quite a lot.

'I don't fancy him!' I squealed, as I hit her with a pillow. 'I've only just split up from the man I love. Jack is the only man who makes my heart flutter.'

'But he's not the only one who gives you goosebumps!' Danielle said, pointing at my arms, which now resembled plucked chickens despite the warm temperature of the room.

'And even if I did fancy him, I'm hardly going to get any-where looking like this, am I?' I said, sighing dramatically. 'Maybe,' I added, 'he'll fancy me when I'm all made over and looking impossibly fabulous,' I mused.

'Maybe,' she said, 'you should take a chance and see if he likes you just the way you are.'

'You're insane, clearly,' I laughed, peering at my reflection in my little compact mirror. 'My hair looks like I've stuck my fingers in a plug socket, my eyebrows are close to becoming a monobrow and I nearly have a small beard.'

'Those, my darling,' Danielle said, throwing first a pair of tweezers, then her mini handbag-sized GHDs in my direction, 'are easily fixed.' She sits there grinning at me as I throw my hands up in the air.

'You're right,' I say, before jumping off the bed and heading into the bathroom.

'Wait!' she says urgently.

'What?'

'You can't do anything to your face or hair, according to this contract.'

'Well, that blows that plan outta the window!' I say.

'No, what it says is YOU can't do anything . . . it's all going to be done for you . . .'

'Great doing business with you, Katie,' Hanna said, as she shook my hand firmly, accidentally digging her long red talons into the palm of my hand. I winced.

'Good!' I said, rubbing my hands on my bum cheeks to take away the sting.

'You can sleep in the guest room here tonight, darling. Here,' she said as she shoved a large cream canvas tote bag with two giant handles towards me, 'gifts for you.' She gestured for me to look inside. Hanna and I sat around the giant oval table whilst Bailey hung back in the corner of the room, surveying the sweeping panoramic views of the city of London at sunset.

'Breathtaking,' I said, as I reached into the bag and pulled out a pair of brand-new pink GHDs and a selection of the most sumptuous shampoos, conditioners, body butters and other designer cosmetics I had ever seen. I delved in further and found silken underwear and a cashmere jumper.

'Gorgeous things for a soon-to-be-gorgeous girl!' Hanna said, clasping her hands together.

'Oh, wow,' I said, as I found more goodies in the shape of CDs, DVDs and a miniature bottle of champagne.

'May I suggest you get yourself an early night tonight, Katie, because Bailey will be driving you to your first appointment at 8.30am sharp? Tomorrow will be the first phase of Project Katie.'

'Which is?' I asked gingerly.

'You'll have to wait and see,' she winked and lay back in her reclining chair. Her phone trilled, she picked it up. 'Hanna Frost,' she said, as though she was gnawing on ice, and with that, she wafted her hand at me to leave the room. Bailey and I got back into the lift for what felt like the millionth time today and rode twelve floors down to the basement.

'So, I guess I shouldn't really tell you this, Katie, but tomorrow . . .'

'Yes, yes, yes!' I squealed. 'Tell me everything! I have to know or I may just simply die right here on the spot in this lift and you really don't want blood on your hands, do you, Bailey? It really isn't attractive,' I said, immediately regretting it, as we both knew that I had spent all of today looking like one of the ugly sisters on purpose. Now I understood why. After seeing myself transformed in the look book, and having been traumatized by the glamour puss who's shagging my boyfriend, plus seeing my massive bum splashed across the pages of a newspaper, not to mention my moustache and my massive spot on my chin, aaaaaaaaaaand my lack of make-up, using the word 'attractive' was a really bad idea. I would now do anything to look as hot as I did in the look book. I knew Bailey would be looking at me thinking I was anything but. The look book was designed to show me how Poets Field PR could redeem my dishevelled self and turn me from not into hot. And it worked. At 5pm sharp, I signed on the dotted line and sold my soul to the Devil. Looking over at the beefcake in his tight, white t-shirt, my cheeks flushed red with shame. My mother was right. Why did I have to look such a midden all the time? Surely I could have used 'natural' make-up, if there was such a thing. No wonder Hanna et al were all twirling around at the thought of giving me a makeover. I caught sight of my reflection in one of the mirrored windows in a corridor down to the power room and grimaced. It was a total nightmare. I made a mental note never to listen to anyone who tells me it's a good idea to go out without make-up on, no matter what the circumstances surrounding that may be. Not even death will come between me and my make-up bag, ever again.

'Well, if I told you I'd have to kill you,' Bailey joked with me. Was he flirting? I couldn't tell. I was so out of the loop when it came to chatting up hot guys, having been in a long-term relationship with Jack for the past two-and-a-half years. A lifetime, it felt. As we made our way to the end of the corridor, Bailey smiled at me. He didn't stare at my chin too much and if he noticed my hairy lip, he never said anything. Thank God. His cute dimples and deep gaze had me melting every time he looked in my direction.

I hoped like crazy that he may consider coming in for a drink or two . . . When drunk he would be at a disadvantage and from then on in, I could work the charm that had landed me Jack Hunter. I was the girl with the bubbly personality, I was funny, I was bouncy and I had an in-depth knowledge of film trivia which made me a very handy asset at a pub quiz. We stood by the guest room, me slightly behind Bailey, admiring his pert bottom whilst he fumbled for the keys. I was still wondering whether I should invite him in.

I mean, we weren't on a date, obviously, but we had just spent nearly an entire day together and he had seen me display a full range of interesting facial expressions and emotions, ranging from sheer horror to complete surprise and everything in between. Just what was the etiquette for trying it on when you've been scooped up by a leading PR agency to transform you into a celebrity, because your boyfriend's done a runner with a movie star and you quite fancy the guy who's been sent to take care of you? Who knows . . . I guess I will have to just make-up the rules as I go along. Here goes . . .

'Would you, uh, like to come in for coffee?' I said, regretting the words as soon as they came out of my mouth. Bailey's face crumpled up and he looked at the floor. 'I can't tonight,' he said.

Fuck, he was totally not interested and I have completely blown it and oh my God, please open up a cavernous pit beneath me full of snakes and monsters to eat me up alive, and do it immediately so I can remove myself from here.

'OK,' I said, as bright and as breezy as I possibly could.

He opened his mouth to say something but I didn't give him the chance to humiliate me further.

'Bye, then!' I said as I grabbed the keys from his grasp, flung myself through the door, locked it behind me and threw myself into the cushions on the bed. My cheeks were bright red and shame was burning a hole in my eardrums. I pulled out my mobile phone to text Danielle.

Asked Bailey in 4 drink – he declined. Booo

Beep Beep

If at 1st u dnt succeed, put the MAC lippy in St Germain on and try try again!

I guess she's right, I thought to myself, pulling my face up and back in the reflection of the giant mirror so I could imagine what I would look like if I had as much Botox and filler as Hanna Frost. Even though I had an abundance of silky, pretty little wispy bits of undergarments and sleep wear at my disposal, I suddenly felt homesick for my little house in Bethnal Green and my fluffy cat, Grum. I missed his gentle purrs as he snuggled up to me at night whilst I splodged out on the couch, stuffing my face with biscuits and watching my soaps. I knew my life was going to change tomorrow, and would continue to do so for the foreseeable future, but just for tonight, it was me and my borrowed pyjamas.

'Obviously, Katie's bum has grown bigger since the days we used to bop around our handbags to the Backstreet Boys back in Little Glove Community Centre. She had that perm done at my mum's salon, Betty Baxter's – HI, MUM!'

Nicola Baxter sat on Lorraine Kelly's sofa warbling on about my style *faux pas* and the fact my arse was now considerably bigger than it was back then.

'Oh, big wow,' I said aloud whilst crunching organic wheat-free muesli with something called almond milk over the top of it. Tasted funny, but I was under strict instructions to eat it for breakfast, after discovering a frightening note all about chemicals in your food and whatnot attached to the fridge.

The phone in the kitchen trills loudly, I reach across the breakfast bar, pressing mute on the telly and answer it, mouth full of muesli.

'Herrro?'

'Darling,' Mum said flatly down the phone. 'I have just seen Betty Baxter's daughter Nicola on television talking about the days you used to smoke ten Royal Blue between you round the back of Jimmy's Bowling Green!'

'Um . . .' I said, swallowing hard.

I heard a sharp intake of breath before she continued with, 'And shoving bottles of alcohol inside her knickers is something no mother ever wants to hear about her daughter.'

'Nicola lied!' I spluttered, as I tried to neck my tea, with one eye on the clock which was ticking towards 8.20am. In ten minutes Bailey, in all his man glory, would arrive to take me to my secret location for phase one of Project Katie.

'I am so disappointed in you, Katie, I thought you were the responsible one out of my two daughters. This is a stunt that Janice would pull!'

'Mum, it was like, fourteen years ago, I'm a grown-up now!'

'And now I also know that it was your footprints in the flowerbeds and not those of a burglar, when you scaled the garden trellis up to your bedroom window at night! What on earth would you have done if your father had caught you!'

'I have to go now, Mum, I really need to . . .'

'I am not a well woman, Katie, I have nerves that are as frayed as the ends of ribbons, what with all this hulla-balloo you're putting me through, and I just don't know what to do with myself and you want to see your sister, dressed up to the nines for her maths lesson today and –'

'I HAVE TO GO!' I shouted at her. Silence enveloped the other end of the phone.

'Well, you could have just said, Kate Lewis. There is no need to shout.'

'Mum, we can talk later, OK? I'll have a word with Janice.'

I hung up the phone and raced into the bathroom to clean my teeth, using the special gold-leaf, minty-fresh floss that sat proudly on the shelf alongside every other fancy product under the sun. I didn't have time to play with them all, so I splashed my face, patted it dry and put on a slick of pale pink lippy. I know they said no make-up but after last night's embarrassment with Bailey, I ought to really make a small effort. I was beyond nervous about seeing him again. I wanted to look semi-perfect the next time he claps his soulful eyes upon my face. I was worried things would be awkward between us, now that he had a slight idea that I could fancy him a little. How will he react to me today?

I needn't have worried – Bailey rapped on the door and began singing to me about what a beautiful day it was outside and had a massive grin plastered on his face.

'Whaasssup!' he said, holding two takeaway coffees. 'For you, *Mademoiselle*,' he said, holding one out.

'Thanks,' I said, pulling the hemline down on the slightly-too-short-for-my-liking dress I had been given in my goody bag yesterday. 'I hope they're organic!' I laughed, thinking back to the note on the fridge about scary evil chemicals in all food.

'Why are you so happy?' I queried, one eyebrow raised.

'Ah . . . we are going on an adventure! Zee car is waiting!' he said, in a rubbish French accent.

I grabbed my handbag and my mobile and made for the door. With the balaclava placed firmly back upon my head, I must have looked a sight walking from Poets Field PR to the luminous white stretch limo which was waiting for us in the car park. Bailey, ever the gent, opened the door for me and I ducked my head to climb into the back seat. Once again, despite my dramatic sighs and evident emotional rain cloud above my head, Bailey failed to mention anything to do with Jack and his real-life Barbie, or the fact my childhood best friend was colluding with the media and ratting me out to my mother on breakfast television with her tales of stolen cigarettes and underage drinking. He kept his eyes on the road as we headed into central London.

Chapter 6

'Daaaaahlllliiiiing,' said fashion guy number one from yesterday's meeting. 'How are you?' he asked, his face etched with concern.

'Great,' I said, still sitting in the limo as the windows were rolled down.

'I'm Aubrey,' he said, holding out a honey-coloured hand with short fingers jangling with coloured jewels. 'I'm your stylist and we are going to have a un-believe-able day today, isn't this just the best!' he said, clasping his hands together and doing a little dance. 'Here, here,' he said, opening the door. He turned to Bailey. 'Be outside Great Portland Street at ooooh, say,' he looked at his massive gold sparkly watch before continuing, '5 pm?'

'Sure,' Bailey replied before throwing me one of those sexy smiles. 'Good luck, Katie,' and off he went.

I stood on the corner of Covent Garden in a flimsy, too-short dress and my father's balaclava. Aubrey takes my hand and whispers into my ear, 'Don't worry, once Ziggy Wang is done with you, you'll never have to go near that hideous headgear ever again!'

'Thank fuck,' I said beneath the material.

'Sorry?' Aubrey said, spinning on his heels.

'I said, what luck that I have got an appointment with Ziggy Wang!' I'd read about him in *Heat!*

'I know!' Aubrey simpered. 'Now come along, we have

a full morning ahead of us, with your roots to contend with!'

Ziggy Wang was the most celebrated hairdresser in London, actually, probably the whole entire world. He was funky, sexy and from Japan. His salon was decked out like a spaceship, everything was cool, chrome and futuristic. Everyone wore white. If I thought I got a gay welcome from Aubrey, Ziggy Wang was off the scale.

'My. God. It's you!' he trilled, spinning me around on my heels – it's hard to be spun when you can barely see for black wool.

'Yikes!' I squealed, as he pulled off the balaclava, the material of which wiped my pale pink lipstick halfway up the side of my face. My hair . . . well, you guessed it.

'Come, come, see,' he said, as they both fussed me into a giant space chair.

'Now, Katie!' Ziggy Wang stared long and hard at me.

'Yeah . . .' I said tentatively.

'I have only so far seen that delightful peach of a bottom with what looked like Cath Kidston underwear . . .'

'Tesco's.'

'Tescows . . . never heard of them . . . are they Italian?'

God, Ziggy Wang really did live on the moon.

'We cut your hair,' he said, making snippy scissor gestures with his fingers.

'I'd really rather we didn't cut my hair, I've been growing it for ages now, please don't cut my . . .'

'We cut your hair, only a little bit, and we,' he turned to Aubrey, 'whaddya think? I'm thinking we colour with honey and beige, infused with . . .'

'Pale sand and biscuit,' Aubrey said without hesitation.

'Pale sand it is. A beautiful collision of blonde and biscuit!' he squealed, spinning my chair violently round to face him. 'You are a star!'

'Great!' I grimaced. As long as they didn't make me look like I'd had a fight with a bottle of Toilet Duck bleach, I was game.

Aubrey had instructed the staff to put blackout props against the windows to prevent any wayward photography before I was unveiled to the world, a better, more wholesome Jessica Hilson.

'Here's some magazines for you to read whilst your colour is setting, Katie,' a stick-thin assistant gushed, as various other bodies slathered dye on my head.

All of a sudden, my heart skipped a beat and very nearly stopped altogether. Right on the front cover of *Scorcher* magazine was my Jack with a whole heap of blonde and tan wrapped around him, gallivanting in the sea! Jack was looking effortlessly chic, a flower garland draped across his chest which looked much more buff than usual. He was grinning like a lunatic whilst Jessica Hilson threw her head back dramatically in the most cringe-worthy pose I have ever seen since, well, this week's *Sizzle Stars*. The headline read: LOVERS ENTWINE IN HONOLULU AS *COWGIRLS* SET TO SMASH BOX OFFICE RECORDS!

'Gaaaah!!!!' I wailed aloud, completely forgetting where I was and abandoning my dignity once again. In an instant, Aubrey and Ziggy Wang were whipping away every gossip magazine that I held in my lap, screeching at the sinewy assistants who saw fit to give me a lovely front-page account of my sodding ex-boyfriend and his stupid new girlfriend.

'Remove!' Aubrey bellowed, his arms flailing. 'Immediately!' Assistants scattered around the room searching out and destroying anything with Jack and Jessica on the cover or in any kind of spread.

'What is the point?' I cried. 'I will never, ever, ever match up to her!' I was fighting back tears. 'There isn't a hair colour in the land that can save me now!' I threw my arms up into the air for effect.

'Katie,' Ziggy Wang said, with an air of Zen-like calm surrounding him, despite the pandemonium of the salon. His eyes were kind and gentle. He got down to my level and cupped my face gently with his hands.

'I know this isn't easy for you right now, I know that I would have committed suicide by now if it were me. But this isn't me we're talking about, and you are made of stronger cookie dough than that. Hair colour can and does save, change and enhance lives all over the world, when done correctly,' he said solemnly.

I sat on my chair and for the next hour and a half I was chopped, coloured, washed and blow-dried, whilst Ziggy Wang continued to pep talk me with a paddle brush.

'You will see,' he said breathlessly, 'that you are . . .'

'Oh my God, you so are . . .' Aubrey interjected.

'Shiiiiit,' I whispered, as I was spun round dramatically to face my new reflection.

'Beautiful,' they whispered together, before erupting into a rush of compliments to each other for having worked so well on completing section one of Project Katie.

Hand waves and twirls galore, Ziggy Wang hissed in my ear, 'Believe me now?!' and with that, he threw his skinny handwoven scarf around his neck, turned on his kitten heels in the other direction and clapped his hands. He didn't look back for confirmation. He didn't have to, I felt like a million squillion pounds and this time, my tears were of pure joy. Ziggy Wang could indeed perform miracles.

I left the salon with hair from an advert bouncing around underneath my balaclava.

'I thought we were going to be through with the face mitten,' I said, upset that my super-shiny, bouncy tresses were now flattened, probably beyond redemption, underneath the offending wool.

'We have to go for some lunchtime plastic surgery,' Aubrey said, as though it was the most natural thing in the world. 'Then,' he continued blithely, 'you have to have manicures, pedicures, a spray tan and we go shopping. Well, you don't go shopping – myself and uber-stylist to the stars, Tom Theodore, will do that for you.'

'Tom Theodore . . .' I mused, 'wasn't he the stylist to mega successful funky girl band Pop Girls?'

'Oh yes, and he styled Jessica . . . ooh . . . Jessica . . . Rabbit . . . uh . . .' he said, trailing off at the end of his sentence, quickly realizing his faux pas.

My stomach lurched at the very mention of her name.

'Never mind, now, here, hop in this cab with me.' And together, we stepped into the cab and headed to Great Portland Street.

'Saggy . . .' Doctor Dickhead said, as he wafted his hand against my breast. It wobbled in response to his touch.

'I see . . .' he continued, prodding the sides of my boob with a pencil.

I sat there on his plush couch, wearing nothing more than my knickers. I shivered in the cold as all of me tensed up with sheer embarrassment. Doctor Vasquez prodded various bits of me, made disconcerting noises, tutted and sighed with a bit of headshaking thrown in, whilst he circled my nipples with bright blue marker pen.

'Ah ha!' he said, stepping back to admire his work. 'We have progress, no?' he addressed Aubrey, who had rudely stayed in the room while my clothes were taken off my back, in what I now realize is completely normal in this crazy world of gay men with a hunger for immediacy. I felt as if these days, bits of me and items of my apparel were whipped off, shoved here, strung upside down and spun round faster than you like. I looked around at Aubrey who had sensibly turned his back to check out imaginary spots and shapes on the pristine white walls. When I looked back, Doctor Vasquez was hovering around a computer screen, muttering to himself.

'We do this here . . . and a little there . . . *et voilà*!' He pressed a button and the giant screen above his head illuminated with a bright picture of my body.

'Now, here,' he said pointing, 'is where age has worn down zee tissue of zee breast which results in this, what I call breast ptosis and what you may call a significant droop.'

I am mortified. Aubrey's face doesn't even move. Must be one of the Botox crew.

'We put small saline-filled implants into zee breast and perform a lift, and you wake up with zee breasts of a twenty-year-old!'

'But I'm only twenty-six. They're not that saggy, are they?'

I look to Aubrey for reassurance but he quickly averts his eyes to the ceiling and whistles a tune.

'OK, so you want to give me breast implants?' I say. 'To get zee look of Jessica Hilso—'

'To get a more enhanced look,' Aubrey jumps in, 'to rival Jessica Hilson. Sorry, love, I know you hate me saying her name but needs must and all that. Take it in context, anyway, you need to be a champion brand, a better version.'

'Sink of it like zees,' Dr Vasquez says. 'You right now are a Burger King.'

'I'm a greasy burger?'

'Enough, darling, don't need to know that much about your hygiene habits . . .' Aubrey attempts a joke, I shoot him daggers. I cannot believe I am sitting here with my tits out in front of one gay guy and another ridiculously accented doctor who's trigger happy about making my chest look more at home in a world atlas.

'We all like a bit of junk now and again, darling,' Aubrey says.

'Speak for yourself . . .' Dr Vasquez says snidely.

'What he means is Jessica Hilson is a twenty-one-day matured Scottish rump steak and you are hovering on the "Do you want fries with that?" side of class.'

I draw my breath in. This is so insulting, I think I am going to cry! My eyes well up in protest.

'Don't cry *ma chérie*!' Dr Vasquez strokes my cheek gently, 'Eet can be fixed, look, see,' he says, as he clicks another button.

Like the look book's computer-generated vision of a

better-looking version of myself, the screen fills up with a noticeably trimmer, perkier me.

'Wow,' I breathe.

'Redemption!' the men chorus.

'We sign you in for Monday morning, you have all weekend to prepare, no food, no drink twenty-four hours before you come in. Now, which size breast would you like?' He addresses Aubrey and not me.

'Uh . . . don't I get a say in this?'

'Darling,' Aubrey says. 'It's really not an option – you did read the contract, didn't you?'

'Yes, of course I did,' I say, in mock horror. Well, if you count getting Danielle to check when I could get my hands on the £10K fee, which wasn't until I fulfilled my end of the bargain, which was an extreme makeover . . . oh, I see . . . but then I have always wanted bigger boobs . . . just on my own terms. Having someone prod and poke fun at me and call me saggy doesn't make me feel all that great about myself. I had been so high from my miracle hairdo. And now I felt grotesque, with Frankenstein lines dotted across my torso. I pulled my arms around my body, concealing my boobs. I suddenly felt even more naked than I actually was.

'She'll have a D cup,' Aubrey says, as they both crowd around my chest to study me intently.

'What about an F?' Dr Vasquez says. 'Her weight could take an F . . .'

'No, because we'll have her in for some lipo next week . . . and then there are the gym sessions.'

'Gym sessions?!' Oh God, oh God, no, no, no, that's a total nightmare! The gym and I have not met since the year

2000 when I bought myself a hideously expensive all-singing, all-dancing gym membership at Buff Bodz, went once, fell over in front of the hot men doing weights, put my hand on to some poor sod's crown jewels to steady myself, which resulted in a sweaty pile-up on the gym mats. Needless to say, I never went back. I shudder at the thought.

'So, an F would be too big, no?'

'TOO BIG!' I squeal.

Both men look taken aback.

'I think we should give her five minutes,' Aubrey whispers, as they retreat from the room. 'She's the emotional type.' The men exchange knowing glances.

I'm left on my own, still sitting on the plush couch with images of myself starkly reflecting in the mirrors hanging on the whitewashed walls. I look saggy, I do. I sigh heavily and close my eyes for a few seconds. When I open them, I can see my 'after' shot. I look luminous, gorgeous. That's the kind of girl Jack wants, not my droopy-boobed, podgy self. These people are trying to help me – they have my best interests at heart. They know what they're doing. Why am I being so ungrateful? I take another deep breath and smile into the mirror. My wonky teeth grin back. My heart sinks. Right, no more moaning, no more feeling awful, I have a chance now, to be someone, to be gorgeous and I am going to take it, even if it means having to suffer humiliating moments with pen-wielding rude men, nothing is going to stop me because I'm going to be gorgeous! I will let them do anything they like to me, anything! My phone trills in my bag. It's Danielle.

'Hey you,' I say.

'Hey, I'm coming to get you tonight, there's no media

outside your house, plus Grum is off his food. I think he misses you. I tried him with a bit of haddock but he was having none of it.'

'He's a fusspot. I wouldn't worry,' I say.

'I don't understand where all the press have gone though, Katie? Jessica Hilson must have farted in Honolulu,' she says sarcastically.

'More likely Hanna Frost has set up some swanky magazine shoot or something with them,' I say back.

'Oooh, get you!' Danielle says, with a smile in her voice.

'I'm sitting here right now,' I say, 'covered in marker pen!'

'May I ask why?'

'I'm having, uh, I'm having some dermatological derm-abrasion skin peel, you know, to recapture my youthful glow!' I lie through my teeth.

'Don't be a banana,' Danielle laughs, 'you're only twenty-six, Christ, I'm turning thirty this year, so if any-one needs a dermadoodlewhop thing it's me!'

I daren't tell her I'm having a boob job. Danielle is so super against any kind of extreme plastic surgery and right now, I really need her support, especially since between them, Dr Vasquez and Aubrey have stripped away any smidgen of confidence I had located back at Ziggy Wang's.

'Shh,' I say to her, 'OK, right, well I have to go, Dr Vasquez is coming back in the room any second . . .'

'OK, sweetie, I will call you later, once I've seen Stewart for an early dinner . . .'

'What?'

'Can't talk now, don't lecture, speak later,' and with that she was gone. I sat and stared at the phone and before

I could think about whether or not any of this was in fact a wise idea, or before I could think about Jack sunning himself with Jessica in Hawaii, Aubrey and Dr Vasquez waltz back into the room.

'Better?' Aubrey queries.

'Yes, thanks, I am excited and very happy and would love new boobs, ones that stay up without a bra . . . you're absolutely right, I do not want to be tucking my boobs into my socks when I reach thirty.'

'Good girl,' Aubrey says, breaking out into a warm smile. Moments later, I am dressed; the face sock is firmly on my head as Aubrey leads me by the hands towards the back entrance of the clinic. I peek out through the eye slits of the balaclava and see an imposing black Range Rover. The window rolls silently down and Bailey pops his head out.

'Over here!' he yells, as we sidle over.

'This is different . . .' I say, admiring the shiny exterior.

'Yeah, Hanna felt it would be less conspicuous to drive around in a four by four than the eye-catching limo.'

'But I like the limo . . .' I whine.

'Madonna likes the limo, too, it's currently in a disused warehouse in Soho being primed for her new music video. It's a popular car.'

'Oh, wow!' I say, as I imagine Madonna's pert gym-honed bum sitting in the same seat I had become accustomed to in the past few days and recalling how Madonna was on the agreed list of acceptable people with whom to cheat on me alongside, oh, oh no! Alongside Jessica Hilson! And Sharon Stone. And anyone from *Hollyoaks*! But everyone knows that those lists are meant to be fantasies, to be jokes, not to be acted upon. Oh God, maybe Jack thinks I gave him permission to slope off with Jessica?

'We often lease it out to rock stars,' Bailey continues, winking at me in the rear-view mirror. I smile, feeling my cheeks flush.

'You so like him,' Aubrey hisses in my ear, as he sits back against the leather seats, buffing his fingernails until he could practically see his face in them.

'Do not,' I hiss back, lying through my teeth.

'You'll be in serious doo doo if you go near that boy,' Aubrey says gravely.

'You can take the mask off, Katie, the windows are blacked out, no one can see in.' Bailey yelled from the front. Why was Bailey off limits, I wondered? Perhaps he was doing it with Hanna after all, although I had so far seen no evidence. Is he gay? After all, he does dress exceptionally well and wears a lot of tight abs-revealing t-shirts.

'Gay?' I whisper to Aubrey.

He raises an eyebrow that suggests not.

'Let's see . . .' Aubrey whispers back.

I pulled the balaclava off my head, distracting Bailey from Aubrey's secret whisperings about him in my ear. My hair, still bouncy from the mega blow-dry, sprang out gaily.

'Nice hair,' Bailey commented, as he twisted the steering wheel down the road, his biceps bulging in the sunlight.

'The wizardry of Ziggy Wang!' I said gleefully, as Aubrey shot me a look. 'And Aubrey chose the colours,' I said, throwing him one back.

'Can you name the shade?' Aubrey questioned Bailey.

'Looks blonde to me,' Bailey shrugged.

Aubrey gave me another look. 'Not gay. Not in a million years.'

'I don't fancy him,' I hissed back in his ear. He raised another eyebrow in my direction. If he wasn't careful, the way he moved them up and down like that he'd do himself an injury. He totally didn't believe me either. Bailey turned on the radio as our conversation came to a natural close. I sat back against the seats and watched the traffic snake around us through the City. Twenty minutes later, we came to a stop outside Poets Field PR, where I could see Danielle in close conversation with Hanna Frost, who looked stunning in a bright fuchsia Galaxy dress. I hopped out towards her.

'Hey you,' Danielle said, quickly turning her attention towards me. Aubrey air-kissed us both, winked at Hanna and bade us farewell. It was far too nippy for him, in his tiny designer t-shirt with strategically placed holes and distressed denim which also had bits of material missing. My mother would have a fit if I came home wearing that outfit and would have it off my back quicker than the stylists to darn and patch with much gusto using navy-blue thread.

'Come on inside, darling,' Hanna thrust her arm into the crook of my own and hustled me into the building. Bailey and Danielle followed.

Hanna looked at me appraisingly. 'Gorgeous,' she simpered. 'Phase one is complete, almost.'

'Almost?' I queried. What else could they have planned for me?

'Tomorrow you will have your nails tended to, your

make-up professionally applied and an outfit will have been carefully selected for you by none other than Tom Theodore, stylist to the stars.'

'Yes, Aubrey said! I am really excited about that, even if he did style Jessica Hilson.'

'Tomorrow is a big deal, Katie. It will be your first test to see whether you come out a winner or a loser. I can't be having you doing an impression of a mentalist on national television, so you need to work on keeping those emotions in check. This means no hysterics if you see a picture of your arse.'

'Which one?' Danielle said sarcastically. 'The one she sits on or the one in Honolulu?'

'Funny,' Hanna said dryly. 'The one she sits on. But my point is,' Hanna said, addressing Danielle, 'that Katie had a full-on hissy fit in the boardroom yesterday, and one today at Ziggy Wang's when confronted with information slash evidence of Jack Hunter's philandering ways, and let's not forget her reaction was the same if not worse to the shots of her being lifted out of Lauriston Gardens on Richard's back.'

'Well, it was a shock, that's all . . . I don't think there is much worse that could happen now, surely?' I said, suddenly unsure of the words spoken.

'Quite,' she said. 'You are doing your first interview tomorrow with *Sizzle Stars* magazine.'

My face dropped and my blood went cold. *Sizzle Stars* ran the leading gossip trail on Jack and Jessica. What if they devoured me? I knew how fickle these magazines could be, one minute we all loved leggings, then next, the

Devil invented them. I know I wasn't a pair of leggings, but the sentiments were the same. What if they noticed the spot that was resident on my chin or they laughed about the size of my love handles? What would I say if they brought up the fact I wear cheap Tesco pants?

'I will be on hand to advise you on everything, Katie, so you don't need to worry. I will have a list of questions that they will ask you and will prep you on answers you should give. You must stick to them.'

Too right, I was going to stick to them, either that or be ridiculed out of London and forced into exile in Little Glove with only my mother for company.

'OK, right, so good stuff, at least you will be there to guide me,' I smiled at Hanna hopefully.

'Right, I must go now, Katie, get a good night's rest tonight. Bailey will pick you up at 10am tomorrow and from there, we will go straight to the *Sizzle Stars* offices.' With that she smiled, turned on her kitten heels and answered her phone which was trilling loudly for attention.

'Blimey,' Danielle said, as we watched her saunter off to the lift.

'I know,' I murmured, 'she's amazing.'

'Right, girls!' Bailey interrupted our moment of extreme envy at the fact Hanna Frost's backside didn't wobble and her boobs stuck solidly to her pencil-thin torso. Her glossy hair trailed in neat waves down to the base of her back. She was a goddess, albeit an unusual-featured woman. She appeared to have no chin.

'I can't work out if she's beautiful or not. Hanna has

everything in the right place, but she still reminds me of a horse,' Danielle chortled.

'I'll pretend I didn't hear that,' Bailey whispered.

'Shhh, we weren't talking about THAT Hanna, were we, Danielle?' I nudged her violently in the ribs.

'Ouch! No, of course not, now let's go eat, I'm starving.'

'I thought you ate earlier with Stewart-small-penis?' I queried.

'Don't ask,' she sighed. So I didn't. If there was a serious need for extreme man decodation and subsequent analysis of his movements, I knew they would come out with the bottle of red we'd surely consume over dinner.

'You girls frighten me,' Bailey says, mocking us, as we clamber into the car.

'We're not that scary!' Danielle says. 'In fact, why don't you find out for yourself?' she says, with a glint in her eye. Bailey looks intrigued, but nervous.

He starts up the engine of the car as Danielle lurches forward, resting her chin half on his shoulder in a playful manner. 'Stay for dinner with us,' she says.

'I can't . . .' he begins to say, before Danielle whips him on the arm.

'Don't be silly, of course you can!'

'Really, it's a big day tomorrow and I . . .' he continues.

'Nonsense,' Danielle says. 'After you have dropped us off, go home . . . where is it you live?'

'Baker Street,' he says.

'Posh,' she says. 'It's not far, go home, freshen up, come back, we'll cook dinner, how about a nice Italian?'

'I'd have one of those!' I joke badly.

'Shh, you,' she prods me in the arm before turning her

attention back on Bailey, whose face has turned a fetching shade of crimson.

'I can't,' he says solemnly. 'Traffic's insane this time of night.'

'OK, well, if you change your mind, let us know.'

Despite the second knock back of the week by Bailey, my resolve was strong in the sense that the look books had shown me the 'me' of my dreams. The fact I wasn't going to put myself into bankruptcy to enjoy the benefits of plastic surgery was even sweeter. The whole shebang made me feel encouraged that despite how dire things looked with regards to reconciling with my beloved Jack, perhaps it could happen, like Hanna said.

We came to a stop outside my house, opened the door and stepped out of the car. No reporters or paparazzi were in sight and aside from some curtain twitching from the direction of Mrs Bellamy's house, all was quiet on the East End front.

'Thanks, and see you soon,' I hollered to Bailey as he revved his engine into reverse, waved his hand and drove off, rather too fast.

'What's up with that boy?' Danielle questioned.

'No idea,' I said, as I got my keys out of my bag and turned them in the lock. It was weird being back at home again, even though I had only been gone less than a week. So much had happened and going back into my living room was like returning to the scene of the crime. The familiar scent of my house made me think of Jack. I looked into the kitchen and intrusive bittersweet memories flooded in of all the times Jack pushed me up against the worktops, hands kneading at my breasts, a leg moved surreptitiously in between my thighs, making me gasp in pleasure. He would lift me up on to the counter and make mad, passionate love to me – all the while his mouth enveloping every inch of my body. The same thing occurred all over the house, the couch, the stairs, the bathroom . . . and especially the bedroom. There were sex memories everywhere. He was insatiable. Is that what he is doing to Jessica Hilson 24/7 in exotic locations? And of course, her body is taut and slender and she earns stupid money for appearing in cheesy films. I struggled for all of five minutes to realize what he could possibly see in her but, of course, what he saw in her aside from her massive tits and honey-blonde hair, was the ability to get exposure, and oh boy, had he got exposure. He was plastered all over the place, playing the role of the tanned, toned adoring boyfriend, in just about every single magazine sold in any newsagent's. He was everywhere. He just wasn't with me, where he should be. My phone rang, breaking the silence of my trip down sexual memory lane.

'Katie,' my mum bellowed down the receiver.

'Hi, Mum,' I replied.

'It has been days now, and there has been no sign of the *Daily Mail* in the front garden. Would you care to explain why your poor father was up a ladder painting the window frames and clearing out the guttering? Why I have been on my hands and knees for nearly two days wearing my Sunday best, weeding and planting and preening? Janice cleaned her bedroom solidly for two whole hours. Can you tell me why there are no promised journalists camped out, wanting to talk to me about my daughter?'

'You say it as though it's a bad thing, Mum! We don't

want to be stalked by paparazzi!' I say to her, incredulously.

'We do,' she says, 'because I told everyone in Betty Baxter's salon, when we went for our trims, that my daughter was on the precipice of becoming a household name and that the *Daily Mail* were going to be scrabbling in the flowerbeds to catch a glimpse of my hairdo and, of course, to gather information on you from us, your loyal, adoring family.'

'Sorry . . .' I said, gobsmacked.

'And now everyone will think I have lied. And they will think it very well runs in the family after Nicola Baxter's scathing interview with Lorraine Kelly on your wild days of debauchery down Little Glove Community Centre. Everyone always thought you were such a cherub, and now we learn that you were anything but, leading Nicola Baxter down the wayward pathway to sin. Really, Kate, heaven knows where you got it from, it certainly wasn't me, must have been a heathen throwback from your father's side. His great-great-grandfather was a cow thief from the Highlands, don't you know.'

'Mum, I'm doing my first magazine interview tomorrow, aren't you pleased about that?'

'Unless it's in *Good Housekeeping* you have no chance,' Janice says.

'Janice?' we both say, as a third person joins in on our phone conversation.

'Yeah, that's me, in the spare room, watching Jessica Hilson snog Jack's face off on a beach somewhere, looks nice, very hot, super jealous.'

'Janice!' Mum barks at her.

'What?' she says.

'I can't deal with this right now,' I say, mournfully, 'I'll call you tomorrow,' and with that, I hang up. Danielle had already poured me a large glass of wine and was scrabbling about in the kitchen for a pizza menu. It was a takeaway night, for sure.

Chapter 7

After a good gossip and some much-needed respite from fashion gays, body scrutinization and my ex with his megastar new girlfriend, I had yet another fitful sleep, peppered with nightmares that included Jack being horrible to me, Jack swanning around with Jessica, her looking amazing and me looking like the back end of a bus. And then I woke with a start to that horrible, head-shattering, dreadful *beep beep beep* of my alarm clock as sweat trickled down my back and down my forehead. So much for being a nightmare, I thought, as reality crept into my sleep-addled brain. Jack dread is actually happening to me right now, I sighed heavily and rubbed my eyes. The sun was shining brightly through the windowpanes, making everything in my bedroom sparkle. I felt a rush of optimism, and grabbed it with both hands. 'Well, not this morning!' I sternly thought to myself as I heaved myself out of my bed and towards the shower, singing shamelessly and using my favourite strawberry-shaped soap that was kind to my skin. I had put MTV on as loud as it would go, sod the neighbours, half of them had hearing aids in anyway, and enjoyed a good hour playing with the make-up in my goody bag from Hanna, all shiny new and Chanel. I wanted to spend at least ten minutes in Bailey's exceptionally good-looking yet slightly morose company looking a little bit attractive. As it happened, disappointingly Bailey didn't show up this morning. Hanna Frost beeped her horn loudly as Danielle peeked through the curtains.

'There's that snooty-looking brunette wearing impossibly big Jackie O shades, fingernails curled around the steering wheel, looking like she's chewing a lemon.'

'So, Hanna's here, then,' I giggled, as I pulled on my white canvas pumps and hoisted my leggings up my midriff, pulling my lovely slip-on dress over my bum and hips.

'Gotta go, D. Wish me luck!'

'I wish you luck, babe,' she said, pulling me close for a quick hug and a kiss.

As soon as I got into her sports car, a packet of baby wipes hit me clear on the side of my face.

'Oops, sorry!' Hanna cooed. 'Accident, my aim has always been bad . . . never join me for tennis, unless you want an eye missing,' she smiled.

'Are these yours, then?' I said, thinking that perhaps she just meant to throw them in the back of the car for safe-keeping.

'No, they're for you. Take the make-up off, Katie, stick the balaclava back on your head and keep yourself hidden.'

The roof of the car was down, the morning was glorious. I wish it was time for the great unveiling. I don't know how much longer I can survive living like a covert burglar.

'Your make-up will be done professionally. Good job, though,' she said, gesturing to the half of my face that still had make-up applied to it. My heart sank a little. One, I was expecting Bailey and wanted to show him that I was as capable as the next girl of glamour, and two, I thought my make-up would go down well. I mean, I've always been good at applying make-up and I thought I looked pretty this morning.

Now, I felt like a minger. How Hanna, Aubrey, Dr Vasquez and Jack all manage to make me feel like a hideous monster, I don't know. At least now I had a nice stylist, I suppose.

The car whipped through London at lightning speed, with the *stomp stomp stomp* of frenetic dance music blasting out of the stereo. Hanna's hair was flowing in the wind as she drove with one hand and in the other held a long, thin cigarette holder with a cigarette popped inside. I guess she didn't want to damage her nails with lovely nicotine stains.

As we rolled up into the bay area of the imposing building that was Sunshine Media, which houses *Sizzle Stars*, a young blonde in vertiginous heels stood waiting. She was chewing gum. She looked fierce.

'Daaahhhling,' Hanna said as she air-kissed the tiny blonde.

'Daaaahling,' the blonde simpered back. 'How are you?'

They exchanged pleasantries before mini-blonde turned to me. 'So, you must be Katie! Bit difficult to see you under there, but let's get you into hair and make-up and I'm sure we'll be seeing a very different version of the one I see before me now!' She grinned. Is she for real? I thought, what is it with these fashion media types, insulting me willy-nilly and getting away with it? My mouth agape, I stood there, silently fuming.

'My name is Frenella.' She extended a dainty hand.

'Hi,' I muttered, 'nice to meet you.' Not, I thought. I hoped my stylist was nicer.

I walked about six feet behind them like some kind of subservient as Hanna and Frenella waffled on about rock stars, Botox and holidays in LA. I hated them so much at this point, with all their amazing apparel, their groomed hair, perfect straight teeth and complete ignorance of me.

We turned the corner, and what lay before me very nearly took my breath away. It was an Aladdin's cave full of Gucci, Chloé and Lanvin, where tanned and toned bodies swayed between rows and rows of bright, expensive, beautifully sewn garments. I pulled the balaclava from my head and stood there gazing at the delights before me.

'And you are the darling Katie!' Fashion guy number two from the boardroom flashed a smile so bright he nearly gave me cataracts. 'I'm Tom Theodore, we met earlier in the week? You are SUCH a pup! Gorgeously voluptuous, like some kind of goddess from a painting, so Rubenesque, so shapely!' He pawed at my arms, ran his hands down them towards my hips, shook me a little and appeared to literally drink me in.

'Hi . . .' I breathed at him, barely taking my eyes off the Balenciaga handbags in the corner.

'I know,' he said, noting my gaze. 'It's just like when Charlie visits the Chocolate Factory, isn't it? Swap chocolate for clothes and you've got the same expression as little Charlie . . . bless you!' he said, hooking his arm with mine and sashaying me into the hub of the garments. Hanna and Frenella continued to converse in the corner, each applying lipgloss like it was going out of fashion.

'Your colouring is Spring, so that means plenty of pastels, greens, blues, baby pinks . . . fab-you-less!' he exclaimed, holding up a variety of stunning outfits. I still hadn't uttered a word, such was my delight at being immersed in Santa's clothing grotto.

'It's all beautiful,' I eventually gasped.

'Right, we'll take this Hervé Léger bandage dress, those Louboutins and the Marc Jacobs shrug, and we're offskis!'

'Off?' I asked as he shimmied me along towards the other end of the room and into an even shinier area of intense glamour.

'Hairdo, baby,' he sang at me, as his long fringe fell on to his eyes. He was a gorgeous man. He had mocha smooth skin, piercing emerald eyes which I suspect were contacts, but nevertheless, they stood out. He wore soft cashmere and tight trousers, showing off his cute bum. Why do these impossibly gorgeous men with immaculate skin, hair and nails have to be gay? Such a waste! I must have been gazing longingly up at him, all six foot of him, as Hanna, who seemed to have appeared from nowhere, said, 'Don't fall in love with him, Katie, he's Aubrey's boy,' and she whisked herself past me and headed towards the nail bar.

'Um,' I said, feeling the colour creep on to my cheeks. I wondered how someone as polite and confidence-boosting as Tom Theodore could do it with the acrid Aubrey.

'SO!' Tom said, ignoring Hanna's attempts to embarrass me. 'Your hair colour is practically illegal, that's how sexy it is,' he cooed. 'I'm thinking, Bardot hair, sixties eye make-up, nude, matte lipstick in a pale rose, *et voilà*, we have our first shoot.'

'I thought I had to wait until I was like, you know, properly glamorous with my surgery and whatnot before I could be seen in public, let alone on a photo shoot . . .'

Tom looked as though I'd smacked him round the chops with a wet fish and denounced pop music.

'Katie, you have curves to die for, an ample bosom, no wrinkles and eyes that could light up a Third World country. You are beautiful already, and all these clothes and what have you will only add to that.' He then embraced me with a hug and I must admit, along with his kind words, I took great comfort from feeling his rippling muscles beat against my chest. This had to be a first – the first time one of these fashion types had actually treated me like a real-life person with thoughts and feelings that could be hurt by scathing comments. He was warm and friendly and gave me respect.

After I was dressed, made up and coiffed, I felt like a princess, sitting on a sumptuous chaise longue, my hair piled up on my head, my lovely pale clothes nestling against my skin.

'Right,' Tom shouted, 'I want you to be looking out of the window wistfully, pull the sleeves of your jumper over your hands, in a cute poor-little-me routine. I want you natural, yet sexy. I want you to look fragile, yet strong because despite being a woman who's been left by her man, you're still a woman in love . . .'

'Christ!' I exclaim. 'How am I going to convey all of that?'

'Easy!' he said, as he produced a picture of Jack snogging Jessica. My face must have looked pure horror, and as my mouth took a downward turn, tears pricked at my eyes, I looked at my feet, and counted my toes, first forwards and then backwards whilst inwardly telling myself not to have another meltdown. Like Hanna said, this was important and I must not screw it up. Tom didn't seem to mind, though, he was actively encouraging a meltdown. Was he some kind of sadist, I thought? No, of course he wasn't, he was just an artist trying to get the perfect shot.

'Lovely, lovely, perfect, oh yeah, amazing, keep going, just to the left, to the LEFT, darling, not the right,' Tom shouted, as he pranced about waving his hands over the photographer's head, 'I want you looking out of the window . . . ahhhh, good girl!' he continued to bark at me.

I moved and pulled the necessary faces, wondering whether he talks like that in bed. Tom was warm and friendly but he was ferocious on this shoot. Still the compliments flowed, which made me feel at ease. After about a million shots with my knees up to my chin, hugging myself and looking longing and at a loss out of a fake window, Tom decided I would now convey the emotion of happiness.

'Good luck,' I muttered.

'Darling,' he snapped his fingers and an assistant zipped across the room carrying a bag which he then presented to me. 'Go ahead, look inside . . .' he grinned at me.

I gingerly opened the black ribbon tying the handles together as some sparkles whooshed out of the top. I reached inside and pulled out two tickets for the most exquisite health spa in London and a £5,000 voucher for Harrods!

'Oh, wow!' I squealed, as my face turned into a beam of excitement.

The camera began to *snap snap snap* as I grinned and looked skywards, not believing my luck, literally thanking my lucky stars.

'Gorgeous, look at you, Katie, how does happiness feel?'

'Pretty damn good!' I smile back, as I notice Danielle in the corner, smiling and snapping away with her own camera. Our eyes meet across the studio floor. I'm a bit blinded by the bright lights, so I hold my hand up to shield the glare and give a little wave.

'Darling, FOCUS!' Tom orders and I quickly resume my

carefree, glad-to-be-rid-of-you poses. In one fifteen-minute time slot, I have gone from miserable, bereft and pathetic to I don't give a shit about you now I have Harrods vouchers. Huzzah! Maybe money can buy happiness, after all?

'Dazzling, baby,' Tom continues, before adding, 'we're done, Katie, *bravo, bravo*!' The lights go down and the people who were watching resume positions towards the other end of the studio.

'Back in a mojo,' Tom says, as he pulls his cigarettes out of his pocket and gulps an espresso. I swear all these people live on is nicotine and black coffee. Danielle walks over and plonks herself next to me on the chaise longue.

'They put me in the tightest trousers known to humanity, and my clothes are covered in clips to pull them into place. I've hungry bum syndrome.'

'Nice, but I know what you mean, I get that with thongs. So,' she says, smiling at me, 'how does it feel like to be a mini celeb, almost?'

'Well, so far it's been hideous! The pants-flashing, my mother giving me grief because the *Daily Mail* haven't been stalking her, Janice's hemlines are getting so short they should come with a health warning, my make-up ban . . . but I suppose once this article comes out, maybe I will feel like more of a celebrated person than the subject of one of those awful magazines that champion women whose errant husbands ate their cats or had it off with their mother or something.'

'I'd love to see Jack try it on with your mother . . . I'd pay good money for that!'

'Oh God, please don't!' I say, shrieking with mock horror. 'That would really tip her, and me, over the edge.'

'Seriously, though, honey, I was having a little chat with Hanna. You're going to be appearing on the decent shows and giving interviews to hot magazines, not appearing on *Jeremy Kyle* in your vest top and old gym bottoms, so don't worry. She seems to know what she's doing anyway, and she seems to have your best interests at heart, so you know, I think . . .'

'Lovely to know you're on my side, Danielle,' Hanna said, as she stepped out of the relative darkness and arranged herself under the spotlight. Although the lights surrounding the actual set were dimmed, we were still under incredibly bright spotlights, meaning we hadn't seen her approach. I wondered how long she had been standing there.

'In a few minutes, Frenella is going to come along and interview you about how you're dealing with being thrust into the limelight and also, how devastated you are about Jack. The questions are normal regular questions such as, how long were you together, did you have any niggling worries about the state of your relationship, did you have any suspicions, what kind of boyfriend is he, that kind of thing. Keep your answers short and sweet, for God's sake, do not go off at a tangent, cry or use the F word. No vulgar language, keep up the pretence that you are a lovely wholesome girl's girl and we'll be on to a winner, Katie.'

'OK, sure, will do,' I say, breathing in deep. This is my first ever magazine interview, what if I accidentally say fuck and call Jack a wanker? What if I cry? Shit, shit, shit, this better go well or I will be eaten alive when *Sizzle Stars* goes to press. Jack only left me a little under a week ago and now I'm pouring my heart out to a woman who sounds as though she has a sexually transmitted disease for a name. I just don't know if I am ready.

'Ready?' Hanna says, looking directly into my eyes. I hate it when she does that staring thing. It's as though she's peering right down into my soul.

I nod my head in agreement. 'Ready,' I say.

'Right, then, let's go.'

Sitting in a pristine white room with massive comfy sofas, vases of fresh flowers dotted about the place and floor-to-ceiling windows which allowed reams of bright sunshine to spill on to the furnishings, I couldn't help but feel as though I was once again part of an advert for cool people whose lives were effortless. My hair was exceptionally shiny, my make-up was perfect, I had on false eyelashes and I smelled divine. I even got to keep the adorable clothes that now, without the pegs to pin them to my body, fell beautifully over my curves, accentuating the best parts and helpfully skimming over the bits I was less impressed with. Danielle wasn't allowed to join me, but Hanna could take a back seat in the room in case I was asked something tricky. Obviously I didn't want to balls it up. Tom had quickly returned just as Hanna and I were leaving in order to air-kiss my cheeks and near enough squeeze me to death in a vice-like hug.

Frenella wafted in, all white linen trousers and a cool cotton shirt. Her hair was shiny and her lips glossy.

'Darling,' she said, sitting down opposite me. 'We meet again, although I would hardly have recognized you with all that amazing make-up, gosh, our staff really are the absolute best, I have never seen a transformation as epic as this. You look like a different woman, what an improvement!'

'OK, OK, stop it, shhh,' I said to her, half joking. She was bordering on the offensive and I really didn't want anything to pull me off cloud number nine right now. Tom had made me feel super hot, and I wasn't going to let Frenella in her posh clothes take that away from me. Besides, she wasn't the only one who could rock Marc Jacobs!

Frenella takes out her dictaphone, pops it down between us and presses play.

'Testing, testing, 1-2-3,' she says into the mic, before pressing stop, rewind and happily listening to her voice as it plays back her message.

'Fab, right, OK, ready?' I nod. 'Let's begin.'

Frenella: [businesslike] 'Katie, as the world knows, Jack Hunter, twenty-five, from Dagenham in Essex, lived a comfortable and happy life with you in your lovely home in Bethnal Green, right?'

Me: 'Yes, as far as I know he did . . . I mean, obviously I knew he was there, he was my boyfriend, we made that commitment to one another . . . but as for him being happy? As far as I know, he was very happy, we both were.' [I bit my lip solemnly.]

Frenella: [eyebrow dancing] 'But he was harbouring the most awful secret, wasn't he, Katie . . .?'

Me: [She totally knows something!] 'Was he?'

My eyes lit up. What did she know that I didn't? I had begun to master the art of eyebrow decodation from the amount of movement that went on from Hanna and

Aubrey, so I knew this particular eyebrow move was an 'I know something you don't know' thing. I felt a little bit sick. OK, a lot sick.

> **Frenella:** [fake smile] 'He had been secretly having romantic love trysts with Jessica Hilson for three *whole* months before the press caught them sneaking out of The Dorchester.' [Sits back with a smug grin on her stupid face.] 'Now, Katie, how does it make you feel to know the man you love has been unfaithful with one of the world's most beautiful and talented women for such a long time, right under your nose?' [Bigger smug grin.]

My face visibly dropped as Frenella cocked her head to one side in mock sympathy whilst plastering a giant smug smile on her collagen-filled lips. Bitch, I thought, fucking horrible, nasty, awful, snotty cow! How the fuck did she think it made me feel? On top of the world? Ready to pen a song and fight for a Number One slot on the download chart? Perform naked cartwheels down Oxford Street? She was clearly insane and I was burning up with humiliation. My face now contorts with anguish as pain stabs at my heart and once again, hot tears threaten to ruin my perfect eye make-up. I'd never get it looking like that on my own, no way, and it wasn't as though I could pick Tom Theodore up and carry him around just for his make-up artistry skills. I look across to Hanna whose facial expression hadn't changed a jot. She looked eerily OK about this little revelation and she didn't seem concerned that I was about to have another meltdown. Then Hanna's behaviour suddenly made sense. She knew all along, didn't she? It suddenly hit me like a sledgehammer and I now had some burning questions of my own such as, why hadn't I been informed by Hanna that Jack had been having it off with Jessica for three months? That's twelve whole weeks! That's . . . lots of days. Why had no one, least of all my PR, told me? Or was it totally obvious and the whole timing thing didn't even occur to me? God, I must be the silliest girl ever to think that it was something quite new. Quite possibly it could have been going on for far longer than three months . . . although the timing made sense. *Cowgirls* was filming for around four months in London. As I processed this new horrible information, I struggled to contain how I was really feeling, which was as though a herd of overweight donkeys had rabbit-kicked me in the belly. As I swallowed the indignity and hurt of it all, I gave Frenella a big toothy smile before taking a big deep breath and answering her beastly question.

Me: 'Obviously it was awful, soul-destroying, oh God, totally beyond any heartbreaking feeling there is when it comes to a break-up. Hearing about Jack's relationship with Jessica Hilson has hurt me greatly. Jack Hunter has made me feel as though I am disposable, as though I never mattered and that he was only my boyfriend until something better came along that he felt fitted in with his wannabe film star lifestyle.'

I sniffed and swallowed a tear. Frenella handed me a box of tissues.

'Thanks,' I said, before taking a deep breath and continuing.

Me: 'I felt like as soon as he got what he needed and wanted out of me, which was designer clothes, money to go out, sex,' [I blushed at this point] 'you know . . . he left me, high and dry, just like that Radiohead song.'

I laughed nervously. Was I saying too much here? Didn't want to slate him too much, after all, my heart ached for him, winced at the mention of his name, broke at the thought of them together. Jack and Jessica. Jessica and Jack. Felt wrong, was wrong, it was Katie and Jack, Jack and Katie, together for . . . oh, who was I kidding? The man was an arse! He was! He had a nice arse all right, and pecs you could bounce tiddlywinks on, and underneath it all, a good heart, but he was still a horrible, self-obsessed, vacuous, emotionally immature idiot who totally turned his back on me when something more akin to his stupid fantasy life came about, without so much as a proper goodbye! The fuckwit broke up with me in a text, for crying out loud. Danielle was right, he was and is a total loser. Why am I so fussed about what his slimy self does? I should have walked out ages ago when he refused to take me anywhere, when he used me like a doormat, treated me like a mug. But I loved him. Still do. Don't know why. I can't give you reasons beyond aesthetics and wishful thinking. There you have it.

Me: 'But to be honest,' I continued, with a smile on my face, 'I am better off without him in my life, and these things only make a girl stronger!' [Lying through my teeth.]

Frenella: 'And you're a strong woman, Katie, our inbox is absolutely chocka with emails wishing you well, encouragement and support, everything, it seems as though many women have this happen to them . . . although not quite on the same scale.'

Me: [poshly] 'Quite.' [Equally smug grin on face, must keep composure.]

Tell me about it, I thought inwardly, I mean, most girls I know who have had love-rat boyfriends have been left for barmaids or secretaries, not movie stars. I give a heavy sigh and wonder if I have had some kind of illness that makes breathing in physical agony, as though I was inhaling razor blades. Is this what lovesickness is all about? Frenella looks intently at me, a face of pure sorrow. She felt bad for me and it was making me feel even bloody worse. Never mind, I thought, at least my face can still move.

The rest of the interview consisted of quick-fire questions about me: what I liked to drink (red wine, copious amounts of it), what was the last film I saw (*Dinner For Schmucks* with the delicious Paul Rudd) and also, would I take Jack back if he asked . . . I said 'Absolutely not' with complete conviction and plenty of gusto. My fingers were delicately crossed behind my back. Hanna sat on a puffed-up white leather chair, filing her nails in her normal violent manner. I couldn't quite work her out. Not telling me about Jack was just mean, almost as if she wanted me to have some kind of horrific reaction involving tears and ruined make-up, splodged mascara all over my cashmere clothes. I am really confused now. Is she friend or foe?

'And that's a wrap,' Frenella clicked the tape machine shut and turned her back to me, facing Hanna whose face now broke out into a sunny smile.

'I'm just, I need some air,' I said aloud to the back of

her head, thinking, I must smoke, get some air, and think things through. The problem with these fashion/media types is they are literally a total whirlwind, they put thoughts and phrases into your mouth, tell you what you think, what's right, what's going to happen next and you end up instantly believing that every word spoken is gospel. What did I think? I didn't know, some extreme smoking was in order. I clip-clopped in my fancy too-high-to-walk-in six-inch heels and almost fell over by the banister of the stairs. I gently removed them and moved with great ease towards the fire exit where I sat back against a quiet wall and removed a Marlboro Light menthol from its packet. I busied myself in my handbag looking for a lighter that worked. As usual I had about a zillion things in my handbag, random things like Vicks nasal sprays, lipsticks, travel playing cards, an old Malteser, a zip, my mobile, a succession of lighters and a photograph of me and Jack when we went boating on the Norfolk Broads one hazy, happy, loved-up summer. After three lighters had failed to light so much as a tiny flame, my patience was wearing thin. I looked at the picture of myself and Jack: his arms were wrapped around my waist and I grinned back a large open-mouth smile, my eyes were gazing up at the sun as he nuzzled my neck. The sky was a bright blue and the water glistened. We were picture perfect. Was all that based upon a lie? Was Jack using me the entire time? Can you fake happiness like the happy look he had in his eyes for me? I just didn't know what to think any more.

'Goddamnit!' I shouted at my useless pink lighter. I threw it in anger and watched it bounce across the pavement where it then came to a stop outside a very large black tyre which belonged to a very large, dark and imposing BMW that seemed to have come out of nowhere.

'Sorry!' I called out, before scrabbling to my feet in order to retrieve said lighter. I guess I'd have to scrap the cigarette for another time. Shouldn't really smoke in these beautiful clothes anyway, but oh . . . what was this? Slowly, the buzz of an electric window came from the shiny black Beamer and I felt as though I was a witness to a spaceship landing. I squinted in the sun, which had come out from behind a cloud, illuminating my stature against the wall behind me. With my hand up against my brow, I could just about make out the silhouette of a man.

'Kate Lewis,' he said as a statement, not a question.

'Um . . .' I said, a little bit afraid. Who is this strange man?

'Come closer, see,' the strange Italian-sounding voice said.

'I'm really not sure I should . . .' I said, nervously backing away from the vehicle.

'Kate. You have just been humiliated by Jack Hunter and his girlfriend, Jessica Hilson, right?' I winced at the word 'girlfriend'. How could she possibly have earned that status so soon! She was his fling, his sex thing, his bit of fluff, I bet she doesn't trim his nose hairs or wax his bum cheeks every fortnight with Veet, no, no I bet she doesn't. And I bet she doesn't trawl the internet and drive to random little places in order to find organic this and organic that and I bet her house doesn't permanently stink of bloody Japanese miso soup! No, she gets the fun bits of Jack, actually come to think of it, I bet he gets his back, sack and crack wax done at the poshest salon in town, she probably doesn't think he possesses any hair on his body that doesn't live on his head, Christ, I bet she also believed that he had stress alopecia on his pubes and that's why he was as bare as the day he was born down there. Yes, OK, it may look bigger, but it wasn't and he just looked weird. But there was no telling him.

The Italian man's voice continued to purr through the wound-down window.

'Hmmm . . .?' he said, prompting a reply from me.

'No, actually,' I lied, still in *Sizzle Stars* mode, fingers crossed, 'I don't care any more, it's yesterday's news. Old chip wrappers, you know, boring, yawn, not bothered . . .' I was waffling now.

'I see.' The words curled along his tongue. 'I would say, that one remarkable thing has occurred in this whole, sorry affair.'

'Really, well, I'm glad you're seeing silver linings on fluffy clouds, whoever you are,' I said carelessly. After all, why should I care what some faceless man in a scary car had to say about my Jack. And then it dawned on me . . . Italian man, rich voice, expensive car . . . Jessica Hilson!! No, her boyfriend, ex-boyfriend? Whatever, it was totally Fabio Matravers! It had to be!

'*Cara, sei bellissima, ti voglio, andiamo a cena?*' he said, confirming my suspicions, as his tanned face came into view at the window. He had large, almond-shaped eyes, framed by dark lashes. He broke out into a bright smile and cocked his head to the side in anticipation of my response.

'Yes, that sounds wonderful, but, um, I don't speak *Italiano*!' I said, in a crap Italian accent.

'I asked you to dinner, Kate, and,' he said, licking his lips, 'I called you beautiful.'

Ooh, that should be pervy but it's not, it's rather nice, he is quite a studmuffin.

'Um,' I said, oh God, what to say, what to say, need Danielle, no wait, need PR, Hanna, need advice, can I accept dates from hunky Italian ex-boyfriends of Jessica Hilson? Imagine the look on Jack's face if he saw me, Katie Lewis, stepping out with Fabio Matravers! 'You're beautiful,' he said. Our eyes locked for a moment. His were narrowed, studying me intently as the skin on my arms went prickly. My heartbeat quickened. I narrowed my own eyes back at him.

'Kate, darling, coffee?' Hanna cooed from the upstairs window which I noticed was wide open. My head spun up towards the window.

'I have to go,' I said, turning on my heels to go back into the warm building and away from Fabio.

'Wait,' he said, his voice urgent. 'Take this, and call me,' and he extended his arm out towards me. Between his thumb and forefinger he held a business card. *Fabio Matravers* it said, in delicate gold writing which I suspect was real gold leaf, or something just as precious. The paper was sturdy yet it felt almost like silk in my hand. The window hummed closed as the car rolled away as seamlessly as it had arrived. Clasping the business card tightly, I popped it into my handbag and thought about what to do next.

I walked gingerly up the stairs. Hanna had sounded OK but female intuition told me something was awry with us, or was I simply being paranoid? No, I just don't know; after all, I wasn't supposed to be talking to anyone unless Hanna or one of the fashion gays said so.

'Kate,' Hanna said angrily.

Shite, I thought. It was a facade, the tone of her voice was severe.

'Let's just get one thing straight,' she screeched.

God, she was frightening. My mother calls me Kate when I'm in trouble, seems as though Hanna's been picking up some tips. Saying that, Fabio called me Kate, but in a sexually arousing, authoritative way, unlike Hanna Frost, the wannabe schoolmarm. She's tapping her foot impatiently whilst Frenella, who's still here, wafts her hands in the background. The smell of acetone from the hot-pink varnish she's been using fills the air.

I swallow hard. I hate it when people shout at me, especially when I'm not altogether sure what it is that I've done to warrant such shoutage.

'You work for me, OK, and as per our signed contract, you do as I say. Did I say you could go on ahead outside willy-nilly with no shoes on in broad daylight, without some kind of apparel to hide your face?'

'Um,' I began to form a sentence in my head. I believe I did ask. I did tell them anyway, I know that much, and no one said anything, and I walked right past them to the door, even stalling for a few moments to take my shoes off. She cannot be serious?

'I, uh, I told you where I was going,' I said meekly.

'You're fucking useless!' Hanna shrieked, her cheeks flushing.

'Exc– excuse me?' I said, my face matching hers in the redness stakes. I was sure to win. My cheeks were flaming red. Frenella said nothing.

'You . . .' Hanna spoke slowly, 'are . . . fucking . . . useless!' She stood still, her face so close to me I could smell the tuna salad she had for her lunch.

'I am?' I said. My confidence had taken a battering what with Jack, and then the succession of stupid gay stylists who had as much subtlety as a brick.

'Yes, and another thing, you better get down on your knees and pray that no one saw you accepting that business card from Fabio Matravers, and it was only I and Frenella who witnessed that and not a rival magazine, such as *London Lowdown*!' she barked.

'Pippa Strong has been sniffing around us for days now, once we'd removed her from your garden – her face was practically invading your hallway via your letter box. She will not stop until she has a story on you and the juicier the better. Kate, you are a fucking liability, do you want to ruin things for yourself?' Hanna was so imposing, all she needed now was a bloody whip to knock me into shape.

'Well, of course I don't want to ruin things for myself, Hanna, I'm just, I didn't think, really I honestly didn't mean to . . .'

'Enough!' Hanna said quietly. Her palm was facing my nose. 'I have heard quite enough from you today. Seriously, I have a migraine. BAILEY!' she screamed, projecting her voice down the hallway. Bailey appeared, clutching a newspaper and a Diet Coke.

'Hanna,' he said.

'Bailey, I need my blue pills.' She sighed and rubbed her temples.

Bailey looked at me, tried to make eye contact but wasn't getting anywhere. My eyes were fixed on my bare feet. I was now hideously aware of my slightly blackened toes from absconding down the fire escape. Note to self, must learn to walk in very high heels. Must not look like poverty-stricken person with no shoes or, worse, like mental patient on day release, barefoot but wearing gorgeous garments. I sigh inwardly, must keep calm. When I think he's stopped looking at me, I look up at him, but then like a bolt of searing hot electricity, I feel his eyes connect with mine, and there is a definite moment. More of a moment than the one I shared with Fabio, which was like a stand-off – who could blink last, who looked away first was a measure of the strength of the pair of us. I half expected Fabio to extend his hand and challenge me to a thumb war. There was electricity flying in all directions today, Fabio to me, me to Bailey, Tom Theodore to my breasts and me, once again, to the clothing emporium downstairs. What a to-do!

'NOW!' Hanna screamed at Bailey, who practically jumped out of his skin at the volume coming from Hanna's pouty mouth.

I could see the tension on his face, he was inwardly struggling to contain the words 'Fuck' and 'You' to Hanna Frost as she looked down her long nose at us. His lips trembled and it looked as though he was about to say something but then thought better of it. He walked off down the corridor, his hand rubbing the back of his neck as he went.

'I . . . I'm sorry, Hanna,' I said, almost gulping back tears.

She cast me a quick glance before waving her hands at me as if she was shooing an annoying child away from her.

'Right, well . . .' I said, looking around the room.

Frenella was tapping away on her BlackBerry whilst Hanna stood looking out of the window, awaiting Bailey's return. Within seconds, Bailey walked back into the room and approached Hanna with the pills.

'About fucking time,' she hissed. 'Now just go, OK?' she said, gulping back the pills with a bottle of Evian.

I shuffled out towards the door, shoes in my hand, my handbag slung over my shoulder and beat a hasty retreat southwards towards the exit of the building. I felt utterly humiliated. Bailey walked a step or two behind me. Neither of us knew what to say after Hanna's outburst. I mean, was this normal? Do media people talk like this to their clients? Which is what I suppose I was? Even though, after all, she knew who I was before I signed the contract, maybe this has made her a bit careless with her words? Maybe that's why she's such a bitch? Familiarity breeds contempt; she could get away with using the C word with me if she wanted to.

'Here,' Bailey said, handing me a new balaclava. This one had a soft cashmere touch, which was a welcome relief after the scratchy woolly item owned by Dad.

'To avoid any more, you know, issues . . .' his voice trailed off.

'Thanks,' I said, half smiling. Was Bailey mad at me too?

We got into the car silently and he set about rolling a cigarette. There was something about Bailey, I didn't know what it was, but I could feel some connection, in the way he looked at me with those dark, penetrating eyes, as though he was looking straight into my soul.

'Want one?' he asked, offering me his tobacco.

'No, I'm a menthol girl,' I said, softly. 'Not that I can smoke through cashmere!'

'Right,' he said.

We drove towards Bethnal Green whilst I texted Danielle.

Hanna had full on strop at me for going outside, V
upset.

Beep Beep

Let's rendezvous 9pm, we need to talk.
K

I put my phone back into my lovely new camel bag that
had long tassels hanging from it. 'We need to talk' sounded
ominous. I wonder what Stewart-small-penis had done
now. Lost in my thoughts concerning whatever topic it
was that Danielle wanted to talk about, I looked out of
the window at passers-by. We continued to drive in silence.
I counted a full thirty minutes before attempting, once
again, to get some answers from Bailey. This was getting
ridiculous. Out of everyone I have met so far, he's the one
I like the most, he's the one who seems to care, he has
kind eyes, a warm smile, he is thoroughly nice. Isn't he?

'Bailey,' I asked him, gingerly.

'Yah,' he said.

'Is Hanna, you know, always like that?'

'Like what?' he said, eyes on the road and not on me.
He's totally not playing ball here.

'Um, nothing.'

'Well, you *were* talking to Fabio Matravers. What do you
expect?' he said suddenly.

'I wasn't talking to him,' I began to speak. Oh my God!

Was Bailey jealous? I narrowed my eyes at him and ana-lysed his body language.

'Yes, you were, Katie. Or is that Kate?' he said with a sneer in his voice. What the hell is up with this boy? Dan-ielle was right, he is weird. And jealous! Hurrah, he does like me after all! Karma was giving me a disco stick.

'He,' I said, standing my ground, 'was talking to me.'

'Same thing.'

'No, it is NOT the same thing!' I said in mock agitation. 'I was minding my own business, trying to light a cigarette after finding out from that weasel of a woman, Fanny or whatever the fuck her name is, short thing, snooty face, you know? The one who gallantly told me that Jack had been potentially doing it with Jessica Hilson for a lot longer than I previously thought. Franny, frrrrigging hell!!' I spit.

'Frenella Balls,' he said, with a perfectly straight face. How does he do it?

I stifled a laugh.

'No wonder she, uh, dropped her, balls . . .'

Even Bailey couldn't resist a chortle, hah, got him at last, he does have feelings and is not, as previously sus-pected, a mutant robot from space, or even a fake human sent to seek out my weak spots and pop them on to a full-colour PowerPoint presentation for a bit of sadistic bedtime reading for Hanna Frost.

'Got ya!' I said, smiling at him through the silky face glove.

He threw me a sideways grin. 'We're here, Katie,' he said, sighing and slapping his hands a bit too angrily on his thighs – total passive-aggressive jealous behaviour, I'll have you know – as the car glided to a halt. Bailey looked at me, and I at him. It was just like the Fabio moment, but more intense.

'Listen, do you want to come in for a cup of tea and meet my cat?' I said, instantly regretting it. Meet my cat? What kind of a loser says that! Although it was much more preferable to, 'Hey, wanna come in and inspect my plumbing?' With those arms, though, I thought, I bet . . .

'No, I can't,' he said. Another grumpy, stand-offish, snappy sentence.

'Righto,' I said, sighing heavily. Rebuffed again, I really ought to just give it up. But I can't. Just when I think he isn't interested in me as a person, as a potential undercover lover, he goes and throws one of those eat-me-up-in-one-go, to-die-for, chocolate-brown, swimming-pool-eyes looks that shoots fireworks to my very core, up and down all over my body in every direction and I melt. I properly, seriously melt and I lose all sense of perspective when he does that 'thing'. He does that 'thing' way better than Jack ever did! For one, Bailey has passion in his eyes and fire in his belly and he appears to me to possess both in abundance. I had to tell him, because what did I have to lose? Nothing. I'd had a large chunk of dignity wiped out, a pinch of humiliation, with a drizzle of hopelessness on top of a slice of heartbreak pie. Deep breath in and . . .

'Bailey, this is weird, you're acting like you don't like me.' Deep breath out.

'Don't be ridiculous,' he says, sparking up another roll-up and winding down the window. 'You're being paranoid.'

'I see you, watching me sometimes and throwing me those looks,' I say, gulping. 'You so totally don't need to be jealous of Fabio . . . There's nothing going on, I mean,

OK, I admit, he asked me to dinner, I took his card out of politeness, but that's it, I'm not going to call him, look, see,' and I take the card, tear it and throw it out of the window. He looks at the card, my hands ripping the paper between my fingers, he looks shocked, surprised, pissed off and confused all in one single go. I am aware, more aware than I ever have been, of myself. More aware of my heartbeat and the prickly arms that I get when I like someone, aware of every word hanging unsaid in the air.

'So,' I say, mustering up every single ounce of courage-type strength that I possess inside of me, 'I will ask you again. Would you like to come in for a cup of tea?'

Silence. The *pit pit pit* of rain begins to spit on to the car windscreen. It's dusk and I can see Mrs Bellamy crawling along the pavement on her mobility scooter, anxious to get out of the rain. A small terrier barks alongside her and makes a feeble attempt to catch up, racing the two-mile-an-hour buggy on his short little hairy legs. His bark echoes down the street. It's as though everything has stopped as the smell of rain wafts into the window, and a bunch of teenagers walk past swearing, laughing and joking amongst themselves.

'Oi, oi!' a scraggly youth screeches into the open window nearly frightening me to death.

'Been on the rob?' he questions, in reference to the cashmere balaclava that I totally forgot I was wearing. No wonder Bailey couldn't look at me! How could he possibly take me seriously as a potential girlfriend in this get-up? He was probably cringing silently, not that I had a full-frontal face view of him, you see. He was still window gazing. I jump, as Bailey himself finally looks up at me briefly before turning his gaze beyond my shoulder, over at the offending youths.

'I'm not jealous,' he says stonily. 'It's just . . .' he begins. 'It's just complicated, OK?'

'Well, you could have had me fooled . . .' I whisper.

'I think you should go now,' Bailey says, dismissively. My heart thumps in my chest, I scrabble for my bag, my keys, and launch myself out of the door and smack bang into a dirty, deep puddle, soaking my delicious new shoes. Oh, it never rains! Before I go, I turn my head to face him and once again, I catch him looking after me. I want to launch myself into his arms and snog his face off, run my hands over what I imagine to be his lovely pecs and a tight, toned, tanned abdomen nestling under his shirt. I open my mouth and look him square in the eyes. I want to shout at him, shake him, tell him I know what passion is, I know that look, I may have missed out on it for the entire time I was in a fake, useless, rubbishy relationship with Jack Hunter, but I'd recognize that look anywhere. I used that specific look on Jack, incidentally, every moment, second, hour and day that I was with my ex-boyfriend. Because I loved him. And although I'm not saying I was in love with Bailey, that first fluttering, those feelings of need, of want, of finally finding . . . well, of pure and simple attraction, I could feel them. And although I have told you often enough about the depth of my feelings for Jack, they were never fully reciprocated, yet here with Bailey, a man who wasn't even in my life last week, a man who has come along and taken all my feelings of hurt and despair and tucked them away from me when he's in my presence, well, things and people and thoughts and feelings like this don't come anybody's way often. He is kidding himself if he doesn't feel it too. This time, whether he wants to admit it or not, we are both playing the game. We hold the gaze for a minute. Eyes wide and expectant, but suddenly Jack Hunter's face pops into my head. Scenarios of me begging him to stay with me over the years when we've nearly broken up, my despair when he hurt me time and time again. Is there any point? Can I do this again? Convince someone to love me? No. I can't. So I change my mind, it's useless, this whole thing was a very bad idea, so I just say, 'Forget it,' because for once in my life, I'm going to try and stop salivating over a bad boy. Whatever is going on in Bailey's head is clearly unfathomable to me, and so I guess I'll take it on the chin and try to bury this shameful encounter in my memory box marked DO NOT REVISIT. In normal circumstances I would be beyond mortified that this pseudo stand-off has resulted in me making an arse of myself once again, but I seem to have developed a couple of iron fists which have been wrapped around the circumference of my heart, never to be swayed by a cute boy ever again. Oh, who am I kidding? I could already feel the pain of recent events combined with this latest knock-back edging its way up into my gullet, threatening to choke the very life out of me. With the rain picking up in urgency, it hits me from all directions and in the distance I can hear a quiet rumble of thunder.

I ran to my front door, opened it up and flew inside, eager to hide from his watchful gaze. The car was still outside. What could Bailey be doing? I thought to myself. Contemplating me? Us? Who was I kidding? This hurt, this rejection stung my body, my skin prickled, not in a good way, my breathing was fast and I was panting big sobs. All the bad things that I felt about myself from the inside courtesy of Jack Hunter's humiliating betrayal and the way Hanna spoke to me today, all came tumbling out.

'I'm useless!' I wailed, as I sank to the floor behind my front door, reminiscent of the day Pippa Strong made herself a resident on my doorstep. I yanked the balaclava off my head and furiously scrunched it up and threw it at the wall in anger. Tears splashed down my face as I sniffed and wiped them on the back of my hand, being careful not to damage my posh clothes. I felt so ugly and horrible and unloveable. Jack had ditched me just like that, no word of warning, for someone who I felt was impossible to live up to. Bailey, I felt, was simply toying with my emotions, pretending to like me so I'd show an interest and then secretly laughing at me whilst rejecting me. Fuck the whole romantic ideal I had of him having the same crazy feelings and not knowing his elbow from his backside when it came to administering them. Who knew any more when it came to a man's behaviour? Whatever was happening, clearly this is what he does on Planet Arsehole, which means he really is a sadist. My cat Grum nuzzles into my legs. 'At least you still love me,' I sniff, as I pick him up and bury my head in his fur. Wiping my eyes on an old hankie that's sitting on the little table by the front door, I pull myself up and over to the living room where I switch on the telly and immerse myself in *EastEnders*.

Chapter 8

'Feels just like the old days,' I say to the cat, as I pull the biscuit tin from beneath the sofa. It's my secret sweetie stashing place. If I can't see the biscuit tin, I'm less likely to open it, thus avoiding those sugary sins on my lips which, of course, go right to my hips. Ah, but they sure taste good. With each bite, I thought a little bit less about Jack, Bailey and Hanna Frost. Sighing, I got up and poured myself a large glass of red and ran myself a hot bath. Now, if only I could find some bubble bath . . . I reached up to the shelf above the toilet and ran my fingers along the sides, looking for something yummy for my bath-time treat. I'd seen Jack put various bits and pieces up there for safe keeping, including his expensive soaps and beauty products that he didn't want me to steal. He knew I stole his Liberty hand cream and his electric mouth-moulding, gentle-vibrate toothbrush, despite my protestations to the contrary. Still, I only ever looked once, and discovered a Diptyque candle and a deep-cleanse summer body wash by Elemental Herbology. I cautiously ran my hands along the top just in case Jack had placed a booby trap for this very reason and then forgotten about it, obviously, because he's fucked off and left me, when all of a sudden a small wicker box tipped over and out spilled the contents first on to my head and then across the bathroom floor.

'Whaaa!' I squealed, pushing my hands up against my

face as trinket pandemonium ensued. I looked down from what felt like a great height, short-arse me on a two-foot-high toilet seat. I gasped aloud.

There on the floor was a picture of me and Jack. It was a cheesy snap of us when we first met, taken at the Poets Field PR summer BBQ. Must have been, oooh, say, 2006? I could see various work colleagues milling about in the background as Jack and I appeared to clink champagne glasses. Yes, it was definitely 2006. Richard had a mullet for starters and I remember they came back into fashion for a while back then. But it wasn't the photograph that made me catch my breath. It was the letter beside it.

I knelt down on the floor and gathered up the bits and pieces and set about placing them together in the box for future inspection. I couldn't take my eyes off this small, perfectly folded-up pink piece of paper that had KATIE CAKES with various doodles of hearts, crosses and four-pointed stars scrawled squarely in boyish handwriting on the front. Should I open it? What if it was my 'Dear John' letter? What if it said horrible nasty things that would take me to the edge of a nervous breakdown? What if it was, like, telling me he was actually going to die a grizzly death very soon and that he had to go and sow his wild oats for the good of mankind? After all, he did have impressive genes. His jaw was chiselled, his stature was long and lean and he worked out so that his six-pack was obvious, but not in the ridiculous muscle-bound Arnold Schwarzenegger kind of way. No, he was solid, sexy, handsome and very easy on the eye. His dark hair was glossy and his eyes, a shining emerald green, were deep and round and . . . rather like Bailey's! Fuck, did this mean

I was on the rebound? Were there any other similarities between Jack and Bailey? Both rather hot, yes. Both dark and swarthy. Does this mean I have a type? I think back to my ex-boyfriends of the past and come to the conclusion that perhaps I do. Matthew Robinson from Little Glove was tall, dark and, um, he used to be handsome, but collected opinions from the village pub last Christmas from the girls who still live there, including the treacherous Nicola Baxter, say he's actually got a paunch, a curly moustache and a twenty-a-day smoking habit. Urgh. So, back to Jack and Bailey . . . What else do they have in common, let's see . . . both, um, have six-packs . . . not so sure about that one, but Bailey does look as though he may possess one. I sat cross-legged now, still in my beautiful clothes, as the bath ran deep with hot water. I reached over to turn off the tap and popped in one of the little round balls of colourful bath bomb-type stuff that had rolled beside the tub and watched as it dissolved like a fragmented rainbow. I know all about feeling fragmented, I sighed. I curl my lips and inwardly prepare myself for what could be in this letter. Here goes. I slowly unfold the creases and begin to decipher the words.

Katie, I love you, soooo much and our little kitten. I think we definitely should call him Grum because every time I pick him up, he says 'Grummm' and I know he's telling us that Grum is his name!

I love u, despite the fact u can't cook, and u always give me warm beer.

Cheeky sod! I think to myself, while allowing a smile to creep up and nestle on my lips. I continue to read, which is a tad tricky, as it's slightly illegible, the written word was clearly not his primary gift.

> *So, I want to say that if u are reading this, my suspishans were correct . . . it is u stealing my posh stuff and not Janice, even thow u bought it, so it shud, technikly be ours, yours, but its mine, you said, we agreed. Anyway, so glad we're together, I miss your silly face, even when I close my eyes. I will 4eva love you, and never leave you for Sharon Stone, even thow she's way hot and please please please can you do that scene from Basic Instinct for my birthday, and then I'll promise to make you cups of tea forever n ever!*
> *LOVE YOU! Jack*

I temporarily forgot to breathe. Happiness bubbled up inside of my gut, he did love me, after all! Maybe this means he'll be back? After all, he promised not to leave me for Sharon Stone! Jessica Hilson is no Sharon Stone! I gathered up the letter, kissed it gently and held it close to my heart for a moment, before shoving it back in the wicker box and placing it in the corner. I wafted happily into my bedroom and selected those awful tartan jammies from the washing basket. They were my guilty fashion pleasure, so warm and cosy. My La Senza sex nightie just didn't have the same soothing effect as the tartan horros. Even with the heating on. I sniffed them. They smelled only of stale me, which was OK as I was only going to be more stale from a night in my stale bed. I really should have washed the sheets by now that smelled of both me and Jack Hunter. I'll be Katie Lewis-Hunter, a double-barrelled girl at the altar, when and if Jack comes to his senses, rings my doorbell and collapses on to his knees, holding out a Tiffany ring and begging for another chance. I will, of course, be wearing top-to-toe Chloé, with Farrah Fawcett curls bouncing along on my shaking head as I give him short shrift.

'How could you, Jack!' I will simper.

'But she's not a patch on you, darling,' he would say, 'she grills my toast too brown!'

'Oh, so that makes it OK, does it? She burns your toast and her bridges in one accidental whoosh of gas mark seven?'

No. I would have to have another think about that fantasy. I peel off my clothes and catch sight of my white body in the full-length mirror. My pants are gaping at the gusset, they've certainly seen better days. My bra hangs like two Dairylea triangles on my relatively flat chest, which reminds me, I better take a good look at my boobs because on Monday, which is only two days away, I would be a busty babe fit for Television X work if this whole 'make me a celebrity' thing goes ahead. At least I will have notoriety, and everyone knows that reality stars, wherever they've come from, do tacky things for oodles of cash. I don't care, it's not as though I have bundles of dignity right now, is it? No, oh no. And if Aubrey, Hanna Frost and Dr Vasquez have their aesthetic way with me, I will not even resemble me much anyway, so it's not like I can embarrass my mother further, who still, by the way, hasn't forgiven me for my teenage vodka knicker-hiding escapades with Ms Baxter and is still curtain twitching and praying for the *Mail On Sunday* to pap the house.

I turn to the side and inspect my belly. Hold it in, nearly look thin, grimace on face . . . aaaand relax.

'Phew, don't look so bad today if you do say so your-self, Katie.' I even like my thighs for once, they look a tad smaller, must be all this stress. I pull my hair up into a lime-green fashion-crime scrunchie and pull an old bleached towel around myself. I so needed to do my laundry. I was rubbish at organizing my life at the best of times. I spied my handbag on my bedroom floor, and the posh envelope from the *Sizzle Stars* shoot poked up through the fabric. Something told me that those precious Harrods vouchers were going to come in rather handy. I could have gold-plated towels, an even better toothbrush than Jack's and I could buy the exact same organic water-activating-mineral-particles facecloth that he possessed and that I adored. But mine would be in baby pink and with KATIE embroidered on it. How posh would that be? Yes, no more skanky stained mouldy pound-shop towels for me – step in angora ones woven with silk and the tears of Jesus. I bet even God has a franchise in Harrods. I moved into the bathroom and couldn't resist picking up the letter once again, along with the glass of red wine I'd brought in with me to help read the letter, before sinking into the most luxurious bubble bath. My feet poked out of the end as I rimmed the opening of the tap with my big toe, being careful not to wedge it up there again. I'd ripped half my toenail off the last time. As I sank carefully into the bubbles, being mindful not to wet my beloved letter, it suddenly occurred to me. Why had Jack referred to Grum as a kitten? Grum is nearly four years old. And . . . oh no, please no! I realized, with the heaviest heart, that this was no recent letter. This was an early days, can't get enough of you, let's have it off all over the house/garden/local park love letter, a can't see straight from too much sex letter. He was blinkered. He was in love. *Was* being the operative word. And sure enough, as my eyes moved up and to the right, he'd clearly marked the date in bold pen.

16th July 2006

'Bastard!' I shrieked at the letter, spilling red wine down on to my boobs. In one angry swoop I scrunched up the love letter and threw it across the bathroom where it came to rest by the loo. How could I have been so stupid? Of course he didn't mean any of that, he'd have said anything back then if it meant getting his jollies three times a day and a round of lightly browned toast for his breakfast. I suddenly felt very stupid. All the gaiety and vigour I felt from just having munched a biscuit and noticed my slender-ish thighs was crushed with the knowledge that I'd been hoodwinked. In the living room, Grum meowed and plonked his furry behind on the remote control, inadvertently changing the television channel from BBC1 to what sounded suspiciously like Radio 2. I was super confused. Yes, I hated Jack so much for faking the last years of our romance and leaving me in the most disrespectful way possible, but I knew he loved me, at one point. Even if it was only for a short while. I loved and hated, hated and loved and then thought about Bailey, my potential Band-Aid boyfriend.

'*And now,*' the dulcet tones of the radio guy filled the room, '*we have a very special evening for lovers . . .*'

'Urgh!' I groaned aloud, before squidging my bottom

downwards so that I could immerse my head beneath the hot soapy bubbles, away from the torture of the radio.

'*A song that never gets old . . .*' he warbled, as the opening bars of my favourite Cure song began to play.

Dit dit doo . . . dit dit doo . . . the synthesizer trilled.

'Argh!' I screamed to myself. Moments later, I emerged suddenly from the water and began to wring my hair dry in my hands as the song continued to play. Our song!

That's it, I thought, feeling sick to my core as I heaved myself out of the bath and grabbed my towel.

'Why did I have to get a cat that could change the bloody television channels with his bum?' I asked Grum as he looked up at me quizzically. Poor sod, he didn't know we were listening to the song that Jack sang to me to make me laugh, to make me melt when he'd been out all night and I was sitting at home waiting for him, as though I was his bloody mother. I switched the channel and was now listening to 'Love Songs for Lovers' on a drive-time show. Good old eighties music, I thought, bittersweet, matches my sombre love mood. I shamelessly joined in the chorus of T'Pau, singing and dancing with Grum, who was struggling to get away from his mad, crazy owner. That's it, I decided, letting him bounce down and into the kitchen en route to the cat flap. I am definitely on a man ban. No more thinking about Jack, I am going to end it with him. I mean, I know it's over, he's ended it, but I am ending it with him *emotionally*. This means no drunk dialling, no drunk texting and definitely no drunk Facebooking. Not that I have done any of those things yet, but give me time. This break-up was still fresh. It was still raw. I still thought about him every second of every day. Life was occasionally made easier by the presence of stuck-up-his-own-arsehole Bailey and the freebie clothes and whatnot, but Jack was still a huge presence in my mind. I would cut the ties with pretend emotional scissors.

I went into my bedroom and violently tore at the sheets. I pulled them off the bed and screamed and grunted and pushed until there was nothing left of him on my bed. I took the sheets and threw them into the laundry basket in the bathroom and tried to shove the lid down over the enormous amount of fabric. I pulled out some horrible old flowery beige jobs from the airing cupboard that Mum had given me for Christmas. They were disgusting and tasteless but they would have to do until I get to Harrods where I will buy the very best kind of sheets that they make. Ones with Egyptian cotton, with 800 thread counts or something equally as extravagant. The flowers lay flat against the bed frame, looking gloomy and brown. I threw off my towel, pulled on my tartan pyjamas and made my way into the kitchen to eat a muffin and have myself another large glass of red. Who cares that it was only 8pm and I was a bottle of Rioja down!

Flopping back on the sofa, I took out my mobile phone and deleted Jack Hunter's mobile number, his Mum's, his agent's and his work's. I scrolled through and deleted every single text I'd sent him and every single text I'd received. I also got rid of all pictures I had of him on my phone. By the end of it, tears were trickling down my face and the music had hit a poetic crescendo. I'd now suffered through two Take That songs, a Texas tune, Barry White and Madness. It must be love? Yeah, right. I was beginning to feel more than a little tipsy now. Where was Danielle? She said she'd be here by nine. I need to bitch and moan and hold a pity party in aid of Katie and her week from hell!

Just then, as if on cue, there was a tiny, just about audible knock on my door.

Excellent, this must be her! I thought. I can tell her all about today's meltdown, what a total bitch Hanna Frost is, how she has a tiny, blonde, bitchy, skinny, nasty, horrible, cow-bag journalist friend whose name sounds like an STD and who, if she was a dog, would be a cross between a mangy terrier and a whippet.

I walked towards the door and opened it to greet her, stopping only briefly to wipe away the smudged remnants of my waterproof mascara and to push my tears off my face. I gave a hearty sniff, took a deep breath and opened the door.

'Am I glad to see you . . .' I trailed off.

'Well, that's a relief,' Bailey said.

'What are you doing here?' I said, rather haughtily.

'Um, I'm sorry,' he said, looking at his toes. I stared back at him. He looked up at me and our eyes connected. My feet were on fire as the electricity shot straight through my eyes and right down to my loins. *Shit, shit, shit,* I thought, catching sight of myself once again in the hallway mirror. My apparel was perfectly acceptable for a turbo moan with my best friend, not so for a hot guy I fancy . . . Why did he have to see me looking like a baboon's backside all the frigging time? I had a lime-green scrunchie on my head containing my bird's-nest hair which was frizzy and wet from my bath. I was wearing tartan pyjamas and my face was tear-streaked and puffy. My eyes looked like two piss holes in the snow. Why was I not wearing my cute little La Senza sex nightie? Where have I put those eye-brightening drops that Janice used to use to conceal the fact she had been down the back of Jimmy's Bowling Green smoking pot? Why don't I think of these things and plan ahead? Ah yes, because Bailey is about as consistent as the winner of the Eurovision Song Contest. You never can tell what's happening with him. Tactical voting perhaps? Voting for his country on account of any wars past or present? Hanna being the war, fought against me for daring to leave the room without permission, even though I did tell them, it's really not my fault if they chose to ignore me. Anyway, let's go back to the brooding hunk on my doorstep.

'Have you been sitting in your car all this time outside my house, twiddling your thumbs?' I ask, my voice now unexpectedly deeper and huskier. Sex thoughts must be transmitting out of my vocal cords. His face visibly reddens.

'No,' he lies. I totally know he's lying because, oh God, his ears! His ears, which stick out slightly, have totally gone bright red. Maybe it's a man thing? A hot man thing? Who knows? I think it's kind of cute. But still, what was Bailey doing outside my house for the past few hours?

'I was thinking,' he says, shuffling his trainers against my doorstep.

'About what?' I ask, hoping, praying, that it's about me. Now I've got rid of Jack officially in my head, it means I can indulge in guilt-free sex, if I want to. Although I had split with Jack, it had felt like I was cheating on him when I felt that pull of my hand towards Bailey's pert bum. I also felt that way every time I saw a movie with Brad Pitt in it, but Danielle soon talked me out of that one. No one should feel guilty about getting their jollies from a Brad Pitt movie. Now standing in my doorway in his trademark tight white t-shirt, his lips curled slightly at one side of his mouth, I noticed for the first time Bailey's freckles on his nose and a dimple on his chin. I decided he could quite easily surpass *Monsieur* Pitt in the gorgeous stakes.

'Can I come in?' he says, half smiling.

'Suppose,' I say, playing hard to get. Can't have him thinking he holds all the cards in this thing, whatever it is, that's charging between us. Even though he *so* does. I flatten myself against the wall to allow him in, his body slides between me and the door. Neither of us moves. He's now looking at me with such intensity I may just spontaneously combust right here, right now, all over my hall carpet. Within a second, his lips are upon mine, feeling his way into my mouth with darting tongue movements. I quiver with excitement and let out a deep, sexy sigh. We kiss, and it's hard, then it's soft, it's fast and then it's oh so slow. He bites my lip gently, then a bit harder, I moan softly in his ear as his lips move down to my neck and he sucks gently, his hands are on my body. One hand moves down towards my bum, and he gently cups my cheek, squeezing, touching me, with such skill. He manipulates the buttons on my pyjama shirt, so that they gently come undone, only one, then two, and then three. My nipples are pressed hard against his T-shirt. I can feel his skin against mine and it's driving me fucking wild. I gingerly move my hands up and down his torso, and oh my God I can't resist, I move my hands down his chest, finding that little line of hair that I love the most on a man, from his belly button, down to his crotch. Sure enough, he was hard and bulging from his tight, skinny jeans. Oh my God, how could I possibly have even considered, for even a moment, putting myself under a man ban? I want to be under this man more than anything. More than life itself. More than Jack? Oh gosh, now there is a conundrum. No, no, no, must not think about Jack. 'Oooh yes, yes, yes!' I whispered, as Bailey's hand snaked along the inside of my elasticated bottoms. Oh, how I inwardly cursed the pyjamas.

'I'm sorry,' I said, breathlessly.

'For what?' he panted back in my ear.

'The tartan,' I giggled, wriggling in his grasp. My hair was damp against the wall.

'Fuck the tartan,' he said, and in one fell swoop, he lifted me up, and proceeded to manoeuvre me, somewhat more gallantly than Richard's impromptu fireman's lift. This one was most definitely a princess lift, oh yes, he moved with grace and ease and made me feel as light as a feather, which was no easy feat. Just ask Richard Dewberry.

'Which way?' he said, and I pointed up towards my bedroom. Thank heavens I changed the sheets! It would have been criminal to have had Jack's DNA mixing with what I'm sure will be the remnants of Bailey's sweat and sex all over my sheets. Bailey kicked the door open gently with his foot and lowered me on to the bed with a bounce.

I was like a woman possessed. My hands were all over him, moulding into the curves of his body as his hands grasped my hair, my breasts and my shoulders. Breaking off from our mega snog, I slunk to my knees and peeled his jeans off with my teeth, OK, and my hands, but I undid the zip with my teeth, which he seemed to take pleasure from. He was naked and ready for me, so I unrolled a condom grabbed from the side drawer and on to his hard cock, also with my teeth, actually. I know he was impressed with that. He pulled me up from my arms and lowered me on top of him where we moved together as he gently pulled on my nipples. I was so hungry for him, hungrier than I had ever been before, and his touch was urgent and needy. He wanted me after all! Our bodies moved rhythmically in heavenly synch until with one final lurch of his body, he came, and I felt him push harder into me until he brought me to the edge, where I let loose and dug my fingernails into his shoulders as I gave in to an earth-shattering orgasm. I flopped back on to the pillow, spent and happy. His breath was loud as his chest fell against mine before he gently kissed me on the lips. We lay in relative silence, entwined, sweating and hot. It felt like one of the most romantic, sexually-charged moments I'd had in my whole entire life. It totally trumped the first time that I had sex with Jack. He was all fingers and thumbs and I had to show him where my clitoris was. But it didn't matter to me that he wasn't as blessed in the bedroom as he was in his looks. I guess this is what happens to most hot men. They can get any woman they want by simply standing next to her. They can be self-obsessed, they can be thoughtless and they can be rubbish in bed, but if he's amazing to look at, you make exceptions. Besides, Bailey and Jack had to make an exception for my wobbly bits. Bailey, however, as smoulderingly hot as he was, didn't need an A–Z to find my erogenous zones. He teased and stroked with great efficacy. Suddenly, permeating the atmospheric ambiance of Spandau Ballet (love songs were still filtering through from the television) Bailey's phone trilled and beeped. Silently, he removed my legs from his thighs and bent over the bed to retrieve it, giving me a full-on view of the crack of his arse. I scrunched up my face and looked away. When I moved my eyes back towards him, he was lying flat out next to me, his hands above his head furiously typing a text. His body was delicious, I thought to myself, but what could be so important that he had to pierce our erotic moment with the *tap tap tap* of a text message? How rude, I thought, but never mind, I was so ready for round two. I slowly tickled his underarms to get his attention and grinned wildly at him. I just knew it, he was special and he quite possibly had fallen for me after all! We'd have to work out a way of telling Hanna Frost, because I'm pretty sure she mentioned that she was setting me up with Danny Divine, the actor from that East End wannabe ganster film *Murked*. Well, I'm sure we can work something out, now that Bailey is no longer denying his feelings for me. I felt on top of the world. He was mine now! Hurrah!

'I have to go,' he muttered, with about as much warmth in his voice as a snowman.

'Um?' I said. Fuck fuck fuck, he wants to go, must play it cool, no wild declarations of love just yet, even though I may be in love with him already. Oh God, look at him, his body is rippling even as he coughs.

'I'm sorry,' he said. What for? I thought. Spluttering beside me or the fact you're upping and leaving me? I instinctively handed him a tissue and he blew his nose. 'Thanks,' he said, barely looking at me. For what? I thought. For the tissue or the shag? Approximately five minutes ago, I was blowing him, and now, he was getting ready to walk out of the door. Fucking wonderful. I har-rumphed a bit, trying to evoke some reaction from him, more than a sorry, a hug maybe, something longing and delicious and with a promise of more naked time. He said nothing.

Hmm. Obviously a man of few words. He pulled his pants on, buttoned up his jeans and stood up as I wrapped myself up in the duvet. My hair was wild, all over the place, and I still had mascara smudged on my cheek from earlier. My lips were chapped from kissing his stubbly mouth.

'I'll see myself out, Katie,' he said, as he leant in for a polite kiss. He kissed me on my cheek and lightly patted my shoulder. Who did he think he was, kissing me like that? That's the kind of goodbye you give to your nan, not your new love interest! Before I could open my mouth to clarify where we now stood, although it was evidently nowhere, he was on his feet and I stayed in the bed, which now smelled of Bailey rather than Jack. The door clicked shut and I buried my head in my hands. I was so confused. I mean, that did happen, right? I did have sex that was insti-gated by Bailey and not by me, didn't I? He made the love move, right? God, men, they really honestly do come from another planet. I sat there racking my brain, wondering why he had to dash off like that so soon after our incredible sex session, when I heard the door click again. Yessss! I thought, clearly he can't keep away and he's back for more.

'Couldn't keep away from me, you big love tiger?' I called out to him.

'Hey babe, I'm so glad you're in, listen we really have to talk about something . . .' Danielle cooed back from the hallway. I could hear her heels on the hardwood floor clip-clopping towards me, along with the jangle of what sounded like bottles of wine in a plastic bag. She sounded happy enough, not like she'd split with Stewart again, so what could this mega important thing be that she had to tell? She had wine so it must require some emotional anaesthetic of the booze variety.

'Where are you?' she called. 'And why are you listening to Duran Duran?!'

'I'm not!' I said, as she edged nearer to the bedroom.

'Yes, you are, "Rio" is my favourite song!' she called before pushing open my bedroom door and flicking on the big light.

'Oww,' I said, as I shielded my eyes from the too-bright glow of the light.

'What are you doing all on your own in here?' she said, as she eyed my get-up which was, um, nothing but a gross duvet set which would have looked more at home in the seventies.

'Honey, either you have a migraine or you've just had sexual relations with someone . . .' she winked and grinned before her expression suddenly changed. 'Dear God, please tell me that Jack Hunter hasn't been sniffing around!' she wailed.

'Noooooo!' I replied, wondering why she momentarily looked as though she was about to keel over with heart failure at the possibility that I may have been shagging Jack. Didn't she want me to be happy, back in the arms of my ex-boyfriend, even if he was a no-balls creep with zero decorum?

'No, nothing like that, it wasn't Jack,' I said, as I felt my cheeks flush red. I was totally going to have to 'fess up.

'And he must have just left . . . judging by your state of

undress plus the fact the door hadn't been properly closed . . .' She plonked herself down on my bed as I reached across to my drawers and pulled out a silky dressing gown. Her face looked relieved. Typical, I can pull out sexy slinky garments in front of someone who doesn't give a toss what I wear, yet hang around the house in tartan pyjamas and very nearly have stand-up hallway sex whilst wearing them.

'It was nothing,' I said, still confused as to why Bailey flew out of here quick as you like. My brow furrowed as I bit on the nail of my thumb.

'Oh, sweetie,' Danielle said, putting her arm around me and drawing me close. I shrugged her off. I'm sure Bailey's call was something mega important and nothing at all to do with me, just unfortunate timing, that's all.

'Forget about me, what was it you had to tell me?' I queried.

'Ah nothing, it's nothing,' she said, looking perplexed and doing one of those 'Everything's OK' smiles that people do when they're clearly hiding something.

'Are you sure about that?' I probe further. Her eyes turn to the plastic bag which she then picks up and heads to the kitchen.

On the way down she calls out, 'Honestly, Katie, it wasn't anything, silly really.'

'Silly sits well with me, Danielle, you know that . . .' I follow her downstairs.

'I just thought we could go to dinner this week, that's all, get some, you know, reality back. We could go to Carluccio's, I know how much you love the focaccia bread!'

'Mmmm, yes I do, God, stop it, food, yum . . .'

'Well,' she begins, 'it's just as well I brought some, isn't it!' Danielle takes the food out and waves it around the kitchen. I'm standing beside the breakfast bar, away from the scene of my wanton sexual crimes. The crime being, he left me before I'd even knotted the condom and slung it in the bin. Should have slung it at him on second thoughts, although I'm sure there is a valid excuse for his night-time sloping.

'Well, as luck would have it, I have two tickets to the most amazing spa plus a five-grand Harrods voucher!' I sing. 'And guess who I'm taking with me?'

'Ooooh, let me guess . . . your mum?'

'You're insane, clearly,' I say with a wry smile. Danielle looks blank.

'It's you, you daft brush!'

'Oh my God, are you kidding me?' she says, open-mouthed.

'Yup, it's true, and nope, I ain't kidding ya,' I grin back at her. 'Tom Theodore handed them to me, that's why I was making kissy-eyes at the camera and acting as though I'd won the lottery on the photo shoot this afternoon.'

'Ah,' she says, 'I see. Well, it certainly worked because, no offence, you didn't look too impressed this morning. Not that you have much to be excited about lately, though . . . apart from your mystery man!'

'There's no mystery,' I wink, 'when I know who he is.' We continue to talk about sex. We talk about Stewart-small-penis and the things he does to make-up for the fact that not only does he have a small penis, but he also arrives at the finishing line before the starting pistol has fired.

'However do you cope?' I ask. I would simply die if Bailey had been a two pumps and a squirt kind of guy.

'I, you know,' she says, rubbing her thumb and fore-finger together, 'I basically make a really big fuss about how great he is in bed, what a stallion he is, how much he satisfies me, I make all the appropriate sex noises, a bit of "Oooh baby" here and a bit of, ahem, don't laugh,' she says, eyeing me up.

'I won't laugh!' I say, stifling a laugh. Must keep composure.

'You're so going to laugh!' she says, laughing herself.

'Come on, come on, it's OK, shhh, just tell me!'

'OK, when Stewart gets really excited, he likes it when I say "Oooh, come on big boy, show me what ya got, big boy!"'

'Bahahahaha!' I laugh until wine shoots out of my nose. 'That's the funniest thing I have ever heard!' I wail. Tears begin to stream from my eyes. 'I need a tissue!' I say, dabbing at my nose and eyes and the mess I've made on the counter.

'See,' she says, 'I knew you'd laugh at me!'

'I'm not laughing at you, I'm laughing *with* you!' I say, still reeling from her shock confession. 'Remind me again why you stick with him?' I say, as she turns and flicks her curls over her shoulder.

'I love him. Simple as that. Don't know why, I just do. So, spill,' she says, sitting down on one of the breakfast bar chairs with her chin in her hands.

'You won't believe this but . . .'

And I filled her in on this evening's developments, including the exceptionally good bedroom skills Bailey displayed, the earth-moving orgasm and emitting the bit about knocking my teeth against the button of his jeans and wincing in pain.

'Oh my God!' Danielle said with a look of surprise on her face. 'I can't believe you actually fucked Bailey!'

'Danielle!' I squealed. 'We didn't *fuck* as you so elegantly put it, we made *lurrrve*!' I purred, before we both erupted into giggles.

'*Bravo,*' she said, raising her glass. 'To the unobtainable.'

'To my sex life,' I clinked glasses with her.

'So, where is he now?' Danielle said.

'Um, well, he had to go, emergency of some sort, will find out tomorrow, I guess . . .' I said, looking into my glass and picking at the focaccia.

'What do you mean, he had to go? Not even an awkward "Do you want a coffee before you go" moment?'

'Not even enough time to make a cross-legged dash to the bathroom.'

'Cripes.'

'What could it mean, Danielle? Does it mean he's not interested? I mean, every girl knows that when a man has sex with a woman he either stays or he goes and the latter means he's had his fun and it's offskis for him, off for a pint or to kill a wild bear or something, never to be seen again.'

'Or he could really actually have a genuine emergency and will call you later . . .'

'But that's breaking the rules,' I said solemnly.

'What rules?'

She tilts her head at me whilst grabbing some bread. She's brought a lovely jar of olives, too, which are now swimming in a side dish of olive oil. Mmm, they taste so good and are a fine accompaniment to the story.

'The love rules according to Richard Dewberry,' I say, squashing an olive in my gob.

'God, Katie, you've not been listening to more of Richard's tripe about how to get a boyfriend, have you? The man's a heathen! He's got as many morals as an alley cat. Who's he stepping out with this week, then? Paris Hilton?'

'No, but another lookalike. She goes by the name of Annabelle.'

'Blonde and slim?' Danielle questions before adding, 'And just as dim . . .'

'Oi!' I poke her in the elbow. 'I'm blonde!'

Danielle rolls her eyes. 'My point exactly,' she says, before moving out of the way of another playful finger jab.

'Richard says that you need to leave it three days between meeting someone, dating them or accidentally-on-purpose having sex with them, before either of you call. Anytime before that and the one who makes contact looks desperate.'

'Are you serious?' Danielle says, eyes wide.

'Yup. So Bailey has left today, which is Friday, this means that he can't talk to me until, um, let's see, Monday. At the earliest. And I must not text him or anything because then I will look desperate and no one likes a desperate girl.'

'Well, Stewart didn't play those stupid games, Katie, no offence.'

'No, he just lied,' I say, a little too bluntly.

Danielle's smile fades as she pours some more wine.

'I'm just saying,' she says, 'that, you know, these games are pointless. If you like him, tell him . . .'

'But I did,' I say defensively. 'Several times. It was only when I practically told him to get stuffed that he dawdled in his car, plucking up the courage to seduce me.'

'Romantic,' Danielle says, with a hint of sarcasm.

All of a sudden, the atmosphere felt really uncomfortable. I knew I'd offended her with my Stewart quip, but she'd offended me looking down her nose at Richard's dating tips. So what if we had to play games to get the men we liked? At least Bailey wasn't married. As far as I knew.

'Listen, babe,' Danielle begins, 'I'm really tired, I've had a tough day in the office, you know how it goes . . .' She begins to gather her belongings.

'Sure, OK,' I say, too tired and consumed with Bailey thoughts to care. God, does that make me a bad friend? All I wanted to do right now, though, was snuggle down in my bed and watch *Will & Grace*. I was feeling rather woozy from the wine we'd been drinking and really, I had just had enough. Too much adrenaline post-row, post-sex and I was feeling rather edgy.

'Listen,' she says, face softening, 'I'm sorry, I'm just tired and a bit stressed and, well, we'll talk another time, yeah?'

'Yes, cool, speak tomorrow.'

'I'll see myself out, yeah.' She smiles and walks out of the kitchen and into the hallway. I put my phone in the oven so I don't accidently wake up and text Bailey, or worse, Jack. At least if it's in a kitchen appliance I will have to physically get up and think about my actions.

I fed the cat and jumped into bed, pulling the sheets up close. I switched on the telly in my bedroom. Ahh, this was bliss!

Before I knew it, I was in a very deep sleep.

Chapter 9

I woke up gently to the sound of a bird chirruping outside my window. I could feel the sunlight streaming through the glass, the curtains swaying gently in the breeze. I knew the floorboards in my bedroom would feel deliciously clean and cool against the soles of my toasty feet. I wanted to reach out and touch the man next to me, feel his soft skin against mine, kiss him gently, feel him rise in my hand and then roll on top of me, silently pulling my legs up around his waist and moving deep inside me. I wanted his dark hair to fall over his eyes, for his touch to command a zillion and one different thoughts and reactions from my body. Once we had romped for hours, I wanted to snuggle up with the weekend papers against his manly chest, I wanted to smell fresh coffee from the grinder, and have an organic grill-up. And then maybe I wanted to have a picnic on Primrose Hill and do some star-spotting. Later that evening, we'd head to Angel, to see Danielle and the girls from her work. We liked to sit around in Danielle's garden drinking fruity wine and giggling about men. Our boyfriends would guffaw at our girly ineptness and complete inability to read a man's mind. We thought we knew what it was all about, ah yes, we had them sussed out, men, you just have to train them like dogs, you see. I stirred gently in the covers of my bed. I felt a thump on my foot, and a *pad pad pad* along the side of the bed, followed by a purrrr in my ear and a wet sandpapery tongue on my face. 'Urggh,' I said, with my eyes still closed. I wanted to remain in this lucid dream for a while longer. Things felt peachy. I was in love and I was loved back. I gingerly crept my hand out across to Jack's side of the bed, searching for him. He wasn't there. All of a sudden, the reality of this past week crashed down upon my weary, hungover, migrained self and I wanted to weep. I opened my eyes, and despite the heavenly morning that said hello to me, the only kiss worth having was Jack's. Where did that put Bailey on my romance chart? I wasn't sure. When I thought of Bailey, I thought about Sudoku, an impossible yet strangely fascinating puzzle. I wanted to learn how to crack it, him, I wanted to be a champion. I got up and made my way into the kitchen, put the kettle on to boil and popped the telly on. Children's TV blasted my ears, seemingly from all directions. The sheer size of the television meant you had to stand six feet away from it to get a decent view. I recalled the cheesy, tear-jerking love songs of last night. What was I thinking, torturing myself with songs of woe, heart-break and unrequited love? I felt like I was living in a soap opera right now – the full force of every single feeling I possessed seemed to be magnified. I didn't just feel heart-broken, my whole world had fallen apart. I wasn't just interested in Bailey, he was the glue that would piece me back together again. I didn't just dislike Hanna, I wanted to catch her in Primark of a weekend, I wanted her to trip over her massive ego and break her ankles on her Gladi-ator heels. Better still, I wanted her to fall over Frenella and snap her in half. I felt like shit. There was an entire building site knocking down walls in my head. I reached for the Nurofen and flipped the channel to Channel 4, searching for a good episode of *Friends* to cheer me up.

'Fuck . . .' I said, wearily. My chest became tight, my breathing slowed. There on T4's *Celebrity Bits* was Jessica Hilson, looking resplendent opposite the gorgeous Welsh muscle-bound hunk Steve Jones. Bitch! I thought, as I grabbed my cigarettes. My strong black coffee slurped over the edges of the cup as I legged it to the living room. I sat there and listened to her gush and simper in front of Steve.

'Yah, I like totally know he's "The One"' she giggles, twirling a platinum-blonde strand of hair round her fingers.

'Well, that's great!' Steve smiles back.

'Yah,' Jessica continues in her stupid sing-song accent, 'like, totally, unexpected, sometimes, you just know when your Prince Charming presents himself.' She gives an all-American porcelain smile.

'And did you always know he was going to propose?' Steve enthuses.

'Yah, like, I totally knew, my mom's psychic, yah, and like, she said, I'd meet someone who was going to see the real me, like, and totally be whacked by that, and yah, Jack Hunter is it.'

'It really sounds like a fairytale. So, how did he propose?'

'How did he propose? Yah, well he like, did it on a giant turtle in Mimi Sparkles Jungle Garden. My ring is like, made of jello.'

'Excuse me?'

'He like, didn't have a ring right now, it was like, so outta the blue for him, and he just acted on instinct, on his magnificent true love for me, yah, so, he had one of those jello cent candy rings, and we used that to symbolize our engagement, which I think is like, really deep and meaningful because like, it represents us in sooooo many ways, like, I'm really sweet, and Jack, he's sweet too, hmm.' She looks vacantly at Steve, licking her lips and applying a fresh coat of neon pink lipgloss.

'Some would say,' Steve continues, 'that it's all a bit fast. I mean, you've only known him a short while . . .'

'No, you see, I've know him my whole entire life, like, this is where people have us SO wrong, like, we are soulmates. We knew each other in a past life, we're like twins almost, he always knows what I'm thinking, we're like, destined, yah?'

'So, have you set a date?' Steve queries.

'Yah, like, no, maybe, you'll have to wait and see!' she purrs back at him, I swear she's flirting. I check out her body language. Her feet point towards him, she's touching her hair, she's giggling at him even though he's not really said much. Hmm . . . wonder if I should call Richard for some help, after all, he knows about things like this? Thank heavens for Virgin on Demand, I can rewind this and play it back to him and Danielle. The next shots are trailers for *Cowgirls*.

'*A woman in peril . . .*' the deep-voiced American movie man says before adding, '*One obstacle she must face in her quest for true love . . .*'

Oh God, I thought, this is over-the-top cheesy.

'*Can Gina Winters defeat rival Cowgirl Tiffany Summers in the quest to save the western town of Mount Dustville?*' Cue some dramatic trumpets.

'*Only time will tell . . .*' A high-pitched string quartet takes over before . . . '*Thrills, spills and action as horses ride over mountain tops searching for the saviour to Mount Dustville before disaster strikes!*' There is lots of 'yee-hah'-type banjo music, guns shooting dust in the air and men in cowboy hats line dancing and as the dust clears, we see a quick shot of the bar area where Jack Hunter smoulders as he wipes down glasses with a dishcloth. The music stalls and we then see Jessica Hilson in teeny-tiny shorts with a gun to her lips, blowing the smoke towards rival Tiffany Summers, who stands opposite her, a good twelve feet apart, glaring like a menace.

'*Battle of the babes,*' the voice concludes.

'Battle of the bimbos,' I add to the cat, who is purring happily on my knee.

'Film looks mega,' Steve trills, as Jessica grins back at him.

Mega shite, I think, gnawing on my fingernails.

'Yah, I love the UK!' she squeals, randomly. 'Go see my movie!' she adds.

'She said it,' Steve says, pointing to the camera before turning back to Jessica.

'Thanks for coming to tell us all about your new film, it looks great and I for one can't wait to see it. Remind us again when it's out?'

'July first!' she twitters. 'And, like, you can join my MySpace page for more information about my next movie, and, like, my other movies too!'

'Goodbye, Jessica, great to have met you,' Steve envelops her for a kiss, before settling himself back down and directing us to the T4 website to catch Jessica on a podcast, her MySpace, her Facebook, blah blah blah. I tune him out and mentally block out any internet details about Bimbo Hilson, do not, repeat, do not stalk her.

'Gah!' I said out loud, sparking up another cigarette.

I settled back with my coffee and my nicotine to watch another bumbling appearance of Matt LeBlanc playing Joey on *Friends*, sharing a laugh about the word boobies. I simply didn't quite know what to do with myself. I mean, normally I would try to do what I dreamt about, which is pretty normal by any couple's standards, isn't it? No work, plenty of sex, lazy brunch, wandering around looking at museums and parks and stuff before going out to a bar. You didn't do clubs when you were with a boyfriend. Too many opportunities to lose them amongst mini-skirted pouty hussies. Mind you, it was rare that I got to have lazy sex with Jack on a Saturday. We normally did the romantic sex stuff on a Sunday morning. He was always, as mentioned previously, seeing to his geriatric crièped-décolletage women from *Emmerdale* or whatever soap it was they came from. Who knows, he never told me. And then it hit me . . . could that have been a cover too? Was he doing it with Jessica Hilson in secret locations under the guise of meeting dames for brunch? Oh, it doesn't bear thinking about. Although, once again, the timing was right. Oh God, I groaned into my hands. The realizations of Jack Hunter's loose ways were coming in thick and fast. Too much to handle with a headache like this. The only thing I could think of that would take the sting outta my tail was some therapy. Intense therapy. Of the retail kind. I jumped off the sofa and raced to the phone. Danielle simply had to come shopping with me to Harrods so I could outbuy

Jack's electric mouth-moulding, gentle-vibrate tooth-brush and get some gold-plated tea bags. And if Danielle's head was as thick as mine, she'd appreciate the spa retreat afterwards – how about the intense hot stone body massage with special essences? Now where did I put my phone?

Brrrriiiiiing! It trilled loudly from the oven, where I suddenly had a flashback of hiding it late last night whilst slightly drunk from red wine, to prevent me from accidentally on purpose sending love texts. I didn't recognize the ring at first because I usually had the current Number One song in the charts as my ringtone. At present, I had one of those old-fashioned ringtones because otherwise any song I loved right now would in the future be the song/ringtone that reminded me of when I got dumped by Jack. Trust me, no girl wants to be reminded of that. The inoffensive chimes rang out as I looked at the screen. Richard's cheesy grin flashed up. I had a BlackBerry, which meant I was permanently updating my status on Facebook when out and about and stalking, sorry, wrong word, checking up on Jack. Except, of course, Jack deleted me from Facebook and isn't searchable so that's that over with . . . aside from Google updates, however, mustn't forget them. I had programmed a picture of my friends' faces to accompany the trill of the phone so I always knew who was calling. If it was my mother, I could divert her to answerphone. Thank goodness for technology!

'Darling, how are you?' Richard purred down the phone.

'Um, hey you,' I said back. Richard was being especially nice. He normally just launched right on in with a full-on conversation, complete with instructions as to what was required of me, what to wear, etc. He was exhausting on the phone, a complete whirlwind. No time for pleasantries. What could he be after? It couldn't be the Space NK products for men. Perhaps he wanted to come shopping to Harrods? No, can't be that, he's got more money than he knows what to do with, which he spends on high-class hookers, vintage rock star t-shirts and expensive West End bar bills.

'I'm outside your door, sweetheart, be a doll and answer it. I don't like standing outside like a common salesperson.'

'You're outside?' I said, confused and pulling my dressing gown tight around my middle. It felt like an age since Richard had seen me with my clothes on.

'That's what I said, stupid, come on, Mrs Bellamy is curtain twitching again.'

'All right I'm en route!' I said, putting the phone down. I padded down the hallway, stopping briefly to check my reflection in the mirror. Hmm, not looking super hot but sod it, it's only Richard.

'Darrrrrrrling,' Richard simpered, hugging me tight as I stumbled back into the hallway with the weight of him. For a five-foot-eight guy with not much to him other than carefully sculpted muscle, Richard had a lot more strength than one would imagine.

'Hey you,' I said in response, hugging him back. 'What's the frequency?'

'Welllllll, how about you pop the kettle on and we have a cup of tea. Here, I brought you some lovely smoked sausage!'

'Mmm . . .' I said, making my way into the kitchen and putting the kettle on the hob.

'Biscuit?' I said, pushing the jar towards him.

'No, darling, and neither should you.' And with that, he picked up my beloved biscuit tin and emptied it into the bin.

'Whoa!' I cried. 'What did you do that for?'

'Carbs. Evil. Banned from now on. FYI.'

'In English please, Rich? IYP?'

'Katie, you can't just make-up acronyms, it doesn't work like that. FYI is a universal code for "For Your Information", and I doubt that IYP . . .'

'If You Please,' I filled in.

'I doubt very much that IYP is part of the celebrity vernacular.'

'Oh God, OK, fine. Why are my biscuits evil?'

'They have carbohydrates in them, sugar, nutritionally dense, addictive, give you cellulite, make you fatter . . .'

'And the sausage?' I queried, bubbling with anger at Richard's blatant disrespect to my Jammie Dodgers.

'Protein rich and full of fat, keep eating these babies and you'll be skinny in no time.'

'Are you calling me fat?' I said, incredulous to his complete lack of manners.

'Yes.'

'Ouch,' I said. 'That hurt.'

'Well, you are, let's not cry about it. Darling, come on, in the celebrity world that you are going to become a part of as of, ooooh, Tuesday when *Sizzle Stars* is in the shops, everyone will know who you are . . . You do read *Sizzle Stars*, don't you, Katie?'

'Of course I do, I'm addicted . . .'

'Then you'll know that they have a section called

"Sinners & Winners" and in the Sinners are pictures of celebrities' sweat patches, their lady gardens, spots, back flab, nose hair . . . the list goes on and on and, honey, you could very well end up in the Sinners bit if you're not careful. Especially with those teeth.'

'Gosh,' I said, aghast. There's no point arguing with Richard, his acidic tongue would win hands down each and every time.

'I suppose you do know what you're talking about . . .' I murmured.

'Yes, I do. I have dated a string of supermodels and even they have the odd pouch of fat that I had to pay to get lipo'd out. Still, I wouldn't ever date a woman above a ten. That's just how I am and it's how most men are and I hate to say it, sweetie, it's probably how Jack was, which is why he's up and off with Jessica size-zero Hilson.'

'Fucking hell, Richard, are you trying to give me an eating disorder?'

He looked genuinely shocked as his forehead furrowed. I saw a line or two crease up and relax as Richard visibly went through a myriad of thought processes before opening his mouth and continuing.

'Katie, I'm sorry, I forget you're not a celebrity yet, you're not used to my world, the world of being a big-time, hot-shot, uber-successful PR Account Manager. I totally forgot that you really don't need to be thin and glamorous because you are the PA, behind the scenes, doing a very important job and we wouldn't do without you, God no, but I do think you just need a bit of education, darling, that's all.'

Richard needed a kick in the face and a swift reality

check. Is this what hobnobbing with Soho media types did to a person? They become shallow and vacuous and unrepentant when they throw insult after insult after insult, whilst dressing them up with bright white teeth and the flash of a Rolex.

'Richard, I am, as you say, a PA and that's it. I am not a celebrity, I don't have hair extensions.'

'Yet, darling, they come Monday.'

'No, Rich, Monday's my boob job! Oh, I can't tell you how excited I am, especially since I've just seen Jessica's chest straining through her itty-bitty top and they looked glorious, all mountainous and bouncy and sexy and I want boobs like that, ones that spill out over corsets and immobilize men from speaking, thinking and anything else that requires a dual process. Everyone knows men can only do one thing at a time.'

'Bullshit. I had two girls last night.'

My mouth dropped open. 'That's disgusting.'

'Filthy bitches, stuff of dreams, very good, shut your mouth, Katie, your teeth are hideous.'

I sighed and literally had to stop myself from wedging the biscuits from the bin where the sun don't shine.

'You're not having the breast augmentation any more, sweetie.'

'What? Why!' I cried out, no, no, no, this could not be happening, I wanted that boob job for, like, ever and I needed that boob job, to get Jack back and to get Bailey's attention!

'It was collectively agreed between the doctor, Hanna Frost and Aubrey that you were displaying overemotional tendencies of a worrying kind. In short, it was felt that you are a little too on edge over this whole to-do with Jack and Jessica, meaning that you have had a couple of meltdowns, namely the one in Ziggy Wang's that everybody saw, and the last thing any of us wants is you crying to the papers months down the line, saying that you hate your tits, they're too big and you were forced into it.'

'I wasn't forced into it, though, I was a little, um, scared and a bit nervous and not entirely sure about the size, didn't know what size . . .'

'You can have a jab to make them bigger. Don't worry, we'll sort you out, it's semi-permanent and if you still want 'em blown up like balloons then you can go right on and book an appointment with the doctor when you make your millions.'

'So,' I said, taking in a deep breath. Must not get sucked in to his warped media brain. Must not listen when he says I'm fat. Size fourteen is not fat! I am athletic! I am . . . bouncy in other bits of me, apart from my chest. I can have a jab that makes them bigger. That, in all honesty, felt slightly less frightening than being knocked out at the mercy of Dr Vasquez.

'To what do I owe this pleasure?'

'Oh, I had to drop by and one, tell you all about the non-boob-job decision so you could eat something tomorrow, and two, I wanted to check you weren't rocking in the corner with a bottle of gin watching *Bridget Jones* after hearing about Jack's engagement to Jessica.'

'Yes,' I sighed, 'I heard all about it, saw her gleaming on T4's *Celebrity Bits*. So that paparazzi shot of them hovering with intent outside Tiffany's was the real deal?'

'Yes, seems so. Although the ring she chose has had to

be made specifically for her very thin and small fingers so she won't have it until mid-week. Just in time for the première of *Cowgirls* on Saturday.'

'He did it with a penny sweet,' I said, picking at the sausage.

'I know, cute, isn't it?'

'You think?'

'No, of course not, I wouldn't be caught dead giving a girl a sweet as a token of my commitment to her, but then this is me, I don't do the C word. God. Right, so anyway, you're OK, you're not a wreck, all is good in the hood and I am offskis, I have a very naughty brunch date to pick up.'

'Annabelle?'

'Yep, she's young, hot, stupid as fuck and up for anything. It's something light on the Thames, I've hired a private boat, going to blow her little tiny mind.'

'Good luck,' I said, as Richard stood up and smoothed his hair down in the reflection of the kitchen window.

'Have fun at Harrods,' he called as he walked down my hallway and opened the front door. 'And, Katie . . .' he said.

'Yes?'

'When I said you were fat, I only meant a little,' and he shoved on his Wayfarer shades and made off to his sports car.

'See you,' I said, under my breath. I plastered a smile on my face, gathered up the cat who had come to stand by my feet for a view of this incredibly self-obsessed, shallow man. He did have a heart of gold, though, and I loved him all the same. Life would certainly be a duller place without Richard in it ... definitely. I walked back into my living room, finished the sausage and opened a new packet of chocolate digestives. I would never give up these edible lovelies, not for him, not for the size of my bottom, not for anyone.

Chapter 10

BEEP BEEEEEEEEEEEEEEEEP!

I raced to the front door, flip-flops smacking against the wooden floor, as I grabbed keys, purse, phone and my light denim jacket. I was wearing loose clothing so I didn't sweat too obviously and a gigantic Stranna hat by Malene Birger that Tom Theodore had suggested would hide my face more stylishly than Dad's balaclava, when worn with a real pair of Ray-Bans. Besides, I bet if I turned up at Harrods in a balaclava, I'd be arrested or shot or something. Now, I thought, looking in the hallway mirror and tousling my honey-blonde locks into a fan across my shoulders, in this classy disguise I was beginning to feel more like the girl in the magazine shoot, the girl who is going to be a star, who's a celebrated person, at least in the world of Twitter and Blogspace. (Yup, I checked out what my new-found fan base have to say about Jack. So far, he's an odious toad and I'm better off without him. Rather apt and I couldn't agree more.) The painkillers for my migraine had kicked in a little and I was ready to indulge myself in sheer designer delight. I took one last look in the mirror and likened myself to a younger version of Goldie Hawn. A younger, chunkier version with wonky teeth, but still, I thought I looked good.

'Finally!' Danielle said, as I skipped towards her open-topped Porsche Boxster. I've always been jealous of

Danielle's pay packet, which is huge and topped up with bonuses which she laughingly refers to as 'love money'. To keep schtum about having it off with her very married boss. No, really, it probably is, but if we err towards the reality of the situation, things get frosty and Danielle gets uppity, making sure I know she works hard and isn't any kind of prostitute lawyer. Oh, no.

'Sorry, I was adjusting this hat,' I say, as I open the door and park my bum on the plush leather seats.

'Primark?' she jokes, knowing full well it is something that cost the best part of a month's wages – hers, not mine, so super expensive I'll have you know – and I laugh and tell her that it was a gift and that I love it very, very much.

'And the shades are real Ray-Bans!' I exclaim.

'Whoohoo!' she says, and once again, I detect a slight note of sarcasm in her voice.

'Yeah, so . . .' I drift off as she turns on Radio 1 and some funky pop music wafts out of the sub-woofers and into the London sunshine as we zoom down Old Street.

'Have you heard Jack's popped the question to Jessica Hilson?' I ask Danielle.

'Yes, I heard. Are you OK? Have you heard from the delectable Bailey?' she queries.

'Yes, I'm fine, never better, full of hatred, bile and despair and no, not heard from Bailey,' I say, feeling a flush of embarrassment. He hadn't called but then it hadn't been long since we exchanged bodily fluids, not even a day. See this face of mine, it wasn't fussed. I checked out my smile in the side mirror to confirm.

'I Googled him,' Danielle continues.

'Oh? Anything juicy?' I ask, feeling a flutter of trepidation as to what she may have uncovered.

'He's un-Googleable,' she says, sparking up a cigarette as we come to a brief rest at the traffic lights.

'What do you mean, he's un-Googleable?'

'I couldn't find him.'

'Well, that's not surprising, we don't know his first name.'

'I do,' Danielle says, as we turn through the city roads. 'It's Sam. Sam Bailey. I searched Poets Field PR, made some calls and looked for dirt . . .'

'Why would you do that?' I say, suddenly angered. 'Dirt? Don't you like him or something? He's not Stewart, you know, there are no skeletons in the closet. No wives there either!' I say, instantly regretting it. I loved my best friend, I didn't mean to be a bitch, I guess this headache was more fierce than I thought.

'I just don't want to see you hurt and really, he is a bit odd, isn't he? You can't deny that,' she continues, puffing on her cigarette and blowing smoke out of the side of her mouth.

'I just, well, I don't know either, Danielle, I just, come on, let's not talk men, gosh, yawn, boring men, let's talk shoes . . . what would you like to buy?'

'Ooh, something special, that's for sure!'

With the Bailey/Stewart situation successfully diffused, I prayed to the gods that I could find a gift for Danielle to appease her that wasn't too expensive because, as much as I loved her, I also loved the Nicole Farhi dress I saw on the telly the other day. We parked up, were robbed by the Kensington & Chelsea council parking meter and made our way towards Harrods.

'Wow,' I said breathlessly, as we stood outside the clothing emporium.

'Come on, then!' Danielle said, linking arms with me as we moved towards the entrance.

'Let's shop till we drop!'

Four and a half hours later and exactly five thousand pounds down, Danielle and I stood outside Harrods, laden down with a selection of boxes and bags (although not quite as many as we'd have contended with had we spent the afternoon in Debenhams). Oh, I think we could quite easily have bought absolutely everything in sight, but as it happens, I made a beeline for the Nicole Farhi dress, which was exquisite by the way, and Danielle had to tear me away from the Fossil & Antique section. If I had eleven grand, I could have owned my very own Freshwater Limestone Plaque with Fish. How cool would that be? I could imagine it now, next time I asked Bailey in for a cup of tea, I could say, 'Would you like to come in and view my Freshwater Limestone Plaque – with Fish . . .' Hmmm, yes, had a much better ring to it than, 'Would you like to come in and meet my cat?'

Struggling back to the car, I listed in my head the items I bought.

There was the magnificent Nicole Farhi dress, and there was the Mike + Ally collection of Gold Trim Ebony Empire soap dispenser, cotton-ball holder and toothbrush holders, a cool £500 for the lot, plus I bought myself some super-amazing princess goose-feather pillows, some 'Katy' collection Missoni bedsheets, OK so they didn't have KATIE bedsheets, but Katy was good enough for me! Besides, it's not as if Bailey knows how to spell my name. Jack can barely read, let alone spell, so I figured it didn't really matter if Missoni was a letter or two out. Finally, I bought myself a Sonata silk charmeuse throw, a bathrobe, some deliciously sexy underwear that would be sure to come off in a minute next time Bailey sees me in all my glory, and as a special present to my cat, I bought him a plush cushion bed which I hope he will use.

Eventually, we made it back to the car, and I checked the time on my watch. It was still only coming up for half past three. It felt like we'd been shopping for years. Thank heavens we had the spa to look forward to. I'd booked us in for an overnight stay from 5pm. On Sunday morning, we would enjoy treatments galore and I, for one, couldn't wait.

'Have you packed your swimming cossie, babe?' I asked Danielle.

'Yes, I've got my swim stuff with me. Are we having treatments tonight?'

'No, we're having them tomorrow. Tonight, we can swim and sit in the jacuzzi and enjoy a cool glass of champers before having one of those posh macrobiotic dinners.'

'Macrobi what?' she said, as we settled ourselves into the car. The engine turned on and the car shuddered.

'Gwyneth Paltrow, Madonna and Jack were all big followers. It's like, where you just eat grains and stuff like that, to aid your, um, what was it again? If I remember correctly, it's to aid your physical, spiritual and planetary health.'

'Sounds dire,' Danielle said, with a look of sheer horror on her face. 'And since when did Jack have a sense of his own spiritual well-being? Planetary health? He lives on

Planet Idiot. Now, shall we get a McDonald's on the way?' she said, with a cheeky wink.

'You should be more open-minded, give more things a try. If it's good enough for Gwyneth, and God knows I'd love a belly like hers . . .' I looked down at my little pot belly straining against the seat belt. I'd eaten far too many biscuits and drunk far too much wine the past couple of days. Emergency food and comfort crisp rations had bloated me up like a balloon. It was unfortunate for my waistline but fortunate for my taste buds that sweeties were my drug of choice for coping right now. Never mind, I had seen a glimpse of my new fabulous self just waiting to be uncovered and I would be damned if I let anyone sway me into a McDonald's! No, must remain strong, smart girls eat salads, not processed food.

'Hmm . . .' Danielle said, unconvinced. She knew me too well. Maybe this time, as part of the brand-new me, I could resist the strawberry milkshakes and the barbecue sauce, maybe this time I could go to a drive-through and order that salad! Yes, a salad, that way I can sleep easy and not feel a fat dollop of guilt which I could very well do without right now, all things considered. Yes, I have made up my mind, leaves and tomatoes and mineral water for me. Must be perfect and thin for the world, especially Hanna et al. They'd have an absolute fit if they caught me in the vicinity of anything that wasn't organic. We drove for a further half an hour before we were edging out of the city, such was the traffic. Like a beacon of dietary respite, a giant luminous M stood in the sky, calling us towards it. I swear I could already smell the satisfying aroma of delicious cheeseburgers.

'Big Mac and large fries, strawberry milkshake and an apple pie to go please,' Danielle instructs the drive-through person.

Salad. Salad. Salad. Salad.

'Sssss . . .' I grapple with the word on the tip of my tongue. Danielle nods with her chin, raises her eyebrow. Time stands still for a second. The cashier chews gum. Danielle turns the music down as the car judders slightly. Thin, skinny me dances in my mind's eye before being eclipsed by chubby me in a kaftan.

'Same,' I agree, before handing over a ten-pound note.

Chapter 11

'Wow, these towels are like snuggling up in giant teddy bears!' Danielle's shouts echoed from the bathroom. Steam rose up from under the door.

'Why on earth are you having a bath when we're going to be spending most of this morning in water?' I yell back as I sit on the massive plush four-poster oak bed, filing my toenails. I have a pretty little jar of posh pink nail polish that I picked up from Harrods and forgot to mention on my list of things I bought. I fell in love with a pink moc-croc beauty bag and bought tons of expensive cosmetics. I couldn't wait to add them to the collection of Chanel and Laura Mercier freebie make-up that Hanna had given me back at the ranch.

'Phew!' Danielle said, as she opened the door wearing the dressing gown, red in the face, her damp hair stuck to her skin. 'Let's get swimming, need to cool down now!' She busied herself with her things, carefully unfolding a bikini and fresh towel.

I looked out of the window at the breathtaking scenery. Lush green fields rolled for miles, birds twittered in the sky, the sun was out, again, not bad for UK weather, and the trees were swaying gently in the breeze. I could see a couple walking hand in hand across the green and felt a small stab in the heart, envious that it wasn't me with the love of my life, whoever he may be. I had managed to only check my phone twice last night. Danielle made me leave it in the bedroom so I wasn't distracted by it over dinner. Still, thoughts of Bailey and whether or not he'd call me, plus what I would say if he did call me, were the two main topics of conversation, aside from Jack and Jessica. We'd been assured that no one in the spa would see us. The pool had been closed off especially for our use all of last night, but we only had it for two hours this morning. The treatments were in private and the staff were under strict instructions not to breathe a word of my presence to anyone else, that is, if they knew who I was in the first place. They didn't strike me as the type to be obsessed with celebrity trivia.

'It's crazy that we're getting the whole pool and stuff to ourselves, isn't it?' I said to Danielle.

'I know, anyone would think you were Jessica Hilson . . . Oh, um, I mean, babe . . .' She looked at me, biting her lip. My stomach churned.

'It's OK,' I said through gritted teeth. She didn't look convinced.

'You're right,' I said, breathing in deeply. 'Jessica Hilson is a Hollywood A-lister with pneumatic tits and my boyfriend on her arm. I'm just plain, old, boring Katie with the droopy boobs and a less than white smile. Urgh, I actually hate her,' I said, throwing myself dramatically into the feathery pillows. I couldn't wait to get my goose pillows on to my bed. Mmm, throwing myself dramatically on to them could become a regular occurrence in my house, whether I was heartbroken or not.

'You're far better than her,' Danielle soothed, as she walked over to my side of the bed, sat down and stroked my hair off my cheek. My face was half wedged into the bouncy pillow, but I could see her concern from beneath my hair, and from the one eye I had open.

'Shhanks,' I said, with a mouth half hidden in pillow.

'Right, come on, Katie, less dwelling, let's go have a bit of "us" time,' and with that she hooked her arm through mine and pulled me up and off the bed.

'Fabulous, you look great, sweetie,' she beamed.

'Thanks,' I said, throwing my arms around her shoulders and kissing her on the cheek. 'You're the bestest friend a gal could have. Whatever would I do without you!' I sank my face into her hair.

'Shh, silly!' she said, hugging me back. 'That's what friends are for.'

We made our way down to the private lift dressed only in the fluffy robes. As we neared the still, quiet pool there was a wonderful smell of aromatherapy essences. Two buff-looking hotties stood to greet us. One held a bottle of champagne in his hands whilst the other held two crystal glasses. They edged towards us and popped them down on the table next to our two loungers.

'Ahh, thank you,' I giggled. 'Isn't it a bit Jeremy Kyle to be drinking at 10am?' I said, turning to Danielle.

'Only if it's Special Brew on a park bench!' she said, as we watched the waiter pour us some fizz.

'Cheers, Katie!' she said, raising her glass.

'Cheers!' I smiled back, clinking glasses. 'To being there for each other,' I said.

Danielle winked back. 'Last one in the pool loves Mick Hucknall!' she said, plonking her glass down, disrobing and making for the water.

'Urgh!!' I shouted, as she dashed ahead of me.

I squealed as I jumped feet first into the deepest part of the pool, sinking fast to the bottom and hearing the chimes of piano music from the underwater speakers. For a moment I was without a care in the world. I opened my eyes under the water, held my breath and looked around. All I could see were Danielle's feet which looked as though they were peddling in slow motion, and all around her, nothing but blue water. It was heavenly. I was running out of air.

'Boo!' I said, as I emerged suddenly behind her, scaring her half to death.

'I couldn't see you!' she wailed. 'I thought you'd knocked yourself out! I was about to call one of those fit muscled waiter lifeguard types to rescue you!'

'Mmm, shall I go knock myself out solely for that purpose?' I smirked.

'Stop it, you,' she said, as she trod water beside me. We moved in circles, ducking and diving, swimming on our backs and mucking about before we swam over to the vibrating massage chairs and settled ourselves down. It was then that the conversation took the inevitable man turn . . .

'I think I am going to end it with Stewart,' Danielle says suddenly.

'Has the crap sex finally got too much for you, darling?' I joke, staring up at the ceiling which is dimly lit and covered in plants to give the look of a rainforest. She doesn't respond so I turn to look at her and notice a small tear escape from her eye.

'Babe,' I say, suddenly sitting up, my legs over the edge of the massage chair. 'What is it?'

'It's, it's nothing,' she sniffles. 'I just don't agree with his morals any more . . . and . . . I know you hate him and think he's a creep, but it's just . . .'

'I don't hate him, D,' I say calmly. 'I just hate that he's married. I hate him in the same way you hate Jack. It's just like you want what's best for me, I want what's best for you.'

'I know, Katie, but you don't always know what's best for me,' she says, kind of sharply.

'Oh,' I say, a bit perturbed. 'Well, I try to imagine what's best . . . but I guess, I'm not you, am I?'

'No, you're not. But all I can say is that I love him desperately. And I thought our love could conquer the differences we have in our views about the world, our core values, all that kind of thing, but lately, there's like, been a major thing occur and I am trying to be supportive, but I'm just feeling so very torn.' She sobs.

'What is it?' I probe gently. She turns to face me, and looks for a moment as though she is going to say something profound, but then thinks better of it.

'Ah,' she says, taking a deep breath. 'It's nothing, work stuff, you wouldn't understand,' she says, with such finality I don't push for further information. What I have learnt over the years that Danielle Kingsley and I have been friends is that if she wants to tell you more, she will. She's not like me. I'm the kind of girl who you'll ask, 'What's wrong?' and I'll solemnly say, 'It's nothing,' and look all moody and upset so that if you prod me a bit more and encourage it out of me, I would normally break and spill, even if it's something I really don't want you to know, like the time I caught crabs, I assumed, from a holiday fling in

Ibiza. I was devastated, itching like crazy and humiliated to fuck, and after some gentle cajoling, I admitted it to Nicola Baxter. We'd gone out there together for our seventeenth birthday celebrations – born within a week of each other, lifelong friends until she blabbed to the press – and ever since, whenever we fell out, her parting shot was, 'At least I never got crabs!'

'Excuse me, ladies,' a silken male voice says above us.

We both turn our eyes skywards and for a minute, in my costume, I feel rather naked.

'Hello?' I say, surprised. A man in a penguin suit stands beside us with a white envelope in his hands. He extends it out to me.

'I can't,' I say, 'I'm soaked, I'll get water on it. You read it,' I direct him with my hand. Now I really feel like a celebrity!

'*Madame*?' he says, questioning me, eyebrows doing a little dance. Reminded me a bit of Aubrey and his techo brows.

'It's OK, go ahead.'

It couldn't be that bad, I thought to myself. Hardly like getting the results of your gynaecological examination in public.

'Ahem,' he said, clearing his throat. Danielle looked on with interest.

'*Katie, how lovely to see you again.*' See me again? What was he on about?

'*You are looking very well and I would like to offer to you, dinner, in The Dorchester, tonight.*'

'What the hell?' I said. 'Who can see me?' I turned to Danielle and she simply shrugged her shoulders. Maybe it's Bailey! I thought, excitement bubbling up inside my gut. My heart beat a little faster, the world looked a little brighter.

'*Please accept the champagne on me,*' the waiter finished.

'So who's it from?' I asked.

'*Mr Matravers,*' he said, looking at me as though I was a total idiot.

'Why would Fabio write me a note and send it all the way over to this secret spa, just to ask me to dinner?'

'Who knows, but it is rather stalkerish, isn't it?' Danielle said gravely.

'*Madame*, may I interject?' penguin-suit man said.

'Sure,' I said, leaning towards him for a better listen.

'Mr Matravers, he owns this spa, it is his gift to you. He will pick you up at 7pm prompt to take you to The Dorchester, should you wish to accept?'

I looked at him blankly. Fabio owned the spa? Hanna had a fit at me for accepting his business card, she'd have kittens if she could see the events unfolding in front of us now. The penguin-suited waiter looked on expectantly.

'What should I do?' I hissed to Danielle. 'Well . . . ?' I said, expecting her to figure it all out for me. I had a man pyramid to contend with here.

'Go,' she said, emphatically.

'What? Are you serious?' I said to her, eyebrows furrowed.

'What have you got to lose?'

'Um . . . my sanity?'

'Questionable . . .'

'Shh! This is serious. This is Fabio Matravers, Jessica Hilson's Fabio Matravers!' I said.

'Katie, I know. And, in my opinion, this is how it looks to an outsider.'

'Go ahead.'

'You're not going to like this . . .'

'So? Let me be the judge of that,' I said, gulping.

'OK, you said it . . .' She turned to the waiter. 'Hey, buddy, can you give us five minutes? Girl chat.'

The waiter was looking all flustered by the sight of the pretty redhead winking at him, lying there in a bikini, legs up to her armpits. Danielle was a real stunner.

'Sure!' he said, edging away from us, near enough tripping over his feet, his eyes upon her magnificent chest.

'Right, this is how it is,' she says, matter-of-fact. 'You will make a huge mistake going back to Jack.'

'But I'm not . . . he doesn't . . .' I begin to explain that Jack hadn't so much as texted me aside from the dumping text so why would he come back to me or even give me the opportunity to patch things up with him? Danielle puts her fingers up to her lips.

'Shh. Don't wanna hear it, my turn to speak, delivering tough love here, sweetie, digest . . . please.'

'OK?' I sigh quietly.

'Jack Hunter is a cheating creep. He's broken your heart. Don't think I don't know that you're heartbroken, and you're reaching out to Bailey as some kind of replacement.'

'But!' I begin to say.

'Shut up, Katie!' Danielle barks. 'Bailey may not call you, and you have to just accept that.'

Bloody hell, she was on some kind of mission this morning, but she was wrong. I liked Bailey for himself, OK, so I didn't really know him as an actual person with a personality, he's just a moody, delicious sex demon in the bedroom and has a chest you could bounce tiddlywinks off, so what? Give us time! It's not even been forty-eight hours since the deed has been done, so really, let's just put this into perspective. I smile sweetly back at Danielle, swallowing my thoughts.

'Fabio, take it for what it is . . . dinner with an attractive man who is clearly interested in you. And he's rich. He'll treat you like a princess. You are a princess to me, babe.' Is she finished, I wonder? No, she's still got that serious look on her face, it briefly softened on the last word she uttered but now, it seems as though she's gearing up for more.

'Jack is history, he's moved on, you need to do the same. If Bailey was really interested, he'd have made contact by now and he wouldn't have just had sex and done a runner. Seriously, that quick, the boy either has severe intimacy issues or . . . well, I don't know what, but if I were you, I wouldn't wait to find out.'

'That's your opinion? Jack is a wanker and Bailey's probably one too?'

'Yes,' she says, and upon noticing my forlorn face she adds, 'But I'm sure he does like you, just, sometimes you have to put yourself first, if he ain't doting on you, dump him. And let's face it, the only one outta the three of them who's put an iota of effort into getting to know you is one silver fox. So, go for dinner, see what he has to say for himself.'

'I guess so . . .' I begin. Maybe she's right? Bailey hadn't texted me or called. Jack has proposed to Jessica Hilson in the ridiculously named Mimi Sparkles Jungle Garden with a ring-shaped penny sweet. I guess that was kind of romantic ... typical Jack, shirking on the cost. He can't really be marrying her, can he? I totally needed to talk to Hanna, Richard, someone, anyone really who knew about these media stories, who really knew what was going on and would give me the truth. I was getting Hanna Frost withdrawal symptoms. No, not in a lesbian way, I meant, that I hadn't heard from anyone at Poets Field PR since our horrible blowout on Friday when Hanna called me a 'fucking liability'. What if they didn't want to work with me any more on account of my stupidity? I thought long and hard. It took all of a minute before I was distracted by the man in the penguin suit. He wasn't as attractive as the other two half-naked, muscle-bound waiters and he wasn't carrying champagne.

'Excuse me, *Madame*, but are we at an agreement?' he said, looking at Danielle. He only briefly glanced at me, even though the question was directed at me. God, maybe I am invisible, so insignificant, that when any major decision about my appearance or my love life arises, it is glibly passed over my head to the most attractive or competent-looking person there, which evidently isn't me.

'I,' I said, loudly, very much in his direction and with what I hoped was an air of authority in my voice, stuff Bailey, Jack, even Hanna, stuff them all, I'm going to this dinner at The Dorchester no less, and I'm going to have a bloody jamming time and, best of all, I will wear my new Nicole Farhi dress!

'I,' I continued, pointing at no one in particular, 'am most definitely going to accept the dinner and also – OW!' I said and shot daggers at Danielle, whose long red finger-nail had left an indentation mark on the top of my arm.

The penguin-suited waiter looked surprised and his eyes darted between us.

'Don't look desperate, for heaven's sake!' Danielle hissed.

'Gah!' I said, rubbing my arm. I curled my lips before turning to penguin waiter. 'I would like to accept, ahem, Mr Matravers' invitation, and thank him also, for his hospitality.'

'Very well,' he said, as he bowed politely, turned on his heels and made off towards wherever it was he came from.

'Sorry, babe, I just didn't want you to be too eager, give the impression you're easily caught,' Danielle half smiled apologetically at me.

'What are you, Richard?'

'What?'

'The love guru with a manual of dating tips at your disposal.'

'Funny . . . no, I just, well, actually, we've got about ten single girls in the office who rabbit on about rules of dating, what to say, stuff that I have no clue about, seeing as the last date I went on before Stewart made himself a fixture in my life again, wanted me to have his children and live alone with him, tied to the kitchen sink in the Scottish Highlands.'

'HAH!' I laughed, picturing Danielle without her power suits and six-inch heels, no pillarbox-red lippy to match her hair, no more Gucci sunglasses, manicures or Pucci maxi dresses. Nope. Try as I might, I simply couldn't imagine Danielle tending to flocks of sheep or, indeed, flocks of babies.

'Yeah,' she said. 'My sentiments exactly. Anyway, I didn't mean to be trite, Katie, it's just, well, sometimes you can come across as, well, as a bit needy.' She took another swig of champagne. I felt as though she'd smashed the glass and stuck a shard of it in my heart.

'Ouch,' I said, swigging from my own glass and reaching for more. 'That hurt.'

'Sorry . . . think I've had too much bubbly. I mean everything I say, with love, you know, lots of love,' she grinned.

I knew she meant it with love, but did she really honestly think I was a loser in romance? I wasn't that bad, was I?

'Am I that bad?' I blurted out.

'No, no, babe, I just think, sometimes you should hold back, like, just be a bit more, self-assured, a bit more like . . .'

'Hanna,' I said, suddenly. Hanna doesn't take shit, I bet Hanna doesn't glue herself to her BlackBerry for it to beep with a message from the man she's currently in love with, or in lust with at the very least, waiting to see if it's him and questioning, wondering, hankering, obsessing over where he is, what he's doing. I bet in Hanna's world, he's the one who's playing the waiting game. In Hanna's world, the men are as disposable as her Wilkinson Swords. I bet Hanna, if she's not a lesbian, commands and dictates and expects the absolute best or else . . . or else she'll make like one of those bitchy spiders that kill their mates after sex. Yeah, that's what Hanna's like, a black widow spider.

'I suppose so . . .' Danielle mused. 'Hanna's not a bad person to mould yourself on, babe, she's smart, cool, successful and I bet she sets the rules in any of her love games.'

'Yes, that's what I thought,' I agreed. 'I doubt she plays any games with boys,' I added.

'She doesn't play with boys, Katie,' Danielle sniggered.

'So, you think she's a lesbian?'

'No, God, no, just because she's a successful ball-breaking bitch doesn't mean she's into women. No, good Lord, I meant, she doesn't play games with boys – she plays them with men.'

The rest of the morning, Danielle and I talked about anything other than men. OK, that's not true, we talked of nothing else, but we didn't talk about Bailey. I wanted to talk about Bailey until the cows came home, but Danielle successfully steered the conversation away from Bailey, and barely involved herself when I attempted to talk Jack. She droned on and on and on about Fabio, to the point where I suggested she give Stewart-small-penis the heave-ho and go on this date herself. An hour after swimming, we lay side-by-side in a dimly lit room whilst two massage therapists pounded our shoulder blades with large oval stones. The heat from them was delicious, my eyes were glazed over and it was all I could do not to fall asleep.

'Mmmm,' I murmured to Danielle, as she continued to babble on about various different things in her life, specifically, her work.

'And so really, I want to get rid of the intern, she's just a little too close for comfort when it comes to making tea for Stewart and he assures me that there is nothing to worry about but, Katie, she's, like, nineteen, boobs like traffic cones, ass like a walnut. I'm jealous. She's blonde too, blue eyes . . . I hate her.'

'Oh, babe, she sounds like a troll. Sod that she's got traffic-cone tits, you have wonderful breasts, the best ones I've ever seen. In fact, let's get a picture of them so I can take them in to show the surgeon when I've made my millions for my boob . . . oh . . . oh . . .'

'Your what?' Danielle is suddenly awake and as she turns to me, the masseuse stumbles backwards. A stone slips off and cracks against the floor tiles.

'My, um, please don't kill me, I was going to have a boob job on Monday.' The room is silent for a minute.

'I see,' she says, before lying back in her previous position.

'Um, I had this consultation and I was going to have the operation, it's in my contract to, um, go with any improvements for the good of my image, but it's OK, no need for shoutage, I'm having Macrolane jabs instead.'

'So, you think if you change yourself, poison yourself even, to become another Jessica Hilson, your life will become amazing and your boyfriends will never ever leave you again?'

'I guess so,' I say quietly. 'Well, it worked for Jessica . . .'

'I beg of you, think some more, buy a Wonderbra, anything, just please don't mutilate yourself, pump your body with chemicals. What would your mother say?'

'She wouldn't know.'

'Katie, don't be a wally, she'll see them! How big were you going to go?'

'I wanted to go to a C or maybe a D with the implants . . . If I go for the jabs they aren't permanent, you can go up two cup sizes . . . Aubrey wants me to be an F!' I attempt to lighten the mood.

'He wants to F-off more like, I mean, who do they think they are? These media types, it's like, fuck off, seriously fuck right off, how dare they think they can mutilate you like this and then tell you it's what you need to be having done in order to "make it" in this world. Please, Katie, think again.'

'I will,' I lied. But I knew that I wanted those boobs, because all the celebrities had big boobs. No one famous had little B cups. No. And I would totally die of embarrassment if I ended up wearing those chicken fillets and they fell out in front of the whole entire world, which they would of course, because this is me, and stupid things happen to me all the time. And I bet you another thing, that stupid, frizzy-haired, big-nosed journalist from *London Lowdown*, Pippa Strong, she'd be there with her long lens, getting the best shot of it and plastering it all over her rubbish magazine.

I hated it when there was tension between Danielle and me and I was struggling, truth be told, to understand what was bugging her. Ever since Friday night when she almost caught me having it off with Bailey, post-coital, alone, and a little bit wobbly, she had something to tell me and she'd been touchy, and a heck of a lot more vocal about her feelings to do with everything from the men in my life, to the bits of me I wanted enlarged. I had to get to the bottom of this.

'Danielle, what on earth is eating you?' I blurt out.

She sighs heavily.

'Nothing is eating me,' she says defensively.

God, it feels like I'm talking to Janice.

'I'm just, I don't want to see you get hurt by these pricks and I don't want to see you go through a very painful operation to change a part of your body that is perfectly fine the way it is. If I can't tell you this as your best friend and as someone who loves you dearly, and cares about your welfare, then so what? Hate me if you like, I'm not going to stand by and watch this. I'll say what I like, and just hope some of it sinks in.'

'Jeez, Louise. I'm not having a boob job right now. I may change my mind in the future and you will just have to lump it either way. I'd rather you at least try to respect me. I have a brain of my own!' I squeal.

'Oh, really? Well, do you want to try using it sometime, Katie?' Danielle shot up off the couch. 'I'm done here, thanks,' she said to the masseuse.

'Danielle,' I called out after her, but she was moving fast towards the door.

'Danielle!' I yelled, as the therapists looked on in vague amusement at the mini drama being played out in front of them.

'I can't talk to you right now, Katie, because if I do, I'll say something I'll regret. It's better we just walk away from each other now, and cool down.'

'I'm cool!' I screeched at her, 'You're the one who's trying to police my life, what with your phone-checking rules and your stupid opinions and your bloody infuriating reluctance to tell me what's really making you act like the PMT bitch from hell!'

'OOOOH, blame it on the period you know I'm having!' she screamed back at me, holding her robe with one hand and pointing at me furiously with the other.

'Need I say more?' I said glibly.

'You know what, Katie, or should that be Jessica mark two? You go desecrate your body, you go moulding yourself on a jumped-up little tart who steals your boyfriend if that's all you think you're worth, but I tell you something, it won't make him love you, and you'll be the one in tears!'

'Like I have any left after all this shit!' I screamed, more hot tears welling up in my eyes. 'What is it?' I screamed some more, 'What is it you can't tell me! This isn't about my boobs, is it!?' I looked at her, exhausted from screaming so hard. My throat tickled and I nervously coughed.

'No, Katie, it's not just about your boobs, it's . . . It's me, it's all my issues, just, I need to go, I'm sorry, this conversation needs to close now, I'm going home, please don't come after me, and you go on this date tonight. Don't wear the Nicole Farhi dress, take it back, you're not a middle-aged Sloaney pony, OK, you need something more hip, go shopping, do what you like, I'll call you.' And she just waved her hands in the air dismissively and padded off down the dimly lit hallway towards our hotel room.

'May I finish the massage, Madam?' the therapist questioned.

'I guess,' I said, as I slumped forward, my face through the hole in the bed, and thought about what had just gone down. What was Danielle's problem? Specifically, why did she hate my dress?

Chapter 12

6.30pm

Brush teeth, spray Impulse body spray all over self and pull up sheer stockings. Do not, I repeat, do not snag them on your costume ring that looks like it's worth a zillion pounds but actually cost £4.99 from Portobello Road market.

6.35pm

Check reflection of hairdo in the mirror. Get vanity mirror to check left, right and back side (of head not bottom).

6.40pm

Peer out of window. Maid comes to the door to collect overnight bag. Can't have overnight bag cramping Nicole Farhi (hah! Danielle) very expensive, camel, knee-length dress.

6.45pm

Check reflection in mirror. Powder nose with Rimmel bronzer and apply pastel-pink MAC lipstick in St Germain. Too bright, so slick a bit of Dior neutral with sparkles on and smack lips on tissue to avoid lipstick-on-teeth disaster.

6.50pm

I wish I had my cigarettes on me. Need to calm nerves. Whiskey shots from minibar will do.

6.55pm
Check phone for texts. No texts. Bah. No missed calls. Bah. No one loves me. Gutted. Check reflection. Looking good, Katie!

6.57pm
Car is here, impressed, he's early. One last check in mirror, looking sophisticated, hair in chignon, teeth free from any macrobiotic seaweed, check.

7.00pm
'Katie,' Fabio growls from the car. 'How wonderful to see you, I trust you have enjoyed your stay, no?'

'Yes, yes,' I say, as I stumble into the car, somewhat akin to a baby giraffe taking its first steps. Not very elegant at all. What was I thinking, wearing six-inch heels? I am used to going down The Dolphin in Hackney with Jack in my plimsolls, not the bloomin' Dorchester with Italian shipping heirs. He takes my hand in his gently and pulls me close for a continental kiss.

'Mwah, mwah,' he says, moving from my right cheek to my left. I sit down on the plush leather seats, which start to warm up my bottom.

'This is nice,' I say, gingerly. I don't want to talk arse with him when we're barely two minutes into the date.

'The seats, they are body reactive, don't be alarmed, my darling,' he winks at me. All of Fabio's bodily actions and face contortions should be screaming out 'creepy pervert scale ten' but they somehow add to his charm. He was a looker, he was smouldering and I could almost smell the money emanating from his person.

'We go to The Dorchester, you like?' he queried.

'Mmm, yes very much so.' I pretended that I had been before. Of course I'd been before, hadn't everyone? No! Of course I didn't frequent Carolina's Pizzas on Mare Street after my Saturday night binge-drinking escapades in my favourite East End boozer. Nah, I was a seasoned professional food connoisseur.

'So, you go there often?'

'All the time . . .' I said.

'Then you will know that the *filet de blaireau* is the finest around, no?'

'Exquisite,' I agreed, not having a clue what he was talking about. It sounded yummy, though!

Fabio began to laugh. A small chortle, but before long, he was howling.

'What is it?' I said, feeling a bit out of the loop. 'Something funny?'

'Yes, sorry, Katie, I'm sorry, I must not make joke with you.'

'What joke?'

'Shh, darling, no matter.'

'What!' I said, feeling perturbed by him laughing at me.

I felt my cheeks flush red and my body temperature was rising uncomfortably, making my calves stick to the leather seating.

'OK, I tell you, but please, don't take it the wrong way, I was making joke, light-hearted, fun, see?'

'I'll see, when you tell me,' I laughed nervously.

'I asked you, Katie, if you had tried the fillet of badger.'

Oh sweet Jesus . . .

'It's OK that you're new to The Dorchester,' he continued, 'I didn't expect you to be a seasoned veteran.'

'Oh,' I said, squirming on the inside. He'd totally rumbled me. Fillet of bloody badger! I just, oh God, I just embarrass myself 24/7 in Kate Lewis world, oh God, how am I going to claw back some kudos now? Must tell Danielle, I thought, reaching for my handbag. Then it hit me, a bit painfully, that I couldn't text Danielle. She wouldn't want to know. After her huff earlier, she told me not to contact her, she's on a cool-down, she'd be in touch. I couldn't tell Richard that I'd told Fabio Matravers I enjoyed eating badger fillets because then he'd tell Hanna and she'd tell Frenella and my life totally wouldn't be worth living. This sucked, being stupid. I must make myself more clever, somehow. Need another stupid boyfriend. Jack made me feel like Einstein.

Eventually, we rolled up to The Dorchester. The driver opened the door for me, I stepped out and Fabio took hold of my hand and led me up to the entrance. Wordlessly, the maître d' led us to a secluded candlelit booth at the back of the restaurant.

'Madam,' a waiter said, as he placed a menu entirely in another language in front of me. It was full of 'Poissons' and such like. I daren't ask what it all meant, no need for further food humiliation. As long as I could work out what was and what wasn't fish we'd be fine. I would vomit on him if I ate any fish.

'Katie, what food do you like the most?' Fabio spoke gently to me, it was clear that he didn't want me to feel awkward, a touching, sweet gesture.

'I like chicken, and um, I like potatoes,' I said, smiling.

His face contorted with surprise and delight. 'You eat the potatoes?'

'Well, yes, if they were here right now, I would eat them, very, um, nutritious,' I say, fumbling with my words.

'Hmm, I see,' he said, still smiling.

'What? Potatoes aren't another word for badgers or poo or something?' Oh God, I'd said poo, this is not good, people don't say poo in The Dorchester, or anywhere else for that fact, especially not out on a date with an Italian studmuffin like Fabio Matravers.

'Heh heh,' he laughed. 'I love your humour, you are so, refreshing, so funny, light, vibrant, you really glow!' he said, gazing at me all starry-eyed.

'It's the excitement of meeting you,' I said, even though I'm positive he was commenting on my Rimmel bronzing glow. Good make-up choice, I thought to myself. Must wear again.

'Potatoes are like, how shall I put it, like, akin to eating poo, I suppose, from recent experiences of dining out with beautiful women,' he mused.

'Champagne on ice,' the waiter appeared and filled up our flutes. I felt really posh tonight. Whole weekend actually. I could most definitely get used to this. But why the potato crimes? What was wrong with spuds?

'Jessica,' he began, and my belly constricted in an instant. I felt nauseous, wanted to be sick, actually be sick on Fabio, not on my new dress, the sheer mention of her sent my guts into a tailspin. 'She was fearful of gaining the weight, so we never ever have potatoes, pasta, chips, pizza . . . food of the staple Italian diet. My mama would take her to the doctors if she were in Italy with me, there be something very wrong with you if you don't enjoy, if you don't love, the pizza, the pasta . . . all Mama made, it's very good,' he continued as he took a sip of his drink.

'I just love all those things,' I gushed, trying to make myself look the very best I could in his eyes.

'And you have an Italian mama's physique. You are very beautiful, Katie, very womanly, curves in all the right places,' he winked. Again, it should be smarmy but it's not, he's adorable, actually, really adorable. My heart fluttered.

The rest of the date progressed nicely. Quaint and polite, Fabio extended his arm for me to take hold of on our walk back to the car, where his faithful driver opened the door for us.

'That was beautiful,' I said, meaning the food.

'Not as beautiful as you,' Fabio said. Smooth. Love it! Feel like million zillion pounds, hah, if only my mother could see me right now, hobnobbing with posh Italian swoon buckets.

'Thank you,' I gushed at his compliments that had been flowing thick and fast all evening. My head was so big I wasn't quite sure how it was going to fit through my front door. Thoughts of Jack and of Bailey had been shoved to the back of my mind as I gazed into Fabio's chocolate, swimming-pool eyes. In a really perverse way, I felt almost like I was getting off on dating Jessica Hilson's ex-boyfriend. After all, in my opinion, it doesn't matter whether you did the dumping or were the dumpee, when the person you are no longer with moves on – or at least makes a very good job of looking like they've moved on – it never fails to sting the heart a bit. And if I could hurt Jessica Hilson even a pinch of how much she's hurt me, then I would go to bed that night a very happy woman. The car came to a stop and I waited for what would most definitely be one of the richest kisses of all time to land upon my primed lips. I had blotted my lipstick so as not to make a mess all over his face. Must do one of those clean-cut kisses, not too much tongue . . . ooh conundrums! Do you use tongue on very rich Italian men? Is that too forward? Should I wait for him to make the first move? If he uses his tongue is that tantamount to wanting to have sex with me? I couldn't, wouldn't have sex with Fabio, must retain the power. Everyone knows a woman's in power until the man has had his wicked way. Then, because of the cruel laws of Mother Nature, I would, along with all other women who surrender their bodies to sexual adventure with attractive hunks, render myself incapable of calling the shots. I would have made a biologically emotional tie to this man, which is why I become obsessed with whoever it is that I have had sex with, most notably, Bailey. So, no sex. No, siree. Fabio's face is so close I can smell the stuffed quail with garlic he had for his dinner. Close my eyes . . . he's coming closer . . . pucker up . . .

'Katie,' he says slowly.

'Hmmm,' I purr in my sexiest voice.

'I would like to see you again, would you like that too?'

Fabio had moved back against his seat away from me. Oh God, prime embarrassment.

'Um,' I said, pretending to think about it. I'd love to go on another date, right away, tomorrow even, ooh, this is soooooo exciting!

'I would like that,' I said, giving away no clues as to how euphoric I felt on the inside.

'I will call you,' he said, as he leant in to kiss me. This is it, I thought, the kiss! I puckered up once again as his lips connected with my cheeks. I near enough knocked his nose off his face in my eagerness to secure a snog.

'Ommph,' he said, rubbing his nose gently.

'I'm so sorry!' I squealed, 'I just don't really do continental kissing, I'm sorry, are you OK?'

'I'm fine, I think,' he said, not looking at me.

Shit, I've blown all chances now. That's the only blowing either of us will be doing from now on. God, I have to remove myself before I cause any more problems here. Not only have I pretended I eat woodland creatures, I've just behaved like a cheap tart. Maybe as a parting shot, I should go all out and flash him my pants?

'See you soon,' he said, patting my arm, with a gentle smile on his face.

'You, uh,' I said, pointing at his nose, 'have lipstick on your face,' I smiled a worry smile and legged it from the car and up the path to my house, shame burning throughout my body from top to toe. Not for the first time in recent days, I scrambled with the keys to my front door, feeling eyes upon me from the waiting car. What a gent, waiting to see that I'd got home safe, gosh, it was only a hop, skip and a jump from the car to my house, not like any passing rapists could attack me or anything. Still, I opened the door – eventually – and as I closed it firmly behind me, I sank back against it and put my head in my hands. There were no tears this time, just sheer humiliation. I really needed to work upon my social decorum. I couldn't go on another date and feign knowledge of posh food only to be caught out again. I totally couldn't close my eyes and pucker up my lips for a kiss that wasn't forth-coming, well, not when I was expecting one, anyway. Poor Fabio. At least his nose didn't bleed. I looked up to the hallway mirror and below it, where my telephone resided, were angry red numbers, flashing loudly, crying out to be heard.

I stood up and pressed play.

'You have . . . eight . . . new . . . messages . . . To listen to your messages . . .' the BT woman said.

I pressed the button. Eight new messages? Wowee, who could they be? One of them had to be Bailey!

'First message . . . received today . . . at . . . five forty-five pm . . .'

'Katie, I'm sorry I left like that, it's Danielle.'

Phew! She doesn't hate me after all, our friendship is still intact and not in the friendship graveyard!

'I'm just feeling a bit weird right now, and this work stuff is bugging me a lot, shouldn't have taken it out on you, will call you tomorrow, love you . . .'

Beep

'Next new message . . . received today . . . at . . . six . . . pm . . .'

'Kate, this is Hanna, please will you call me on 07887 . . .'
Beep

'Katie, please come home. Mum's driving me mad. She thinks I'm going to become a high-class escort because my hair's now blonde. You have blonde hair. You're not a hooker . . . as far as we know . . .'
Cheeky sod! I thought. Delete. Bloody Janice.

Beep

'Kate, sigh, this is Hanna Frost, will you call me on 07887 . . .'

Hmm, I thought, as the remaining messages were all

from Hanna. What could she want? I wonder if she knew about Fabio?

The phone rang. 07887 . . . flashed up on my call screen.

'Hanna!' I said, picking up the receiver and answering her, bright as a button.

'Katie,' she replied, cool as an Icelandic winter.

'I've been trying to get hold of you, where on earth have you been?'

'Harrods . . . and, um, the spa trip that was given to me by Tom Theodore on the photo shoot, you know?'

'Fabio's spa,' Hanna confirmed. Shit. This is the bit where she kills me, right?

'Yes, I believe that is correct,' I said, gulping down my anxiety.

'And how was dinner?' Hanna said, coolly. OK, I'm rumbled, she knows, heaven knows how she knows, but she knows . . . must not lie.

'It was lovely thanks, Hanna, how did you . . .'

'Katie, relax. I organized the trip to the spa. Fabio is a good friend of mine, we mix in the same social circles, we have a vested interest, specifically, in you.'

'Then why did you have, you know, um, why did I upset you so much taking his business card?'

'Because, Katie, you really need to understand how PR and publicity campaigns work. I'm the one busting my backside for your benefit right now. And haven't I been over the top beyond, over and above good to you, what with the Harrods gifts, the expensive cosmetics, the free clothes and now a date with Fabio Matravers?'

'You set me up?' I said, feeling the wind knocked out of my sails.

'Why, yes, Katie. You didn't think he actually liked you, did you?' she said, all matter-of-fact.

'No, course not, I had an inkling myself,' I lied.

'I didn't want anyone to take pictures of you taking his business card and run stories willy-nilly about how you are dating him undercover. I'd rather break the story sometime this week with the collected pictures of you and Fabio emerging from The Dorchester in that hideously ageing dress of yours. I'd prefer not to, seriously, I hope you kept the receipt for it. Swap it for something more current, will you? The pictures of you in a couture dress with Fabio Matravers would be simply to die for. But we have to give the press something to play with, otherwise things could get a lot nastier,' she said, gravely.

'Nasty in what way?' I queried, feeling fear in my belly. What could they have on me other than dodgy trims and teenage escapades?

'You caught crabs in Ibiza when you were seventeen.'

'OH MY GOD!' I squealed. 'How did you get that information! This cannot become common knowledge!'

'Quite. It was one Nicola Baxter.'

'I knew it!' I hissed angrily. That silly cow seemed to have it in for me right now. Just what was her problem? I totally needed to knock on her door next time I was back in Little Glove.

'I'll do my best to contain it,' Hanna said. 'I will do my best if you do your best for me, Katie, and that means, you wine and you dine and you do whatever it takes to get your face all over the magazines with Fabio Matravers. I have it on good authority that Jessica Hilson is still in love with him, so there is a very high chance you can get Jack Hunter back in your life and in your bed by parading about like love's young dream. There's nothing like a bit of jealousy to help seize the day. God knows, you will make yourself a packet with subsequent stories such as 'My life of hell without Jack' which we will be doing with *Sizzle Stars* this week.'

'But my life isn't hell without Jack, actually, I am not altogether sure I want him back . . .' I said, thinking about Danielle's words of wisdom. She was right. With Jack, I did think so little of myself that his needs came first, I never came at all. So what's the use of having Jack in my life? Let's see, I thought, rummaging in the side dish for the PRO and CON list I made about Jack when we first broke up. It was scribbled down on the back of my note-pad the night Danielle came over to keep me strong in the face of the paparazzi who had camped in my street.

Pros for going out with JACK HUNTER:
Gorgeous (very)
Yummy body including six-pack he owned that
wasn't actually beer in the fridge
He was going to be mega famous and we were
going to live in the Hollywood Hills
He was sweet and thoughtfully recorded *Jeremy Kyle*
& *Airline* for me to watch
I liked to steal his Space NK products
I loved him

Cons for going out with JACK HUNTER:
He was rubbish in bed
He skipped Saturday morning sex with me for
brunch with other women

He never bought me any presents
He never invited me anywhere
I never met his family
He made me feel like I was an embarrassment to be
seen with
I never felt good enough for his wannabe media
lifestyle
He always forgot about me and never put me first
It was always about him!
I never met any of his friends
I felt like Jack Hunter's personal therapist at times
He never appreciated me or paid me any compliments
Whenever I had a problem, he'd conveniently
disappear on me
I unfortunately loved him

I slowly digested the note and my heart sank. I was living in some kind of rose-tinted land of ex-boyfriend admiration. It was not good. Code Red.

'Katie?' Hanna said loudly down into my ear, making it ring slightly. 'Are you still there?'

'Yes, sorry, Hanna, I'm here, where were we?'

'Katie, this is how the week will pan out. Tomorrow you do nothing, Tuesday is *Sizzle Stars* release day so Richard will drive you to your mother's house in Little Glove for some respite, because the media will no doubt be camping outside your house again.'

'Richard's driving me?' I queried, feeling confused. Richard wasn't my driver, Bailey was, and I totally needed to talk to Bailey, find out where I stood with him. Yes, OK, I know I must be some kind of psycho glutton for punishment, but I still held on to the glimmer of hope that Bailey really did like me and that our passionate encounter meant something more than just two people sweating all over one another in an animal embrace.

'Bailey is busy this week,' Hanna said.

'Doing what?'

'Why ever do you need to know, Katie?'

'I'm just curious, I quite liked having him around, you see, for the time that he was, um, around . . .' I was stuttering. I hoped Hanna didn't guess about the sex.

'If you must know, Katie, Bailey is in Soho right now with our new girl, the Big Brother evictee, Carolina Fernando, opening a new cocktail bar, the Wu Bar.'

'What?'

'He's stepping out with Carolina Fernando, raven-haired lingerie model. They are opening the Wu Bar. Now, can we go back to business? This week *Sizzle Stars* comes out and you'll need to prepare yourself for that. Let me get my thinking cap on re possible questions for you and I will get back to you. Must dash.'

The phone went silent. I stood there holding the receiver and all I could hear was the dull *durrrrr* of a disconnected phone line.

Bailey was with Carolina Fernando? Arguably the best-looking, mocha-coloured beauty that the series had ever seen. She had the legs of an athlete and the body of a goddess. No wonder he hadn't called me! I half thought about hotfooting it down to Soho to catch him in a clinch with this Carolina Fernando and announce to the paparazzi that we'd had it off only two days ago all over my seventies fashion-crime bedding in my tartan pyjamas, but then thought better of it. What is it with the men in my life of late? Cloak and dagger dating, whereabouts unknown, get your end away and leave me pondering the end of my love life. I hated men right now, Jack Hunter marginally being overtaken by Sam Bailey, modelizer. I walked into the kitchen, put the kettle on and opened the biscuit tin. The rest of the night passed slowly. I had a zillion and one thoughts in my head about Fabio, Jack and Bailey. Fabio seemed so genuine, how could I fall for it? He really seemed to like me. Was he ever going to tell me our date was a set-up? What if he told Hanna Frost that I embarrassed myself with the badger faux pas? What would I do then? At least Hanna was talking to me. She hadn't apologized for using the F word on me, though. Still, what did I expect? For her to send me flowers and beg at my slippers for mercy? Nah, this was prime-time bitch features in full flow. Can't for the life of me think why Danielle would prefer me to model myself on horse-faced, chinless Hanna. Oh well. I switched all the lights off, checked my phone, tried really, really hard to expel all thoughts of Bailey writhing around a bedroom that was all white and pristine with posh art hanging on the walls and doing complicated sexual positions with Carolina Fernando, because in my mind, that's what the beautiful people did, in places like Notting Hill and Mayfair. I sighed, pulled my Sonata throw up and over my head and attempted to go to sleep.

Chapter 13

Trrrrriiiiiiiiiiiiiiiiiiiiiiiiiiiiiiiiiiiiiiiing

I nestled against my super-expensive bedsheets, trying to block out the sounds of my doorbell. I'd slept like a princess in the Harrods bedding.

Trrrrriiiiiiiiiiiiiiiiiiiiiiiiiiiiiiiiiiiiiiiiiiiing

'Gah!' I muttered, pulling one of my sumptuous goose pillows on to my head and pretending that there wasn't someone at my door. They could sod off, I was in no mood to wake up right now.

Riiiing . . . Riiiing went my phone.

'*Meow!*' went the cat.

Trrriiiiiiiiiiiiiiiiiiiiiiiing went the door.

Ooooh, baby! Nobody hurts me like yooooou! went my alarm clock radio. *Beep Beep* my phone growled against the bed-side table with a text message.

'For God's sake!' I screamed as I sat bolt upright. The cat sprang off the bed and ran down into the kitchen, mewing as he went.

I turned down the sound of the alarm clock and noted the time: 9am. That wasn't such a terrible time to be awake, but oh, I was enjoying my nightmare-free dreams about clothes shopping and chocolate cake. I picked up my phone and opened the text.

Triiiiiiiiiiiiiiiiiiiiing . . . bang bang bang

'KATIE!' Richard's voice bellowed through the letter-box. 'Open the door immediately, it's all systems go!'

'Shit,' I thought, getting out of bed as I heard Richard scuffle with folk outside the front door. I pulled my brand new plush white fluffy robe around my body and checked my reflection in the hallway mirror. Didn't look too hideous, so I pulled my hair into a messy bun and screamed, 'I'm coming, I'm coming,' through the wooden door to placate a very uppity-sounding Richard Dewberry.

'Thank the Lord you've finally awoken,' Richard said breathlessly in his usual over-the-top manner. 'I've been standing out there for fifteen minutes! What did you take last night? A truckload of Valium?'

'No, just some warm milk. Where's the fire?' I said, rubbing my sleepy eyes.

'Coffee, immediately,' Richard said, throwing himself down on to my sofa and switching on the television. Some low-rent news hacks were on your doorstep, I told them to come back tomorrow for an exclusive.'

'Are you for real?'

'No, stupid, of course not. But they believed me.'

Lorraine Kelly stood next to a fat woman crowing about her miraculous diet plan that had helped her shed ten stone in as many months. She still looked like she had eaten a small town.

'Coffee, toast?'

'No, Katie, God, how many times do I have to tell you? Bread is evil. Do you have any eggs?'

'Sure,' I said, popping two slices of white into the toaster.

'Egg-white omelette, please, and if you have any cress, that would do nicely.'

'What did your last slave die of?' I called through to him above the noise of the kettle.

'Disobedience,' he winked.

'Hah, very funny.'

'Darling, it's Monday . . .' Richard cooed.

'Yes, I am aware of that,' I said, rubbing my temples. I could feel a headache coming on after the cacophony of appliances and Richard's incessant banging on my door. What a way to wake up, not pleasant, I tell you. I popped some ibuprofen into my cool glass of orange juice and I poured a glass of tap water for Richard.

'No worries,' he said, as I approached him with the glass. 'I have San Pellegrino.'

'So, to what do I owe this early morning visit, Rich?' I said, stifling a yawn. I lit up a cigarette and offered him one. He took it and sparked it up before pulling out a copy of this week's *Sizzle Stars* from his man-bag.

'Here,' he said, pushing it across the coffee table towards me.

'Gosh,' I said, breathing in sharply. For once, I looked a million zillion pounds. My hair was so glossy and bright, with various shades of blonde running through the tumbling bohemian waves. My face was light and happy, my lips were pink and shiny and my eyes were large and emerald green, framed by luscious long lashes.

'You look absolutely amazing,' Richard said, with a smug grin on his face. 'I would,' he winked.

'Urgh, you would not,' I mocked. 'I don't know where you've been!'

Ignoring me, he inspected his fingernails the way posh people do, fingers splayed out, knuckles slightly curled towards his body. 'Hanna, myself, Aubrey, Ziggy Wang, Tom Theodore . . . we're the best, don't you agree?' he simpered.

'Yes, yes!' I said, feeling a bubble of excitement in my belly. Everyone was going to see me looking like a super-model on the front cover of *Sizzle Stars* magazine! I have never in my wildest dreams looked so perfect in all my life as I did on that cover.

'I look . . .'

'Unrecognizable,' Richard mused. 'It's amazing what photography and airbrushing can do!'

'Ouch!' I said, jabbing him in the ribs. 'I look like that, that's me!'

'Yes, obviously, but a heck of an improvement! I mean, look, darling, look at you now . . .'

'I've just got up!' I squealed in my defence.

'Rocking the slob look as usual . . .' he continued.

'Hang on a cotton-picking minute, Mr Dewberry, you asked, no sorry, you all DEMANDED that I look horribly unkempt and sans make-up on purpose for like, ages, plus you made me waft about last week wearing a balaclava!'

'Yes, well, we had to do that so as not to spoil this glorious moment, and as for your face, we had to let your skin breathe and it worked, no? I haven't seen a pimple the size of the one you had on your chin last week since I was in the sixth form. Seriously. And now look at you. One spa trip later and you have the face of an angel, with skin as smooth as my perfectly taut *derrière*.'

'Yes, well, I look great, please don't piss on my chips,' I said, as I got up and moved to the kitchen to finish Richard's eggs. They came out looking like squashed ghosts, all wobbly and uneven.

'Here,' I said, plonking his breakfast in front of him and stealing *Sizzle Stars*. I sat down with my toast and flicked through the pages until I found my interview. I gasped.

Katie Lewis is an overnight sensation, a champion brand for real girls everywhere! the headline screamed, next to a picture of me looking like a supermodel. My teeth looked really white!

Katie Lewis rocks Marc Jacobs! another splash across the page, with me, once again, looking soft and feminine, yet sexy and delicious. I wanted to look like that all the time. I wished that everyone in the world could see through the eyes of a soft-focus lens instead of harsh reality.

The interview was great. Frenella didn't make me sound or look like a total dipshit. Which I was thankful for, I tell you. Maybe Hanna Frost, for all of her arsey mannerisms, really did know what she was doing. I decided right there and then on the spot that I would never ever question anything she said again, I would simply believe her. My faith was now entirely in the hands of Poets Field PR team.

'I love it!' I squealed, grabbing hold of Richard. He nearly choked on his eggs.

'Yes, it's excellent, I can't wait for it to come out tomorrow, such positive PR, your life is going to change dramatically, darling.' He grinned wildly.

Triiiiiiiiiiiiiiiiiiiiiing went the door.

'Whoever could that be?' I questioned.

'Don't know, darling. Unlike Jessica Hilson's mother, I am not psychic. May I suggest you open it?'

'Funny,' I said, standing up and shaking toast crumbs from my robe. 'I meant, maybe you had some kind of thing going on for me today that I don't yet know about.' I went into the hall and opened the door.

'Mum!' I said, taken aback.

'Kate,' Mum said, standing there, arms crossed. 'We need to talk.'

'Um, we do?' I said, feeling a bit uneasy. What could I have done now?

'Well?' she said, staring at me, an eyebrow raised.

'Well, what?'

'Are you going to invite me in, or is it now customary for you, as an almost famous person, to leave your poor mother standing on the doorstep of her elder daughter's house?'

'Mum, unlike you, my neighbours don't care about every single microscopic move I make,' I said, opening the door wide and standing back to allow her entry.

'Well, that's not strictly true now, is it, darling?' Richard purred from the living room. 'You probably still have bum prints in your flower beds from where the journalists were sitting last week. Plus, I saw an empty packet of chocolate digestives blowing about on your lawn.'

'That was mine,' I said, blushing.

'No wonder you can't keep a boyfriend!' Mum said, prodding my hips.

I silently seethed. Richard said nothing. Traitor.

'There are two things I need to speak to you about,' Mum said, harrumphing as she laid her massive handbag on the floor and plonked her backside down on my armchair, which strained under her weight. She was one to talk, her bottom was three times the size of mine and her hair was so frizzy she looked as though she'd stuck her fingers in a plug socket. Still, she had an ethereal, matronly beauty about her and my father still adored her after thirty years of marriage, so she must be doing something right. 'First, Janice has become obsessed with showing her particulars on Spacebook,' Mum chuntered. 'Have you got any biscuits?'

'Sure,' I said, as I got up. Spacebook? Was I hearing her right? I stifled a laugh.

'You mean Facebook, Mother,' I said, as I filled the kettle for another cup of tea.

'Whatever it is, she's putting indecent pictures of herself on the World Wide Web for all and sundry to see. Her bosoms are pushed up right under her nose. Your father is on the edge of a coronary. As we speak, he has in his hands a copy of a Reader's Digest PC guide and is trying to disable her account. I'm so upset, I can't tell you,' she said, pulling a hanky out and dabbing her eyes for effect. I hadn't the heart to tell her that Janice is the only one who can disable her Facebook account.

'I'm sure they're not that indecent, Mum,' I said, trying to placate her.

'Oomph,' Richard said, pulling his collar in the way men do when they're hot under it.

'What?' We both swivelled our heads round in his direction. Richard was twiddling with his BlackBerry.

'I see what you mean,' he said gravely.

'Richard? Since when have you been friends with my seventeen-year-old sister?' I shrieked.

'Well, she added me and I thought it would be rude not to,' he coughed. I know Richard so well. I know as much as I know night follows day that he's absolutely dying to say something about her being legal, or that if there's grass on the pitch you can play the game. His lips curled as he visibly repressed his vulgar jokes.

'I'll talk to her, OK? I'm sure once she knows how upsetting it is for you, she'll have a change of heart and remove them.' I patted Mum on the arm. The kettle whistled a loud tune.

'Well, you're hardly the beacon of respectability, are you, young lady?' Mum sniffled. I poured the tea and carried it through to her on a tray, complete with a proper cup and saucer and even some posh sugar lumps. I kept Queen's crockery for such times as when my mother decides to swoop upon my house uninvited. Ever since I'd given her a cuppa in a novelty mug that had a fully clothed man on it which became a very naked man when filled with hot water, I'd never heard the end of 'Kate and her pornographic mug'.

'Thank heavens this is a respectable set of china,' Mum said, tutting. Anyone would think I was born from Hyacinth Bucket. Honestly, what a drone she could be.

'And what is it that Katie has done to warrant being called "young lady" when she is anything but?' Richard winked.

'Excuse me,' I said, aghast, 'twenty-six is not old, Richard, just because you date prepubescent girls . . .'

'Your friend is a paedophile?' Mum shrieked, toppling her teacup all over herself and the carpet.

'No! Good Lord, no!' Richard squealed like a girl.

'Is that why you are on my younger daughter's Facespace

profile?' Mum snarled. 'I've always thought you looked shifty!'

'I'm not a paedophile, Mrs Lewis, I love a mature woman. Tell her, Katie, I am obsessed . . .' he looked at the television for inspiration, 'with Lorraine Kelly!'

'What?' I said, turning to Richard.

'Lorraine Kelly?' said Mum.

'Lorraine, yes, gorgeous, just my type . . . um . . . I don't like children, Mrs Lewis, I mean, obviously I *like* children, my sister has two, delightful creatures, but obviously, I don't *like* them like them, in a sordid way, oh gosh . . .' Richard visibly squirmed, his cheeks flushed. I'm sure she knows he's anything but, but she's really playing him now. Her face is an absolute picture. She sits there scowling at him, eyebrows raised.

'Mum, shh, I was joking, it was a joke, Richard likes to date girls in their early twenties, he is by no means anything akin to being a paedophile, honestly. Calm down, and hang on there a minute, let me get you a towel. Are you OK?'

Mum said nothing. She continued to glare at Richard, who now looked like a very naughty schoolboy being reprimanded by the headmistress.

'I'm sorry for the confusion,' Richard said, gallantly. His phone beeped in his pocket but he didn't dare answer it.

'Here,' I said to Mum, mopping up tea dribbles. Luckily, I had put half a jug of cold milk in it so that her tea wasn't scorching hot. It wasn't the first time she'd got herself in a tizz and dropped beverages down her front.

'So, um, Mrs Lewis,' Richard began, totally frightened by my over-zealous mother.

'You can call me Jo, dear,' she said, her face softening.

'Jo,' Richard replied, tepidly.

'Go ahead,' she said.

'Well, what was the second thing you needed to speak to Katie about?'

'Kate, I have it on good authority that you were riddled with beasts when you came back from your holiday with Nicola Baxter in the year 2000 and, in turn, had to sneak one of Betty's nit combs from her salon to dislodge the creatures from your person.'

The room goes silent. I want to die. Richard is sitting there with his eyes as wide as saucers, a look of sheer disgust on his face. I was beyond embarrassed when Hanna Frost became privy to my unfortunate brush with crabs, but this was on another level entirely. At least Hanna could kind of understand, what with being a woman and having to deal with other itchy personal issues like thrush, or burning pain when using that erotica stuff that's supposed to make your bits tingle with pleasure but in fact has you squatting in a cold bath for an entire evening, thus ruining an entire sex-game night. Trust me, don't ever put anything on there that isn't naturally secreted.

'How, um, how did you know?' I said, flabbergasted. I knew that Nicola was on some kind of mission to make me look as stupid as possible in the press, but I didn't know why. We'd been friends since childhood, we'd gone to the Friday-night discos together, I'd snogged Matthew Robinson so she could snog his best mate round the back of Jimmy's Bowling Green. 'I was weeding the garden, minding my own business, looking out for the promised *Daily Mail* to take pictures of the house and ask us questions about you, when some youths rode past on their BMXs shouting vulgarities about your sexual health, my girl,' she said sternly. 'Well?' she said expectantly.

Richard perched on the edge of the sofa.

'Well,' I said, lying through my teeth, 'it's not true. It was Nicola who had them.'

They both stared at me.

'How could you possibly think it was me?' I said, affronted.

Mum seemed to be swallowing it, as did Richard. Phew! I was a good actress. Maybe I should look into a new career. That would be the stuff of dreams, wouldn't it, for me to take off as an amazing show-stopping actress and for Jessica Hilson's abysmal snore fest *Cowgirls* to sell no cinema tickets, rendering her prematurely on the acting scrapheap. Hah! That would be sweet revenge. Indeedio.

'So it wasn't you who had the pubic lobsters, then?' Mum said, nonchalantly.

Oh God, I wanted to die. Richard spluttered his water all over himself.

'No, Mum, I did not have pubic lobsters!'

'But you did have crabs, didn't you?' Richard hissed as Mum began faffing about with the *What's On* TV magazine.

I shot him a look. 'Maybe,' I hissed back. 'It was super long ago!'

We both smiled. I was pretty sure Richard was riddled with disease, the amount of escorts he had sex with on a weekly basis. Let us pray he stuck something on the end of it and that my assumptions were hideously incorrect. Especially if, as I feared the worst, he ended up having it off with my sister. I'd seen the way Janice wiggled her hips and threw him backward sex glances. I'd seen the way he'd lapped it up and twinkled his eyes back at her. I hoped to God that I could keep her away from London, and I would most definitely make her remove him from her friend list on Facebook. How? I hear you ask. Because as all elder sisters know, the amount of dirt I had on Janice would be enough to make my mother tie her up and have her reside in the basement until her twenty-first birthday.

'Jam tart anyone?' I sang lightly.

'That would be lovely,' Mum said, 'and if you've got any iced buns, that would be even better!'

Triiiiiiiiiiiiiiiiiiiiiiiiiiiiiiiiiiiiing the doorbell rang again. We all looked around.

'Aren't you going to answer the door?' Mum questioned.

Trrrrrrrriiiiiiiiiiiiiiiiiiiiiiiiiiiiiiing! Triiiiiiiiiiiiiiiiiiiiiiiiiiiiiiiiiiiiiiiiiiiiiiiing!

'Ach!' she said, putting her hands on her ears. 'My eardrums are going to perforate if you don't get a move on and answer your door!'

'OK, OK, I'm coming,' I huffed. I didn't have octoarms. I couldn't do a zillion things at once. There I was trying to appease Mother, Richard, make more tea and locate iced buns and jam tarts in the fridge, praying they were still in date or else I'd never hear the end of it.

'Bailey?' I said, shocked to the core. Once again, I looked like I'd been dragged through a hedge backwards.

'Katie,' he began.

'What are you doing here?' I said, completely taken aback. Oh my God! I twirled round in my mind's eye. He was here, he clearly hadn't forgotten about me, he looked as fresh as a daisy and most unlike someone who'd been up all night partying and having complicated *Kama Sutra* sex with an impossibly long-limbed lingerie model.

'So . . .' I began to speak, my cheeks flushed, a large smile spreading all over my face. A warm glow was rising from the tips of my toes, up and all over my body. Bailey stood there, looking sheepish.

All of a sudden, he was shoved out of the way by a pint-sized blonde. Frenella. What on earth was she doing here?

'Katie, darling,' Frenella simpered before turning to Bailey. 'Offload the rest of the things now please, Sam,' she said as I noticed for the first time that in his hands, Bailey held a large steel box. He passed it to me.

'It's heavy,' he warned.

'What the . . .' I began. Bailey shrugged and turned to go.

'What's going on?' I demanded.

'Ooooh, tinkles, it's *soooooooooo* super exciting.' Frenella jigged on her vertiginous heels. This time they were bright pink. She was wearing cut-off denim hotpants and a loose shirt. Mum would probably faint at the sight of so much leg. Bailey stood by the car, smoking a cigarette and looking forlornly at his feet. Hanna Frost emerged from the back seat along with Aubrey. What on earth was going on? Why was half of the Poets Field PR team here? Another car whizzed up and parked neatly behind Bailey's black Range Rover. Hanna passed Bailey another box and shoved several long clothes carriers on to his shoulders. He nearly buckled with the weight of it all. His cigarette smouldered by his feet.

'Darrrrllling,' Hanna cooed, as she opened the door

and air-kissed Magenta Rubenstein. God, it was full-on PR royalty here. Curtains were twitching next door as Richard came up behind me and rested his hands on my shoulders.

'I didn't know about this,' he said softly.

'What's going on?' I turned to him.

'I don't know, Katie,' he said, squeezing my shoulders.

Magenta, Hanna and Aubrey moved up my garden path towards my front door with Bailey trailing behind them laden down with various bits and bobs of the fashion and beauty variety. Frenella B had already pushed past me and was now getting acquainted with my mother. Oh God . . . I thought. I plastered on a fake smile and prayed my mother didn't bring up STDs or call me useless and fat in their company. It was a daily struggle to appear as though I was 'one of them' and now, thanks to *Sizzle Stars'* glorious interview and the photos of my flawless and peachy self, I finally felt like I was making some headway.

'Katie,' Magenta said, bringing me close for an air kiss on both cheeks.

'Come in, come in,' I said gaily.

'Remember, don't offer them carbs!' Richard said quietly in my ear. 'I'll go to the shop now and buy in some salads and salmon for lunch later on,' he said, squeezing past me and acknowledging the women and Aubrey before throwing a manly nod to Bailey.

As Hanna, Aubrey and Magenta busied themselves with the bags, boxes and clothing hanger things, I noticed as I closed my front door that Richard appeared to be in deep conversation with a worried-looking Bailey. I wondered what they were talking about. I prayed that Bailey was simply going with Richard to Waitrose and not to the corner shop, where all they could buy was pork pies, stale sandwiches and a selection of crisps. I also prayed that Bailey wasn't going back to bed with Carolina Fernando for more exciting posh sex. Before I had the chance to watch where they were going, Magenta had hooked her arm through mine and pushed me into my living room.

'Gosh! What a marvellous surprise!' I said, standing above everyone who had, without asking first, taken a seat and made themselves very comfortable. My mother was chattering away to Frenella, using her irritating posh voice that was reserved for the residents of Little Glove, the vicar and anyone else important with an air of authority. Everyone else got short shrift most of the time, but if she encountered anyone she deemed to be slightly above us, out came the Queen's English with the crossed legs and the pursed lips.

'Kate,' Hanna began, 'I appreciate that this visit is unexpected and for that I sincerely apologize.'

'It's really OK, there's no need . . .' I began. What planet was Hanna Frost living on? She was acting completely alien! She was friendly, her voice was soft and she was wearing gloss instead of her usual brash scary lipstick. She had on cotton trousers and a plain t-shirt. She still looked good, albeit slightly dumpy without her massively high heels. Hanna Frost was actually, beneath all the make-up and the strange designer clothes she wore, a very plain woman. There was nothing special about her, apart from the selection of expensive accessories and her super-duper fast sports car. For the first time in the entire time I'd known her, I didn't feel like the ugly one.

'Now, darling, I know that I said nothing would be happening for a few days but unfortunately in this crazy, fast-paced, uber-glamorous world we live in here at Poets Field, things can change at the last minute.'

I looked at her blankly.

'We're here because today you are having the makeover to end all makeovers.'

'Seriously?' I breathed. Did this mean they were going to make me look as hot as I did in *Sizzle Stars*? If that was the case, then I prayed that this time Bailey could stay away until I was complete. That way, for once, I would get to show him my fabulous side. God knows, he so needed to see it.

'Aubrey has brought you some Botox.'

'What?' my mother shrieked. Argh! I cringed. I knew that she'd find some way of embarrassing me to death. 'Botox?'

'Yes, Mrs Lewis, it's a wonderful addition to Western women's beauty regime.' Aubrey said politely. What is it with everyone being super nice? Could it be Mum's presence?

'Darling,' Mum wafted her hand dismissively, 'Kate doesn't need Botox. As you can tell from looking at my wrinkle-free face, we Lewis women have followed the family secret of soap and water for generations and remained free from looking our true age.' Mum winked around the room. 'You would never in a million years guess that I am actually a woman of fifty-six,' she said smugly.

Actually, we would. She did look her age, she did have wrinkles, but in all honesty, she didn't look haggard or worn out. But then she didn't smoke, rarely drank and used a heck of a lot of moisturizer. She never went out in the sun without a hat on and hadn't ever graced a sun bed. I wondered how awful I was going to look at her age, with the amount of sunbathing I had already done. Thankfully, Hanna et al humoured her and the conversation took a positive turn as everyone began to swap beauty secrets and tips. With Mum suitably tied up waffling to Magenta about Olay Regenerist, Aubrey and Hanna took me into the kitchen to discuss cosmetic surgery.

'As you know,' Hanna said gently – how strange, Mum is out of earshot, yet she's still being over-the-top nice to me. Maybe I'd just run into her the week she had severe PMT or something? Maybe her PMT lasted a fortnight? Who knew? Hanna continued, 'You failed to get the go-ahead from the Brand New You clinic for a breast augmentation.'

'Yes, I know, stupid decision,' I muttered. Aubrey shot me a glance and prodded me in the back.

'But all is not lost,' Hanna said, as she pulled out a couple of leaflets with happy-looking women on them looking incredibly line-free, buxom and radiant. Slogans were splashed across them.

I have the confidence to go outside my house now, thanks to Botox!

I don't have to worry about showing up my mega young boyfriend, now I have Botox to chase away my wrinkles!

'Mmmm,' I mused. 'Interesting. So how long does it take?'

'It's instant,' Aubrey said, as I noticed him opening one of the silver boxes and a packet of antiseptic wipes.

'Um, I'm not really comfortable with my mother being privy to this, um, get-together, you know . . .'

'Oh right, as you wish, Katie,' Hanna said.

'So, how do you get rid of her?' Aubrey blurted out.

I was about to answer when there was a clattering by the door as Richard stumbled through, laden down with shopping bags.

'Lunch,' he announced and pushed his way past Hanna and Aubrey to dump the plastic bags on the breakfast bar. Disappointingly, Bailey didn't follow him inside. Where could he have gone?

'We have salmon, eggs, salad and green tea!' He looked around, smiling.

'That sounds disgusting,' my mother said.

'Well, you don't have to eat it,' I snapped. Where is Bailey? I wondered, gazing towards the window before turning back to face Mum.

'Let me fix you something else up?'

'No, dear, I want to go home.'

Thank the Lord!

'Can you call Janice for me? She gave me a lift on her way to her sixth form thing this morning.'

'Bit of a detour?' I said, surprised. I assumed Mum had come by train.

'Yes, well, apparently she had a trip to a museum this morning, so I allowed her to take the car on condition she drove me here first.'

School trip my arse, I bet she's shopping in Topshop as we speak, with a gaggle of her friends.

'Bailey will take your mother home,' Magenta announced, as she tapped some numbers into her BlackBerry Pearl.

'Nooooooo!' I said a bit too loudly. All heads swung round to look at me. 'I meant, I'm sure that Janice will be more than happy to drive Mum home, after all, it is lunch-time, and I'm sure her trip is over by now. I mean, how long does it take to look at a few fossils and paintings?' I smiled sweetly.

'No trouble at all, Katie, after everything you've done for us, and what you are doing for us in the future, it's absolutely no problem at all for us to lay on your driver to accommodate your family's needs.' I look to the window and spy Bailey, finally, tapping his mobile phone with no idea he was about to be rudely interrupted.

I'm gobsmacked. Magenta is tripping over herself to be nice to me, I feel like a princess, and as I look around, everyone aside from my sour-faced mother, is glaring at me like a Stepford Wife. I wondered, what could they know that I didn't? I got the distinct impression that something was amiss. Call it gut instinct, but something was up.

'Bailey, darling, can you drive Katie's mother back to her house in Little Glove please? Yes . . . Uh huh . . . the same place as before. Straight away. Yes. Fabulous.' She snapped the phone shut.

'Your carriage awaits,' Richard said, holding out his hand for her to lean on as she pulled herself to her feet. He handed her her massive bag, which she took and slung over her shoulder.

'Bye, Mum,' I said, moving over for a hug.

'Take care,' she said. 'I will call you later, heaven knows why I bother, though – you never answer your phone.' She said her goodbyes and waddled off to the car.

I raced out afterwards. Maybe if I could whisper something to Richard about asking Bailey what was going on with us, he could intervene on my behalf and decipher all this crazy business with Bailey and his moods. On second thoughts, Mum was still wittering on about the perils of leaving messages on answerphones and Richard, ever the gent, was humouring her gently. I could see Bailey over their shoulders looking taught and tanned, leaning casually against the car, smoking another cigarette. No wonder he was inwardly stressed, all that nicotine can't be good for him. Also, I could hardly ask Richard about Bailey when I hadn't 'fessed up about what had actually happened between us. 'Safe journey,' I called out after them as they manoeuvred my mother into the back of the car. I imagined she would be furiously waving out of the blacked-out window, so I waved back. Bailey slammed her door shut and went to get into his side of the car. Richard was striding back across the road and up towards the garden path. Bailey gave me a salute and winked. Cheeky, I thought, and gazed longingly back at him.

'OK, what's going on?' Richard said, standing next to me on the step as I watched them drive away.

'What do you mean?' I smirked.

'I saw that look – that was a wink that said he'd had you naked and that was a gaze that said you wanted more . . .'

'How on earth did you get that from just a wink and a look?' I said, suddenly feeling really exposed. How did Richard guess? And if he guessed, had anyone else? No, surely not – for one, we'd hardly spoken in front of anyone.

'Darling, I am an expert in love games,' he said.

'How did you know?'

'It was pretty obvious.'

'Oh . . . well . . . Now the cat's out of the bag, what should I do?' I looked up at him, a worried expression on my face.

'What do you mean?' he said sarcastically. 'I haven't seen a cat aside from your mangy one inside. God, Katie, no one buys moggies any more, you import pedigree ones from abroad.'

'Shut up, there's nothing wrong with my cat,' I said grumpily. He was avoiding my question.

'So, you had sex with Bailey?' Richard said, pulling a cigarette out of his pocket.

'I did,' I said, sinking down on to the doorstep. Richard joined me, and held out his cigarette packet for me to take one.

'Thanks,' I said, lighting up. The nicotine sure helped me in times of stress.

'And he's acting really weird, like, he left really suddenly after we'd, you know, done it,' I blushed furiously. 'And he hasn't called me . . . no explanation as to where he went and then he just shows up on my doorstep says "Hello", buggers off to Waitrose with you and throws me a wink.'

'I think,' Richard said slowly, 'that you had fun and you shouldn't think about it, just enjoy it and if anything else happens then great, if not, well, you had a good time, right?'

'Yeah, but . . .'

Gah! Richard was totally avoiding my questions. Why couldn't he analyse? Why couldn't he give me some darned hope? This was a girly conversation and most of the subtle hints about how wretched I felt inside went up and over Richard's head. Oh, how wonderful it must be to live on Planet Boy, with no emotional quandaries, faffing about through life, seeing everything through black and white spectacles. They have it so easy. Non-emotional, commitment-free sex, nothing open to interpretation, straight down the road, simple love life. Argh! I wanted to hit him out of pure gender envy.

'But nothing. It's sex, Katie. Do you want him to be your boyfriend?'

'Um, gosh, that's a bit soon after Jack, I really don't know about that . . .'

'Well, what do you want from him?' Richard said sharply.

'Erm, I don't know. I mean, I guess an explanation, I'd like to know how he feels about me . . . what he thinks . . . if he'd like to go on a date with me?'

'Are you serious?' he said, flicking ash into my plant pots.

'Well, yes. Why not? What's wrong with that?'

'Nothing. It's just a bit like opening your presents before Christmas.'

'Oi!' I said, nudging him. 'It wasn't like that.'

'How was it, then?' Richard said dryly. 'The world's biggest romance? Hearts and flowers? Poems and songs?'

'No, but it was electric. We had dynamite sex.'

'Katie, you do know that Bailey is, how shall I put it, popular and sociable?'

'You mean he's a player? I fucking knew it! God, this means I've been played, doesn't it? Oh, it's so bloomin' obvious now, I hate players!'

'Don't hate the player . . .'

'Excuse me?'

'It's a man thing. You need to understand. Don't hate the player, don't hate the game . . . hate yourself for taking part.'

I looked at him blankly.

'Katie, think of yourself as a roast dinner. You know how you wait for hours and hours before you get your roast dinner?'

'And it's over in five minutes?' I sniggered.

'No,' Richard smiled wryly. 'I mean, if you package yourself as a microwave meal, easily accessible, quick to prepare, cheap . . .'

'Oh, I see where you're going with this. So, you think Bailey now thinks of me as a Pot Noodle or something? Dirty and grubby but undeniably tasty,' I said, humouring him. I just don't believe that all men think like this. It can't be true.

'I'm saying that if you offer yourself on a plate, he's not going to come back for seconds unless he's going through a dry spell.'

'So now I'm tantamount to a box of Micro Chips. Do I have no hope of getting Bailey to take me to The Dorchester like Fabio Matravers?'

'You went out with Fabio? How are you still alive?' he said, in reference to Hanna's strop at me for accepting Fabio's business card back at the ranch.

'Hanna knew. She orchestrated it, apparently.'

'Interesting,' Richard said, pursing his lips.

'What?' I said. 'What is it? What is it you know that I don't?'

'Well, it's just that Fabio Matravers doesn't have anything to do with Hanna, as far as I know, in fact, I would go so far as to say that he dislikes her, but then I could be wrong.'

'Why would he dislike Hanna?' I said.

'You have to ask?' Richard laughed.

'Well, she seems perfectly fine to me today,' I shrugged.

'That's because you're winning for her. Your fabulous interview has reflected greatly upon Hanna. This means Magenta sucks up to her, Frenella continues to dance to her tune and as for Bailey, well, less said about that the better.'

'What do you mean?' I said, worried.

'Well, let's just say . . .'

'Kate?' Hanna said, standing behind us and looking down her nose.

'Hanna!' we both said in unison.

'We were just talking about you,' Richard said, as he flicked the end of his cigarette into the neighbour's garden.

'No, we weren't,' I said.

'Just joking,' Richard chortled, as he clambered to his feet and pulled me up.

'I don't care what you're doing, but what I do care about is that Magenta is inside sipping green tea and awaiting the presence of our little soon-to-be celebrity. And what is she doing? Smoking like a chav on her doorstep with you, the biggest lothario London has seen since Darren Day was in town.'

'Sorry, we were just getting some air, my mother can be a handful at times,' I said quietly.

'I see where you get it from now,' Hanna sniped, as she turned on her heels and walked back into my house.

'The cheek of it,' I muttered to Richard.

'Ignore and smile, ignore and smile . . .' Richard said under his breath.

'Just one more thing, is Bailey interested in me?' I said, looking at Richard, dying for his opinion.

He opens his mouth to speak, but doesn't get the chance. Frenella has now wafted in, hooked his arm and dragged him to the sofa for a chat. He doesn't seem to mind – as I watch him scan her body, taking in her little curves and plastic boobs.

'Don't look so alarmed,' Aubrey says, as he stands there in a white coat with a syringe in his hand. He looks like something from a horror movie.

'Listen, I never got to ask earlier, but why are you all here?' I say, hoping I don't sound ungrateful.

'Darling! How awful of us not to say!' Magenta coos. 'It's the film premiere of East End gangster flick *Murked* in Leicester Square tonight and you have been invited by Danny Divine, the most attractive and suave Bond-a-like man on the British film scene at the moment!' She clasps her hands together in pure delight. I make a mental note to escape to my bedroom to Google Danny Divine. Now it made sense. They wanted me to cosy up to this actor guy for good publicity. Hmm . . . well, let's just hope he's as gorgeous as all the other actor-type men in London.

'I am here to prep you on how to behave,' Hanna informs me. 'Aubrey is qualified to give cosmetic injections.' She nods over at Aubrey who smiles back at me.

'Frenella's going to do your mani-pedis – it's her sideline – and Magenta is here to oversee everything. Ziggy Wang is coming over to give you a blow-dry and style your hair into something totally out of this world and Tom has selected some outfits for you to choose from for tonight's extremely important soirée. You must look absolutely flawless. No food stains on your outfit, which means you have to say "No thank you" to the canapés. Besides, no up-and-coming celebrity ever eats, certainly not in public.'

'What do you mean, no one eats?' I say, shocked. I have to eat! I would die without my food.

'Come off it, Katie. Your fans may identify with you because you're tipping the scales the wrong side of eleven stone, but the fatty fan base is minute compared to the legion of lithe teenagers who eat, sleep, breathe and shit Jessica Hilson.'

My stomach lurches. Coffee . . . that will help. I move to the kettle and fill it up with more water.

'And let's not forget the teenage boys, their elder brothers and their fathers!' Aubrey interjects.

'Yes. One, you have successfully managed to achieve the dream that the ordinary girl can make it, even at a size fourteen.'

'Yes, and I'm happy about that!' I say, smiling.

'You had your cake, you've eaten it, now it's time to diet,' Aubrey says, grabbing my back fat. God, it's not like you can even see my back fat unless you grab it like a bloomin' pincher.

'Two,' Hanna continues, 'you have to begin to live the dream. It's not attractive in the world of celebrity to be normal. It's not attractive to be blubbery. It's not attractive to have anything less than the utmost perfection. You now have to model yourself on starlets like, and I hate to say it, but it's deathly true, like Jessica Hilson. She's the one who everybody, including your beloved Jack Hunter, loves, and she's the one whose name is on tons of merchandise, she's the one who has her own reality show starting at Christmas and she's the one that everybody, including you, especially you, wants to be like.'

I gasp. This is unreal. Reality show at Christmas? Jack really will be famous. I feel sick. What are they doing to me? Is this bad? Or is it good? The jury was still out on that one.

'Um, well,' I begin.

'Let's make no bones about it. Thin and beautiful and perfect is in, and that is what you will be. You're incredibly lucky that you have the best in the business helping you live the dream. Tonight, you are stepping out in the most expensive clothes, with the most attractive man in London, and you are going to dazzle and shine and every girl in the country is going to be lapping up your interview in *Sizzle Stars* tomorrow. This is how you are going to get revenge on Jessica Hilson, you will surpass her, YOU will be the BEST!' Hanna is tomato red. She thumps her hand on the table.

'What about Fabio?' I say meekly. Aubrey raises an eyebrow and looks away. Magenta is immersed in my *What's On* TV guide, and Frenella is busy giggling at Richard's bad jokes.

'Forget him, it was one night, get over him, move on . . .' Hanna says, a little too knowingly.

'Right . . .' I say, feeling slightly bruised. Did she mean Bailey or did she really just mean Fabio? Fabio! I thought I had a date with him, ooooh gosh, when was it? Ah, that's right, I remembered. He will call me. Where did I put my phone? I scrabbled in the pocket of my dressing gown. God, I really ought to get dressed!

'This all sounds perfect and mega exciting,' I said to Hanna, whose face lit up at my reaction to her crazy, celebrity, image-obsessed, vacuous outpourings. 'I'll just go get changed, won't be a minute,' I said, leaving them to it.

'Don't be too long, the jabs are ready now,' Aubrey sang after me.

Right, I thought to myself as I entered my bedroom and closed the door quietly behind me. The cat purred on the bed, sleeping cosily amongst the goose pillows. I flicked open my Mac and set about doing some extreme Googling. Whilst the machine was powering up, I pulled on my black sweatpants and a Gap t-shirt and took out a packet of baby wipes and removed last night's make-up.

Ding! The computer indicated that I had messages.

One from Janice, about what colour highlights I have had done and whether or not I could wangle her an appointment at Ziggy Wang's. Not on your nelly, I thought.

No important emails. Hmm . . . I wondered. Why had none of the girls I sat with at work emailed me to ask for the gossip? I also wondered whether I could locate Nicola Baxter on Facebook and find out why she was sabotaging my credibility. Bitch, I thought, she always did have a nasty streak in her. I typed in her name and about a dozen different Nicola Baxters popped up. I found the one I was looking for, pressed 'Add as a friend' and forgot about it. I'd check later. I scanned my room for my phone and found it on the bedside table. I picked it up and scrolled through my messages.

U looked cute 2day, B

Ooooh!! I giggled. It was from Bailey! Saying I looked cute!! He wasn't an arsehole after all! Right, must text back . . . but what to say? I wanted to ask him how he felt about me, whether his tummy did flips at the mere sight of me in my posh dressing gown. I already figured out that clothes were not all that important to him. He had ravaged me, after all, on disgustingly unfashionable bedsheets while I was wearing tartan pyjamas. Also, he only seemed to own one very tight, easy-on-the-eye, white t-shirt. He always wore his skinny jeans and he always had on his white trainers. He always looked ripped and sexy and smouldering. He always looked as though he had literally fallen out of bed and into his clothes, yet his tousled hair and easy-going aura suited him down to the ground. Richard and Jack, however, would give Cristiano Ronaldo a run for his money on the metrosexual-o-meter. Jack was always *always* in a pair of tight Levi's with a variety of tight t-shirts imported from America (on my credit card) over which he wore a blazer. He would top it all off with his ridiculously overpriced leather jacket that looked as though he'd picked it up from Whitechapel market, his Wayfarers and a distressed-leather man-bag. He didn't smoke, preferring to chew gum and ponce about with fruit and bags of macadamia nuts. He wore pale pink t-shirts, had a diamond stud in his left ear and used hair straighteners. Jack was the colour of David Dickinson. Richard was slightly more macho, preferring to wear navy-blue suits, often with a low-slung shirt so you could get a glimpse of his chest hair. Richard didn't wear earrings, was the colour of golden sand and had his hair cut so short it looked as though he was wearing a helmet. It was thick and short, a bit like Jack. They both had short man syndrome and delusions of grandeur. Richard, however, was confident, arrogant, in love with himself, but with a roguish charm and a loveable nature. Jack simply thought only of himself, how he looked to other people and about being seen in the West End bars – without me. I wasn't quite so cool in my food-stained clothes, my oversized sweatpants, my scruffy hair and my penchant for ripped tights. Honestly, I thought they made me look edgy. When I asked Richard if he thought I looked like a hooker he gave a resounding 'no'. The hookers, sorry, high-class girls he picked up for £300 an hour, wore stockings woven with gold. As for me, I looked like a Hoxtonite. So what, it was my style and I didn't care. Before I had a chance to text Bailey back, there was a quiet knock as the door opened.

'Danielle?' I said, surprised. What was it about people coming over today uninvited?

'Hey, honey,' she said, 'can I come in?'

'Sure,' I said, and she walked towards me for a hug before sitting down on the bed.

'Gorgeous sheets, are these the ones we bought the other day?'

'Yep, the very ones.'

'I tried texting you to see if you were in . . . wasn't sure what with all the crazy stuff that's been going on around you this past week. I'm sorry I've been so weird with you . . .'

'Hey, it's OK,' I said, as I sat down next to her to comfort her. She really didn't seem herself. I glanced at my phone and sure enough the other two texts were from Danielle, along with one from Richard demanding I open my front door this morning. Nothing from Jack, but then I had almost given up on hearing from him.

'I brought you a gift,' she said, passing me a parcel wrapped in swirly pink paper with a glittery pink bow on it. Totally girly and over the top – I loved it!

'Oh my God, Danielle, you shouldn't have!' I squealed, as I took the parcel from her hands and began to rip it open.

I pulled out, from beneath lashings of tissue paper, a beautiful black velvet diamanté . . . bra?

'It's a Wonderbra,' Danielle smiled. 'You know, I thought it was fitting.'

'Wow,' I said, fingering the little white diamonds. 'Thanks! And yes, it is fitting. Oh, babe, you're so sweet, I can't believe you did this for me!'

'Well,' she said, grinning, 'I'd like it if you could give this a whirl before you, well, you know how I feel . . .'

'Babe,' I began, before the door creaked open again. We both looked up.

'Kate, the jabs are ready now.'

Danielle's face dropped as Hanna stood in the doorway.

'Jabs?' Danielle queried.

'Botox,' I said to her, feeling really anxious now. I totally didn't want a stand-off between us here, right in front of everyone.

'OK,' she said, looking a bit forlorn. I could tell she was mega unimpressed and was battling not to show it. I had felt distant from her since last week. I knew something was bugging her, but she wouldn't give it up and tell me.

'HANNA!' Aubrey wailed from the kitchen. 'These jabs need to be done!'

Hanna turned her head briefly, spun back and gave me a look before turning once again back downstairs towards the kitchen.

'Danielle, are you OK?' I said, putting my arm around her shoulder.

'I'm fine, but I have something to tell you and I don't think you'll like it, but I swear to you, I'm doing my best

243

to have the right thing happen, but sometimes, you just can't control how people feel and before you know it, certain relationships are formed and there's no going back . . .' Danielle looked on the verge of tears.

'Babe, you're talking in riddles, what do you mean? What relationships? Has Stewart let you down again? Is that what this is about?' I queried. Nothing made any real sense at the moment. All I had to go on were cryptic clues and tearful confessions These lawyers didn't half dress their issues up.

'OK, in simple terms . . .'

'Kate, NOW,' Hanna barked.

Danielle and I sprang back. She pulled a tissue from the box on my bedside table and blew her nose. She took another and wiped her eyes. She smiled brightly. 'I'm going to go now, call me when you're free,' she said, standing up.

Before I could protest, Hanna was saying her goodbyes and practically shoving Danielle out of the door. I swear I heard Hanna hiss, 'How did you get in here?' to her, but I couldn't be sure. All I knew was my confident, full-of-life, ball-busting bitch (but in a nice way) bestest friend in the entire world was in some kind of trouble and I should be there to help. What kind of a friend was I, just letting her go off into the afternoon without giving her a chance to tell me what she came here for? I got up and looked for my trainers. Maybe if I leave now I can catch up with her.

'Hanna, I won't be long,' I said, heading for the door.

'Where are you going?' she questioned.

'To catch Danielle. She's upset, I just know it, and I'm her best friend and I need to be there for her, I'm sure you can all wait for fifteen minutes. I know this is inconvenient for you, I'm sorry, but I have to do this.' I pulled on my denim jacket.

'Sure, I understand,' said Hanna gently.

'You do?' I said, surprised.

'Yes, of course I do. If she was my best friend and there was something wrong I would be out there too, trying to find out what it was and offering her my undivided attention, my unwavering support, regardless.'

'Oh, right, then,' I said, feeling a little uneasy.

'But my best friend isn't about to become an overnight celebrity. Is she?'

'Um, I don't know . . . I mean, I guess . . .' Hanna had me rooted to the spot. I was so incredibly torn between wanting to be with Danielle and also being super aware of the fact that there were people here, for me, to help me, to get one over on Jessica Hilson and my stupid ex-boyfriend. They'd gone to so much effort too. Over and above, beyond and all that jazz, that's what Hanna said the other day, wasn't it?

'Personally, I think Danielle has a lot to answer for,' Hanna said, snidely. 'She came over here unannounced.'

'But . . .' I began to tell her it wasn't entirely unannounced, Danielle had texted me, it's just my phone had been in the bedroom. Besides, that's how our friendship worked, it wasn't like how I imagined Hanna's friendships would work, I didn't have to page her or call her weeks in advance or book into her diary or check in with her PA, no, we always turned up unexpectedly to see each other and it was always a priority to make time for each other. We'd been known to throw sickies here and there in aid of emotional crises of the boyfriend kind, where chocolate cake and trips to the salon were necessary for the broken-hearted. Man problems were in such abundance that we were on first-name terms with the beauty therapists and would get free cakes from the cake shop on our birthdays.

'She is a very selfish friend,' Hanna continued, shrugging.

'No, she's not! She's a wonderful friend, she's thoughtful and caring and kind and . . . and . . .'

I wanted to scream at her, 'Everything you're not!' but refrained.

'Sorry, Hanna, I'm just worried and I really ought to catch her up.'

'Well, you can't,' Hanna put her hand up.

'I think you'll find I can . . .' I said, nudging past her to the door.

'Well, unless you have rockets on your shoes, an exhaust poking out of your backside and an engine in your belly, mind you, with all that water retention you carry, it's not impossible . . . you won't catch her.'

'What on earth are you talking about?' I said, my blood pressure rapidly rising. Engine in my belly? I was becoming sick of the fat jokes. So bloody what, honestly anyone would think I was a Ten Ton Tessie. And there I was, thinking it was only geriatrics and pre-menopausal family members who saw fit to make comments about my shape.

'Kate,' Hanna said softly, her face rapidly changing from smacked in the face with a trout to calm and angelic.

How did she do it? I wondered.

I pursed my lips.

'She got in a car and drove off.'

'Ah,' I said, realizing, duh, of course she got in her car, she wasn't car-less like me, she didn't take the smelly Tube or the packed bus to work, she drove in her sexy sports car.

'Silly me,' I said, looking at my feet. I could feel my cheeks flush red.

'Darling,' Hanna said, putting a hand on my shoulder, 'I admire you, I respect you even, your keenness to be there for your friend, your courage in the face of celebrity-boyfriend-stealer adversity, your determination to fit in with the elite.'

'You do?' I said, thinking, was that just a barrage of back-handed compliments complete with barbed wire wrapped around them, or was she actually, honestly being nice? I zoned out as she steered me towards the living room and into the kitchen. I noticed Richard giving Frenella the thumbs up as she twirled in a bright blue backless dress and giggled some more. Some journalist she was, I thought. She was supposed to be intelligent, good with words, all I ever heard from her was 'Fierce!' 'Tinkles!' and 'OMFG!' Seriously. Stupid bimbo.

'Thank the Lord, I was about to declare you MIA.'

'What?' I said, puzzled. Seriously, these guys needed to come with a translator. 'I'm not down with the kids,' I said, attempting to make light of the situation and sounding less like a cool person and more like a bad Ali G impersonator.

Hanna and Aubrey both ignored me and sat me down on my breakfast-bar stool and wiped my face with antiseptic wipes.

'Can I have the boob-job jab too?' I asked, feeling slightly nervous but also tingling with excitement.

'Botox first,' Aubrey said, administering the drug the way psycho doctors do in horror movies.

Drops of the liquid spat out into the air.

'Macrolane is out for now,' he said, concentrating on my brow bone.

'Don't move, Katie, unless you want a paralysed cheek,' Hanna said.

'Ouccchhhh,' I said, as I felt the needle sting my temple.

'Nearly done . . .' Aubrey said gently. 'The Macrolane is out for now because although I was more than happy to give you 100ml in each breast, which would have taken you up to a size oooh, um, what size are you now? An A?'

'B.'

'OK, well it would have taken you up to a D.'

'Oh, wow, please, please, please give me bigger boobs, Aubrey, it's so mega important to me, go on, please!' I begged shamelessly.

'No,' he said as he pulled the needle from my head and refilled. 'Macrolane will hurt.'

'I don't care!' I said. God, had I been brainwashed or something?

'It will hurt a lot, it will feel as though you've been kicked in the chest by someone really fat wearing wedges, and it will take about three days before you won't scream every time anyone tries to hug you. It's just not a good option when you are going to have to move with complete ease and grace with Danny Divine across the red carpet on Leicester Square this evening.'

'Ooh,' I said, pondering that fact. He did have a very good point. And he wasn't telling me that I could never do it, he was just saying that it wasn't going to happen today. I thought about the Wonderbra sitting on my bed. That would have to do for now.

'We brought you these,' Hanna said, slapping two clear jelly balls into my lap. They looked like chicken fillets.

'Breast enhancers,' Hanna said. 'They fit into your bra, *et voilà*! Bigger boobs and a cleavage to die for.'

'I use them!' Frenella twittered. 'My turn now, Dr Aubrey!'

'You can get down now, Kate, you're done,' Aubrey said, blushing at Frenella. 'I'm not a real doctor.'

'Cripes!' I said. 'I hope you knew what you were doing!' I felt a little bit freaked out.

'Don't have a cow, Katie, he's a doctor of beauty, he's a cosmetic doctor, he's a doctor all right, just not a proper one who gives you Valium or whatever,' she simpered as she sat back on the chair and clipped her fringe away from her eyes and forehead. I stood there, unsure as to what I should do next, holding a pair of boob enhancers.

Triiiiiiiiiiiiiiiiiiiiiiiiiiiiiiiiiiiing the doorbell went for what felt like the zillionth time that day. I walked to the front door and opened it.

'Darrrrliiing, oooh you look peachy!' Tom Theodore almost did one of those little ankle click jumps famed by pixies in the forest. He kind of looked like one too, although as mentioned previously, Tom Theodore had a face that could melt a million women's hearts. He was super stylish, which was obvious of course, because that's his job. He gripped me tight against his hard body.

'Ooomph!' I said, holding tight to the jelly boobs.

'I have with me the most fabulous gown!' he said, and I smiled warmly.

'What happened to your face?' he asked, pointing to my forehead.

'What? Oh that? It may not move for a while, I just had Botox!'

Tom looked traumatized. 'Ewwwww!' he said, pulling a tissue from his pocket. 'You're bleeding!'

'OH MY GOD!' I squealed, as blood trickled down the side of my head. I raced to the mirror and mopped it up.

'Chillax,' Aubrey called from the kitchen. 'Hold the tissue on it for five minutes, hard, and you'll be right as rain.'

'You so didn't need to do that,' Tom said, looking at me, concern swept across his face.

'I didn't?' I said, feeling really confused.

'She totally did,' Hanna said, appearing like a spectre in the corner. They shared a look. I sensed that something was going on between them and not in the *I love you* sense.

'No, she didn't.' Tom stood his ground. Hand on hip, he minced into the living room, knocking Hanna out of the way.

'*Excuse me*!' Hanna said, a look of horror on her face.

'*Excuse me*,' Tom spat back, 'but the last time I checked, girls in their mid-twenties didn't need their faces ironed out by Botox. What were you thinking, Frost?'

Hanna stared at him. I thought, this is it, any minute now he'll turn to pure stone.

'Tom, you totally need to catch up with what's hip and hot right now. I think you'll find that eight out of ten women under the age of thirty are familiar with a vast array of cosmetic enhancements and I will also tell you Tom, FYI, I have plenty of aesthetic practitioners attached to plenty of young girls on my list.' She stood there with her hands on her hips.

'Whatever,' Tom wafted his hand at her and turned his back. Hanna's face was a picture. Honestly, if looks could kill, Tom would be totally dead.

'Darling, I have for you beauty in a bag!' he said. '*Au naturel*,' he winked, as he laid out the sheath on the sofa and carefully unzipped it.

'But I've already got all these other choices,' I said, gesturing to the pile of clothes that had been brought in earlier. But before I could protest too much, I noticed the fabric glitter and twinkle.

'Ooooh!' I gasped.

'Isn't it,' Tom cooed, as he pulled the garment out fully, 'to die for!'

There in front of me, was a long, beautiful, white bustier gown. It was stunning!

'I'm in love,' I said slowly, hands clasped together. I was rapidly picking up gay body language as the days went by. I stroked the fabric of the Naeem Khan gown and swooped it from his grasp in order to hold it against myself in front of my hall mirror.

'Whooaah,' Tom shrieked.

'What?' I squealed, nearly jumping out of my skin.

'Food! Make-up! Blood!' he pointed furiously at my face. 'The gown must not be worn under any circumstances until you are completely clean and shiny. The silk in this dress is to die for, the design is unlike any other, the colour is exquisite and the price . . .' Tom gasped theatrically, 'is unmentionable.'

He gathered the dress from my arms and carefully zipped it back into its cover.

'Oh God, Tom, do you have to act as though you're an extra from *Les Misérables*.' Hanna goaded him. Tom ignored her.

'Gross,' Frenella exclaimed, as she held a cotton-wool pad on her swollen forehead.

'We're done here,' Aubrey said, packing up his needles and putting them into his carry case. Magenta put the TV-guide magazine down and sighed dramatically. 'Katie, darling, you are in safe hands now. I believe it is time for me to attend to other, more pressing engagements.'

Beep!

We all look towards the window and see a shiny black limo pull up outside the house.

'Wow,' I exclaim. More posh cars, who is in this one? For a fleeting moment, I wonder if it's Fabio Matravers.

'Our car's here,' Aubrey huffs as he gathers up the rest of his belongings. His coat-tails swing as he lifts his man-bag over his shoulder and wafts out into the living room.

'M'lady,' he says to Magenta, who whinnies as he extends his hand. I swear he said her name through gritted teeth.

The two of them go into the hallway.

'Go,' Hanna says, and I move swiftly after them.

'Thanks for coming and, also, thanks for the head,' I say before quickly realizing my faux pas.

Aubrey's eyebrows shoot up so fast they look as though they are launching into space.

'I mean . . .' I say, my cheeks flushing. I can hear Tom giggling. 'Thank you for the procedures to my head and also, the advice and support, it has been a great honour, Magenta, Aubrey.' I smile at them, baring my teeth.

'Urgh, Katie, you must see this friend of mine,' Aubrey pulls a pen from his top pocket and scribbles a name and number down on the pad beside my, ooh, beside my pros and cons list for dating Jack Hunter. I pray, Please don't notice, please don't notice . . .

'He's a top dental hygienist, will turn those tombstones into pearly gates in no time,' and with that, he flashes a smile that's blinding, and hot-foots it out of the door after Magenta, who is already settling herself into the car. I breathe out deeply. He didn't notice the list, oh God, he would have humiliated me, I know he would have done, it's what he does best. My confidence was like a roller-coaster, up, down and loop the loop. So were the contents of my stomach. So much to think about. What was bugging Danielle? What was Bailey playing at? Why hadn't Fabio called? I closed the door and my eyes for a moment and collected my thoughts. Deep breath in. I had to now walk into Battle Zone Galactica Glamour and negotiate my afternoon with Tom Theodore and Hanna Frost – two giant egos, one living room. However were we going to cope?

Hanna and Tom were getting along as best as they could. There were fake smiles and insincere arm pattings all round. Tom was explaining the 'look' he was going for with me, and Hanna was paying attention. Frenella sat perched on a breakfast-bar stool with one hand on her phone sending text after text and the other on a bloodied cotton-wool pad pressed to her head.

'So,' Hanna said, brightly. 'The look we're aiming for tonight is pure classical glamour girl.'

'You get classical glamour girls?' I said, thinking, surely you just get one or you get the other, not both, not together. Classical, to me, said no boobs. And I sure as hell wasn't going to waste an opportunity to enjoy having a different set of boobs with my Wonderbra and enhancers. No way, they were going to have their moment of glory!

'But the cleavage?' I say, mimicking a pair of boobs with my hands, moving them up and down like some kind of perverted Charlie Chaplin.

'You can still have class and tits,' Tom says, smiling. 'The gown is ultra classy, but with a modern twist, the bustier has an inbuilt corset, we'll wire you in and make a gentle mound on either side, so you won't end up looking like you have two Mitchell brothers stuffed down your top, oh no, we're thinking . . .' he rolls his eyes up to the right-hand side of his brain, splays his hands out ahead of him, '. . . perky,' he says, finally.

'Perky,' I say, deadpan. 'OK?' I look to Hanna. She's not saying a thing.

'Sounds great to me!' I say, clasping my hands together. God, I was getting so good at this. I throw in a little twirl for effect. Tom's face lights up.

'Excellentey! Let's begin!'

The rest of the afternoon passed by in a happy fuzz of hairspray and backcombing. Frenella was absolutely out of this world amazing at doing manicures, my nails were perfect and square tipped. I'd never had posh nails before! I couldn't stop looking at them, all white tipped and sophisticated. Frenella made my feet look resplendent with baby-pink varnish and a full-on scrub of all the hard skin on my heels. Once again, my face was decorated with the best products money could buy. There was even a mineral make-up thing with diamonds in it worth zillions. It's totally true, though, about getting what you kind of pay for. I mean, I hadn't actually paid for any of it, but still the difference between a powder with diamonds in it and my Boots own brand was astonishing. Oooh! It felt so good! Tom painted my lips a beautiful light pink and swept gloss over the top. My eyes were a cream colour with just a dash of black smudged on the outside to create a very light, smoky-eyed look. Long fake eyelashes were glued on and once my blusher was applied, I was done. By the end of the pampering, I felt so unrecognizable I didn't even know my own name. Ziggy Wang arrived to fix my hair, adding a spray that lifted my hair up into voluminous waves. He then fixed in several clip-in hair extensions, and honestly, my hair was as glossy and long as the tail of a horse. I was totally about to outdo Jessica Hilson in the style stakes! I had visions of us both in *Sizzle Stars*, 'Katie v Jessica, Style Wars!' As long as I had this team of beauty magicians behind me, I was confident in winning. Finally, everything was applied and brushed and to top it off, a little shoulder massage from Ziggy Wang's assistant left me suitably relaxed. With a hairdo that bounced with body and was so uber-primped and preened to perfection, I felt as though I was messing it up by simply existing within it.

'Wow,' Tom cooed slowly. 'I have never seen a vision *so* super stunning as I see before me right now!'

'Shh,' I giggled, 'you're making me blush!'

'The dress,' he said dramatically, 'is awaiting you.' Tom unzipped it for me to put on. 'Katie Lewis, for tonight and evermore,' I stepped into the dress, excitement bubbling out of every single pore, 'you are . . . a real celebrity!' He gasped and did a little jig as Frenella appeared behind me to zip me into the beautiful gown.

'Jack's going to totally die when he sees this,' Frenella squealed.

'So?' I said, spinning round to face Hanna. 'What do you think?'

'You look . . . exactly how a brand-new, up-and-coming, celebrated person should look,' she said and smiled.

Wow, I thought to myself. I've really arrived if Hanna thinks I'm good.

As Tom and Ziggy Wang busied themselves fixing the last bits of Frenella's beehive, Hanna sidled up to me and whispered, 'You've done Poets Field PR proud, Kate.'

I smiled warmly, she does like me after all!

'For Christ's sake, don't fuck it up,' she hissed, before turning on her heels and walking up to my bathroom.

Chapter 14

8pm

Frenella sits with one leg over the other, wearing an Elie
Saab dress, holding a Lulu Guinness bag. She looks like a
tiny little princess, with glitter dusted upon her tanned
shoulders and little crystal jewels in her blonde beehive.
Hanna stands poised to perfection against the backdrop
of the white curtains of my living room wearing a Hervé
Léger bandage dress. She looks fierce. Amazonian goddess, albeit with no chin. However, she did appear less
horsey than normal today, and her brown chestnut hair
was curled in ringlets which fell loosely down her back.
She had a sensual glow to her which matched her coral-
pink lipstick to her charcoal grey dress. Her heels were so
high she was in danger of going through the ceiling.

Tom Theodore wore a dapper suit with his hair groomed
to within an inch of its life and Ziggy Wang, who had
decided last minute to come along for the ride, wore distressed leather with a fitted shirt. I couldn't quite work out
whether it was a fashion disaster or not, but then I wasn't
exactly skilled at spotting designer this or designer that.

'I'll be back in a minute,' I said, as I lifted my dress from
the floor and shuffled up to my bedroom. Everyone had
their eyes fixed on the window, waiting for our limo to
arrive. For once, they barely noticed me leave the room.

Safe and secure in my bedroom, I gently sat down upon

the beautiful KATY sheets and rubbed the material of my Sonata throw between my fingers. It felt so luxurious. I glanced up and caught sight of myself in the full-length mirror. I didn't recognize the reflection staring back at me for a minute, but I saw my eyes, underneath the false lashes, I saw myself, and I saw for the first time in months, a happy version of myself. I was glowing. My dress really was amazing. I sighed heavily. I was afraid, but of what?

'What are you so scared of?' I whispered in the mirror.

8.30pm

'Can I come in?' the voice of Tom Theodore wafted through the crack of my door.

'Sure,' I said, standing up to greet him.

'Ahhhh, Katie, darling,' he said, pulling me in for a hug.

'Careful!' I yelped. 'My hair!'

'Ahhhh, you are already talking like a celebrity, darling, "Oooh! My hair! My dress!"' he mocked me gently.

'Oi!' I jabbed him in the arm. 'It's taken hours to get me looking like a superstar, baby!' I said, moving my head to one side and grinning wildly.

'We only enhanced what God gave you, my darling,' he said, winking.

'I am so nervous!' I said. 'On a serious note . . .'

We sat down next to each other on my bed and enjoyed a moment of comfortable silence.

'I'm just not so sure I'll fit in, you know . . . all this glitz and glamour and impossibly skinny girls and, you know, the biscuit dodging. I don't know if I can keep it all up, long term. You know?' I look up at him for support.

'Katie,' he says, reassuringly, 'I have been in this business

many, many years, and it is so rare to come across such natural beauty, so raw, your skin, your hair, your body, so real,
both inside and out. It is sad to see you go down the Botox
route but I understand why you did so . . .'

'You do?' I feel a little humbled by Tom. His vibe is so
caring and nurturing.

'Of course! Girls like you, they arrive fresh-faced and
innocent, and in the end, they become a product of Hanna's circus of celebrated persons. I hate to see you go down
that route,' he takes my hand and places it on my heart.

'See this?'

I nod.

'Feel it.' I nod again, as he closes his eyes and makes the
sound of a heartbeat with his mouth, 'Wawhoosh,' he says,
repeating it under his breath. I close my eyes too. Ooh,
we're really having what one would call a moment. If he
wasn't gay this could quite easily topple any Jack Hunter
sex moment and even my passionate clinch with Bailey.

'It's your heart,' he says, opening his eyes to meet my
gaze. I am enthralled by his passion.

'Listen to it, and always, always, be true to it,' he removes
my hand and kisses it gently.

'I will,' I promise him. 'I promise.'

9pm

This is it, girls. This is it. Deep breath. Must not fuck up
what is potentially the most important night in the entire
history of my social calendar. There is a limo here, and a
door is being opened. Mrs Bellamy is curtain twitching as
predicted. Everyone else is walking ahead, they are walking with grace and they don't appear to be in any danger

of tripping over their own feet, a favourite of mine. Just ask Danielle. She has been embarrassed by me on a zillion different occasions when I have tripped over my own feet in public, often grappling with whoever happens to be near me to avoid collapsing in a heap. Collapsing is so much more endurable if done in twos. Perhaps don't ask Danielle about that one.

I'm nestled in the car, my gown splayed out along the seat. The limo is so large there is enough room for my bottom and another bottom on either side of me. Hanna's skinny rump parks itself in the corner and she gazes out at the bright lights of London town as we snake through Old Street towards Leicester Square. I am so nervous an entire swarm of butterflies are currently doing the rounds in my belly.

'Stop here, thank you,' Hanna barks at the driver.

'What are you doing?' I query. 'We've only just left Shoreditch.'

She turns to face me as the car rolls to a stop.

'What? Did you seriously think that you'd step out on to the red carpet arm-in-arm with Ziggy Wang?'

'Um, well, I don't know, it's not like I do this often, is it?' I mean, just what is the protocol for going to film premieres?

Bzzzzzummm

The window rolled down seamlessly. Another car lay in wait opposite us, a mere three feet away.

'Your car,' Hanna said, pointing, 'awaits you.' She smiled swiftly before her chops turned back to their usual sour look.

'Toodles!' Frenella giggled and waved.

'Good luck, Katie,' Ziggy Wang said. 'Your hair is so

fabulous, keep it fabulous, no tweaking, darling. Here's a compact to check with,' and he slid a mirror into the palm of my hand.

'Thanks,' I replied, a worried look on my face. Why was I being separated? I already felt like peeing all over my seat with nerves, my stomach was in knots, the salmon and salad we had for lunch doing little somersaults, it was a precarious situation, and one that commanded a cigarette, but I wasn't allowed to smoke until after the film which was, like, zonks away.

'Be true,' Tom gestured to his heart with his fisted hand.

I felt as though I was going to war. The door opened before I got the chance to do it myself.

I gasped as a man in a suit and a posh hat on his head beckoned me to follow. I looked back at Tom, whose chocolate eyes met my gaze. He mouthed 'Your heart' at me and thumped his chest. Oh gosh, this was all getting terribly emotional. Must not cry, I thought, as little tears pricked at my eyes. Posh driver quickly ushered me from one car to the other, opening the door and gently shoving me on to the leather seats. My old car geared up and sped off down the road.

'Hey, chick, I'm Danny,' a mawkish-looking geezer boy, who didn't look anything like the most attractive and eligible brand-spanking-new movie star on the London scene, held out his hand in order for me to shake it. I extended my hand.

'Na naaah!' Danny Divine pulled his hand up sharply before I even had a chance to shake it and made a finger-waggling gesture on his nose. He puffed on a rolled-up cigarette.

'Gotcha,' he said, smoke billowing out of his nostrils. I looked at him in complete shock. Oh. My. God. I am one of them! I caught myself pulling a face that my mother would be proud of and thinking thoughts that were well beyond my twenty-six years about respectability and standards and whatnot.

'Hi, I'm Katie and . . .' I think you are vile. No, can't say that. What about, 'Hey, I'm Katie and you're a twat?' No, can't say that. Must smile.

'Yeah, I dig you,' he said, as he slicked his greasy hair off his face. 'You're the hot chick whose dawg left her for an even hotter chick with massive guns, innit?' Danny said.

My eyes widened at the sight of this guy. This pasty chump was talking like he was from the ghetto. Was this how people talked outside of Bethnal Green? I mean, I was as East End as they came, I counted Hackney as my second home, I drank in The Dolphin, I drank shots of Jagermeister and had been known to throw up from drinking too many and then continue. I wasn't exactly posh, not like Hanna Frost and Magenta Rubenstein, oh no, but was this guy for real? He moved closer to me and placed his arm around my shoulder, squeezing me tight. If he so much as touched my new pushed-up mountain-ous boobs, I'd take his ear off.

'Yeah, like, innit?' he continued to puff. Was that? No, it couldn't be?

'Are you smoking pot?' I asked him. I sniffed the air, trying to identify the offending whiff.

'Yeah, want some?' he said, shoving the roll-up into my hand.

'No,' I said, pushing it away. 'Thank you, but no. I'm not to smoke until after the film.'

'We ain't seeing the film, baby girl,' Danny smirked. Urgh. I hope I didn't have to shag him to please Hanna, God no, that was going way above and beyond the call of duty. For a brief moment, I had a hideous thought that it could quite well be nestled in the contract I signed with Poets Field PR between 'new hairdo' and 'Botox'.

Must partake in sexual adventures with Danny Divine. One sex tape must be produced by August – or else! Mwhahahah! I could see Hanna cackling in my mind's eye. I shook my head free of this hideous idea and shoved Danny's stale, sweaty, too-much-Issy-Miyake cologned self as far as he would possibly go across the leather seat.

'Whoah, Shorty,' he said, hands up. 'Whagwan?'

'Excuse me?'

'I said, ahem,' he coughed, 'um, what's the matter?' He looked at his shoes and scuffed an imaginary bit of fluff around the carpet. 'Champagne!' he said, lifting his head, his eyes lit up.

I wasn't entirely sure that Danny Divine wasn't in cloud cuckoo land, dipped in acid. His behaviour was disturbing me. If he touched me again I decided I would scream.

'Yes,' I said, thinking champagne would be a wonderful idea. One, it would take the edge off how nervous I was feeling and two, it would make being in the company of this pseudo gangster a little more bearable. We drove along silently for around twenty minutes, stopping and starting at traffic lights, exchanging wry smiles and kneading our fingers into the car seat. I sipped my drink slowly.

'So,' I said, thinking of polite questions to ask him. 'Is this your first film?'

'Yeah, it's like my first big gangster film.' Danny became animated, his voice high-pitched and loud, and he continued with great gusto. 'Having so many accomplished actors play massive parts, like, against my character, Jealous Mike, well, it's a big deal, which is why I needed a fly girl to be on my side tonight, for publicity,' he winked.

'I see,' I nodded. Fly girl? Shorty? Was he for real? I was at least five eleven in these heels.

'We ain't seeing no film, though,' he said, winking.

Before I had a chance to ask him exactly what we were going to do, the car was surrounded by flashing white light.

'OH MY GOD!' I squealed. 'What's going oooooo-oooon?'

'Shh,' he said, putting his arm around me and drawing me close. I was so freaked out by the commotion outside, the car was rocking slightly, the light was dazzling and there was a dull roar outside, I let him hold me tight. Had we accidentally driven into a riot? I wondered.

'Shh, baby girl,' he pulled me even closer, so that my nose was level with his nipples.

'We're here, this here, Shorty, is the paparazzi, and we gonna step out of this limo to a crowd of fans all here to see me, baby girl, so get with it! Bounce!'

The door flew open and I gulped air into my lungs. He leapt out to rapturous applause.

'Wahoooooooooooooooooooo!' Danny screamed as he unfashionably played air guitar on the red carpet. I was rooted to the spot. There was absolutely no way on earth

I could get out of the car while this guy careered from genre to genre, imitating God knows what on the red carpet, the RED CARPET of a film premiere, my first, the only one I had ever seen that wasn't on the telly. Never fear, Danny was already strutting towards the entrance, before stopping a good ten yards ahead of me. Phew, I thought, time for the grand entrance! I put my hand into a fist and I placed it on my heart. I felt it beat hard and fast in my chest. Listen, feel it, be true. I felt like an advert.

Deep breath . . .

'Let's do this!' I whispered as I lifted one leg and then the other out of the open door of the limo.

OMFG!

Flash! Flash! KATIE!! KATIEEEEEEEEEEEE! *Flash! Flash!* SMILE HERE, OVER HERE, KATIE, AAH THATTA GOOD GIRL, SMASHING, FABULOUS, GORGEOUS, OVER HERE, KATIEEEEEE! *Flash! Boom! Flash! Flash!*

I smiled and I turned every direction there was when I heard someone shriek my name. I posed, looking gorgeously coy with my head cocked slightly, one knee ahead of the other, a glance over the shoulder, a hand on the hip, a big grin. Not too much teeth, lots of pout. Shove boobs forward, not too much. They love me! I am loved! Fuck them all! Who needs Bailey! Who needs Jack Hunter! Who needs a man when you have this!

I felt a hand on my arm, Danny wannabe rude boy Divine laced an arm around the small of my back and posed alongside me for pictures.

PAP! PAP! FLASH! KATIE!! DANNY!! ARE YOU SEEING EACH OTHER?

'You can keep guessing,' he winked, as he steered me towards the entrance.

'In your dreams,' I smiled and hissed through gritted teeth.

Bright lights and flashing bulbs sparkled and dazzled all around me, so much so that I was positively blinded.

'Radical,' Danny said, switching accents.

'Amazing,' I breathed, too overwhelmed to care.

'Follow me,' he said, as he led me towards a darkened staircase.

Uh oh. This is the bit where he demands I have sex with him for art or something ridiculous like that.

'I don't really know, think, uh, this isn't really what I had in mind,' I began, before being stopped in my tracks once again. This time, though, I had clearly just entered heaven.

'Is that?' I hissed in Danny's ear, as he stood there, legs apart, a massive grin smacked across his face.

He clicked his fingers and a waiter appeared. 'Champagne and two shots of whiskey on the rocks,' he barked. 'Yes,' he said, turning to me. 'Yep, film stars, everywhere, you dig?'

'Oh my God!' I squealed as quietly as possible. I scanned the room. Every single person here appeared to be from a film, my dreams, *EastEnders* and *Sizzle Stars*.

'This is beyond cool,' I said, as the waiter reappeared with our drinks. I took the shot and downed it in one. Before Danny had the chance to protest, I necked his drink too.

The bar area was intimate, meaning it wasn't too big but it wasn't so small you were wedged up against random people although, personally, I had had very rude dreams about most of the famous men in here and could think of worse things than to be sandwiched between these rippled hunks. Soft music swayed the crowds of people as I glanced to my side and felt the warm glow of a fire. I felt as though I was in *Arabian Nights*. The waiters and waitresses were decked out in saris and jewels hung from their arms and ankles. The smell was of sweet saffron with candles burning on pillars dotted around the room and on each table. Everywhere I looked I saw sequins set against rich reds and burnt oranges, bright yellows and vibrant purples. It was absolutely breathtaking. Everyone was beautiful, slender and wearing shoes to die for. I was in awe.

'Ahh,' I said, smiling. 'So this is why we didn't see the film?'

'Girl, no one sees the film,' he grinned back.

'Gotta fly, there's some booty with Danny D's name on it,' he said, swigging his champagne and wandering off. He managed to squeeze my arse before he left. I was about to protest, but suddenly stopped. Bailey stood in the shadows surrounded by a bevy of beauties. For once, he wasn't wearing his tight T-shirt and skinny jeans ensemble. He smouldered in a fitted dark suit, the shirt was Richard-like, meaning it hung loose from his neck, buttons undone, giving a glimpse of his hot chest. I had a very naughty sex flashback of Bailey laid out on my bed, me looking down at him, growling, pawing at him, him pulling me down on to his chest, pure lust. My heart beat a little quicker and as he caught my eye, I felt a bolt of electricity shoot right into my knickers. Unfortunately, his timing was out because our eyes connected right at the moment Danny's hand removed itself from my *derrière*. His face dropped and he looked away.

Fuck, I thought. I hoped that Bailey had the good sense

to realize I wasn't linked to Danny Divine in any way shape or form. I would rather have a repeat of the crabs/Ibiza incident with the double-crossing Nicola Baxter than bump uglies with Danny Divine. On another point entirely, what was Bailey, the hired help, Hanna's busboy, the dogsbody, doing here? I'm not, like, an overnight snob or anything, but I suppose it's only natural to wonder, because let's face it, aside from being criminally good looking, he is there to service Magenta Rubenstein and whoever she directs him to take care of, and I suppose, he kind of indirectly works a little bit for me, what with taking care of my mother's transport back to Little Glove and driving me here and there. Aubrey also commands him, so you know, it just seems odd to me that he's here, right now, in the same room as all these celebrities and me, an almost-famous brand-new celebrity. I thought this was exclusive?! None of the other office staff are here. Then it dawned on me. He just had to be sleeping with or was at least the date of one of those freakily gorgeous whippet girls. I looked back at them. Their vacant eyes rolled back and scanned the room whilst looking effortlessly cool in skyscraper heels. They towered over the men in their company. Now I understood why Jack was obsessed with his Tom Cruise shoes.

Should I go over? I looked at my own shoes, all cream and sparkly and high, and thought about it. When I looked up, he was gone.

'Katie!' Hanna said, as she glided across the room towards me with Frenella in tow. 'You did very well on the carpet,' Hanna smiled.

Should I ask Hanna about Bailey's presence here? Or

would she suss what had happened and tell Magenta and ruin my life and . . .

'Yeah, haha, loving the moves, oh yeah,' Frenella pulled some weird shapes.

'There should be *some* useable pictures on our desk by tomorrow.' Hanna sneered.

'Canapé?' a passing waiter offered.

'Mmm, yes,' I began extending my hand. Hanna smacked it away.

'Naughty, naughty, what did I tell you?'

'Shit, I mean, yes, of course, how silly of me, you said, no eating in public.'

'No eating, full stop, if I were you,' she said, looking down her nose.

'Sure,' I said. My stomach was churning at the thought that I could have given Bailey the wrong impression. He couldn't possibly think I was having it off with Danny Divine? The guy was the biggest idiot I'd met since my university days, where immature idiots were ten a penny.

'Anyway, the press went wild for you, Kate, you must be very happy about that.' Hanna stood sipping her Cosmopolitan with one eyebrow raised.

'Well, to be totally honest, Hanna, I don't really know what I'm doing or what to expect.'

'Shhhh!' she hissed.

'What?'

'For God's sake, fake it, Kate, you seriously don't know what you're doing by now? Are you completely thick or something? It's not rocket science, you turn up, you look good, you stand at an angle that doesn't accentuate your triple chin and back flab, you play the fame game, darling, and if you don't know the rules, you fake it till you make it, *comprende?*'

'Understood.' God, why was she being so evil to me again? I was really honestly beginning to hate the woman. And then she went and changed her approach again.

'Kate, you are gorgeous, funny, articulate and charming, I just want you to maximize your potential, sweetheart.' She smiled.

'Thanks, Hanna, I mean, I don't know what to say to all these compliments.'

'Kate,' Hanna said firmly. 'I do not give compliments. I just tell the truth, plain and simple, no more and no less.'

'OK,' I said confidently. Fake it, fake it, fake it. That should be easy. I faked enough orgasms in bed with Jack-useless-in-bed-Hunter. Still, he was a dream . . . Looking around, I desperately tried to spot Bailey whilst checking to see if Jack and Jessica had shown up. I'm sure there would have been a whole circus performance if Jessica was there and we'd have known all about it from the cacophony of whistles and bells and banners and flags and whatnot that came associated with La Hilson. But no, must not be negative, Jack is probably still at Mimi Sparkles Jungle Garden in Honolulu with the Barbie doll, sharing Haribos (when not proposing with them, of course) and Bailey, well, he was probably off getting another drink or networking or, oh my, oh nooooooo!!

There he was, sitting in a booth, surrounded by women, one of whom, identifiable as Carolina Fernando, sat on his knee, giggling and flicking her hair over her shoulders. His tie was loose around his neck as she fondled the material in her hands. She caught sight of me and casually looked away. I stood there between Hanna and Frenella, staring at him. I watched Derren Brown programmes. I knew that if you stared at someone long enough they'd sense it and look round.

'Katie, are you OK?' Frenella said quietly before adding, 'You look like you have wind.' Another waiter passed us and all three of us simultaneously reached for another drink.

'I'm fine,' I said, bright and breezy. They both swung their heads round to face the direction I was looking in. It didn't take them long to figure out that I was gazing at Bailey.

'Sam Bailey,' Hanna tutted. 'Well, I never . . .'

'Oh. My. God.' Frenella exclaimed as she picked the olive out of her cocktail glass and popped it into a tissue. I went bright red. I could see my face in the reflection of one of the panelled mirror walls by the bar.

'You're a brave woman,' Frenella said, rolling her eyes and smirking.

'What?' I said, trying desperately to pretend that there was nothing going on. Nothing to see here, nothing to understand from my body language. I tensed up, I couldn't help myself. I shuffled nervously and tapped my foot. I swirled the olive in my dirty Martini around my glass, knocking it against the sides. I never took my eyes off Bailey. He looked happy. Happy without me. Honestly, if he was fussed one iota about witnessing my bottom being manhandled by Danny Divine, he didn't show it. I was beginning to wonder whether I'd made up the sex that we'd had. Perhaps all these crazy situations I'd found myself in during the past week had created some kind of mental psychosis, where I'd fantasized about Bailey to replace the awful kicked-in-the-stomach feelings Jack Hunter left me with. Did I dream it up to protect myself or something? No, I remembered it well. Stop now, I chastised myself. This is not healthy. Lusting after unsuitable, unavailable (emotionally, physically or otherwise) men is not for one second a healthy thing to do and is something that I am forever reading about how to stop doing in my girly magazines.

'I hope for your sake you didn't sleep with Bailey, Katie,' Frenella smirked some more.

'I haven't,' I lied. 'But if I had, why would that be so bad?'

'Bailey broke my sister Lydia's heart,' Hanna said stonily. 'He broke her heart after dating her for some time.'

'Well, that's too bad I guess, but still, Hanna, no offence, people break up, and more often than not that hurts one of the couple. God, I should know, Jack Hunter wasn't the best boyfriend in the world, but he was the only one I had, and I loved him all the same.'

'That's nice, Katie, thanks for your little trip down memory lane there, but I think you would do well to remember that Lydia, like me, is uber-successful and attractive. In our world of extremely uber-successful and attractive women, we don't get dumped, our hearts don't break and the sun always shines on TV. If we get dumped and our hearts get broken and there's a massive rainstorm, then clearly, this is all the man's fault and obviously has nothing to do with us. As soon as they've left us, we're back to our glamorous, show-stopping best. So what if it hurts? There's always a pill for that.'

'Hanna, I don't understand you. What do you mean?'

She sighed dramatically.

'Kate, Bailey is a user. He used Lydia for a step up the career ladder. He used Lydia to get ahead of the game, he used her for sex and he used her for her money. He's one big, horrible user.'

'Right,' I said, my heart sinking. He's just like Jack.

'We can't get rid of him,' Hanna said, twirling her hair on her fingers. 'He knows too much. He knows too much about how the company works, if he was to jump ship, he'd sell our commercial strategies to our rivals, probably sell stuff to the papers, ruin us, effectively. And I've spent too long . . .' she trailed off.

'She's spent, like, oh, too long,' Frenella concurred in unison. 'Too long, Hanna,' she gave her a solemn pat on the arm.

'Building up Poets Field PR to what it is today, a thriving, successful, shiny, smart business, with me at the forefront, how can one fail? Waiter,' she snapped her fingers and one came running. 'More drinks.' She didn't say please.

This is all a little too much information for me to digest right now. Must get rid of the gruesome twosome.

'I'm off to powder my nose,' I smile brightly.

'Oooh, goodie, I'll join,' Frenella says linking arms with me.

'If you must, I'd prefer you to go to the VIP section, darling.' Hanna wafts her hands towards a scary-looking bouncer. She clicks her fingers. Seriously, the woman clicked her fingers. As if any self-respecting man would come running to a . . .

'Katie, this is Gabe.' She gestured to a seven-foot Hispanic giant.

'Hello,' I smiled sweetly and held out one of my perfect-looking, manicured hands. It was all I could do to stop myself going 'Oooh' every time I saw them, such was the novelty. I decided then and there I would never go back to my old nails, which were chewed with chipped, pink splodges hanging around on them.

'This way, *Madame*,' Gabe said, as he walked a pace or two ahead of Frenella and me. When I turned back to question what Hanna was going to do with herself, I noticed Danny Divine approach and thought better of it.

'Quick, run!' I hissed to Frenella.

'What? In these heels? Are you insane?'

Clearly, I thought to myself, if I want to spend any amount of my free-ish time here with Little Miss Plastic. I carried on following Gabe with Frenella by my side to a dark stairway, lit only by incense cones and pillar candles scattered with wild purple flowerheads. As we neared the top of the stairs, a long cloaked purple velvety curtain hung heavily in front of us. Gabe grunted and all of a sudden, the curtain was drawn back and, inside, I could see beautiful people swaying in time to the music. I noticed several actors from *EastEnders* and got all mega excited. Must not drool over anyone famous, I am after all, almost famous myself, listen to the wisdom of Tom Theodore, what was it? Listen to your heart? I smiled at anyone and everyone in one of those cool facial expressions that you kinda have to learn fast, which I learned from Ziggy Wang. He nailed the smile, all right. Tom Theodore's smile looked as though he'd met the Wizard of Oz, Hanna Frost looked angry, Aubrey looked constipated or surprised, depending on how much Botox he'd had. Too much in the wrong place resulted either in a permanent frown or looking as though he'd stepped into a room full of naked Chippendales. Frenella giggled too much and God, there were no words for Danny Divine. Mmm, yes, my smile was from a mixture of an 'I know I'm cool as fuck' Ziggy Wang and an 'I'm hot as hell and you want me' Sam Bailey.

'Katie, are you OK?' Frenella nudges me.

'Hmm, yes, why do you ask?'

'Your face . . . you look a little startled.'

'I guess, I am, uh, excited,' I murmur as we turn a dimly-lit corner and find ourselves placed neatly between two hot male models. They sat there smouldering by candle-light in their open-topped shirts, tanned, toned, muscle peeked from beneath the fabric. Note to self, if it doesn't work out with Bailey, who clearly prefers skinny mod-els . . . God, he is just like Richard, I thought. A modelizer. Only dates models. Just like that episode from *Sex and the City*. And they say that was all fictitious!

Well, anyway, my whole point was that there appeared to be about fifty Bailey/Richard/Jack Hunter-type men in here and the law of averages suggests that if I were to drunkenly hit upon them all, one by one, after I've finished this lovely bottle of vintage champagne that's just been placed on my table, one of them is bound to say yes.

'Katie Lewis, right?' A tall blonde hunk in a ripped t-shirt appeared in front of me and sat down uninvited in the chair opposite. 'I'm Brad, I'm a model,' he grinned. He looked especially pleased with himself.

'So,' he drawled. 'Do you come here often?' I looked at him as I took in the words just spoken. Do I come here often? Is he serious? I look around the room, half expecting

Jeremy Beadle to jump out and 'fess up to setting me up with a himbo who's swallowed a copy of the *Little Book of Cheesy Chat-up Lines*.

'Um . . .' I say, trying to think of a reply. Must not lie, look at what happened the last time I tried to pretend to be something I wasn't. Hmm? Refresh your memory here, let's see . . . The Dorchester, yep, go there aaaall the time, fillet of badger is my favourite. I really wanted to say that I frequented film premieres, in particular, this swanky VIP room five nights out of seven, but the truth was . . .

'No,' I said, still smiling. Must not look insecure. 'I don't come here often.'

He had the most delicious blue eyes . . . long eye-lashes . . . such a beautiful man.

'I didn't think I'd seen you in here before,' he said, one eye half closed, sizing me up. 'But I have definitely seen you someplace before, your face looks awful familiar to me . . .' he said in his American twang. He sighed as he pondered where he'd seen me. He'd seen my arse over Richard's shoulder and, probably, he'd seen awful pictures of me half opening my door, gawping at the paparazzi outside my house from last week, after all, the gorgeous pictures of me weren't released until tomorrow, the day that *Sizzle Stars* hit the shops. But I wasn't about to admit to that because then I'd have to admit that my boyfriend left me for Jessica Hilson and God, no one wants to start talking about their ex-boyfriend and his philandering ways twenty seconds into a potential hook-up with a male model from across the pond, now do they? Huh? Do they? No, of course they don't.

'Can I buy you a drink?' he said, sweetly. Aw shucks, he

wants to buy me a drink. I wasn't entirely convinced that I fancied him. For one, he was blond and blonds don't really do it for me.

'You can buy me a drink, yes, uh,' What was his name? What was his name again? 'Brett!'

'Brad.'

'Sorry. Brad. I would like . . . a Singapore Sling, please.' This was the only posh cocktail I could remember from one of the only times Jack Hunter took me out in public.

'Nice,' he said, winking and then he made his way to the bar. I topped up my champagne glass. Well, no harm in warming oneself up on free booze, is there? I'd have the hangover from hell at this rate anyway and besides, I doubt I could tell the difference between a shit hangover and a really shit hangover. Sod it, I thought as Brad returned with one Singapore Sling for me and a tall frosted dark-looking drink for him. It was ultra posh in this gaff. No umbrellas in the glass here! Brad waffled on about his life, which consisted of parties, parties and more parties. He modelled for some fashion house I'd never heard of and got to fly to tons of exotic locations.

I was trying really hard to be interested in everything he was saying, but was totally unsuccessful. I couldn't get Bailey out of my head, my thoughts were whizzing around and around in my poor boozey brain, and as I was an excellent multitasker, I managed to thank God for this, silently. I made the appropriate verbal nods and facial gestures so Brad felt as though I was hanging off his every word. Brad was one of the beautiful people. Beautiful people, I've noticed, don't have to develop much of their personality beyond having the basics that one needs to get by in a variety of social situations. For example, Brad didn't have a clue that I wasn't really listening. Brad hadn't asked me anything about myself, how I felt this evening, where my dress was from, even, who I was beyond my name, meaning, who was Katie Lewis when she was at home? Not literally at home because, oh God, can you imagine if *Oh Yay!* magazine did a shoot with me in my rubbish boring old house in Bethnal Green? They'd get the dusty wooden floors, the ripped James Dean posters curling from the kitchen walls, CDs splattered around the ghetto blaster – yep, I still had one of them and no, I don't want to upgrade – Bob Dylan, The Cure, Joy Division smiled up at me from the sleeves of the music cases. There were bizarre antique photo frames that stood on curled wooden tables next to my two big old browny-beige couches that were littered with cigarette burns and red wine stains from many a silly evening with Danielle, moaning about men, specifically Stewart-small-penis and, of course, the day that my life had seemingly changed for-ever, the morning of THAT TEXT. Like an ultra famous person dying a hideous death or a natural disaster, there was clearly a shift in polarity the day that Jack Hunter left me. The world had changed and nothing in it was ever going to be the same again, least of all me.

Beautiful people didn't pick up on subtle tones of voice, turns of phrase or subliminal body language, because they never had to decode potential partners. Everybody wanted to shag them. End of. They didn't have to make half as much effort as I did in my normal life, even just getting ready for a night out took an entire day. I wished my life was as easy as it must be for a person like Brad, a beautiful person. They just look pretty and everyone panders to them, because beautiful people are positive people and everybody needs a bit of sunshine in their lives, right?

Suddenly, Frenella plonked herself down next to me, wild eyes and talking ten to the dozen. Thank the Lord, I thought, as now Brett/Brad/whatever his name is, was now being backed into a conversational corner by the increasingly hyper Frenella. What on earth had she had to drink in the past half an hour? I wondered.

Brad's flimsy attention was turned to Frenella, the compact blonde in the tiny dress. Her eyes were as wide as saucers. Hmm. I know what that means. I read it in a magazine, that when someone's pupils dilate, it means they are insanely attracted to the person they're talking to. I checked Brad's eyes. Hmm. They weren't so big. Oh well, I thought to myself, as Brad and Frenella started talking LA and chemical peels. I allowed my eyes to wander around the room, taking in the beauty of the faces, the sleek and sexy bodies and the clothes that adorned them. All of a sudden, I locked eyes with a tall, dark, familiar Italian – Fabio Matravers. He winked at me. Urgh, must not fall for his slimy tricks of pretending to fancy me when really all he wants is to piss off Jessica Hilson. Already had enough humiliation to last an entire lifetime. I looked away. Before I could formulate anything of any great sense to say to him, he stood beside me, his shadow falling down the length of me. I looked up and glared at him. I pouted my lips and huffed.

'Oh,' I said. 'It's you.'

'Kate?' Fabio purred. 'What's the matter?'

'I think you know very well what the matter is,' I replied.

'Darling . . . let me buy you a drink and let's talk, why not?'

'I already have a drink, um, Brett bought me one.' I smiled smugly.

'Uh . . . it's Brad,' he interjected.

'Whatever,' I said. Brad and Fabio looked a bit perturbed but were soon distracted by Frenella, who was singing along with the music.

'Hey, do you think anyone actually really landed on the moon?' she said randomly.

'Dunno, why?' Brad shrugged, before turning himself to face her.

'Listen, darling, that drink is empty, let's leave them to it, I have a table over there, you can order a drink, anything you want, please?'

I looked at my options. Himbo and the Brainiac sitting there discussing conspiracy theories, albeit in some crazy, childlike, thicko kind of way. Hanna, thankfully, nowhere to be seen, safe for now. Bailey was probably humping Carolina Fernando against a wall or partaking in some kind of beautiful-people sex orgy. Danny Divine, oh God, who knows, let's keep it that way. And here I was, with the only half-decent, extremely attractive option standing in front of me, wearing what I now know, thanks to many a gay fashionista's teaching, is a made-to-measure Manning & Manning Savile Row suit. Nice.

'OK, you win,' I said, standing up and flattening down my gorgeous gown.

'Katie, there is no game,' he said, looking directly into my eyes.

'You sure about that?' I snorted.

'Quite sure,' he replied. He looked slightly confused and a lot concerned.

'Come,' he said, as he rested his hand gently on the small of my back and drew me closer to him. We almost floated towards his table. His touch was that of a gentleman and not that of a pervert, like Danny Divine and his octopus hands. Unlike Danny, Fabio didn't squeeze my backside. Although what with the fuzzy, confident, happy feelings the Singapore Sling had given me, I was not really all that opposed to a bit of bottom groping. I steered my hands towards my clutch bag and twirled strands of my hair over and above my perfect fingers.

A suave, silent man arrived at the table.

Fabio muttered something exotic and the waiter nodded and turned on his heels.

'What did you say?'

'I asked for a surprise for the lady . . . and for me.'

'Well, I don't like Amaretto, just so you know,' I said haughtily.

'I'm sorry I haven't called you, Katie, I assume that this is what your antagonistic mood is for?' He looked into the middle distance and sighed.

'No, I mean, yes, there is that . . .'

'You see, Katie, I had to go back to Italy to see my sick mother.'

'Oh, really,' I said. What planet was this creep on? Sick mother? I'd bought that line too many times from Jack to fall for it again.

'Pull the other one,' I said, smirking at him. I shrugged my shoulders and stuck my nose in the air.

'Pull the other what?' Fabio looked rather taken aback.

'Leg!' I said, nudging my head to prompt him into the famous saying.

'I understand not?'

'Leg! Pull the other leg!'

'Why?'

'It has bells on it!' Fabio wasn't going to get the better of me!

'I am unclear?'

'You and me both. Listen, forget it, it was a joke, doesn't matter.'

'Mr Matravers,' the waiter appeared and laid two crystal frost-rimmed glasses on the table in front of us. He coughed nervously before turning to Fabio and saying, 'I am so sorry to hear about your recent loss, please accept the drinks on the house.'

The two men exchanged respectful nods. I felt really stupid. Again.

'Fabio . . .' I began apologetically.

'No matter,' he said, gently taking my hand in his and gazing longingly into my eyes. 'Now, tell me?'

'Well . . .' I began, unsure as to which bits I should tell him about and which bits I should exclude from the conversation. After all, I didn't want to go upsetting Hanna and who knows whether Fabio was trustworthy or not?

I turned my head in mock carelessness and clapped eyes on Bailey, who'd clearly just jumped up the stairs to the VIP room two at a time, judging by the slight sheen on his forehead and his startled eyes. When he spied me, the bolt of electricity between us could have blown up the entire room and all of its occupants. He stopped in his tracks like a rabbit in the headlights, looking at me, my face, my eyes, then, down to my hand. Fabulous fingers entwined with Fabio Matravers'. It looked as though I was in a lovers' embrace with another man. Across the room, Bailey's face dropped, and he just shook his head slightly and turned to leave. No! I thought and accidently said the word out loud.

'What is it, Katie? Are you OK?' Fabio queried, as concern swept across his chiselled features.

'No, I , I'm sorry, listen, I will be right back, OK? Wait there!' I leapt up as fast as one can in a floor-length gown, belly full of expensive alcohol and wearing six-inch heels. I clumsily toppled over into the side of the couch and stuck an arm out to steady myself.

'Whoooo . . .' I squealed quietly.

'Kate.' The unmistakeable acrid voice of Hanna Frost barked my name, albeit under her breath. I looked up at her and saw double.

'Have you been taking advantage of the free alcohol?' she hissed.

'No!' I said. In my defence, the champagne was a gift and how could I refuse himbo Brad/Brett's drink or, indeed, Fabio Matravers'? Fabio shot daggers through his cavernous dark eyes as Hanna leant into me, hooked her arm beneath me and pulled me up straight.

'Gorgeous, darling!' she cooed. 'You are a real show-stopper tonight, darling, real showstopper!'

Gosh, I must be drunk. Is Hanna cooing on me? She totally is. I smiled back. I felt more steady on my feet now and the previous dizzy moment appeared to have washed right over me. The silent waiter appeared and handed me a cool glass of water. I took a big gulp and glanced over to the table where I had left the model with the tiny terror. They were literally eating each other. Both were undistinguishable from one another, their mops of peroxide blonde hair embedding on one another's faces, lips locked, sucking for dear life. He had one hand on her boob and the other on her thigh, her dress was riding halfway up to netherland. Her eyes firmly shut, head tilted, she had one hand on the scruff of his neck and the other steadying herself on the chair. 'Thanks,' I said to the waiter. He nodded and retreated back to the bar.

'Ms Frost,' Fabio was on his feet now, extending a hand, to Hanna's sheer delight. Gosh, he was so polite.

When neither of them was looking, I made my escape. I bent over, pulled my shoes off, held them in my hand and shuffled towards the exit. I looked in my bag for my mobile. Game over, I'd left it at home. Now where could he be? To go faster I lifted the hemline of my dress, the way princesses do in fairy tales and made for the downstairs dance floor. It was flooded with people, in stark contrast to the quiet buzz of the VIP room. Gorgeous people were dancing to funky house, the eclectic beats allowing sylph-like bodies to sway in time to the music. I searched frantically for his face, to let him know it wasn't me with Fabio, well, it was me, but I didn't want to be there with him, I wasn't bothered about him, I was bothered about Bailey, more than anything else in the entire world. I don't know if it was the combination of the alcohol or the music or my first film premiere, I really didn't know, but I simply had to find him on pain of death. I crept around the perimeter of the floor, being careful not to tread on any broken glass. People jostled, boobs were thrust up into my face by passing glamour models. On closer inspection, I noticed that there were no more mega famous people swanning around the vicinity, just trashy celebrities from reality television. Or something like that. I couldn't really tell. Faces were swimming out of focus as the beats of the tunes grew more frenetic. And then all of a sudden, the funky house tune hit a euphoric pitch, with strings and bongo drums and it felt as if people on the dance floor were moving out of the way without me having to ask them, like the parting of the Red Sea but with disco beats. A hazy glow of spotlights criss-crossed the dance floor before right there, all of ten yards away from me, stood a dishevelled Sam Bailey. He was looking right at me, and I at him. I was about to take those steps towards someone you know you've fallen in love with, but for one reason or another have not managed to tell them, when Carolina Fernando grabbed him from the side and kissed him square on the mouth. My heart almost died. It almost stopped. My blood ran cold as I looked at him. His face was all squidged with the force of her kiss, yet he twisted round to look at me. His hands leapt up away from her and in a vain effort to appease me, his mouth moved, he said my name, he tried to give chase, to reach me, to get to me. But it was too late, I was already gone.

Chapter 15

My eyes are refusing to open. I know I am in bed. Whose bed, I was unsure. With whom . . . God only knew. My head thumped. My mouth was dry. I stretched one leg out under the covers and was met by a hard, leg-shaped lump. I inhaled deeply and smelled the scent of my bedsheets. I was at home, phew, this was a good thing, but who was occupying my space?

'Darling, you know I like kinky sex, but this is taking it too far. Please stop kicking me,' Richard growled from beneath the Sonata bed throw, and thankfully not the duvet I was under. I opened my eyes.

'What are? How did? Oomph!' I said, slapping my hand on to my forehead.

'You can't remember?' he said, still half snoozing beside me.

I sat up. I was still wearing my dress. A large glass of water and a packet of paracetamol sat next to me on the bedside table.

'Swallow those and I'll explain,' he said, lifting himself up, still dressed. He went down to the kitchen and as I smudged my eyes open, wiped the crusty dribble from my mouth and surveyed the bedroom for any sex clues, I heard the kettle begin to boil. I pulled the door to and shed last night's outfit, sliding it from my body. I pulled on my tartan pyjamas and walked downstairs into the kitchen.

Richard stood there with a pan, cracking eggs.

'Ah, lovely, how are you feeling?'

'Shit,' I said and I actually really truly meant it. My eyes felt like sandpaper, red and raw. I sniffled.

'Oh, please, not more crying . . .' Richard lamented.

'Sorry,' I said, as my chest gave one of those little shudders that you get when you've been sobbing dramatically.

'Well . . .' Richard began, moving towards me, taking me by the shoulders, steering me into the living room, and plonking me on to the couch.

'You called me last night, totally rat-arsed, sobbing incomprehensibly down the phone, said you were on some random person's mobile, could I come and get you immediately, you'd lost your shoes, you were babbling about being seen doing something you hadn't actually done, feeling rubbish, not being good enough to model Grattan's granny pants let alone posh teeny-tiny, G-string-type pants such as, who was it you said, Carolina Fernando? Hmmm . . . I know her, Brazilian, legs up to her armpits, boobs like little mountain peaks.'

'Not helping . . .' I sighed, pulling a woolly throw around myself. I felt terrible. I couldn't remember anything of the previous evening past seeing Fabio.

'You said you were in love with someone who didn't love you back because you were short without your heels, but then you said he wasn't worth loving anyway because he had it off with Hanna's sister and used her for money, sex and God knows what else.'

'Eek!' I squealed. 'I told you all my secrets!'

'Quite. You were a scene, I'll give you that. But don't worry, Bailey didn't see you. Well, he saw the back of your head but I thought it best not to tell you at the time. Who knows what you would have done?'

'He came after me?' I whispered, suddenly remembering the intense disco dancefloor moment in which we once again had a love stand-off across a crowded room.

'I'm sorry, Kate, but if you ask me, I did you a favour. You were in a horrendous state, you were emotional, incoherent and frighteningly drunk. Bailey would have run a mile. Seriously, he would have freaked.'

'So now he thinks I am aloof and mysterious and hard to get instead of paranoid, needy and insecure?'

'Well, I wouldn't put it quite like that but yes, perhaps he does.'

'God . . . and us, we didn't . . . you know . . .'

'No. Absolutely not.' He winked.

'Thank God!' I cried.

'And what's that supposed to mean?' Richard huffed.

'It means that I've already embarrassed myself enough lately and the very last thing I needed was to have an accidental shag with you.'

'Sweetheart . . .' Richard began in a philosophical tone, 'I may not know anything about how to sustain a healthy long-term monogamous relationship, instead, preferring to sow my wild oats with blondes and models and the more in the bed the merrier, you know . . .'

'Too much information . . .' I groaned.

'Shh,' he said, sitting down next to me. He put his arms around me and pulled me in close, so close I could hear his heart beating. He sighed and kissed my mop of hairsprayed hair that stuck up in all directions on my head.

'Life would be so much easier, darling, if all you girls

stopped expecting men on white horses to rescue you, and realized that not all men come equipped with shining armour and the ability to read your mind. In turn, us boys would realize that we're not all going to pull a Victoria's Secret model and would happily ignore your wobbly bottoms and not ditch you for Hollywood megastars.'

'I thought you pulled a Victoria's Secret model last weekend?'

'I said not *all* men . . . some of us can,' he winked. I laughed and fell back into his chest for a hug.

'And Jack . . . he, he, he pulled a megastar!'

'Well, I didn't say *all* men . . . Jack and I are clearly the exceptions.'

'Oh, Richard,' I sighed, 'what am I going to do?'

'Well, young lady,' he said, ruffling my shoulders, 'you're going straight into the shower to wash your sins away.'

'Cripes,' I said, turning to face him, 'I'll be there all day!'

'Take as long as you need, Kate, and when you get out, your fabulously low-carb protein-rich star breakfast will await you with a steaming cup of coffee.'

'You're letting me have coffee?'

'You haven't hit the gym yet, darling, therefore this coffee, although a total cellulite giver, won't honestly make a difference to your *derrière*,' he said with a little smirk. I shook my head and smirked back at him.

'All right,' I said and I padded on upstairs.

The hot water stung my tired skin. It sure felt good, though. I stood there, feeling pretty pathetic, wiping mascara down my cheeks, opening my mouth and allowing the water to bounce in, off my tongue and down my throat. I hummed a tune while running a flannel over my body. Bubbles trickled down my elbows on to my belly. When I was done, I stepped over the side of the bath and stood naked on the bath mat, shivering slightly. Refreshed and rejuvenated, I wrapped myself up in my posh towels and pulled the skin on my face taut. It made me look a lot younger. If only I could walk around like that all the time, I thought. I sat down on the loo seat and just thought about my life. After a few minutes I let out a big sigh, got up, opened the door and with a spritz of posh body mist, I felt more than ready to face the day. After all, I had only made a tit out of myself in front of Richard and he was kinda used to that by now. I was a disaster around men, this much was clear. Yet I had Brett/Brad model guy interested in me, well, he was more interested in himself, but he made the effort, a big effort considering the amount of time it took to tear himself away from reflective surfaces and towards my movie star made-up face – well, it was last night, thanks to the tribe of fashionistas in my living room all day – and let's not forget Fabio Matravers, although I hadn't actually forgiven him for taking me on a pity/let's piss off Jessica Hilson date. I didn't need a pity date, nor did I want to be used as a way to help Fabio gain Jessica's attention. No, siree!

'Coffee, darling,' Richard said brightly. A little too brightly, actually. He looked dodgy.

'Thanks,' I said, nervously sitting at the breakfast bar. Richard's mouth twitched. He tapped his foot. I looked up at him and caught him looking at the ceiling randomly. I sipped my coffee. He drummed his fingers.

'OK,' I said, looking him square in the eyes.

Richard said nothing.

'What's going on?'

He opened his mouth wide and began to say the word 'Nothing' when I cut him short.

'Don't lie to me!' I shrieked.

Richard looked startled at the force of emotion behind my voice. I had the hangover from hell, a short temper, a zillion crazy thoughts in my head, flashbacks from the night before and, God forgive me, but I'm not Superwoman and I am still trying to digest that the love of my life has walked out on me for a celebrity. I had no headspace for more deception, even if the truth hurt more than stubbing your toe on a door.

'Joel Farthing,' Richard said, gulping down his coffee.

'Oh God, I know him,' I sighed. Joel Farthing, Jack's agent, couldn't stand him. Last seen schmoozing on *This Morning*, giving the insider's scoop on my ex-boyfriend's sex life.

'Yes, well, Joel Farthing just called me to let me know, so that I can let you know, that Jack has given a scathing interview in *Oh Yay!* magazine that includes information about you. He's saying you were cheating on him and he was driven into the arms of Jessica, a woman who apparently puts him first.'

I felt like I'd been hit by a sledgehammer.

'Cheating?!' I whispered, incredulously. 'Who with?' I said, confused as a confused person.

'Uh . . .'

'Cheating with who?!' My voice grew louder.

Richard visibly stiffened.

'How the fuck can him running off with tit-face Jessica be MY FAULT!' I screamed. I needed Danielle, so *so* much right now. I ran around looking for my mobile and found it half under a cushion in the living room. I picked it up and marched back to the breakfast bar.

'Who are you calling?'

'JACK!' I said, not meaning to. The whole point of getting the phone was to call Danielle, but now I had a burning urge to phone Jack Hunter and call him a massive arrogant horrible arsehole liar who was also, for the record, shit in bed, a total drain on my emotions and a complete twat!

'NOOOOO!' Richard says, dive-bombing me. I pull the phone closer to me as though it's a small child that needs intense protection. Richard hits me like a heavy-weight and I go down to the floor like a feather. If anyone saw us now, God knows what they'd think. There we were, on the floor, my robe open, the granny pants and comfort bra that I'd pulled on after my gloriously hot shower on display, wrestling over my BlackBerry.

'Give me the phone, Katie!' Richard growls.

'FUCK OFF!' I scream. 'He needs to know,' I finish quietly.

'Know what?' Richard shouts back at me.

'He NEEDS TO KNOW GODDAMNIT!' I squeal with such force my throat hurts.

'Anything he needs to know we do through Hanna Frost and we do it with style, Katie, we don't go calling him up, screaming and hissing like a banshee!'

'WE DO, BECAUSE HE NEEDS TO FUCK-ING KNOW!'

'KNOW WHAT!' Richard screeches.

'HOW MUCH HE'S . . .' I sob, relinquishing the

phone into Richard's grasp. He releases his grip on me and I flop to the floor, defeated.

'How much he's hurt me! He's broken my heart!' I cry, tears streaming down my face. Richard just sits there for a second as I remain on the floor, flat on my back, crying.

'Oh, darling . . .' he says quickly and quietly.

'And . . . he's totally moved on within what, a fortnight, he's been long gone before that I know, cheating, horrible, nasty, beautiful, gorgeous man, oh I love him sooooo much, I really dooooooo,' I wail.

'Nooooo, you don't, poppet,' Richard soothes. He gathers my wretched self up from the cold wooden floor of my kitchen and like a knight in shining armour (heh! they DO exist after all!) he carries me through to the living room as I lean into his chest and grasp the collar of his shirt. That manly scent, comforting, secure and exactly what I needed. All my pent-up anger came thrashing out on to the lapels of Richard's Prada shirt. Mascara and all. Why is it, no matter how many eye make-up removing lotions I use, there is always some left over ready to smear on people when I cry, or to leave marks on my new bed-sheets?

'I'm sorry,' I sniff.

'It's OK. This fresh make-up stain can join the long queue of last night's make-up stains,' he says gently.

'You don't love Jack Hunter, Katie, you really don't. This isn't love, what you're feeling.'

'Then what is it?' I mean, I made a pros and cons list for going out with Jack and the one pro was that he was good looking but that was about it. The rest of the pointers on the list were in the cons bit and they were all things about how disrespectful he was and how unhappy he made me.

'Why do I love someone like Jack, who doesn't love me, or loves me with, with a list of conditions?' I sniff.

'It's not love.'

'Is too.'

'Is not, darling. Love is wanting someone to be truly happy, with or without you.'

'I want Jack to be eaten by someone really fat or to trip up and fall over into the path of a lorry carrying pig manure or something.'

'Hmmm,' Richard nods. 'Me too.'

'I just, I feel like what was the point in having a relationship with me if it was always going to be a bad idea? I look back at photographs of us together, and he has a smile in his eyes that stretches all the way out to the corners of his mouth, a real, honest, genuine smile, one that you can't fake.'

'And any recent photographs?'

'Yeah, actually. And oh,' I look up skywards and sigh, 'he's . . . he's not smiling in any of them.'

'So, darling,' Richard says gently. 'He's broken your heart, but did it ever really belong to him to break? That is my question.' Richard raises an eyebrow.

'I loved him . . . still do. He's on my mind all the time.'

'But you don't, darling, you think you do but you really honestly don't. What you're feeling is longing, it's lust. You can't tell me anything about Jack that made you love him that was about HIM. All you can say is that he's hot. The rest is about meaningless stuff. None of those words or phrases equate with loving someone, no matter who they are or where they may be.'

'God,' I say.

'Yes, my child,' Richard gently jokes.

'Shhh,' I say, sitting up straight, pulling my dressing gown tight around my middle. 'I've just had an epiphany!'

'Go on?'

'You're right, I don't love Jack Hunter – I loved the thought of him, the Jack Hunter I built up in my mind, and he was never ever it, because if he loved me even just a teeny-tiny bit he'd never have dumped me by text message, he'd have given me warning, sat me down, anything other than humiliate me across the national press and shove his new happy relationship in my face! He may as well have invited me around to watch them have sex, THAT'S how little he respected me and how much he shoved this whole to-do in my personal space.'

'Eureka!' Richard says, sparking up a fag. He offers me one, I take it.

'Then, if I thought I loved Jack Hunter, does that mean I haven't got a clue about love?'

'No . . .' Richard thinks. I puff furiously on my cigarette, I was on some kind of deep and meaningful roll here, I couldn't stop.

'What is love, Richard?'

'Gosh, darling . . . love is, well, it's being able to list a million reasons why you love someone that mean something . . . and you never running out of reasons why you love them.'

'Hmmm.'

'Like last night.'

'Oh God, please don't, last night, I talked rubbish, disregard anything I said, stupid talk . . .'

'They do say the truth comes out when inebriated . . .'

'Nooo, no, that's simply not true and do you know how I know that? Because I once told my next-door neighbour's husband he had a great sense of style when I was coming back from the Electricity Showrooms . . . and he's an octogenarian!' I giggled.

'Last night . . .' Richard said with a wry smile, 'you said that you loved the way Bailey shuffled on his feet when he was nervous, how he lit his cigarettes in the side of his mouth, how he sighed and scrunched up his nose when he was frustrated, how he looked at you, how he felt, how he touched you, how he made you feel like a zillion pounds, how you loved the way his white t-shirts clung to his body and how the brown in his eyes went hazel in the sunshine.'

'I did?' I said softly. I tilted my head to the side.

'Yes,' Richard said, tapping his cigarette into the ashtray.

I said nothing and listened intently.

'You said that you loved the way he spoke, his accent, the way he ordered his coffee, the way he shoved his hand on the back of his neck and rubbed it whilst pulling a face whenever he was thinking about something. You said you loved how he always saluted magpies on the way to your house.'

'Oh my God,' I said slowly.

'You know, Katie, what this means.'

'I do.'

'See,' Richard said, shrugging his shoulders.

'I love Bailey!' I screamed. Suddenly the clouds lifted, birds sang songs, 'Let's Hear It for the Boy' played loudly in my head, the room was sunny and Richard was a fucking love guru.

'Mwah!' I kissed him square on the mouth before bounding off the sofa and into the kitchen.

'What are you doing, you mad woman?' he laughed.

'I'm going to get my man!' I hollered back. 'Wahoooooo!'

Chapter 16

Wearing a silk, slashed-to-the-navel wrap dress, thick black tights and Mary Jane shoes, I spritzed myself with Marc Jacobs and touched up the puffy bags under my eyes with some Touche Éclat. I completed the look with a white cashmere bolero.

'Gorgeous,' Richard said, still sitting in my living room. 'Do you want your phone back before I drive you to Bailey's?' he enquired.

'Nah . . . I'll just call Danielle later, when I know where I stand with Bailey. Hopefully we won't be interrupting him having an orgy, or having it off with Hanna or someone . . .'

'Hanna?' Richard's head spun round.

'Yes, Hanna. You know the one, horse-faced, grumpy, acid-tongued . . . calls me fat alllllll the time.'

'Yes, darling, of course I know who you mean, but what I am confused greatly about is how you could possibly think that Bailey would be anywhere in the vicinity of Hanna, in a romantic slash sexual way.' Richard looked aghast.

'I'm confused . . . I mean, I know Hanna doesn't like him because of . . .'

TRIIIIIIIIIIIING

The doorbell screamed down the hallway, making me,

Richard and the cat, who was rubbing against Richard's trouser leg, jump.

'Who could that be?' I said, pulling an 'I don't know' face.

'Well . . .' Richard said, rubbing his chin. 'It could be the press . . . after all, Jack's *Oh Yay!* magazine interview is out, as is your glorious *Sizzle Stars* interview.'

'Well,' I sighed inwardly, 'at least I'm wearing Donna Karan and have fabulous Ziggy Wang blonde hair . . .'

'Hmmm,' Richard agreed. 'Pale sand and biscuit by the look of it,' he winked. 'Good choice.'

I gasped! Before I could say what that meant to me, the doorbell gave another urgent ring, so I quickly made my way to the door, stopping to check for lipstick on my teeth in the hallway mirror.

'Um . . .' I said, as I opened the front door. A mass of blonde frizz stood in front of me. Drizzle was seeping from the heavy clouds above us. The wind picked up, as Pippa Strong from *London Lowdown* held an umbrella which was clearly losing the fight between staying open and upright and being a crumpled, useless contraption. She also clutched a large Manila envelope.

'Katie Lewis,' she said gently. Softly spoken and very dishevelled, Pippa Strong smelled strongly of incense cones and turnips. I sensed she lived on a farm somewhere, which was unusual for a gossip journalist. They were normally single women who lived in the cool parts of London. She looked like a downtrodden mother.

'I need to talk to you urgently,' she said, trying her best to be strong, like Hanna et al. Her voice shook slightly.

'It's not a good time. I need to be going somewhere . . .'

'To see your long-term lover Fabio Matravers?' she said suddenly.

'Excuse me?' I said, eyebrows furrowed.

'Jack Hunter's interview, as I'm sure you've seen, includes accusations that you have been cheating on him for a very, very long time with one Fabio Matravers.'

'Whahaha!' I guffawed. 'That's the biggest heap of shite I've ever heard!'

Richard appeared behind me.

'Unless you want an audience, may I suggest you invite her in,' he hissed in my ear.

'But what about Hanna?'

'What about her?'

'I'm not to do anything without her say-so, remember?'

'Without Poets Field PR say-so, and I am a senior PR account manager.'

'Of stuff that isn't celebrity related!' I hissed back.

'Methods of execution are still the same.'

Pippa Strong stood in my doorway, teeth chattering, wind whipping up her dress to reveal her woolly purple thick tights.

'You'd better come in,' I sighed. By the time we had got through this, my post-hangover confidence would have worn off and the moment to profess my new and what I was sure would become undying love to Sam Bailey would be well and truly lost. Never mind . . . I suppose, what's meant to be will be, right?

'Tea? Coffee? Biscuits?' I queried.

'Tea, one sugar, milk and what biscuits have you got?' Pippa's eyes lit up as she gently lowered herself on to my couch. Oooh goodie, she wasn't a carb-dodger, good stuff, I was in good company. I certainly liked her miles more than Hanna Frost, and she'd only been here five minutes. Pippa Strong just didn't seem like a hack. She really truly didn't. She was just like someone you'd meet at Weight Watchers or aqua aerobics, you know, normal. Just a regular kinda girl I'd happily have a cuppa tea with and tell my problems to. She had matronly, married and mortgaged written all over her. Quite a stark contrast to the women in my life, such as Danielle, who was fiery, passionate and as clever as they come, and Hanna Frost, ballsy, sophisticated, clever and hard-faced. Even Frenella was tip-top of her game and knew her Jimmy's from her Luella's.

'This chat, Katie,' Pippa began, 'is strictly off the record, woman to woman.' She looked directly into my eyes. My bottom squirmed slightly on the sofa. I didn't really like folk who eyeballed me like that.

'First, I wanted to show you this week's edition of *Oh Yay!* magazine as I'm sure if Jack sees any paparazzi shots of you buying it he'll know you still care, and you could possibly look desperate and also –'

'Jammie Dodgers or Digestives?' Richard cut in quickly.

'Digestive please,' Pippa delved into the biscuit tin. She ended up with one of each in her hand. 'Oops!' she said.

'Never mind, plenty to go around, do help yourself!'

'Thank you,' she said, crunching into the Dodger. Richard placed cups of steaming hot tea on the coffee table and took a seat in the armchair. He never took his eyes off her once.

EXCLUSIVE – JACK HUNTER TALKS CANDIDLY ABOUT KATIE LEWIS INFIDELITY, BREAK-UPS AND HIS NEW-FOUND FAME

'Oh my God!' I gasped as I read through the interview, spotting another headline.

KATIE WAS AN ANGEL WITH A DIRTY FACE

'*It was clear that all along she had been having it off with Fabio . . .*' said Jack, wearing all white, actually, similar to my attire in *Sizzle Stars*. He looked clean, smooth and a little bit heart-broken. My heart jumped for joy at the thought that Jack could be in a little bit of emotional turmoil regarding me, his ex-girlfriend. The more I read about him, though, the less I felt good.

'*Jessica knew it, too,*' he stared right up at me from a white fluffy bed that had feathers floating down all around him, white of course. He looked like he was in heaven.

'*We confided and clung to one another as our hearts broke in tandem, but then healed as one.*'

'Oh, I'm going to be sick!' I whispered. He totally didn't say that.

'Right . . .' Pippa said, sipping her tea. She surreptitiously moved her hand towards the biscuit tin, which was just a little bit out of her reach.

Richard nudged it towards her.

'Jack wouldn't know the word tandem if it came up and hit him on the forehead,' I stated. Still, I continued to read.

The interview was seven pages long. Half of it was him gushing about his 'Haribo Princess' and the day he proposed, that his life had moved on 'tremendously' since his relationship with me, how happy he was, how much he loved plastic-tits Jessica Hilson . . . their wedding plans . . . and then back to his 'utter hurt and betrayal' by me, and my affair with Fabio Matravers, a man I have only met three times, and one of those through a rolled-down, blacked-out window in a futuristic beeping car round the back of Sunshine Media's offices!

'I've only met Fabio Matravers three times!' I said defiantly.

'Is that so?' Pippa shuffled uncomfortably, before adjusting her shirt buttons.

'Yes, it is. This entire interview is fabricated!' I said. 'Well, the bits about me having it off with Fabio behind Jessica and Jack's backs! Let me get this straight, Pippa, I had no idea that Jack was going to leave me, least of all for a movie star.'

'She's right,' Richard interjected. 'What she says is the truth. None of us knew what was going on and I can assure you, Jack is lying about this whole affair thing.'

'Yeah, the only affair anyone had was the two of them!' I shouted. 'This is ridiculous!' I exclaimed to Pippa, who didn't look as though she believed a word I said.

'I believe you,' she said earnestly.

'You do?' I said, surprised. No, she still didn't look like it. She looked odd.

'Then, what's with the "I totally don't believe you" face that you have going on here,' I said, drawing an 'I don't think so' diagram over my own face, like I'd seen on *Jerry Springer*.

'You'll see.' Pippa pushed the Manila envelope she'd been nurturing towards me.

'What's this?' I said, my heartbeat quickening, what could it be? What *could* it be?

'Open it, but be prepared for something you may not like . . .'

'A different story in what way?' I asked, with the envelope on my lap. I was too afraid to open it until I knew what I would find. This was like a sadistic Christmas present.

'Open it,' she gestured.

'No,' I said firmly. 'Not until you tell me what's inside it.'

'Open it and see.' She wasn't budging.

I looked at Richard. He nodded his head for me to open it. I said 'no way' telepathically. Richard sighed, huffed and then guessed.

'Is this something to do with Samuel Bailey, Hanna Frost's assistant?' he asked.

'Who?' Pippa queried.

'Phew,' I muttered under my breath. No Bailey surprises of the horrible kind.

'Doesn't matter. May I ask, then, is this to do with Katie and Jack?'

'Just open it and Jack Hunter's little cheating ways will be exposed. It appears that despite being clad head to toe in innocent white, he is anything but.'

'I could have told you that!' I said, laughing as I ripped the envelope open with my fingernails.

Before I delved inside, I looked up at Richard. His face was expectant. Pippa had a face on her like she'd turned to stone. No one made a sound.

'Well, it can't be that bad, can it . . .' I said, as I pulled out some black and white photos, the kind you see in James Bond movies or on those shows where people get followed by private detectives or whatever.

My mouth opened as my eyes focused on the shapes in the shadows.

I made no sound. The world crashed down around me. I held the very worst thing that there could ever be, right there, in my hands.

'This is what she was trying to tell me,' I whispered. My body shut down, white noise surrounded me, I could hear Richard talking, Pippa asking questions, my head blocked them out as I focused on one picture of my best friend, Danielle Kingsley, gazing up into Jack Hunter's eyes, her body tipped towards him, in an embrace, his arms, hands, placed upon hers.

'No!' I gasped. 'No!' I said, louder this time. 'This is insane! It cannot be true, you've totally doctored these pictures, you can do anything on Photoshop these days, can't you, Richard! Tell her, Richard, tell her, tell me, it's not true, it's not true, it CAN'T BE TRUE!' I wailed.

Richard came and sat down next to me. He took the pictures from me and looked through them one by one. Clear as the nose on my face, my best friend and my ex-boyfriend were pictured talking, embracing, coming out of her office, another of them on the pavement exchanging knowing glances.

'Katie, I'm sorry, I knew nothing about this,' Richard said gravely.

'Fucking BITCH!' I swore. 'She's been a nightmare lately, cagey, weird, acting out, she was a total cow in the spa, little digs here and there about this whole drama of mine. She bloomin' well hated Jack with such a passion and and and, and another thing!!' I was pointing furiously at everyone.

'When she let herself into my house and she thought I'd been having it off with Jack her face dropped and she went green, she was, like, super not impressed to the point where she looked like she'd seen a ghost at the thought of me and Jack having hooked up again. NOW I know why, she'd clearly been having sexual relations herself with MY EX-BOYFRIEND!'

'Pippa, is that all?' Richard said, as I stood up and walked to the kitchen. I took down the emergency vodka and poured myself a stiff drink. And then another. And another. So much for my perfect 'I love you, Bailey' day. Fucking ruined now. Shit shit shit!! This cannot be happening to me, God, no one gets this amount of rubbish friends and ex-boyfriend dramas in one month, do they? Surely not? The vodka warmed me up from the inside and numbed the pain that was ricocheting all over my heart and brain and back again.

'I think I should stay, you know, woman to woman,' Pippa said, with much sincerity.

'Perhaps . . .' Richard mused. He was clearly torn between staying with me to mop up more tears or, I don't know, going to have sex with someone to release some of this tension, change his clothes, do some fast manly driving, who knows?

'I need a breather from this girl stuff, darling, nothing personal,' he said stiffly. I could see he had moist eyes. I know everyone has moist eyes but his were shimmering. They weren't quite crying eyes, but I think he actually was close.

'Must dash, I'll be back in a couple of hours,' he said, kissing me quickly on the cheek and making for the door. He stopped suddenly and turned to Pippa.

'Take care of her, Pippa. If I find out . . .' he said warningly.

'Richard, is it?'

'Yes.'

She extended her hand for him to shake.

'Listen, I'm not like the other journalists, I'm a down-to-earth girl, a friend, I just want to help, and I think I can do that, right here, right now, probably better than any man. For one,' she said, opening her crocheted bag, 'I have chocolate!'

'Well, in that case,' Richard said slowly, 'chocolate will help right now. I will be back, please stay with her, as you can imagine, she's, well . . .' he shook his head. 'That will be all,' he said, before letting her hand go and heading out of the front door. He closed it with a bang. I laid my head in my hands and let out the kind of noise my cat made when I stood on his tail in my stilettos. A guttural, pained sob.

'Shhh,' Pippa said, rolling kitchen paper around her hands and passing it towards me to catch the tears that rolled silently down my cheeks and dripped into my vodka.

I gulped back emotion.

'I'm fine, honestly, nothing surprises me now,' I said through gritted teeth.

We sat for a good ten minutes, my head resting on the ledge of her gigantic squashy boobs. Reminded me of my mother's maternal embrace. She stroked my hair gently and made reassuring shushing noises, which made me feel supported and slightly better. I sniffed and sobbed some more.

Triiiiiiiiiiiiiiiiiiiiiiiiiiiiing

The doorbell went again.

'Fucking hell. Not now, not today, cannot deal with this,' I moaned.

'It's OK, I'll get it,' Pippa edged towards the hallway before stopping and turning back to me. 'If you don't mind?'

'Go ahead,' I said, lifting my head. I smoothed my hair back from my wet face. I necked another vodka shot. Need limes, I thought, and got up to go to the fridge, picked some off the shelf, popped them on the chopping board and grabbed a sharp knife.

'Whoah there, Katie, things aren't that bad, surely?' Hanna Frost stood at the breakfast bar.

'What?'

'The knife, your face . . .'

'Hanna, don't start, I've just had some incredibly, insanely awful news, delivered by Pippa, and I can't deal with your comments right now,' I said, waving the knife dismissively. I grabbed hold of a lime and sliced it in half. Hard.

'Katie, I'm sorry, darling, if I came across as criticizing

you, that totally wasn't my point. God no, honestly, honey, please, what's wrong?' Hanna said, rubbing her temples.

'I got a call from Richard,' she said, before glancing at Pippa. For someone she had never spoken fondly of, they looked fine in one another's company. How odd, I thought to myself, but quickly let it pass. Now wasn't the time to potentially inflame any kind of journo-war.

'I don't even know where to begin,' I sighed. I poured out three neat vodkas and placed a slice of lime in each. 'I'm having mine neat, but I have some cola or lemonade or whatever.'

'Do you have tonic water?' Hanna questioned.

'No. Do I look like a bloody pub?' I snapped. Hanna said nothing.

'I'll go to the shop for some,' Pippa said brightly. 'Maybe, Hanna, you could come with me and I can bring you up to speed away from Katie's ears, that way she doesn't need to go through it all again.'

'Good idea,' I barked.

The two women shuffled out of the kitchen and down the hallway. Seconds later I head the door close gently.

'Oh, Danielle!' I shouted to the empty house. 'Why did you do this to me? How could you do this to me!'

'Meow!' Grum said, nuzzling my hand, which was placed firmly on the bottle of vodka.

Right, I thought, I'll go delete her from my Facebook. That way she'll never know what's going on in my life, what I like, what I don't, who I'm having it off with, where I'm going, anything! She can be deleted! This was the twenty-first-century way of ending friendships, after all. One click of a mouse, bye bye Danielle. Bitch! I traipsed up the stairs and caught sight of myself in a mirror. Weirdly, despite being emotionally tortured with photographs, my make-up had remained intact. My tears had not ruined my face. I even looked quite edgy. Even though I was wearing the most beautiful salmon-pink, slashed-to-the-navel wrap dress. Yeah, well, I was planning on declaring my love for Bailey and then he was supposed to take in the *bella vista* which was *moi*, in silk, by Donna Karan, a J-Lo dress. It was sexy, classy, gorgeous. It was the image I wanted to give him of me. And now I was knocking back vodka in it, alone, with my cat, like a saddo. I sighed heavily. It hurt to breathe. Razorblade breathing. Stomach tight, in knots, I logged into my Gmail.

FACEBOOK: Nicola Baxter has accepted your friend request.
Jan.Lewis@hotmail.com: HIGHLIGHTS PURRRLEASE!
Do YOU Want To Perform Better In Bed? You Can with COCK-A-RAMA!
Danielle.Kingsley@yahoo.co.uk: Lunch in London Baby!

Fuck off! I hissed under my breath. I didn't open it, not right now. First I wanted to find out what Nicola Baxter's problem was. She was being ultra bitch blast from the past and I had no reason at all to explain her behaviour. I mean, OK I nicked a lipstick in Boots and blamed it on her back when we were thirteen, yes I might have snogged Barry Wilmslow in year eight, deliberately, knowing she fancied him, but come off it, this was like donkey's years ago and we'd had tons of fun times since then, including Ibiza for our joint seventeenth, despite the crabs incident, which in the end came from the hotel's dirty towels, not from a boy because neither of us pulled on that holiday, on account of having extreme sunburn. Mum was right, in a way. Although we didn't get lobsters, we certainly looked like them. Still. We were friends, weren't we? But then again, after finding out about Danielle's odious actions, could I really be sure of any loyalty, love or honesty? I clicked on her page.

Nicola is . . . in the Cow's Hoof beer garden with the gang.

Hmm. The gang. I suppose she's referring to the rest of the village idiots. I flicked on to Info. So, she's in a relationship with Jamie Entwhistle. Hmm, he was a geek at school, wonder what he's like now? He wore jar-bottomed glasses if I remember correctly and was obsessed with *Star Trek*. Nice choice. Mind you, seems as though they're all stable and happy in love and stuff, judging by the number of photographs of everyone arm-in-arm, having a laugh. Yeah, the men were ugly. But who was uglier? Them, or Jack and Danielle? Sure, Jack and Danielle looked stylish and pretty, but they were black on the inside, they had to be, for what they'd done to me. I fought back tears and, in my anger, wrote Nicola Baxter an email through Facebook, containing a piece of my mind.

Dear Nicola, Delete, delete it out, way too formal.

Nicola . . . No no no no no, too accusatory, need to lull her in.

Hey Nicola, Yes, good start, not too horrible or scary, she'll keep reading.

Thanks for telling the fucking world about my crabs, you double crossing cow!

Can't help myself . . . this anger has to go somewhere!

Thankfully I have decent PR who contained that bit of nasty, horrible information that wasn't, for the record, entirely true anyway. I mean, the hotel admitted it was the towels and it's not like I could pull any boys with your bright red face shining out in the club like a radioactive beacon of light. God. Ever heard of colour correction foundation? So, yeah, anyway, I mean, I know we had our differences and all that, but seriously, Nicola, why on earth do you want to cause me pain? Don't you think I have been through enough humiliation lately? Some friend you are, Nicola Baxter!

Send.

There, that's Nicola dealt with, now on to Danielle . . .

'Katie!' Hanna shrieked from the hallway. Great . . . they're back.

Danielle would have to wait.

'Darling, we have vodka, tonic and nibbles!' Hanna continued.

'Are you OK up there?' Pippa joined in.

I said nothing. Let 'em stew, I was in no mood to be courteous. I looked towards my computer, logged off and walked to the top of the stairs, straightening my dress as I went. My beautiful, gorgeous dress. Seemed to be the only true thing around at the moment. Least I knew my dress wasn't a big, fat, fake phoney!

'Is she, you know, into the glamour of celebrity suicide?' I could hear the distinct whinny of Frenella. Where had she come from? I wondered.

'Don't be stupid,' Hanna hissed. 'She's just, you know, had to cope with seeing Jack pawing her best friend. The Little Miss Perfect best friend Danielle who actually was a female snake in the grass, albeit in a very nice tailored suit.'

'She was a snake, wasn't she?' Frenella mused. 'Didn't see that coming. You're right, though. About the suit. Did you see those sexylicious Glads she had on that time? Stunning.' She nods knowingly at Pippa who stands at the bottom, shuffling on her sensible heels.

'Darling?' Hanna calls, with a note of concern for my well-being in her voice.

'Girls!' I say, bright and smiley at the top of the stairs. I edge my way down.

'Frenella, I am peachy, Pippa, thanks for telling me, and Hanna, you have nibbles?'

They all nod in unison and smile perfect, bright, flashy smiles. Except Pippa. Her teeth are normal, the odd crooked one here, a coffee-stained one there.

'Great then, so who's drinking?' I say as we all get comfortable around the breakfast bar.

'Well, we thought you could do with some company, you know, considering . . .' Hanna trails off. She tinkles her bright pink nails on the kitchen counter.

'Ooh, your nails are to die for!' I exclaim. Well, if you can't beat 'em . . .

'Yes, darling, they are, would you like a little mani/pedi before we go out?'

'Um, yes and go out, where, what? Like this?' I said, totally forgetting I actually looked pretty hot, despite the emotional pain that must have been etched across my face . . . and then I remembered . . . I'd had Botox! This meant my face didn't move! Hurrah! No one knew my inner turmoil! No wonder I thought I looked remarkably composed for someone who feels as though she's from one of those chav magazines about best friends running off with husbands and boyfriends turning into women. I held out my hands for Frenella, who had already unpacked her nail bar in anticipation of me saying yes. She was beginning to know me too well.

'We need some music,' Hanna said, wandering around my living room, playing with the remote. She flicked through the channels on my television. 'Jesus, Katie, how big is your television?' she said.

'Jack's idea. He wanted it to be big. Bigger the better, he said.'

'What was up with him?' Frenella quipped. 'Couldn't afford a sports car so had to have the biggest telly instead, to help him deal with his small willy?' she giggled.

'Something like that,' I said. I didn't stick up for him. I was past caring about Jack Hunter and his torrid love life. Or his penis. Honestly, I was totally over it, him, her, them, the whole lot of them. Even Bailey. Who even though he had run out to catch me the other night, still hadn't bothered to call me, or turn up here or anything. So that says it all really, doesn't it? I remembered this bit of advice I got from a random bloke outside a club one night, where I was once again crying over some guy treating me like shit. I sobbed into my handbag, mascara dancing down my face, lips chapped from the cold. It was always cold.

'You know what, if a man wants to contact you, he will.'

'But what if like, his computer is down . . .'

'He'll find one.'

'Or his phone's run out of battery and he's gone to a party on a mountain so even if he had a battery he couldn't get a signal, could he, you know . . .'

'Bullshit.'

'Commitment issues.'

'Rubbish.'

Crestfallen, I looked at my shoeless feet, grubby and bloated.

'Listen up, if a man wants you, he'll let you know and he'll find a way. And if he doesn't, then discard him, forget it, and move on to one who does.'

'Thanks,' I said, mentally recounting the times boys had told me they'd had no signal, no battery, computer crashed. Oh God, I'd been had, multiple times, and not in a fun way.

'So, if he doesn't call me?'

'I think you know the answer to that, girly,' he said, puffing smoke into the dark night. 'Always make yourself a little bit unavailable, hold something back . . .' he said and then he drifted like an archangel on acid (this was the late nineties) into the night, never to be seen again. I hadn't heeded his advice. Stupid girl that I was, when a man appeared he was always 'different' to the last one, or anyone else's man experience that there ever was in the history of love civilization. You know it, I know it. The difference is, we're always going to make excuses, no matter what.

Eventually Hanna settled on Heat radio and we got in a happy mood. Well, I was getting happier with every empty glass of vodka tonic that was topped up by a concerned-looking Pippa Strong.

'Everything OK?' I nodded to her.

'Yeah, it's just I don't really have anything to wear, you know. I may have to go home and change.'

'Don't be stupid, Pippa,' Hanna said in her evil, caustic,

you're sooo below me tone that she normally used on me. 'You're fine as you are, besides, we've got VIP.'

I looked at Pippa's shape. She was bigger than me. What a feat in the world of media, this woman was at least an eighteen. There was nothing here I could lend her. I was only in a slinky Donna Karan, slashed-to-the-navel J-Lo dress thanks to the heartbreak diet. I'd shed half a stone, perhaps a bit more. Just as well, because magic pants totally didn't go with this outfit. I'd also been banned from carbs. Maybe that had something to do with it? I thought, admiring my slimline physique.

'We're going to Mahiki tonight,' Hanna announced, sipping her vodka.

'Mahiki?' I exclaimed. 'Isn't that where, you know, royalty and really mega famous movie stars go?'

'Yes, Katie, and you know something? You will fit in like a dream!' She smiled warmly at me.

'Oooh!' she said, grabbing her massive Hermès tote in pale turquoise. 'I nearly forgot, your official copy of *Sizzle Stars*. What do you think!' she passed it towards me, jubilant.

'Oh, I've already seen it,' I said.

'Oh really?' she said.

'Richard brought it earlier. I love it. It's great, isn't it?' I said, looking into Frenella's eyes and smiling. 'You write well, I came across really good, thanks.'

'No problem.' She smiled back.

'Well,' Hanna said, still smiling. 'That's perfectly OK as long as you're happy with it and you are, so that's just fabulous.' She took another sip of her drink. 'Can I smoke in here?'

'Sure,' I replied, 'if you open the window. Grum, my cat, he's not a fan.' I smiled. My nails were in desperate need of fillers, thank heavens for Frenella and her vanity case.

'Shouldn't take too long tonight, Katie, only the tips need sorting,' she said, furrowing her brows and concentrating hard.

'So what happened with Brett?'

'Brad?'

'Was it Brad?'

'Not sure if it was actually, come to think of it!' Frenella giggled.

'Whatever,' I said, wafting my freshly painted hand under a little plug-in UV lamp to dry it off.

'He was a good kisser,' she said, coquettishly.

'And the rest!' I squealed. This vodka was really making me feel good!

'Shut up!' she joked with me. 'Get outta here!'

'How big was it?!' I laughed.

'Not telling,' she said. 'My lips are sealed.'

'Oh, go on . . .' I nudged her with my foot. 'Tell me!'

'OK . . .' she giggled, 'it was this big!' she said, holding her hands a ridiculously large length apart.

'You get outta here!' I said, laughing.

'Seriously,' she confirmed, pushing her hands into a willy-shape. 'It was mammoth, massive, the biggest, like, ever invented.'

'Yeah, yeah,' I said dismissively, let her have her fun.

'He was actually, you know,' she said, quieter this time.

'Sure he was,' I replied.

'Look,' she said, producing her phone and scrolling

down the pictures. 'See!' she said, smirking, handing the phone to Pippa first who went beetroot red.

'Oh, my!' she said, shuffling on her seat.

'No way!' I breathed. She was right, it was an incredible appendage.

'I wouldn't have believed it myself unless I'd seen it with my very own eyes,' Hanna chipped in, smoking in the corner whilst applying fresh make-up in her compact mirror.

'There's a bigger mirror in the hallway, Hanna, if you want to use that one,' I pointed in the direction of the mirror.

'Bigger!' Frenella sniggered.

'Shh!'

'Was he a porn star, then?' Pippa queried, nibbling on peanuts.

'Nah. I totally told him that he should be one, though, he was like, stoked about it. We couldn't have sex, though, unfortunately.'

'Why not!' I squealed. 'You'd have to, those don't come along often, men like that, good looking, ones who have the, uh, no pun intended here, whole package!'

'Katie, that was the problem. Did you see the size of him? Both in his height and in his trousers. And have you seen the size of me? I'm like five foot nothing, if that.'

'I see,' I said, wafting my other hand.

'We're done here, just let 'em dry,' Frenella continued. 'I didn't want to fuck him in the toilets, no way, and I wasn't taking him back to my house, my boyfriend was home.'

'Your boyfriend!' I whistled in surprise. 'You're a disgrace!'

I joked. Although I totally meant it. There I was warming to her, beginning to like her, finding common ground and it turns out she's as duplicitous as the rest. I smiled a fake smile and thanked Aubrey from afar for giving me the ability not to give anything away with my facial expressions. Botox, the potion of choice for faking a friendship!

'Enough about this stuff, honestly, Frenella, learn some decorum,' Hanna said, laughing under her breath.

'Decora what?' Frenella said, genuinely flummoxed.

'Nothing,' Hanna sighed. She looked resplendent in a bright red dress. Her heels were sky high. Frenella had on a little electric-blue boob-tube dress and with me in my salmon pink we looked hot to trot. The only problem was Pippa Strong. Her big nose and frizzy curls and frumpy dress were *so* totally not West End Girl material. I actually felt a bit smug. Now I understood what Aubrey, Hanna and the like got out of feeling this way about others who had on the wrong shoes. I felt better than her. Instantly I pieced together outfits in my wardrobe that I had been given for free by Tom Theodore etc. and imagined how Pippa Strong would look should she be given a makeover. She could be the journalist version of Susan Boyle!

'Katie?' Hanna said, walking over as though the length of my wooden flooring from one end of the kitchen to the other was a catwalk runway in Milan.

She laid a hand on my shoulder.

'I saw the photographs and I just wanted to say, I wish I had known sooner so we could have talked about this, you know, in only the way good friends can . . .' she drifted off. 'I hope you now see just how much of a friend I have been to you.' She paused for effect. 'And I know you think

I am mean to you and unnecessarily so sometimes, but honest to God, it's because I saw the potential in you and to be frank, I want you to be a ball-busting babe yourself. Fuck Jack Hunter, from what I've heard he's useless in the sack anyway, like finding a needle in a haystack . . .'

We all giggled. Vodka shot out of my nose.

'That's like the oldest put-down in the book, isn't it?' I said as I wiped my nose clean. 'Boyfriend dumps you, he's rubbish in bed, small knob anyway,' I trailed off. 'But seriously, he was and, you know, I can't tell you how disappointed I was but, you know, in the end it didn't matter, we learnt how to do it right, for us both . . .' I blushed. This wasn't the kind of conversation I wanted to be having with Hanna, Pippa and Frenella. They just giggled with me. There was such a good happy vibe in this room, despite the day's events, I couldn't help but imagine my troubles marooned on a desert island, never ever to be touched on again.

'That's it!' I said, raising a glass. 'No one is going to double-cross me, humiliate me, break my heart, spirit or anything else for that matter!' I wobbled my glass against the others as we all clinked for the toast.

'Too right, girl!' Frenella squealed.

'And Danielle is a rubbish friend,' Hanna said, coming over and giving me a hug. 'I always knew it, but I didn't want to say anything. I knew how much you loved her.'

'Thanks,' I said, hugging her back. Maybe I had it wrong all along, maybe with all of Danielle's subtle put-downs of Jack, of my new Stranna hat by Malene Birger that she accused of being from Primark. Then she was pushing me into the arms of Fabio, perhaps she was in cahoots with the press! That's how those photos of me with Fabio got out! Yes, on page six and seven of Jack Hunter's 'Exclusive' with *Oh Yay!* there were grainy pictures of me walking into The Dorchester with Fabio, emerging from The Dorchester, coming out of the spa, and one of the back of my head with what looked like Fabio kissing me, which was actually the nose-bashing moment.

Fuck! That could be the reason Bailey didn't call or come over! He'll have read *Oh Yay!* today and he'll have jumped to the same conclusions as the rest of the celebrity gossip-reading planet. I must tell him, clear it all up with him, soon. But not tonight, tonight . . .

'Tonight's all about the girls!' Hanna said, laughing. She raised her glass again. 'It's about having some fun, looking gorgeous and forgetting all about our troubles!'

'YEAH!' we all said in unison. 'FUCK MEN!'

'That too!' giggled Frenella.

'Shut it, potty mouth!' Hanna nudged her. Pippa smiled as she stuffed her gob with more peanuts.

'Right, well, I've texted my driver, he's on his way and in ten minutes, ladies, we'll be cruising down the West End ready for a night of intense action-packed glamour!'

'Awesome . . . so, who's your driver?' I queried, hoping it was Bailey, but then kinda hoping it wasn't Bailey, because then I'd have to talk to him or ignore him and things will get even more mega complicated and, arghh, not tonight. I sighed.

'His name is Ed, he's cool. Old chap, don't worry, Katie, it's not your man-crush, Sam Bailey.'

'I don't have a crush on Bailey,' I said, smoothing down my dress and adjusting my tit tape.

'Whatever.' Frenella quipped.

'Yes, well, even if you did, remember I told you he's bad news,' Hanna said gravely. 'And I was right about Jack and Danielle, wasn't I, Katie?' she said knowingly and with such conviction that I guess, well, she probably was right. In that case, I really ought to believe her more, because the people I loved and cherished and trusted implicitly have broken my heart into a zillion little un-put-back-together-able pieces. I was like a glamorous Humpty Dumpty. All the camp queens' clothing and all the fit men, couldn't put Katie Lewis together again . . .

Triiiiiiiiiiiiiiiiiiiiing!

The doorbell went. I wondered if it was Richard, back with a fresh Prada shirt or something. I went to the door.

'Danielle?' I said, shocked to the core. My blood ran cold. She stood there happy as Larry, bottle of Rioja in one hand and what smelled suspiciously like Chinese food in the other.

'You know I don't eat carbs any more,' I seethed, eyes narrowed.

'Jesus, Katie, what's eating you? That is, if you eat any more, you're all skin and bones.'

'Hardly,' I snapped. 'This is a Donna Karan dress, and Donna Karan does not dress people who are skin and bones, she dresses women with fabulous figures, like *moi*,' I said haughtily.

Danielle stood there dumbstruck. I knew what she was thinking. Who was this girl, where was podgy Katie Lewis, pushover Katie Lewis, her best friend?

'I don't think you're a pushover, Katie,' Danielle said, matter-of-fact. Fuck, my thoughts did a detour past my brain and tumbled out into the cold night air.

'I don't think you're podgy, either. I was joking. You know, that was a thing we used to do before all this . . .' she shrugs her shoulders.

'Before this drama?' I screech at her.

'Well, yes, Katie, if you must know, yes, before this drama.'

'Right . . . and you have, like, no idea do you, of the damage you do, do you ever take responsibility for anything in your life, or do you just go about fucking other people's boyfriends and husbands?'

Danielle visibly reddens and then pales. Stewart-small-penis was Danielle's Achilles heel. She's trembling and her voice cracks with the weight of her emotion.

'I do NOT fuck other people's boyfriends and I have zero clue what you are talking about, Katie. What is your problem, exactly?'

'What is my problem?!' I shout louder, waving my glass around in her face, one finger pointing at her as the vodka sloshes over the edge of the glass and on to her shoes.

'Fucking hell, Katie, these are suede!'

'So!' I spit. 'Fuck your shoes!'

'What?'

'Like you fucked Jack!' There, I've said it.

'Katie, are you on drugs?' Danielle says slowly.

'Don't be stupid,' I wobble.

'What the hell is wrong with you!' she screams back. 'I absolutely did not fuck Jack, you silly girl!'

'Well . . .' I begin, sneering at her.

'Jack,' she continues, pointing furiously at me, 'by the way, is NOT your boyfriend and hasn't been for a while now, so I could fuck him if I felt like it, which I don't . . .'

'So you did!' I shriek, ignoring her words.

Danielle's face twists with incredulous disbelief and her eyes dart back and forward.

'Talk about jumping in my grave! How long has it been going on?!' I bellow, shaking her by the shoulders.

'I don't know what you've heard, Katie, but it's not how it looks, or how it seems. Jack and I . . .'

SLAP!

My hand stings hot against skin. Hearing her refer to herself and Jack as a couple, as two people in one sentence, platonic or otherwise, was just way too much for me.

A sharp silence fills the air.

I just hit my best friend. Oh shit! Shit, shit, shit! What have I done? I stand backwards and bite my lip hard. I taste a bit of blood in my mouth.

Danielle gasps.

'Oh my God,' she whispers as she stares right at me with a look of pure disgust. Despite the fact I have just slapped my best friend for apparently sleeping with my ex-boyfriend, she should hit me back, do something, anything back to me but she can't do anything. She's rooted to the spot and her eyes are filling with tears. Her hands are full of food and alcohol, she's a rabbit in the headlights and I'm driving the car. I'm crying now, in full force.

'You fucking awful nasty double-crossing slag!' I scream at her.

'Kate?' she says, stuttering. 'I am so beyond hurt right

now, so absolutely, insanely upset with you right now, I haven't done anything wrong, what you think, is not how it was, how it is, I'm sorry that you . . .'

'Too late for apologies, Danielle, you cow!' I shout. Hanna appears behind me, holds my shoulders and stops me throttling Danielle.

'This is insane, Katie, you're wrong, I don't know what lies you've been fed, but this is totally outrageous and you are so completely out of order, but I'm willing to forgive you.' She measures her words. I can tell she is furious but she's hiding it, kind of. She breathes deep and places the food she brought by her feet. She continues.

'We need to talk some more about this, when you are sober, as you clearly have no idea what you're doing right now . . .'

'I know what I saw!' I shriek, not knowing exactly what I saw and wanting to stop, to listen to her explanations but fuelled by the booze, the glamour of my evening, the dresses, the promise of a new life. I couldn't stop, I couldn't just say 'OK' and invite her in, we were going out, and I was going to make it big and show the world exactly what I was made of. The mention of Jack still hurt a lot and I couldn't possibly imagine what it would be like if I really had seen Danielle having it off with Jack. It looked bad, you can't deny that those photographs did Danielle no favours. And so what if she was right, that they weren't shagging, it still doesn't explain what the hell they were doing together. I'd need intense therapy for evermore if they have even so much as air-kissed each other. But what if I was wrong? I had to save face in front of my new friends – there is no way I will back down now, not when they're hearing every single word we're saying . . .

'But . . . oh my God . . .' she begins, as it dawns on her that I won't be budging. Hanna cuts her off.

'Why don't you take your nasty, poisonous self away from Katie?' she sneers.

'Yeah, get outta here!' Frenella calls from the living room before bursting into rapturous laughter.

'You're so drunk,' Danielle says.

'And you're a bitch!' I retort. 'Hanna was right all along.'

'Well,' Danielle says, shoving the wine into my hands and gesturing to the bag of Chinese food on the floor. 'So, you don't want to talk to me right now about this stupid, crazy idea you have in your head that, for the record, isn't true, and you will know this, when you are back on this planet.' She attempts a laugh.

Why is she being so good about this? Is she mocking me? She must be!

'So, you're not interested in talking about this?' she says, as a small tear escapes down her face and nestles on her lips, which are quivering slightly with emotion. 'Are you serious? You really, honestly, truthfully swear on the cat's life?' she pleads.

I stare back at her through narrow eyes.

'Come on, Katie, this is so silly . . .' she reaches for my arm.

'No,' I say, turning away.

Frenella passes me the envelope. 'Want these?' she whispers.

'Yes,' I say politely to Frenella before turning back to my ex-best friend. 'Want to know why I can't even look at you right now, you lying cow?'

'Tell me!' she screams back, her voice shaking.

'Here!' I shriek, with one final vitriolic rant. 'Take these, Danielle Kingsley,' I say, pushing the file into her arms, 'and shove them up your fat arse!'

Danielle's eyebrows furrowed, her eyes filled up with tears and my heart broke once again, that very moment, for real, as I turned my back on my devastated best friend, as, clutching the envelope, she sobbed into her sleeve.

'Why Katie? Why?'

'I ask myself that all the time,' I said. And then I closed the door on Danielle.

'Give me a minute,' I said to Hanna. Wordlessly, Hanna retreated back into the living room, closing the door tight. I reached for my phone.

'I told her where to stick those photos,' I text Richard. *Message sent.*

I fought back the biggest tears in the entire world. I loved Danielle more than I've ever loved anyone, even a man. Not in a lesbo way, just she was my best friend, we'd been through so much together, which is why I just can't fathom how she could do this to me. She knew how much Jack meant to me. Lord, give me strength, I prayed, for the first time in my life.

'Right!' I said, standing up and wiping my eyes on a tissue. I looked good still, nothing a bit of lippy and Touche Éclat wouldn't fix. I opened the door to see the girls carrying on as though nothing had ever happened.

'I'll take that!' Hanna said, grabbing my phone and putting it in her bag. 'No drunk texting, dialling or Facebooking from that BlackBerry!' she said sternly.

'Good thinking, Batman,' I said, wincing at the memory of a phrase I used with both Jack and Danielle. Neither of whom is any longer present in my life. Hanna just stood there, glowing. She seemed so happy. I wonder what it's like for folk to be that happy all of the time. I really had her wrong, you know, and tonight just proved it. She stood up for me, she supported me and she's arranged for us to go to the most exclusive place in London, probably, and you know, she's just been amazing.

BEEP!

'Oooh, tinkles,' Frenella said, jumping to her feet. Her little legs moved fast towards the window where she peeked out into the night. 'Ed's here in the Hummer!' she squealed with delight.

'Great, fabulous, let's go, darling, oh and tonight,' Hanna winked at me, 'I have you something extra special lined up to cheer you up on what has been a crazy day for you.'

'Oh, yeah, you got that right,' I said, feeling suddenly sober. All the adrenaline that had pumped through my system from my altercation with Danielle had subsided and I felt as though I'd climbed a giant mountain. I felt both heady and exhausted.

'Here,' she said, pulling me close for another hug. 'I have you a room booked, the very best room there is, in The Mayfair, no less,' she said, smirking.

'The Mayfair?' I said, unsure as to which one that was.

'It's super classy, darling, and *très* expensive, thanking me, no?' she said, with mock sorrow.

'Of course, thank you, Hanna, that's a wonderful gift!'

'You're very welcome,' she smiles as we all trot outside to the Hummer.

As I leave I notice the Chinese dinner left in the hall. It was a symbol of a friendship gone wrong, in all its sugary carbohydrate glory. Everybody who was anybody famous knew that carbs were bad for you . . .

Chapter 17

'KATIE!! OVER HERE, LOVE! AAAAATTTTA GAL . . . SMASHING!'

The paps were, like, *all* over me. Totally chaotic, people I didn't know screaming my name, wanting my picture. I looked hot, so they got what they wanted.

'SEXY HOT GAAAAWJUSS, LAAAHHVV!'

Oooh this is good! My problems melted away with each camera flash.

'Mwah!' I blew a kiss to the press.

'Come on, star girl, don't want to be overexposed now, do we, darling,' Hanna whispered in my ear whilst posing provocatively next to me.

'QUICKLY, KATE, WHAT DO YOU THINK ABOUT JESSICA HILSON'S ENGAGEMENT TO YOUR EX-BOYFRIEND, JACK HUNTER?'

My stomach churned.

'I'M SORRY!' I called back over the noise of the flashbulbs. 'BUT I HAVE NO IDEA WHO YOU'RE TALKING ABOUT!' And I threw them an over-the-shoulder wink as I sashayed into Mahiki, bypassing the queues.

'Right, girls, what are we drinking?' I said, rubbing my hands together with glee.

'Table,' Hanna says, as a muscle-bound attendant comes

towards us. He bypasses Hanna and addresses me. Whoah! This is the first time this has happened! I look at Hanna, but she's looking the other way, pretending that she's not just been snubbed by Mahiki staff.

'Katie Lewis, I am a huuuuuge fan!' he gushed.

'Thanks!' I said, blushing.

'Let me take you to the most amazing table we have. It's way up here, on a top level, you can see all the action, but no one can really see much of you!' he said, as we followed him to a round table with seating and a curtain that we could pull around us if we wished.

Suddenly, he pulled my arm sharply towards him and whispered, 'Keep this on the down low, but two of your most favourite people in the whole entire world may be arriving here, just so you know, the place is crawling with undercover showbiz types looking for the juice on you . . .' he said with a smile plastered across his face. He turned to the group.

'My name is Ryan and I'll be your personal slave this evening,' he winked. 'First drinks are on the house,' he said as he moved off in the direction of the bar. The music was pumping loud with cool funky house beats. I felt truly euphoric, despite everything that had happened to me of late. Hanna's hard-nosed personality seemed to be rubbing off on me. As I gained power and status through fame, she became more subservient towards me. Just the little things I noticed, like looking out for me and saying nice things, the look in her eyes now suggested respect instead of pity. And they say it's what's on the inside that counts? Bollocks, it's all about what you look like, why else would my friendships have suddenly blossomed into the kind of friends I've always wanted? Why else indeed.

'This is HOT!' Frenella shouted above the bass-line beats. She stood up and started dancing on the podium next to us. She was pretty good. Her body twisted and turned with the rhythm of the music.

Pippa Strong fiddled with her shirt for the zillionth time this evening as Hanna huddled closer to me and flashed megawatt smiles at all the hunks checking us out from every direction. Fame tasted great. The drinks were placed upon our table in huge glasses full of sparkling alcohol with frosted rimmed tops. Amazingly intricate decorative fruit pieces adorned the top of the drinks.

'Mmmm!' I grinned, taking a sip.

'The cocktails in here are to die for,' Hanna said breezily. She'd been here a thousand times before, I suppose she knew what she was talking about.

'Worth the £200-a-round tab,' she said, as though she was discussing the price of fish.

'Oomph' I said, spluttering slightly. Hanna raised her eyebrow in alarm.

'Don't worry, darling,' she soothed. Hmm. I was half expecting her to shoot me down like she normally does when I shoot alcohol out of my nose, fall over my own feet or accidentally say the word 'fuck' in public.

'First round's on the house, remember?'

'Are you serious?'

'Yes! Do you know how much positive PR you will bring merely just by sitting your peachy *derrière* on that seat?'

'No . . . well . . . I guess?'

'No guessing about it, baby cakes, you're a star now, don't you forget it!'

'I know!' I said, drunkenly letting it slip out. How vain of me! I wasn't drunk, though. I mean, I was but not in the way I was last night, slipping and sliding all over the place. Bad times. I felt properly in control and *très* smug.

'Thanks, Hanna,' I said, feeling a rush of happiness.

'What for?' she replied, smiling bright red glossy lips.

'For . . .' I was about to say, for being a shit-hot PR, for kicking my butt into losing weight, for putting me in touch with the amazing hair god Ziggy Wang, for making me feel good about myself for the first time since all this Jack Hunter debacle began, for introducing me to Tom Theodore, the most stylish man on earth, for Aubrey and his Botox, for Frenella and her writing and her nails, for Bailey . . . I wanted to say all of those things and more, but I remembered watching and cringing at the Oscars circa 1999, when Gwyneth Paltrow's acceptance speech went on for an age . . . No, must not be gushy. Thinking about all the help I'd had to look this amazing, it was a great wonder to me how half the mega famous movie stars even got out of the house of a morning. I wonder what they'd look like pre-stylist, pre-zero carb and pre-high maintenance. I couldn't imagine shopping in Boots ever again for cosmetics. So *passé*.

Hanna looked at me adoringly.

'I wanted to say thanks,' I began again, forgetting about not wanting to gush and totally gushing all over her, 'for being you, my new best friend!'

I felt like I'd just told the man of my dreams that I

loved him for the first time. My words hung not so silently in the air, due to our club surroundings, and there was that split-second moment when the fear of rejection makes you pull a weird face where you're getting ready to say, 'Only joking, God, don't take me seriously, booze, too much, makes me love eeeeeeveryone, honestly, hah, aren't I silly?'

Except Hanna Frost didn't reject me.

'I love you too, and you're totally my best friend!' she giggles and pulls me in for a hug. I belong here, I think to myself. I really do.

'I'm just going to go to the bathroom,' I say above the noise to Hanna. 'Come with?'

'No, darling, I'm going to stay here,' she says. 'I have my eye on a very naughty-looking man wearing Lanvin . . .' she licks her lips.

'I'll come,' says Pippa.

'OK, cool,' I say and Pippa alights, arranges her shirt and we walk towards the ladies' loos.

'There's no queue?' I exclaim in surprise.

'VIP,' the loo lady says, as she chews gum slowly.

About a dozen perfumes were laid out on the side next to a large box of lollipops.

'Thanks,' I said as I looked in the mirror. My hair was perfect, my lipstick and all other bits of make-up were intact and I still looked every inch the immaculate starlet.

'Just nipping to the loo, won't be a minute,' I said brightly, as I opened the cubicle door and sat down. Just then, I heard the outer door swing open and smelled the strong, sweet scent of perfume. Which kind, I was unsure . . . I sniffed the air. Bubblegum?

'OH MY GOD,' the unmistakeable voice pierced the air.

'I was like, sooooooo out of there, those vibes, badness.'

No. It couldn't be.

'Jack like, you know, he's a doll and all that but when I saw Fabio I nearly D.I.E.D. It was beyond badness.'

'You totally still love him, Jessica,' an unknown female voice chirruped.

'Like, duh, Hayley, of course I do.'

'And Jack?'

'Jack has totally worked out for me, did you, like, see the look on Fabio's face when he saw me! It was, like, totally a picture, right?' I heard her smack her lips.

'Oh God, yah, a total picture, OMG, like, what are you gonna do, Jess?'

'See, yah, I was thinking, Jack's downstairs by the bar with his agent . . . Fabio he's, like, right over in the corner . . . I guess go dance with you in front of Jack so he thinks I'm dancing for him, but, like, throw some looks over at Fabio to remind him of how absolutely amazing I am. That will make him put that giant rock on my finger . . .'

'I like your style, girl,' Hayley said.

'Ready?'

'Ready.'

'No, wait, how does my hair look?'

'Gorgeous, as always.'

'Yah, you're right! I totally am gorgeous!'

The door swung shut as I stood up and flushed the loo. I opened the cubicle door to see Pippa standing there with her mouth wide open.

'You didn't hear that,' she said.

'Uh, yes, I so totally did!' I replied, confused. What was

335

she talking about, of course I heard that, I was sitting right there with only a toilet door between me and the bitch that ruined my life, but then, I can't hate her too much, she inadvertently made my life 100 per cent fashionably better.

'What are you going to do?' Pippa breathed. She looked genuinely afraid.

'Well, I need to talk to Hanna,' I said, my heart beating rapidly.

Hanna will know what to do. Hang on, I need to tell Richard! Basically from what I've just gathered, Jack is about to be publicly humiliated by Jessica, unless . . . I step in. Could I really help him? Suddenly, memories of how he's hurt me infiltrate my brain. Could I help a man who broke my heart without a second thought? All the nights of crying, the tears that have fallen to the floor, joined more often than not by me. I don't know if I can forget about the day of THAT TEXT, when I opened the wardrobe to find rows of empty coat hangers dangling like bats in a cave, my heart pounding as I ransacked the bedroom, hunting for evidence that he was still present in my life, finding nothing, nothing at all but the dregs of his posh soaps, bathroom stuff and an ancient love letter. And let's not forget about Jack having it off with my best friend and humiliating me even further by professing to be the 'wronged' party, a victim of my 'cheating' with Fabio Matravers who, if you remember, I didn't even snog! Of COURSE I could bloody well let Jack Hunter get shafted by Jessica, in fact, I want to watch with a side order of canapés.

'Jack Hunter has been P.L.A.Y.E.D!' I shrieked to Hanna over the beat of the club music.

'He's what?' she called back, pushing her long, dark hair behind her ears and leaning in.

'He's been had!' I squealed.

'Explain,' Hanna said, as Pippa attempted to butt in. Hanna put her finger to her mouth in a shushing motion and waved at Pippa to sit down. Frenella was deep in conversation with a strapping hunk in a tight white vest top. Made me think of Bailey and his fondness for tight white t-shirts.

'He's about to be screwed over by Jessica Hilson!' I said, with one eye on the guy's butt and the other on Hanna.

'She's here?' Hanna visibly paled.

'Yes, she's here!' I exclaimed excitedly, before raising an eyebrow (with some difficulty thanks to the Botox) and nodding towards her cheeks. 'You need some more blush, here, let me sort you out . . .' I began pulling my bag open.

'I'm fine,' she said, pushing my hand back on to my bag. It snapped shut.

'Suit yourself, but I have to go now, I have to do something mega important!'

Hanna looked at me blankly.

'God, Hanna, I have to warn Fabio!' I said, quickly standing up. Fabio had always treated me with respect, even when I was ice queen central and then did a disappearing act on him the night of the *Murked* premiere. Besides, I wasn't going to miss an opportunity to saunter past Jack Hunter in a clingy Donna Karan number, was I? I bet he thinks I'm sitting at home with ultra-hairy legs, stuffing my face with biscuits and having threesomes with Ben & Jerry. Hah, well, I'll show him, since Jack Hunter had been out of my life I had become a better, more positive person. I was no longer constantly on edge about when would be the next time Jack Hunter was going to go cool on me. No longer did I have to wait up for him to get back from his evenings out without me, no more did I have to pander and pay and listen endlessly to him moaning about wanting to break into the acting world. No, I was thinner, happier and altogether more together than I'd been in a long time. He can see me, and weep.

'Oh no, you don't,' Hanna screamed, pulling my arm down violently. I staggered on my heels and flopped back against the seating.

'What the fuck did you do that for?' I said suddenly, my confidence still strong enough to swear at Hanna without fear.

I was still reeling from the Danielle and Jack escapade, although that totally didn't make any sense at all now that I had given it more than five seconds' thought. The alcohol had allowed me to face up to my worst nightmares ten zillion times easier than mulling them over with just a quiet cup of tea. I could think in great detail about the whys and wherefores of Danielle and Jack's dalliances. It didn't really make much sense. Except that Danielle had been trying to tell me something since the spa trip, hadn't she? This must be it! It had to be her sex confession involving Jack. But then, the pictures were taken outside her office – what would Stewart-small-penis say, or indeed do, if he'd seen them together? I'd never met Stewart, but I did know he was a forceful man with a lot of power and money at his disposal. He may have been pushing his late fifties and he may very well only have been five foot seven, but he was a pocket-rocket power demon. I knew this much. Jack would have been shot in his Tom Cruise heels for so much as touching a follicle on her head.

Sitting back, a little bit winded by Hanna's forceful pull on my arm, I pushed my hair behind my shoulders, looked her square in the eye and lifted myself back up again. Hanna stood up and we were boob to boob. I noticed in the corner of my eye that Frenella had broken off from the beefcake and was now watching us with trepidation.

'You're not going down there to make a scene,' Hanna snarled.

'Yes, I am,' I said, before realizing my mistake. 'I mean,' I backtracked, 'I'm not going to make a scene, Hanna, I'm going to talk to my friend downstairs, Fabio.' I sniffed.

'Please, darling, don't leave me,' she said mournfully. I scrunched up my nose. She continued.

'It's just, well, I've been meaning to tell you something all night, there was more than one reason for us being up here . . .' she said, sadly. Is she about to cry? Her voice wobbled. 'It's just that Fabio behaved, uh, inappropriately towards me, after you left the other night at the premiere.'

'What?' I said, stopping in my tracks. I turned back to face her.

'He, well, he looked at me in a way that suggested predatory sexual intent.' She looked at her shoes.

'He perved on you?' I whispered.

'Yes. I believe he did . . . and . . .'

'What else?'

'And, well, it wasn't the first time,' she said, bowed head still only glancing up to look at me.

'Oh God, that's just not good, is it?' I gasped.

'I don't want to come between you or anything, but I just thought you should know. To be honest, he's one in a long line,' she simpered.

'Really? Hanna, you poor thing!' I said, lending her a hand, I rubbed her shoulder gently. We both sat back down again.

'I've been in this business for an age,' she said, wafting her hand.

'I think this requires more cocktails,' I said, hoping to defuse what was potentially an explosive situation. Hanna's oracular presence toned down a notch as she solemnly gazed into the middle distance. I swear she even shed a tear.

'Who else?' I queried. The star-struck attendant glanced over and I tipped my empty cocktail glass in his direction. He nodded and made his way to the bar area. I could get used to all this fuss and splendour, oh yeah, but now, more pressing issues were in front of me in the shape of Hanna Frost and downstairs, God, well, the whole love crew. I had to tie this up and give her the slip. As much as I admired and revelled in my new best-friend love affair, I couldn't just sit there and be privy to the dramas about to unfold and not even watch Jack Hunter get his comeuppance! Yes, I suppose I ought to be the bigger, better person, Lord knows I was the bigger before, but now, well you name me a girl who doesn't secretly want to outdo her ex if he's shat on her from a very great height and then proceeded to watch it splatter? His ego totally needed to come down a peg or two and I'll be damned if I miss it.

Meanwhile, Hanna dabbed her cheeks with a serviette.

'I'm sorry, it's just, he,' she whispers dramatically, 'he really scared me!'

'Well, I would never have expected anything like this from Fabio,' I sigh. 'He was always so gentle and unassuming and chivalrous.'

'Lucky you,' she says, deadpan.

'Well, yes, lucky me, if this is what he's really like! Was he drunk?'

'What are you saying?'

'Nothing! Why?'

'Are you saying a man needs to be drunk to find me attractive?' She had that glint in her eye, one that suggested malice. I was ricocheting between trusting her with my shoes and wondering whether she was the full shilling.

'Look, Hanna,' I sigh, whilst simultaneously rubbing her arm to soothe her. 'I had no idea and I'm so sorry that you felt so upset and uncomfortable but it doesn't detract from the issue at large now, does it?' I say firmly.

'Which is?'

'That Jessica has been using my ex-boyfriend to get to Fabio and she's down there right now about to play both of them against each other and I just can't let it happen to Fabio, because, despite what he's done to you, he didn't do it to me.' I pull my face taut, fully expecting a verbal assault of some kind, but instead Hanna looks contemplative.

'OK, Kate, do what you have to do.'

'Thanks,' I say, getting up on to my feet to leave. 'I mean that.'

'I understand,' she continues, 'that you have a skewed perception of what constitutes loyalty in a best friendship,

341

after all, you only have to look at the cards Danielle Kingsley and Jack Hunter brought to the table, so one can't really blame you,' she says, sipping her drink. She looks, once again, on the edge of tears.

'What do you mean?' I say, annoyed that this conversation is preventing me from going downstairs.

'It's just, I am so super used to it,' she sighs, swirling her cocktail glass.

'Used to what?' I was rapidly losing patience with her cryptic whinging.

'I'm so used to girls pretending to like me for what they can get. Girls pretending to be my best friend when really, all they ever have in mind is themselves and their own agenda.' She pauses.

I look at her and shrug my shoulders. 'I'm not like that,' I say.

'Hmm,' she muses. 'I don't think you know what loyalty is. Don't think anyone does, not in this industry.'

'OK,' I sigh heavily, sitting back down. 'You win.'

'Really?' Hanna's entire face lights up.

'I love you,' I lie through my teeth. 'I will be here for you, and no one else.'

'That's just fab, darling, see I underestimate all the time so that I can be massively surprised. Katie,' she says, patting my leg, 'I knew you had it in you!'

At that moment, Richard pulled back the curtain of our private booth.

'Katie, thank heavens,' he said, out of puff.

'What is it?' I said, glancing at Hanna, whose face didn't move. She barely looked at him.

'We need to talk,' he said, pulling me up.

'I think Katie wants to remain here,' Hanna barked.

'I think I do, too,' I said, making eyebrow gestures to Richard.

He stared back blankly.

'You know, stay here and enjoy the company, girl stuff,' I said, furiously arching my brows, attempting to gesticulate that I knew what he meant, I'd be there.

'I'll follow you on later,' I said, arching them some more.

'Katie, why are you staring at me like that? You're freaking me out.'

'I'm not!' I said, 'Ah, come here, a hug is needed, thanks for being a great friend earlier!' I said, pulling him in close and whispering, 'Go wait for me at the top of the stairs and give me five, I was trying to prompt you with my eyebrows!'

'But they don't move!' he hissed back. 'Botox princess!'

'See you later, Richard, maybe,' I said and waved.

'Yes, probably tomorrow,' Richard pushed. 'Annabelle has accompanied me here tonight, mustn't leave her too long now,' he nodded and backed out towards the exit. 'Bye then, Katie,' he nodded in the direction of Frenella and Hanna, 'ladies,' and then he was gone.

'Phew, that got rid of Richard!' I said with gusto, to convince Hanna that I was on her side. 'I'm on your side, you know. That Fabio, what a creep!'

'Thanks, Kate, I knew you would be.'

Frenella stood at the balcony with the hunk, she looked round and we locked eyes for a second, she was checking I was OK and I was truly touched. I gave a subtle nod. She smiled and returned to the guy.

'Hey, Katie, I need to go to the bathroom. Will you wait

here for me? I won't be long,' Hanna said, standing up. She held her mobile in her hand.

'Sure,' I said lightly, as she moved off in the direction of the Ladies. She didn't take her handbag. What was she up to? I wondered. Any girl knows that if you go to the bathroom you sure as hell take your bag with you, to apply touch ups of make-up. Especially a woman like Hanna. I looked at her little clutch bag nestling between the drinks on the table, wondering whether I should follow her and give her the bag, save her the trip of coming back to get it. All of a sudden, something began to glow through the fabric.

My phone! That glow of colour was my phone either ringing or with a text. I remembered she took my phone to prevent me from drunk dialling anyone I shouldn't. But then I realized, the people I'd drunk dial if I was in one of those moods, which I wasn't, well, my point was, if I edged over to the balcony, I'd see them for myself, so there was no reason now for Hanna to take care of my phone. I gingerly opened the bag and pulled the phone out. Missed calls. Twelve of them. Richard, Danielle and Bailey. Bailey! He called me! Woop! I thought. I wonder, is he here? The distinct no-nonsense chimes of Hanna's voice could be heard coming towards me.

'And yes, I have put you on the list for this season's handbag, yes, you are ahead of . . .' she continued to placate a client before heading straight over to the edge of the balcony.

I snapped my phone shut and looked around quickly for a place to put it. Can't put it in my bag because only have teeny-tiny bejewelled clutch thing in the shape of a sea creature. I had on no bra, with simply tit tape holding my boobs in place. Only one thing for it, I thought, gazing down the length of the split in the front of my dress which went down to my navel. I shoved it in my very tight French knickers and sat very, *very* still. I prayed that no one would call or text me, causing my nether regions to light up and letting Hanna discover I had stolen my phone. She'd only take it off me again. She'd become like one of those suspicious chavs I watched on *Jeremy Kyle*, wanting to know my movements, not wanting me anywhere near Fabio et al downstairs. Not even around Richard. She had grown possessive and dramatic and I wondered whether everything was as it seemed with her. Stop it, I chastised myself. Hanna Frost was being so good, had been so good to me, I mustn't assume she's a conniving, backstabbing cow, just because it turned out my last best friend was. Still, I had to find out what Bailey wanted, must meet Richard, must give Hanna the slip.

'Sorry about that,' she said, as she returned to the table and sat down opposite me. I strategically placed my bejewelled sea-creature clutch over my own jewels.

'I had something else to tell you,' Hanna said gravely.

Oh God, what could it be now?

'It's about Bailey.'

Someone texted me, I'm buzzing, oh God, oh God!

'Katie, is something up?' Hanna queried. 'You just shuddered rather violently.'

'I'm fine!' I said, a little too shrilly.

'Right, well, you know, I have a confession,' she said, scratching her nose.

'What is it?' I said, my voice ridiculously high-pitched.

My phone vibrated against my skin.

'Aieeeeekk!' I involuntarily screamed.

'Good Lord, Katie, whatever is the matter?' Hanna exclaimed.

'I love this song!' I screamed, held one arm out as though I was ready to go on a march.

'It's not that good,' she said, before her body heaved with another dramatic sigh. 'It's Bailey,' she said, looking down and then up at me. She fiddled with her fingers.

'What about him?' I said, a little bit too interested. I was useless at pretending I didn't like Bailey, heck, I was supposed to have gone over there today and laid all my cards on the table, after Richard so expertly managed to get me to face up to my love for him. I'd hoped he would then lay me on the table, ravish me, undress me, pull me closer until . . . ! And then I thought, what does it matter? I don't have to lie about my feelings for Bailey, it's not as though she's had a relationship with him or, you know, fallen in love with him now, is it?

'Bailey and I, we, well, we've been having an affair.'

'You've what?!' I said, shouting. Frenella's head spun round to watch us. The man she was with kept trying to entice her back to his embrace by pulling at her chin, he'd move her gaze to face him, she'd pat him playfully and turn back towards us girls. I looked up and nodded to her to let her know all was OK, even if I didn't know what the hell was going on or indeed if it was actually OK.

'We've been having an affair for ages now,' she said, wafting her hand. 'I had to keep it secret because Lydia, my sister, would totally kill me. But she's moved to Australia for a year as of today . . . so I figured it wouldn't really matter if I went public with Bailey, after all, one can't help who one falls in love with, can one?' she smiled.

'Oh my God,' I said, my breathing shallow. This cannot be happening!

'So, why are you telling me this?' I said.

'Because I know that you and he were, how shall I put it, getting close, and I didn't want you to get hurt again, God, not after what you've been through with Jack Hunter and Jessica . . .'

'Don't say her name,' I said, with venom.

'Why ever not?'

'Just don't say it. It makes me feel physically sick. Please don't say it.'

'Whatever,' Hanna said.

I decided to let her blatant disregard for my feelings go right over my head. From now on I was going to pick my battles carefully.

'I had to tell you, because remember when I told you the truth about how Fabio took you on a date to gain Jessica's attention? Well, Bailey had to find someone to use as a decoy,' she smirked, 'for us.'

'Are you serious?' I said, dying a little more inside.

'Fraid so, Katie . . . I hate to tell you this, but I knew and counted on the fact that if Bailey got close to you, you'd tell Richard, he'd probably tell Aubrey, who would tell Tom Theodore and all the attention would be detracted away from me and placed on you, which in turn created the ideal opportunity for Bailey and me to spend time alone together,' she put her fingers up in quotation marks and continued with, 'working late, and no one would be suspicious of us because of you, oh God, Katie, you know how it goes . . .'

'How could you do such a thing to me?' I said.

My stomach felt as though I'd inhaled broken bottles.

'I feel . . . humiliated, I mean, Fabio was humiliating, Jack Hunter was beyond humiliation central, and what, now Bailey?'

'Well, no one expected you to get over Jack Hunter in the time it takes to boil an egg now, darling, did they? Did you even?'

'Who says I am over him?' I said, desperately trying to claw back some dignity. No one knew how I felt inside about Jack, aside from Danielle. You can be over someone but that doesn't necessarily mean you're over what they did to you. I was over Jack Hunter but I hadn't yet fully come to terms with the way in which our relationship ended. Hanna didn't know that. She didn't have to. What is it with this woman? Did she not want to see me happy? I decided there and then that Hanna Frost was the ultimate frenemy. She was like a doll, a totally amazing wonderful friend when I was on my knees, suffering, heartbroken, frizzy and in awful clothes. OK, not entirely true, she was mostly acerbic and yada yada yada, but I get that, it was from being around the fashion gays. God knows, Aubrey has a heart of gold and Tom Theodore and Ziggy Wang especially have their hearts firmly in the right places. And tonight Hanna demonstrated that she cared for my welfare, she organized a hotel suite for me for Christ's sake, she hugged me, she stood up for me, stood by my side when I was going bananas at Danielle for her hideously awful love crime against me. She was here, and she needed my support and I should be giving it to her. I mean, of course I will give it to her, but something hurt when she spoke to me, deep inside. Something ached when she spoke about her and Bailey in a romantic way. The very idea of them together made me want to retch. And then Jack Hunter, I was over him romantically, I did not want him as a boyfriend, partner, someone to love, cherish and share my life with, Jack Hunter had fulfilled a role and now he was gone, but we all know he'd been gone a long time before we broke up. We had died a long time ago but neither of us had the courage to admit it. I didn't hate Jack Hunter. I didn't have it in me to feel that way about him. Which made the following decision easy. I'd rapidly changed my mind throughout the evening, with each and every conversation that took place between me and Hanna, I just became more and more confused as to what was real and what was not. I did know firmly who I was, though. I had to do something. I was going to tell Jack. I was going to go downstairs, and I was going to tell Jack Hunter and spare him humiliation, because underneath the make-up and the fancy clothes I was Katie Lewis. I was a good person and good people don't let other people, no matter who they are or how much hurt they've caused, get hurt themselves. It was totally bad karma. I was then going to go home. Not to The Mayfair. No, Hanna and Bailey could go and have sex all over the hotel for all I cared now. I was going to catch the bus home to Bethnal Green, Lauriston Gardens, my house. I was going to get into my bed, alone, wear my pyjamas and snuggle up with my cat. I was then going to book a one-way ticket to the Caribbean, fuck it, I'll take my mum and Janice, and we'll all go someplace nice, away from the drama and fast-paced, two-faced crazy life of being almost famous. OK, pretty much famous now that *Sizzle Stars* was out and Jack had blabbed to *Oh Yay!* magazine. I gazed at Hanna who was applying a fresh coat of lip gloss, her eyes glistening, not a care in the world; I looked at Frenella, happy, flirting her little feet off. Pippa was sitting so quietly in the corner that I'd all but forgotten she was there, which means ... she must have seen me put my phone in my knickers! But she's not said anything to Hanna! Yet. Which brings me to this dilemma. If I move, Pippa will totally tell Hanna that I stole my phone back, which means Hanna will probably steal it off me for my own good. I know what Hanna is like, meaning she's forceful, she's patronizing and she'll bloody well do what she likes, especially when it came to matters of love. Particularly my love life. Did she want to go on down to see Jack herself and offer him an evening with her? Just to spite me? That's how it felt when she told me about Fabio and our 'pity' date, the one that Fabio pretended not to know anything about. I felt like a really small version of myself (not in a good way) whenever Hanna came out with these revelations, which were always preceded with a sigh and dramatic hand gestures. I had never felt so lonely in all my life.

For the third time, my knickers shuddered with the vibration of a text. I couldn't sit here in this position any longer. I had to leave.

'I feel sick,' I announced to Hanna, as I stood up to go. 'I'm going to go get some water and then I think I'm going to head home,' I said.

'Are you sure?' she said, unperturbed. I was sure. I was through with all these games, the bitching and the shit that comes with being fashionable and gorgeous. I didn't know who to trust any more in this mad world aside from my cat and my family and that's why I was absolutely resolute that the decision I just made a second ago was totally the right one.

'I'll see you get out OK,' Pippa said, as she leapt to her feet.

'Thanks, Pippa,' I said, turning to her. Her warm, kind and open face spoke volumes. She really didn't belong in this world. She belonged in a world full of knitting and baking and book clubs. Bless her. I linked arms with Pippa who, strangely, sprang back from me.

'I don't bite,' I said, joking.

'I know you don't, Katie, it's just I feel a bit ill myself, don't really want to infect you, think it's some kind of chill . . . the one where it hurts to be touched, nothing against you.' She trailed off.

'Kate, finally!' Richard came into view at the top of the stairs.

'Hey, you,' I said, patting him on the back. 'You didn't have to wait, I'm going home.'

'No, you can't,' he said.

'I think I can . . .' I half joked.

'Kate, we need to talk.'

'Leave her alone!' Pippa squealed ferociously, pushing Richard out of our way. He jumped back in surprise, his hands in the air. A couple of burly-looking bouncers looked over.

'Jesus, Katie, what the fuck is going on?' he said.

'I, I . . .' I rambled. I'd never seen this side of Pippa. She was like a rabid terrier, nipping and bouncy. She was glaring at Richard. Why didn't she want him near me?

'What the hell has he ever done to you?' I demanded of her.

She ignored me and with one eye on the bouncer and the other on Richard, she screamed really loudly, 'STOP TOUCHING ME!'

Richard's face went white and his hands, once again, were up in the air. 'I'm not touching you, you fucking lunatic! You're a mad woman, I'd have to have drunk the entire bar dry and been starved of a woman's touch for eternity before I'd even consider touching you, you scraggly hag!' he snapped.

'Move along, sir,' one of the big bouncers said. 'Don't want any trouble.'

'Well, neither do I! Just for the record, I haven't laid so much as a manicured finger on this troll,' he said with his nose stuck up in the air. The bouncer looked at me. I shrugged. I didn't want to get involved but then Richard hadn't done anything wrong, had he?

'He's done nothing wrong. This woman,' I said, pointing at Pippa, 'is lying.' I recalled that Pippa was a bitch when I first met her. She was intrusive and she didn't give me an easy time, what with camping on my doorstep and sticking her nose through my letterbox. She was the one who printed massive pictures of my arse and then circulated them in *London Lowdown* for the whole of the city to see! Could I trust her? No, of course I couldn't, and just seeing her now, trying to stitch Richard up for goodness knows what reason, made me wonder if I had any character-judging skills whatsoever left inside me.

'Pippa, just leave,' I said dismissively, before hissing in her ear, 'I don't know what you think you're doing, but

Richard is a good friend of mine and you have absolutely no right to go accusing him of things he hasn't even done, nor ever will do. So please, may I suggest you either go back up to Hanna and remain there, away from us, or I will have you removed. I can do this now, you see, now that I am famous.' I smiled one of those awful fake nasty smiles I'd seen day in, day out, on Hanna Frost.

Pippa grimaced. Richard took me by the arm and as we began to take steps away from her and down on to the floor, I felt a sharp pull against my other arm.

'NOOOOOO!' Pippa squealed, launching herself at me. I toppled on my heels, missed one step, two, oh fuck, I was heading for one gigantic and potentially life-threatening, face-maiming fall down these incredibly steep stairs in front of, oh God no, let this not be happening to me, in front of Jack and Jessica!

'What is wrong with you? You psychopathic freaky bitch!' Richard wails. He pushes Pippa away from me, she releases her grip and then he grabs her arm by the elbow and attempts to reach round and save me from falling flat on my face . . . by one strand of my long blonde hair, he misses.

'Waaaaaaaaaaaaaaaaaaaaaaaaaaaaaaaaaaaaaaaaaaaaaaaaaaa aaa!' I scream at the top of my lungs, as I tumble down the stairs. I haven't hit one yet, just sail down like I am taking a ride on one of those vertical flumes you get in water parks. I close my eyes and brace myself for what is going to be a pretty nasty fall.

'Waaaaaaaaaaaaaaaaaaeeeee,' I yell, tears racing up into my eyes. This is it . . . THUMP!

Oh! That wasn't so bad after all . . .

'GOTCHA,' he says, pulling me close. I fall back

against him and we collapse in a heap on the nightclub floor. Everybody stops and everybody stares. I can see Hanna leaning over the balcony, screaming my name. I can't hear a word, I just watch, helplessly lying in the arms of this man. Frenella has seen the whole thing, and she's moving away from Hanna, heading for the curtains.

'You're OK now, Katie, I've got you,' Bailey says. He nuzzles into my neck. Mmm, feels good . . . but no! He's having an affair with Hanna! She just told me, so this is wrong, he can't go doing the whole public displays of affection thing whilst his not-so-secret girlfriend is standing up there watching!

'What kind of a sicko are you!' I squeal and shove him off me. 'Thanks for breaking my fall,' I say, back in full-on Hanna mode. 'It's the very least you could do.' And as I stand up and smooth my dress down, I notice my phone, which has been harassing my lady garden from its place wedged in my knickers, now lying in two halves across the floor. Frenella races down the stairs towards me and scoops up the pieces, and my sea-creature clutch.

'Here,' she says. 'Oh my God, are you, like, OK?'

'I'm fine,' I say. 'Richard?' I call, looking up to where I'd last seen him.

He stood, nose-to-nose with Pippa Strong, holding what looked like a lighter in his hand. It was small and black and it had . . . wires coming out of it? What the fuck?

'Richard!' I screamed, loud enough for him to look at me. Pippa was bright red and the black, wired lighter thing was clutched tightly in Richard's firm fist. He glared at Pippa before pacing downstairs towards me where he enveloped me in a hug.

'She bugged you,' he hissed.

'Too right, she bloody well did, silly cow,' I said, hugging him tightly back. 'She's been bugging me for the past week until tonight, she was like, really different, you know, what with the photos and everything . . .' I was rambling now. Must be the shock of falling arse over tit in front of everyone. At least Bailey broke my fall . . . and this time everyone witnessed expensive pants. Not a Tesco pair in sight, I was in Agent Provocateur tonight.

'No, I mean she was recording everything you said this evening.' He looked me in the eyes.

'She what?' I said, confused to the hills.

'She's been taping everything, to stitch you up, to do an exclusive with one of the major Sunday newspapers, now that you're a celebrity, the papers will pay six-figure sums for exclusives, and what could be more exclusive than your heartache over Danielle's supposed encounters with Jack Hunter?'

I gasped. 'Oh no! This is insane, clearly!' I yelped.

'It means she was privy to the monster meltdown, the necking of the vodka, and anything else you said or did when I was gone from the house.'

'Oh God . . .' I breathed.

'It's OK, though,' Richard smiled.

'How is it OK? The woman has heard, like, everything and I mean everything and she's seen me do things . . .'

'Like what?'

'Like . . . take my mobile phone from Hanna's bag and shove it in my knickers!'

'Saucy!'

'Wasn't, actually – uncomfortable, especially when I received a text,' I grumbled.

'So, you got no calls?' he said, eyes narrowed.

'No. Hanna took my phone. When I got it back from her bag, I saw the missed calls, lots of them actually, but then I had to shove the phone, you know, down there, because Hanna reappeared from the loo.'

'It all makes perfect sense . . .' Richard mused, as his eyes darted skywards. Pippa stood at the top of the stairs, edging down, one by one.

'What does?'

Richard opens his mouth to explain but Pippa jars between us, pushing him, pulling my arm and saying, 'I can explain! I can explain!' but I am in no mood to hear it. Bailey stands there next to Richard. I notice they exchange a knowing glance and I am seriously about to grab the two of them and shove us all in a toilet cubicle to get to the bottom of all this insanity, when out of the corner of my eye I see a whole lot of blonde and a whole lot of pink heading in my direction.

'OH MY GOD!' it shrills.

My stomach has now officially frozen over. It doesn't move. It's now located somewhere between my lungs and my gullet.

'Katie Lewis. You are, like, so not as fat as you look in the magazines.' Jessica Hilson stands there, tiny and skinny with long hair extensions falling over her little Malibu Barbie brown shoulders. I'm stunned.

'And you,' I begin, but my mind goes blank. 'And you . . . really should stop using sunbeds. Didn't anyone tell you that the look of a well-worn-DFS leatherette sofa was so 2007?'

Jessica's mouth fell open.

'Oh my God, you totally didn't just say that!'

'She totally didn't just say that . . . ' Hayley echoed.

'I soooo totally just did, you dizzy cow,' I said and pushed past her.

'I'm so totally through with even sharing the same oxygen space as you, darling,' I said in my faux piss-taking accent. Jessica Hilson was nothing. She was nothing. She had nothing I wanted and she was somebody I would rather die than be like. What was the big deal about her anyway? Up close, she actually did have leatherette skin. She was fake. Totally fake. Beyond the hair extensions, the plastic boobs, the mahogany glow and the make-up, she was just like anybody else with a bit of effort. She was just a girl, not a demi-goddess, not a supermodel, not better than me.

'I told you the airbrush is a girl's best friend,' Richard hissed in my ear.

I stood there, and looked forward. Next challenge was Jack Hunter.

For a minute I took in my surroundings. Behind me stood Richard, next to a confused and incredibly sexy-looking Sam Bailey. Frenella stood next to her flirty friend and Pippa stood sweating and gawping at Richard. Jessica Hilson had long gone with her little doppelgänger and ahead of me, Jack Hunter stood casually at the bar, nursing a whiskey on the rocks. It was now or never.

Deep breath in.

I strode across the dancefloor, moving my hips, sashaying. I flashed him my best 'You want me but you ain't getting me' smile. My cheeks flushed pink.

Boom, boom, boom, boom, boom went my heart.

'Jack Hunter,' I said crisply.

'Kate,' he said nonchalantly.

'Jack,' I replied.

'Uh . . . Kate,' he said, looking at me as though he couldn't quite place me. I had figured it out, during the time I spent falling into Bailey's arms, hearing about Pippa Strong's odious plans and facing off with Jessica Hilson. I was going to give Jack a moment to say the words I've been longing to hear for such a long time. The three little words that could take away all this pain and give me the closure I so totally need, in order to move on in my life. Well, I mean, I'll move on, have moved on anyway, but hearing these important words would definitely help. I felt he owed me that at least.

'So . . .' I said, frantically prompting him to say the words in my head, say it Jack, come on, say the words, goddamnit!

'I've been meaning to call you,' he said, half looking at me, half eyeing up . . . no! Half eyeing up Frenella, who was walking towards us.

'Stop it!' I squealed. 'Do you have to be a total prick 24/7?' I spat.

'Katie, let's not get personal here . . . so what, we broke up, big deal, move on, get over it, this is so boring now . . .' he yawned. He actually yawned.

'But saying that,' he quickly changed tack, 'you look amazing.'

'Thanks, Jack,' I said, smiling by accident. No, I thought to myself, must not fall for his faux compliments.

'I meant to call you,' he began again. Frenella stood beside me. Good, I wanted her to hear him beg for my forgiveness, for my love. And I wanted to reject him! No, wait, this is madness, that's not what I came here to do . . .

was it? It all seemed well meaning and charitable to warn him of impending love doom but now I was face-to-face with the man who broke up with me in a text message, who walked out without a backward glance, who'd been cheating on me with another woman for God knows how long, and worst of all, who had moved on from me and our relationship without even having the decency to tell me. In the cold glow of the disco daylight I now felt as though I was looking at Jack Hunter for the first time. I could see now that his eyes looked shifty. That his stature was sinewy, not defined. That he had shaved off a patch of his eyebrow and I wanted to tell him, now armed with a stack of fashion knowledge, that modelling yourself on the style of Keith Duffy from Boyzone circa 1996 was so not a good look. It was neither edgy, cool, nor retro and it looked ridiculous. And in that moment, I knew that I had the power. If I told Jack all the fashion mistakes he was making, including the double denim monstrosity he was wearing as he stood before me now, his green eyes glinting in the light, his foot tapping and his tongue clicking against his teeth nervously, I knew I could crush him.

'I meant to call you to say,' he began.

'Yes . . .'

'To say, had you by any chance kept my organic mineral-particle-activating facecloth that I left at yours? It's just it was a once in a lifetime product made from the skin of baby seals and the real-life tears of the natives. I have scoured the planet and I just can't find one and . . .'

SPLASH!

Jack stood there, soaked to the skin, a large glass of something or other I'd taken out of Frenella's hands now trickling down his face and on to his top. Partygoers giggled and pointed.

'All you had to do to avoid this,' I said slowly, quietly, not wanting to make a scene, 'was apologize!' I said, louder now. 'ALL YOU HAD TO DO WAS SAY THOSE THREE WORDS TO ME!' I lost my temper. Jack was furious, I could tell, beneath his skin, he was incandescent with rage, but he wouldn't dare say anything, not here, not in front of all these people. But I would.

'I'M SORRY, KATIE!' I screamed at him.

'Well, you don't make it . . .'

'FUCK YOU!' I said, as his eyes stared coolly right into my soul. I stared right back into his shallow, self-obsessed, selfish, arrogant, stuck-up, vacuous soul.

'And for the record . . .' I said, '*Jessica Hilson* –' I began as he swivelled his head round and gasps.

'Lordy, Lordy,' Frenella nudges me. 'Would you look at that!'

I look. Frenella looks. Jack squeaks like a girl.

Tongues wrapped around one another, arms grappling with clothes, blonde hair falling on to dark skin, entwined on a velvet chair in the far corner, hungrily latching on to one another as though that kiss was the very kiss to bring them to life, romp Fabio Matravers and Jessica Hilson.

'I don't believe this!' Frenella giggles. And as I turn to Jack, I see his face crumple, his hands splayed out in abandonment, his eyes dart between them, his mouth falls open in shock, pain etched across his face.

I silently walk away from him, and I don't look back.

'It's time to go,' I say to myself, and I head towards the door.

'WAIT!' Richard squeals, and pushes his way past clubbers to get to me. 'We still need to talk!' he says, breathlessly.

'Richard, I'm through with talking,' I sigh, walking on ahead. We come to a quiet chill-out area and he pushes me hard up against the wall.

'Richard? I never knew you felt this way . . .' I say, half joking. What was he doing to me? Now was not the time for love confessions. I was so totally through with anything to do with love.

'I won't let you go, not like this, not until you've heard the truth about your life as it stands right now.'

'Go on, then. What more awful, humiliating, shitty things have you got to tell me? Have you been having it off with the delectable, irresistible Hanna Frost too?' I laughed sardonically.

'What on earth are you talking about? No one likes Hanna, let alone shags the deranged woman!' Richard said with gusto.

'I don't get it,' I said, pushing my hair off my face.

'Hanna was in on it with Pippa Strong. She planned on taking a cut of your exclusive bugging tape that Pippa had shoved down her shirt all evening.'

'So that's why . . .' I began.

'Shush. I'm not finished.'

'Go on . . .' I said.

'Hanna, as you know, is a plausible, confident, well-respected woman who, I hate to say it, holds a lot of power with the knowledge she's got. She gets things done, but she's a manipulative, dangerous, lying bitch, Katie.'

'Whatever, she's got her faults, God knows, and yeah, maybe she was in on the Pippa bugging thing . . . but it doesn't make sense. What would she have to gain from doing that to me?'

'I already told you, half of a hundred grand plus per dramatic story about you. Darling, I hate to say it, but you do have many . . . And by keeping you onside you're going to form the kind of girly attachment you ladies do to unsuitable boyfriends . . . and sometimes your friends. She needed you, you loved the drama and God knows, we all love to be needed . . . She played you perfectly.'

'No way!' I said. I just wouldn't believe it.

'And another thing,' he said gravely. 'After I saw those shots of Danielle supposedly with Jack Hunter, my gut instinct was that it was a set-up. I knew something fishy was going on, so I decided to pay her a little visit.'

'You did?' My head spun around. 'But I saw those photos, I saw her resting on him, in his arms, that can't be Photoshopped, it simply can't be.'

I hung my head in my hands. Hanna couldn't have lied, it was wishful thinking to imagine that she had, I had already ended the friendship between me and Danielle in my heart and in my head and put my faith in Hanna . . . I was willing to give Hanna the benefit of the doubt when it came to Fabio Matravers and the like making inappropriate seedy advances towards her . . . I could even have understood her Bailey indiscretions . . . Maybe, oh God, I don't know really if I could have forgotten about my love feelings for Bailey . . . Oh, it was all such a confusing mess!

'Danielle fell over,' Richard said, his arms placed on either side of my shoulders. His look was intense.

'If you look a bit closer you can see she's only wearing one shoe. One very high-heeled shoe. The other is close by, snapped in half. Jack Hunter was catching her as she fell. It was by no means a romantic clinch.'

'Oh. My. God.' I breathed slowly. Like an episode of *Columbo*, Richard began to piece together the mysterious photographic evidence of Jack and Danielle.

'Jack Hunter's media lawyer is one Stewart . . .'

'Small-penis!' I said, in surprise.

'Darling, don't need to know.' Richard screwed up his nose. 'I went to see Danielle after remembering where she lived from dropping you both off there one night over Christmas after a party. I just had to go and find out exactly what was going on. She scrunched up her nose, cute, and then she gave one of those weird half laughing, half can't quite believe what I've just heard laughs. She's dreadfully hurt but I think I managed to help her understand how you've been feeling lately. I think she listened . . . it's not easy being in the spotlight, especially around people like Hanna, you know, all focused on looks and presentation. I think she'll be OK. Eventually. Quite an attractive woman, your best friend . . .'

'She'll hate me,' I squeaked.

'Well, as I was saying, Stewart is Jack's media lawyer, and Danielle had a major problem with this, had some big falling-out with Stewart, from the penis quip you just gave me I assume they're lovers, no?'

'Yep.'

'So, they have a lovers' tiff over Jack Hunter being

Stewart's client . . . which makes sense as she's being loyal to you and doesn't want the man she loves to represent the man who broke your heart.'

'I'm a big, nasty, horrible bitch and I don't deserve any friends ever again!' I wailed.

Richard sighed and put his arms around me. I leant into his chest.

'Hanna set the whole thing up. Pippa took the pictures, not realizing what was going on. Hanna knew that it was innocent, I mean, all it was, was Jack . . .'

'Going into her office and she's a clutz like me, she snapped her heel, it looks suspicious to anyone who didn't know Danielle the way I know her . . . Oh God, I really have let her down, haven't I, Rich?'

'Sorry, Katie . . .' Richard squeezed me.

'So, what next?'

'Pippa had the photos, Hanna manipulated the situation to her advantage. They were going to make an awful lot of money out of you, darling.'

'I can't believe it.'

'Believe it, kiddo. I've been trying to call you all night, to tell you the truth about Hanna. I had no idea about Pippa until our little showdown on the stairs, but I have the bug, so you don't need to worry about her any more.'

'And Danielle?'

'She'll understand. She loves you, she's your best friend.'

'Even after everything I've done to her?'

'Even after everything.'

'And that's why she was calling me?'

'No, she was calling you for another reason – Bailey.'

And suddenly, it all became clear. Bailey wasn't having

it off with Hanna. No way. Hanna had totally lied to me, and if she'd lied to me about Bailey then she must have lied to him about me! I cast my mind back to all the times where Bailey had accidentally on purpose walked in on me holding hands with Fabio, seen Danny Divine's hand on my backside, the episode with the business card.

'He . . .' I said, standing up.

'I told him I'd explain it to you. He's in the VIP area.'

'And Hanna?'

'Ejected. I'll fill Magenta in, don't you worry.'

'And lastly,' I said, gulping back air in anticipation of future events, 'Frenella?'

'Frenella had no idea, bless her little socks, and her boyfriend, luckily for me, is just as dumb.' He winked.

'Oh, Richard!' I laughed.

'She's safe, don't worry.'

As I look up I see Frenella waiting at the end of the lobby. She gives a little wave.

'Tinkles!' I smile and turn to Richard. 'I have to go now.' He stands up and gives me a hug before gently whispering in my ear, 'I know you do, go get your man.'

'This is it!' I squeal in Frenella's ear as she totters along beside me, holding my hand, her little legs running to keep up.

Together, we raced back up the stairs I'd previously fallen down, past the helpful bartender who nodded in my direction. I nodded back politely and stopped suddenly, just for a minute, to compose myself.

Behind that curtain, my life could change.

Deep breath . . . I pulled the velvet sheath back.

'Danielle!' I gasped. She walked towards me.

365

'I'm so sorry!' I said, tears welling up in my eyes. She looked beautiful, her hair was straightened and glistened red under the lights.

'It's OK, I can forgive you, just this once,' she said, taking me in her arms.

'You silly sausage, how could you think I'd ever go near a slimeball like Jack Hunter!'

'I know, and I'm so sorry, honestly, God, all those mean things I said. You, have permission to do anything you like to me from now on, I'll do anything to prove to you how sorry I am for ever doubting you.'

'Shhh,' she said, stroking a tear away from my cheek. 'You're my best friend, Katie, I knew deep down you didn't mean it. I knew once Richard explained we'd be all right, and of course, when I saw Bailey . . . well, I understood.'

'Thanks,' I said, 'OOH, look!' I giggled. 'Is that Stewart-small . . .'

'Smallthwaite!' he said, hand outstretched. 'I don't believe we've met!'

'Hi!' I said, shaking his hand.

'Well,' he said, in his brusque tone, 'love to stay and chat but I've got to take this young lady home now . . . Can't have me rattling around my brand-new one-bedroom loft apartment all alone now, can we, my darling?' And in that moment, I knew that Stewart Smallthwaite had finally done the decent thing, for himself, and for my best friend.

'No, wait!' I said, hurriedly. I delved into my sea-creature clutch bag.

'Hanna gave me this before we got here.' I produced a plastic card.

'What is it?' Danielle said, taking it from me and studying it intently.

'It's a room key.'

'Gee, thanks.' She laughed.

'To The Mayfair. The Penthouse Suite, it's all yours.'

'Get outta here!' She squealed, embracing me again.

'Take it, before I change my mind!'

'Well, it IS the least you can do!' she joked and before I know it, she's pulling back the curtain and walking off into the club with Frenella and Stewart.

Finally, I am alone. I take a deep breath and look around the table area. Empty. My heart sank. Bailey was supposed to be here, this was supposed to be an epic love moment! And then I heard it, slowly, a deep sigh, a sniff and a cough. I turned in the direction the sound was coming from and saw him, the big green eyes, long lashes and a half-hearted smile.

'Surprise?' Jack Hunter said.

'What are you doing here?' I gasped, gripping the chair. 'She's not here too, is she? Honestly, Jack, I thought we had our chance to . . .' I said, looking around once more. No one appeared to be here, least of all anyone American and blonde.

'Put things right?' he finished my sentence. I inwardly chastised myself for allowing him to fall back into effortless synchronicity with me. He always finished my sentences.

'I'm leaving,' I said, standing up and smoothing my dress down.

'Please,' he began, sniffing again.

'No,' I said, rolling my eyes and moving towards the curtain.

'Katie cakes,' he simpered and my heart fluttered a little at the memory of us.

'For heaven's sake, Jack, I have to find someone, it's important!'

'That guy?' he said, meekly.

I stopped in my tracks and turned to face him. He looked so small, so pathetic, so . . . upset. My stomach churned. I felt something for him, looking at his face and into his eyes, there were feelings there that I'd not normally have ever associated with Jack Hunter. Those feelings were pity. I pitied him and because he cut such a pathetic figure, standing solemnly in front of me, clutching at metaphorical straws to grab my attention, I let him speak.

'The good-looking, well-dressed guy wearing that beautiful shirt, those shoes . . .'

'Richard? No.'

'The one you fell upon on the dance floor,' he said, shuffling on his feet.

'Yes, that's Bailey, I have to go, find him, talk to him, most important,' I shrugged and pushed my hair behind my ears. 'Sorry . . .' I offered.

'I saw him leave with a dark-haired woman about ten minutes ago,' Jack said.

'Are you sure?' I asked, feeling stressed out to the max. He can't have done what I think he's done, not after everything Richard told me, but then perhaps he has done it. Could anyone blame him, walking out with another woman, a woman with no drama attached to her, a woman with no agenda.

'She was wearing a scarlet dress.'

Thump. That was my stomach enduring one final descent

on the road to glumsville. Talk about your past making itself present in your future, like some kind of twisted guardian angel, Jack had potentially saved me from any further embarrassment with Bailey. He'd gone home with Hanna. Perhaps that was only one thing she had been telling the truth about.

'Listen, Katie, this is all a bit too heavy, shall we split?'

He's not suggesting . . . he's not serious . . .

'I believe we already have . . .'

'Come on,' he said, and he grasped my arm in a surprisingly strong grip. We sped effortlessly out of the club, hailed a cab and were making the journey back to Lauriston Gardens, my house. Oh my God, I was in a black cab with my ex-boyfriend, the duplicitous pretty boy Jack Hunter, the Jack Hunter who broke my heart into a million little pieces. The Jack Hunter who got a taste of his very own heartbreak medicine very publicly this evening.

'I just want to talk, no funny business,' he said quietly.

'You can come in for one cup of tea,' I said firmly. I was not so desperate that I would let him touch me again, no way. Oh, but he looked amazing, gorgeous. His features had softened. Perhaps the blow of being treated worse than an amoeba had changed him? Often, men change when they have been in love and when they have experienced loss. Difficult for him to fathom, that he ruined my life. Or maybe he's come to his senses and is hoping for a reconciliation? And if so, is this something that I want? The taxi came to a gentle stop outside my house, what used to be our house, and I paid the fare. Jack hopped out the other side and loitered at the bottom of the steps whilst I fumbled for my keys.

'So, uh . . .' he began.

'Here we are,' I said brightly. The key turned and the door opened. We both walked through the hallway and into the living room which smelled divine from earlier, us girls getting ready.

'It's just the same as when I left,' he said. 'Apart from it smells less like cat food and more like . . .' he sniffed the air, 'Valentino, excellent choice.'

'Tea it is, then,' I said, ignoring him. I walked into the kitchen, kicking my skyscraper heels off on the way.

'You look different,' Jack mused as he walked towards me. He stopped a few paces behind me and looked me up and down.

'Do you mind?' I said, perturbed. This was not what I had in mind for us. I had to put a stop to this, immediately.

'Look, Jack,' I said, rubbing my temple. 'Tonight's been fucked up. I know you got your heart broken by Jessica Hilson in front of like, everyone, and I know how sensitive you are to public humiliation.'

'It wasn't ideal,' he coughed, 'but I was only ever using her for what she could give to me, which was fame. I have always wanted to be an actor, and she made it happen for me.'

'Oh, really,' I said, with a note of sarcasm. I knew it would be lost on Jack. 'So, you've had more acting jobs come through, then?'

'Not yet but, like, Joel is mega excited about our future, only a matter of time, he says.'

'Hmm,' I said, tapping my foot against the floor. The kettle began to whistle.

'Why couldn't you have dressed more like this when we

were together?' he said suddenly and without a hint of shame.

'Excuse me? Would that have changed what you did to me?' I half joked. I didn't want to engage him any further than I had to. It was uber-weird. How can a girl spend so long, so many hours, days and lonely, long, stretched-out nights crying and wondering and analysing so much about one person? And now Jack is doing the one thing I have internally begged him to do, which is to be here, in front of me, ready, willing and able to unlock the door to my pain, to provide the answers I so desperately need to move on in my life. Here he was, the man who broke my heart, playing with the buttons on his denim jacket, without a care in the world, wanting, needing somehow to talk to me, perhaps to find answers of his own, perhaps to release some of his own pent-up guilt, so he and I can part ways having learnt a little bit about life, love and each other. His look was intense. Maybe he did really love me after all?

'Oh, Katie, I can't stand here and watch your nipples poke through that dress like piglet snouts,' Jack growls, and launches himself towards me.

'I'm sorry, babe,' he mutters as he snorts and sniffles into the side of my neck. I am so shocked I can barely move.

'Mmmmmm, you smell divine, your skin is so soft,' his hands snake around my bottom. 'Have you lost weight?'

'Yes, Jack, I have,' I say, hesitating slightly, pushing his hands away. He ignores me, pushes them back. This attention from a man such as Jack is definitely not lost on me.

He lifts his head and whispers in my ear, 'I still love you, Katie, always did, never stopped in fact, please, I need you, can't live without you, let's go to bed,' and he puts his fingers on my chin and nudges my lips towards his. He places his own lips upon mine and sucks furiously.

I tried to resist, but gave up trying, falling into his grasp. This man I used to love was all over me, his hands were like an octopus, his breath hot and heavy, his hard-on jabbed into my thigh as he moaned and groaned and attempted to mount me on the breakfast bar. The kettle whistled loudly in the background, bringing me sharply back to reality. My phone trilled from the living room where it lay next to my sea-creature clutch on the sofa.

For all of five seconds I thought that this was what I wanted. But when I opened my eyes, I felt nothing. Whatever we had, it was gone. I pushed him away from me, shook my head, but he ignored me, continued to paw at me.

'Jack! Gerroff!' I screeched and lambasted him with a fork I grabbed from the side, straight into his bum cheek.

'Ouch! Katie! What did you do that for?!'

'You were on me like a rabid terrier,' I said, shuffling backwards towards the kettle to relieve it of its duties. The whistle abated.

'I thought you loved me?' he said, springing back and clutching his arse with both hands.

'I did, yes, I used to love you,' I said, gently. 'I thought you were all that I wanted, the man I loved, but actually you're just a thick, egotistical turd and I would rather like you to leave now, Jack Hunter, because you don't go with my wallpaper any more, not in those denim horrors!'

He went bright red and scowled at me.

'Fine, Katie, but you just wait, I will do the world's most horrific kiss-and-tell on you and everyone will know that you are so desperate for a shag, you took home with you the very man who left you for a movie star and humiliated you for fun!' he spat, his male ego clearly getting the better of him.

I glared at him.

'This isn't over!' he squealed, whilst pointing at me.

'Oh, it so is,' Richard purred, stepping out of the shadows of my hallway. Danielle stood behind him with her arms folded.

'What the . . .' Jack said, backing up.

Richard held the bug in his hands. With an emphatic click, he stopped the tape running.

I stood there, grinning. My friends, God knows how they got here, what they were even doing here, but my lovely, wonderful friends had just saved my bacon.

We all stood looking at Jack and he just looked back, defeated and humiliated for the second time this evening.

'Please don't ruin my career,' he bleated.

'Get out!' I screamed, before throwing an apple at him from the fruit bowl.

'But, Katie, what are you going to doooo?' he squealed, as he narrowly missed being decapitated by a banana.

'Kill you!' I screamed so hard that he legged it out of the house and down the front path. The door gave a heavy slam.

'Cup of tea, anyone?' I said brightly, as Richard and Danielle collapsed into hysterical giggles.

'That was amazing!' Danielle laughed as I succumbed to the fun.

'What are you both doing here?' I asked.

'Well, it's my fault really,' Danielle said. 'Despite everything you did to me, I just had to check you were OK . . .'

she trailed off, half joking, eyebrow raised. She wasn't angry with me, just hurt and trying to make the best of it.

'I know, I know,' I begged, 'I feel terrible, awful, the worst there is, and don't think you're not in line for something mega amazing, in fact, fuck it, I will tell you now, how does a trip to the Caribbean sound, on me!' I exclaimed.

'You're serious?' she asked, smiling. 'Yes, yes, YES!'

'Of course, except, only one thing . . .' I said, as I noticed my house phone flashing with an answerphone message.

'Leave it,' Richard said.

'But it could be important.' I leapt to the machine and pressed play. I smiled up at my best friend who smiled warmly back at me. I knew as much as I was certain that night followed day that Danielle Kingsley was at that moment mentally packing a suitcase full of very expensive and *très* glamorous outfits.

'Kate, darling, this is your mother here, remember me? No, thought not, not now that you are thin and well dressed, of course I always knew you'd take after me in the end, that's what I tell everyone after all. But still, when you have a moment between film premieres and having your picture taken, do call me, at the very least, to tell me where you got that jumper from. Anyway, I have had a very good-looking young man appear at the house this evening searching for you, I nearly sent him back to London as heaven knows when you will grace our doorstep again.'

'Bailey?' I gasped. Richard shrugged.

'I said nearly sent him back to London [heavy pause] *His name was James Watson from the* Daily Mail's Femail *section,*

OOOH it's tremendously exciting and he's coming back to do an exclusive on us, your loyal, adoring family, Kate. I am so over the moon, I can't tell you. Aunty Fiona is coming over to take me to Boden for a new outfit and Betty Baxter will be making me over to look just like the brand-new you!'

We all sniggered.

'Anyway, darling, Janice informed me of your little getaway to the Caribbean, but in light of the Daily Mail *interview and Janice's exams, I'm afraid we can't make it . . .* [muffled sounds] *NO, young lady I am NOT telling you where your passport is! Toodles!'*

'Well, that's that problem solved, no Janice, no Mum, just you, me and a couple of Sea Breezes!'

'Yay!' Danielle squeals as she gives me a giant hug. 'You're totally forgiven!'

'So,' I say, turning to Richard. 'What's the 411?'

'Well . . .' he begins, rubbing his neck, 'I bumped into Danielle and Stewart as I was leaving and then all of a sudden a certain Hanna Frost went past in the arms of one Sam Bailey, shoeless and screaming about injustice, revenge, heads will roll . . .'

'I thought she'd been ejected?'

'Must have snuck back in . . . Anyway, she was ranting and raving about you.'

'I had a spare key – the cat, you know,' Danielle said, pulling it out of her pocket. 'Thought she might have come over to cause trouble . . .'

'So you thought you'd babysit me?' I said.

'Look out for you . . .' Danielle interjects.

'And aren't you very well glad we did!' Richard says, smartly. 'There's everything on this little bug, everything . . .' he continues. 'It's up to you what you do with it.'

'Nothing for now,' I say, taking it and popping it in the kitchen drawer. I sigh heavily and rubbed my eyes.

'Well, all's well that ends well,' Richard says, clasping his hands together.

'It's late, Katie, go to bed, everything will feel better in the morning,' says Danielle.

'Here,' Richard says, picking up the fruit from the floor and handing it to me.

'Thanks, not just for the fruit, but for everything,' I say, and I mean it, I truly, honestly have the very best friends there are in the whole entire world.

Chapter 18

I woke up the next morning feeling surprisingly refreshed for a girl who'd ingested half of Oddbins plus various different concoctions from a plush nightclub only twelve hours earlier. Despite Hanna's insidious behaviour, and Jack Hunter's smarmy manhandling and the news that the *Daily Mail* are doing an exposé of my early years through my shameless mother, I was feeling decidedly bright-eyed and bushy-tailed. And then I remembered. Last night, as my best friends left my house after spending an evening rescuing me from the evil clutches of various pop tarts and lipstick bitches (Jack Hunter included, of course) I had come to the conclusion that I had what I wanted all along . . . I then had such a restful sleep, having let go of my so-called dreams and aspirations, my designer demons, I suppose. Bailey was a fervent pain somewhere between my gut and my heart and Jack Hunter was always going to be a pain in my arse. I knew, though, that an indeterminate amount of time sunning myself surrounded by Hawaiian Tropic men in the Caribbean, family-free and with just my best friend and copious amounts of alcohol, would make significant tracks in sorting out my wonky love life. The sun shone through my windowpane, illuminating my bedroom, my cat stretched out on the rug, I stifled a yawn and shifted my gaze to my laptop which sat upon my desk, the screensaver dancing across the front. Cripes! I remembered that I'd sent an evil email to Nicola Baxter last night. I wonder if she's replied? I shuffle along the end of my bed and move to the desk, click the mouse and my Gmail begins to load up on the screen.

Six emails.

DAILY MAIL! from Mum . . . read later . . .
Excusemoi! From one Nicola Baxter.

Dearest Katie,

I'm not altogether sure what you're talking about with regards to my exposé of our crabs incident in Ibiza . . . back when? Good Lord, I can't even remember when. I was, however, approached by a sinister-looking woman in a so tight she couldn't possibly be wearing pants dress and I know that in London, what with it being cosmopolitan and all that, there must be some kind of invisible G-string/underwear ensemble that's not been seen this way yet, to excuse the fact she was not only knickerless but very much bra-less too, just ask my Jamie, who got an eyeful of her peanut smuggling. I wasn't impressed, I tell you. I will inform you though that this hookeresque woman with the plummy accent offered us an undisclosed amount of money for tales about our friendship back in the nineties. I am engaged now, your invitation to the wedding is at your mother's although I'm not so sure I want to invite you after your little outburst. Honestly, the money means we can get married in some place other than Little Glove village hall, so I hope you can see where we're coming from. If I have upset you by talking about the questionable hygiene habits of the El Codo Playa beach huts, then for that I'm truly sorry.

Nicola

I smiled. Oh deary me! Hanna had done it again ... I knew with 100 per cent certainty that I had been in the presence of the most manipulative individual I had ever had the unfortunate luck to meet. Even with the Prada shoes and the killer dresses, she was wrong on just about every level. Still, knowing what I knew about Bailey, I couldn't fathom what made him take her home – or indeed how she even got back in the club in the first place. Oh, who cares! This is so passé it's ridiculous. I continued to check the rest of my emails, found nothing exciting, so shamelessly Googled myself to get the gossip on my crazy life. I was still worried in case Jack went to the press with made up stories. But nothing new came up on the search. I closed my laptop and made my way downstairs. Popping the kettle on the boil, I flicked on the telly and listened as the chef waffled on about organic muffins. Mmm, I thought. Sounds good, must make mental note to download recippppeeeeeeeeeooooooooooooh!!! I dropped my teacup and in a scene reminiscent of the day I discovered Jack Hunter had walked out on me for a real-life blow-up doll, aka Miss Jessica Hilson, I was once again gobsmacked.

'OH MY GOD!' I squealed as my gaze fixed on the television screen.

JACK HUNTER CAUGHT WITH PANTS DOWN IN HIGH-CLASS HOOKER ESCAPADE!

'I'm so sorry . . .' he pleaded to the camera. 'All I ever wanted was a kebab!'

Bzzzzz! Bzzzzz!

My phone jittered from beneath the sea-creature clutch that remained on the sofa from last night's throwage. I picked it up and discovered a ton of texts from Danielle warning me about Hanna, a pleading one from Pippa about whether I was going to rat her out, several from Richard about Danielle and Hanna and one from Bailey . . .

'Check your messages,' it said.

Check my messages? I was checking them. There was nothing else left I hadn't checked . . . except my actual voicemail! I stood dialling the number while Jack Hunter sat looking like a naughty schoolboy on the television sofa, images of Hugh Grant and Divine Brown popped up behind him. A helpline ran along the bottom of the screen, followed by the strapline: Things we do when dumped, inviting viewers to call in with their own horror stories. God . . . the man still came out on top. I swear if he had a face like an infected backside he'd have been dropped quicker than a hot potato by all media, just goes to show, looks are everything in this fame game.

'You have one, new, message,' said the answerphone lady.

I wish it told you who from, so I could prepare myself. My heart stopped beating. I felt the familiar rise of tense, anxious sweat . . . Could it really be Bailey? And if so, what did he have to say? Everything had been so chaotic, I wouldn't have blamed him for running a mile . . .

His voice was rich and dark, butterflies rose and fell inside my belly.

'Kate, it's me.' Ooh, rather brusque, not liking this.

'We need to talk.' Fuck, I know what that means, it's along the same lines as 'It's not you, it's me!'

'I know everything there is to know about Hanna, Fabio . . . but there are certain things that you don't know about me.'

I was beginning to feel like a weapon in a Cluedo game. Here we have Katie, she had her heart broken by a big tool in the drawing room, who is the culprit?

'It's not true, whatever Hanna said, says, maintains, whatever . . . look,' he sighs deeply. 'I'll be outside the South Bank television studios at midday, I'll explain everything . . .'

Explain everything? What did he have to explain? Was my contract now terminated by Poets Field PR? Was Magenta Rubenstein going to smother me with her pashminas and feed me to Hanna?

'And Katie . . .' he said, warmly.

'Yes?' I said, forgetting I wasn't actually having a conversation and that I was actually only listening to him on my voicemail.

'I suppose I should tell you that . . . well . . . I think I love you and if you love me too, then that's just awesome.'

Oh my God! This totally trumped anything good or amazing that had ever happened in the entire twenty-six years of my being present on this planet. Bailey said the L word! He said I love you! I sat there, dazed, confused but deliriously happy! Not only had I seen Jack Hunter humiliated thrice over, the club, my house and now kebab-gate, I'd moved on, really honestly moved on.

Beeeep!! Beeeep!!

I raced to the living-room window and pulled back the curtains. There in a sea of paparazzi that hadn't been there half an hour ago, was Richard's sports car, Danielle waving from the seats, Frenella perched beside the door, beckoning me out. My phone rang.

'What are you waiting for, tinkles!' Frenella squealed.

'I don't have any clothes on, just tartan pyjamas . . .' I gasped, as I took it all in.

'Fuck the tartan!'

It was now or never. This was the stuff of dreams, he loved me, he wasn't going to care about my outfit!

'I'm coming, world!' I said, fired up with happiness. I ran out of the front door, blinded by the light, blinded by love.

'KATIIIIIIIIIIIIIIIIIIIIIIIIIIIIEEEEEEEEEE!! OVER HEEEEEERRRREEEE!!'

FLASH! FLASH!

'Hellooooo!' I waved as I stood in my front garden in my tartan pyjamas and a pair of flip-flops, a camel shawl around my shoulders, bed head, smudged eyes, the lot!

'Wahooo!' I squealed and did a little jump, whilst grinning manically at everyone taking pictures plus the neighbours who'd come out of their houses to gawp at my crazy self.

'Always knew she had a screw loose,' I heard Mrs Bellamy bellow.

I skipped towards the car and Frenella stood aside to let me in. As Richard revved up the engine, Danielle passed me a bag.

'What's this? It's not for my head, is it!' I said, as the wind picked up, pulling my hair in all directions.

'Look . . .' she winked.

'Oooh, *très* exciting!' Frenella wittered.

I gingerly delved into the bag and tore at the silver

382

tissue paper as the figures of the paparazzi faded into the background until they were first tiny and then out of sight.

'Never mind them,' Danielle said, pulling my focus back into my lap. The paper was off and in my hands I held the most gorgeous dress I think I had ever seen in my entire life!

'Present from me, chosen by Tom Theodore,' she smirked.

'Oh my God! I don't know what to say!'

'Well, you didn't think we'd let you go out to meet the man of your dreams in those, did you?' Danielle said, pulling at my sleeves.

'Bailey . . .' I whispered, 'I don't get it, this declaration of love, this whole thing, makes . . . no sense?'

'He called me just after I left,' said Danielle, 'you weren't answering your phone . . .'

'The sea-creature clutch!' I exclaimed. 'Left on the sofa!'

'When Hanna crept back into the club, I guess to cause trouble, what she got was Bailey on his way to get to you. She was drunk as a skunk, so he carried her out to the taxi.'

'But they were seen canoodling!' I wailed.

'No, they weren't! She sat on Pippa who was stone-cold sober in the back of the cab, pulled Bailey down for a snog and he pushed her off. He then ran back in and . . .'

'Oh God! He saw me leave with Jack!'

'Got it in one, but never fear, he was coming to say that he was in love with you.'

'So, what now?' I queried.

'He knows everything, thanks to us,' Richard interjected.

'And luckily for you, he's an understanding chap and certainly not as stupid as your ex.'

'Thank the Lord!'

'No problem,' Richard laughed.

We all rolled our eyes.

'Well, darling, we're here,' Richard said as he spun into the car park on the South Bank. 'Don't fuck it up this time, Katie,' he said.

'I won't!' I said, as I kissed the girls and smoothed my hair down. My heart was doing somersaults as Bailey came into view. He stood there looking gorgeous, in a pair of tight jeans, his trusty tight white t-shirt and an open blazer which flapped in the gentle breeze of the summer wind. He smoked his usual roll-ups in that sexy, cool fashion that was so typical of Sam Bailey.

'Go get him, girl,' Danielle nudged, and I did. I didn't even open the car door, I leapt out and skipped all the way to reach him. He flicked his cigarette, opened his arms and I fell into them, and just like in the movies, I kicked a flip-flopped foot out as we kissed the most delicious kiss that there ever was.

'Wahooo!' Danielle and Frenella clapped from the open-topped car. Richard gave a one-handed salute of approval.

'I wanted to say . . .' I began, but before I could finish, he was cupping my face in his hands.

'Shh,' he said, pulling me close, his hands reaching out for me, his lips nestling into my neck as he planted butterfly kisses all over my skin, making me tremble. What was I thinking, letting Danielle have the Mayfair suite! But then

I got it, Bailey wasn't about money, or being seen here or there, he wasn't about labels. He was honest, genuine and he liked me for exactly who I was, spots and all.

'I . . .' I breathed.

'Love . . .' he whispered.

'You . . .' we said in unison.

'I have a confession . . . but it's a nice one, don't worry. There are no skeletons in my closet,' he winked.

I smiled, thanking the Lord that skinny minnies Carolina Fernando and Hanna Frost weren't any kind of fixture in his boudoir or his life. As if reading my mind, he laughed.

'And no, I never did do it with that chick from *Big Brother*, or with Hanna.'

OMG, we were in perfect synch already!

'Thought stealer,' I giggled.

'Seriously, darling,' he continued, while gazing into my eyes, 'since I met you I haven't been able to stop thinking about you. You're everything I want in a woman and then some. I'm crazy about you . . . and so I have to tell the world about you, about us. It's time to stop faking it and come clean to Phil and Holly about what's really going on in our world.'

Oh my God, this is what I've always wanted – a boyfriend who took me places! But I only ever meant a cocktail bar, or the cinema or something, not on television, not for everyone to see! I'd have settled for a trip on the London Eye or something like that. This was absolutely out of this world.

'Don't worry, honey, we're going to have a blast!'

'But I still don't get it . . . how come you get to go on telly and waffle about us? Who are you?' I narrowed my eyes and cocked my head.

'You'll see,' he said, and with one giant scoop, Bailey picked me up, kicked open the doorway to the building and carried me in.

Epilogue

One week on . . .

SAMUEL BAILEY RUBENSTEIN, MULTI-MILLIONAIRE FASHION PR COMPANY HEIR, FINDS REAL LOVE WITH MODERN-DAY RAGS-TO-RICHES 'REAL' REALITY GIRL, KATIE LEWIS!

Who knew? Bailey, the dogsbody, my driver, the tea boy, my future boss. Forget his mother, ah! His mother, Magenta, no wonder, he almost curtseyed in her presence . . . I cast my mind back, looking for clues. Even though there were many, for example, the way Magenta would demand and he'd comply with no obvious resentment towards her for her brusque intonation . . . just the kind of intonation your mum uses when she nags you. You just get immune to it, you get on with it, like he did. I simply hadn't twigged that Bailey was anything other than a lowly assistant, much like myself. Would I have treated him differently had I known he has squillions in the bank? Nah. Not I! But it did explain why Hanna Frost was absolutely desperate to bed him and even more desperate for me not to bed him. Aside from her very obvious attention-seeking, jealous behaviour, Hanna couldn't stand not to be the one the boys fell for. It wouldn't surprise me in the slightest if it came to light that Fabio had never so much as glanced at the woman for longer than a second, let alone perved and stared at her with such frightening intent. Bailey explained to me the reasons for his undercover behaviour, under the, uh, Sonata bed throw on my bed back in Lauriston Gardens. Seems he was very well used to women like Hanna digging their claws in and hanging on for dear life and all the monetary joys that being involved with a rich boy brings. Hanna could have married him and then taken him for all he's worth, perhaps, even owned the entire company. Especially if she had his children. What a witch! Personally, the bells rang out for me with regards to this relationship, because for once it looked as though I wouldn't have to keep my man, instead, things could be equal in all aspects, for the very first time. I assured him I had my own money, and he assured me that he already knew it – especially since my £10K Poets Field PR cheque for honouring my contract hit my bank that morning. Now I was taking some time out, some 'me' time, before my extremely exciting life took another interesting turn. With a frappuccino in hand, I walked through Soho with my gossip magazines. Some things will never change!

I couldn't stop looking at the gorgeous glossy pictures. I mean, I was as addicted to *Sizzle Stars* as the next girl and seeing my lovely, airbrushed, near-perfect face on the front cover no less, with straight teeth and hair in golden sand and pale biscuit swishing over my shoulders, next to a man even better looking than Jack Hunter (is that possible? It *so* totally is, trust me) I felt like I imagine Posh

Spice felt when she graced the cover of *Vogue*. Stuff of dreams, man of dreams, living the dream . . . I was officially a smug chick. I clutched the magazine to my boobs and sighed gently. In times of extreme happiness and/or things going extremely well, it does a girl good to be reflective, count her blessings and give a little nod to whoever makes these fabulous things happen. It's an epic moment for a girl like me, I was used to things nearly going right, being close to going my way, but ultimately fate never getting enough of a wriggle on to make it OK. A bit like being promised a hot day and getting drizzle, like expecting the world to spontaneously combust just because a scientist guy says so, you can't go ahead expecting the best because you'll almost always be disappointed. I had been plucked from the depths of despair, to find something a zillion times better. Sam Bailey.

It was incredible how much my life changed since I got rid of Jack. They do say that everything happens for a reason, that what goes around comes around and although I have never really been one for karma and the like, I couldn't help but wonder if there was some truth in it, especially when confronted with the news that Jack Hunter was now in the Priory for sex addiction (are you insane, Jack Hunter? You can't even do sex properly!). I was also pleased to hear that Jessica Hilson's movie had bombed so badly that any movie she ever does again will probably go right to DVD. The best news of all that I read in *Sizzle Stars* was that Fabio Matravers, sweet, polite and mega rich Fabio Matravers, had finally seen sense and dumped Jessica Hilson in a very public and humiliating way, albeit by accident. Carolina Fernando (remember her? Tall, enviably curvaceous lingerie model from *Big Brother* who I thought was having it off with Bailey in complicated *Kama Sutra* positions all over her, I imagined, white, posh, plush, minimalistic apartment) had stolen his heart after toppling from her vertiginous heels and very nearly ending up underneath a different kind of undercarriage to the lingerie she models, one black cab. Their chance meeting had occurred outside Mahiki, of all places, and according to this week's *Sizzle Stars* their eyes connected and in the space of seven short days, they had fallen desperately in love. He had proposed with the biggest, most expensive diamond the world had ever seen and literally dropped Jessica like a hot potato. I could almost hear the irritating scrape of her voice shrieking OH MY GOD NO WAAAAY from my bench here in Soho Square. Jessica's sob story was, of course, splashed across Jack's favourite, *Oh Yay!* magazine, detailing the most intimate sexploits of the pair of them, plus what Jack was like in and out of bed. What a sell-out! I could tell you this for free, in bed he's clumsy, lazy and he snores. Out of it, he's clumsy, lazy and he grunts.

Meanwhile, on planet *moi*, I was totally enjoying that enthralling can't-get-enough-of-you stage with my new boyfriend, Sam Bailey. I was about to get on his private jet and fly to his father's very own slice of Tropicana for an idyllic fortnight away from the lens, just the two of us, without a balaclava, Botox injection, boob-job leaflet or vacuous entity in sight. After that, Danielle and I were off to the Caribbean for more hazy, lazy living, drinking the most deliciously blended Caribbean cocktails the world has ever seen. Bliss! After all, it was the very least I could do. It seemed as though everything had worked out the way it was supposed to, and as I turned the pages of *Sizzle Stars* to read all about my happy new life, I thanked my lucky stars for Hanna Frost because, after all, if it wasn't for her, perhaps things could have been very different . . .

Acknowledgements

With special azzzome thanks to my friends who, without their patience, support and hilarious anecdotes, this book wouldn't have been half as much fun to write.

To Danielle 'Fluffykins' Levy ... well what can I say? You're really something special, honeybee, so here it is. Woop! This book is definitely for 'us'. To my agent, Ger Nicholl, for taking my thoughts, dreams and aspirations and turning them into reality. To Richard Salt, you're one of the bestest friends a girl could wish for – this book is also, in part, for you. To Ellen, my godson Freddie, and to Kelly, thank you for welcoming me into the family. I love you very much. To my family, with thanks for the support: Grandma, Grandad, Mum, Glen, Lucy and to my uncle, Peter Walsh. I've actually done something with my life!

To my Wimbledon Wombles, Lisa Kiddie and the lovely Paul, (he's *so* your 'One'!) thanks for putting me up and making me feel like I've come home. To Lucy 'Don't Stop Believing' Fisher, your anecdotes are priceless ('Too fast? That's no good!'). Thanks to Sarah Kate Ramsden for reading parts of the book in draft, and to all the others who pitched in with feedback. To Caroline Naharnowicz, you're incredibly special.

To Sophie 'Daaaahling' Leigh, you are *so* Katie and if we make it Stateside, I'll pimp you out for the lead role!

And also to Nick, you are the best. Thanks for taking care of me, both of you, going forward to good times.

To Paul Donnelley, for all the advice on how to be a proper writer over scampi and chips in Elephant and Castle back in 2008 but especially for that one comment you made after my first rejection letter: 'You don't have to use everything you've got you know, you can just write something new ...' And so I did – this book. Cheers!

To my talented friend Grum, with tons of love. You are the most inspirational, funny, wonderful person, seriously. Your unwavering support and one hundred per cent dedication to helping me shape this book (falling asleep in front of David Attenborough on the TV, covered in paper with scenarios for Jack and Katie, anyone?) has definitely made it infinitely better. To Greg Harrop Griffiths and Natasha Gaynor, my oldest and very much wisest friends, thanks for keeping me on the straight and narrow. Can't wait for us to walk past Waterstone's armed with a camera – and is it OK to go up to folk who are reading your book on a train?

To Janice and Simon Zutt, there are no words for the love I have for you both. You're both one in a kazillion! To Magda Knight and all the girlies at Mookychick for giving me a platform to write my random thoughts about life, love and everything in between, and to *Maxim* for giving me my very first break – the experience writing sexy columns and erotica certainly helped when it came to the 'steamy scenes'. To the very sexylicious Jessica Underwood and Lucy Hilson, two of the most glamorous girls I know, the inspirations (in looks, not personality!) for super-diva-bitch Jessica Hilson's character.

To my new London friend Alex 'Modders' Modley,

you're a dove amongst the crows. You know why I'm thanking you. And I can't forget my Scottish friends: to Billy Camlin (what a wonderful friend you are, I wish I could be there more. Let's open a Stoli!) and to Lindsay Thain and Steph Doull, my wee lasses!

Thanks to Hayley Gunton for putting up with my moaning about men and the unglamorous lifestyle involved in writing a novel – love you lots, we're going to live the dream m'dear! To my (brief) Ibiza girlies, Kim Gardner Edwards and Laura Summers for being awesome and also for marking the celebrations with Jagor bombs and Sangria way back in May 2009 (that's if any of us quite remembers it!) To everyone I worked with at the Royal Mail on Old Street, and particularly to my old boss, Simon Burman, for providing much needed guidance throughout my time in the marketing department and for always encouraging me to follow my dreams. Thanks to Simon Hunter, Ian Moore and Martin K. Smith, you're all absolute stars and I can't thank you enough just for being yourselves. And to my lovely talented artistic friend Ben Hurlie of the Graffiti Life Company (check us out!)

And to Sparky. You'll shine again. Promise. ('We're on an adventure, Charlie!')

A really special mention – and you'll definitely know who you are when I say this – 'to the one who believes'. Thank you for helping me sleep, for introducing me to films and, for a brief moment in time, showing me how it was supposed to be. And yes, you do deserve it, you butt-kicking ninja!

Finally, last but by no means least, to my editor(s) and all the wonderful people at Penguin for loving this book almost as much as I do. HUZZAH!!